PRASE FOR CHR )

Praise for *Wha.* ... .. ~~Darkness~~

"*What Lies in Darkness* is a riveting story about the love of family, the devastation of loss, and the secrets we keep. And it has earned Christina McDonald a place in the pantheon of thriller-writer greats. Change your plans for the night because you won't be able to put this one down."

—Alex Finlay, *If Something Happens to Me*

"Jess Lambert is my new favorite detective! Christina McDonald's *What Lies in Darkness* is a must-read. Every single character leaps off the page. The story grabbed me on page one and didn't let go until the last shocking, twisty page!"

—Debra Webb, *USA Today* bestselling author of *All the Little Truths*

"*What Lies in Darkness* is both a smart and edgy mystery and a searing portrayal of loss and betrayal. In Detective Jess Lambert, McDonald has gifted crime fiction with an unforgettable lead, a woman both in love with and struggling against the ghosts that haunt her. I tore through this, mesmerized by the dueling perspectives, hypnotized by McDonald's prose, and shocked by twists that kept coming all the way to the very last page. This is the perfect book for readers who love their thrillers fast paced and deeply emotionally intelligent."

—Ashley Winstead, author of *Midnight Is the Darkest Hour*

"Eerie and evocative, Christina McDonald's genre-bending police procedural / paranormal mystery masterfully (and beautifully) explores grief, loss, longing, and healing. The stakes are high, the tension is palpable, and the secrets are explosive. Be prepared for breath-hitching twists you never saw coming."

—Marcy McCreary, author of *The Summer of Love and Death*

"With richly drawn characters and striking imagery, Christina McDonald delivers a taut, thick-with-atmosphere puzzler that doubles as a meditation on resilience in the face of trauma and an exploration of the sacrifices we make for those we love. Don't miss it!"

—E. G. Scott, internationally bestselling author of *The Rule of Three*

"Utterly compelling. In Detective Jess Lambert, McDonald has captured the perfect mix of gritty determination and haunted soul. With twists and turns everywhere, *What Lies in Darkness* delivers the kind of page-turner you don't just read but devour."

—Lisa Gardner, *New York Times* bestselling author

"Shocking, atmospheric, and tense, *What Lies in Darkness* is an emotionally powerful and twisty page-turner. With rich prose and multi-faceted characters, McDonald has expertly crafted a genre-bending supernatural thriller, making it an absolute must read!"

—Jeneva Rose, *New York Times* bestselling author

Praise for *These Still Black Waters*

"Atmospheric and inventive, Christina McDonald's *These Still Black Waters* pulled me in on page one and held tight. In this haunting and beautifully written thriller chock full of secrets that won't stay buried, McDonald is a masterful storyteller. A truly nightmarish trip to the lake guaranteed to keep readers enthralled."

—Heather Gudenkauf, *New York Times* bestselling author of *The Overnight Guest*

"*These Still Black Waters* has it all: electric writing, complex characters, a touch of the supernatural, and whiplash twists guaranteed to keep you up long past your bedtime."

—Jess Lourey, Amazon Charts bestselling author of *The Quarry Girls*

Praise for *Do No Harm*

"Gripping and unflinching, *Do No Harm* explores the ferocity of a mother's love—and shows, in heartbreaking detail, how she'll risk everything to save her child."

—Sarah Pekkanen, *New York Times* bestselling author of *The Wife Between Us* and *You Are Not Alone*

"*Do No Harm* is a pulse-pounding deep dive into the dark heart of addiction. The stakes couldn't be higher in this smart, breathlessly paced, and emotional novel about love, family, and how far we'll go when our child's life hangs in the balance. Riveting, ripped from the headlines, and not to be missed."

—Lisa Unger, *New York Times* bestselling author of *Confessions on the 7:45*

"Christina McDonald has a real talent for bringing suburban domestic suspense to life and showcases it to great effect in *Do No Harm*. Tense, taut, and absolutely unmissable, you'll find yourself wondering how far YOU would go to save your child's life."

—J. T. Ellison, *New York Times* bestselling author of *Lie to Me*

"McDonald takes the heart-wrenching premise that has become her trademark and ratchets it up a notch in *Do No Harm*, blurring the lines between good and evil in a doctor desperate to save her sick child. A gripping, emotional roller coaster with a sting in the tail."

—Kimberly Belle, internationally bestselling author of *The Marriage Lie*

"Christina McDonald knows how to pack an emotional punch! *Do No Harm* is a riveting, thought-provoking novel that keeps you reading even as it breaks your heart. This might be my favorite book by McDonald yet."

—Samantha Downing, *USA Today* bestselling author of *My Lovely Wife*

"A gripping page-turner with a heart-wrenching moral quandary at its core. *Do No Harm* is tense, moving, and disturbingly relevant."
—Robyn Harding, internationally bestselling author of *The Swap* and *The Party*

"Devastating, heartbreaking, and incredibly timely—this risky and brilliant examination of when the ends justify the means will captivate you from moment one. The talented Christina McDonald dissects the crumbling marriage of two good people, and reveals how love and obsession can combine to destroy even the most perfect family. As a doctor's vow of 'do no harm' twists into 'do whatever it takes,' you'll be riveted by this thought-provoking and tragically believable story."
—Hank Phillippi Ryan, *USA Today* bestselling author of *The Murder List*

"With her trademark emotionally gripping, outstanding writing, Christina McDonald tackles the moral and ethical lines crossed by a doctor desperate to save her child. A stunning gut-punch of a suspense novel, *Do No Harm* expertly merges the dangers of the opioid crisis with a mother's love, leaving readers gasping for more. A breathtaking read."
—Samantha M. Bailey, #1 bestselling author of *Woman on the Edge*

"*Do No Harm* is a gripping and unflinching novel. Christina McDonald demands an answer to the ultimate question: How far would you go to save your child? One thing is for sure: your heart will be ripped out as you whip through each page to discover the answer. Highly recommend!"
—Liz Fenton and Lisa Steinke, authors of *How to Save a Life*

"A family-driven medical thriller that's unique and propulsive, *Do No Harm* by Christina McDonald is as gut-wrenching as it is jaw-dropping. Not to be missed!"
—Hannah Mary McKinnon, bestselling author of *Sister Dear*

"Grace Fraser and *Do No Harm*'s Emma have a lot more in common than what meets the eye . . . From the outside, selling opioids sounds like a horrible and irresponsible idea, but readers will quickly become fans of Emma, Christina McDonald's protagonist . . ."

—PopSugar

"*Do No Harm* is a cross between *Breaking Bad* and Kohlberg's theory of moral development."

—CrimeReads

"[A] complex medical thriller that will have the reader asking themselves what they would do if they were in Emma's position . . . McDonald explores the many perspectives of the opioid crisis with insight and compassion . . . Readers looking for a fast-paced and emotional story will enjoy *Do No Harm* and be thinking about it long after the last page is read."

—*Seattle Book Review*

"This raw, emotional story echoes fear that would result when denied necessary available health treatment due to lack of funds. And it brings into question how far a parent can morally go to save their child."

—*Authorlink*

"A deftly woven blend of suspense, family life, amateur sleuthing, and an opioid epidemic, *Do No Harm* is an inherently fascinating and engaging novel by Christina McDonald that examines whether the ends ever justify the means—even for a desperate mother."

—Midwest Book Review

"In her suspenseful new thriller *Do No Harm*, Christina McDonald brings a controversial topic right out of the real-world headlines and displays a fantastic ability to truly examine it from all sides . . . *Do No Harm* is an absolute page-turner! McDonald has once again perfectly balanced little twists that the reader can feel clever for figuring out with big, sudden, gasp-out-loud moments. Fans of the author's previous books, *Behind Every Lie* and *The Night Olivia Fell*, should be ready to jump right into this intense new thriller!"

—The Nerd Daily

"*Do No Harm* poses morally gray questions . . . McDonald's novel doesn't just tell a story of a doctor trying to use the opioid crisis as a quick payday, she examines different angles of the crisis and how it plays out for different people, exploring who benefits, who suffers, and who is left behind."

—*Fairfield Citizen*

Praise for *Behind Every Lie*

"*Behind Every Lie* is a deep, suspenseful novel packed with family secrets. Christina McDonald has a true gift for creating characters that are so well developed, it feels like you know them. An outstanding achievement!"

—Samantha Downing, author of the #1 international bestseller *My Lovely Wife*

"In *Behind Every Lie*, Christina McDonald brilliantly intertwines page-turning suspense with jaw-dropping family secrets. An emotionally charged domestic thriller that is sure to please!"

—Wendy Walker, national bestselling author of *The Night Before*

"A riveting collision of motherhood and memory—where a sinister and inescapable past haunts those struggling to make sense of their lives and protect their children. What's *Behind Every Lie* is a shocking truth—and for readers, a jaw-dropping, page-turning whirlwind of a thriller. Instantly captivating and endlessly surprising! Christina McDonald is a star."

—Hank Phillippi Ryan, *USA Today* bestselling author of *The Murder List*

"A clever, tense, and absorbing novel—this tale of family secrets had me racing toward the final pages."

—Emma Rous, bestselling author of *The Au Pair*

"Christina McDonald follows up her smashing debut *The Night Olivia Fell* with another winner. McDonald starts with a bang, then builds the action steadily, a gradual unfolding of secrets and lies that will have you constantly switching alliances. Read it like I did, in one sitting and straight through to the end, because you won't want to put this one down."

—Kimberly Belle, international bestselling author of *Dear Wife*

"Christina McDonald's *Behind Every Lie* is a layered, gut-wrenching domestic thriller that explores the complexities of mothers and daughters and the secrets families keep. Smart and intense, and with more than enough twists to give you whiplash, McDonald's beautiful, emotional storytelling will leave you breathless. I don't think I exhaled until the end."

—Jennifer Hillier, author of *Jar of Hearts*, ITW Award winner for Best Novel

"Told in alternating narratives from Eva's traumatic life and her mother's mysterious past, the story twists and turns with one shocking revelation after another until it threatens to career out of control. But behind every lie there is always a reason, and there is a satisfying ending once everyone's hand is played out."

—*Booklist*

"*Behind Every Lie* is a page-turner and an entertaining read. Many readers will enjoy Eva's breathless race of discovery and journey of survival."

—Bookreporter

Praise for *The Night Olivia Fell*

"*The Night Olivia Fell* by Christina McDonald is a stunning thriller that instantly grabbed me by the throat and wouldn't let go until the final, poignant sentence. McDonald artfully brings to the page the emotionally fraught, complex relationship between mother and daughter in this atmospheric, absorbing page-turner. *The Night Olivia Fell* cracked my heart into a million pieces and then slowly pieced it back together again."

—Heather Gudenkauf, *New York Times* bestselling author of *The Weight of Silence* and *Not a Sound*

"In Christina McDonald's *The Night Olivia Fell*, Abi gets the call every mother fears: her daughter has fallen from a bridge and is brain-dead . . . but was it an accident or a crime? McDonald reveals the answer in steady, page-turning increments, a gradual unfolding of truths and long-held secrets that culminates in a heart-wrenching resolution. A suspenseful debut that packs an emotional punch."

—Kimberly Belle, international bestselling author of *Three Days Missing* and *The Marriage Lie*

"McDonald ratchets up the suspense with every chapter, including plenty of gasp-worthy twists and turns as Abi and Olivia's story pushes toward its devastating conclusion. The suspense is supplemented by relationships of surprising depth and tenderness, providing balance and nuance to the story. A worthy debut from an up-and-coming domestic-suspense author; readers who enjoy mother-daughter stories in the genre should line up for this one."

—*Booklist* (starred review)

"This book is a tearjerker, so have tissues at hand. A well-structured story of how lying corrupts from the start that will keep pages turning."

—*Library Journal*

"A thrilling page-turner you have to read."

—PopSugar

WHAT
LIES
IN
DARKNESS

WHAT LIES IN DARKNESS

A JESS LAMBERT THRILLER

CHRISTINA McDONALD

THOMAS & MERCER

Text copyright © 2024 by Christina McDonald

Published by Thomas & Mercer, Seattle

www.apub.com

Amazon, the Amazon logo, and Thomas & Mercer are trademarks of Amazon.com, Inc., or its affiliates.

ISBN-13: 9781662511646 (paperback)
ISBN-13: 9781662511639 (digital)

Cover design by Sarah Congdon
Cover image: © Cosma Andrei / Stocksy; © Antagain / Getty; © borchee / Getty; © Umomos / Shutterstock; © MICHAEL CUTHBERT / Stockimo / Alamy

Printed in the United States of America

*For my sister, Sheri, who's known all the versions of me
and loved every one of them.*

Dear Reader,

If you know me at all, you know my books are always very personal, and *What Lies in Darkness* is no different. The idea behind this story came from a recurring nightmare I had as a kid, reflecting a deep-seated fear of mine: coming home after school/work/socializing and my entire family being missing.

This nightmare lessened as I got older, but it still appeared randomly. One morning I woke after having that nightmare, filled with the shivery, foggy feeling you get after a dream that's too real. But instead of turning away from it, like I usually did, I leaned in and started writing about it.

From that came Alice, who wakes after a car accident to find her entire family is missing. I knew that this was the story I wanted Jess Lambert to investigate: the story of a girl who'd lost her family, much as Jess had lost hers, showing Jess in her endless quest to put her life back together again.

If you loved this story, come find me on social media. I love connecting with my readers!

Instagram & X: @christinamac79

Facebook & TikTok: @christinamcdonaldauthor

And don't forget to sign up for my book club newsletter for deleted chapters, book club discussion questions, and monthly giveaways: www.Christina-McDonald.com/book-club.

Writers are only writers because of readers, readers like you, and I have the best ones. Thank you.

Christina McDonald

P.S. I haven't had that nightmare since writing this book. I don't know if the book exorcised that fear or if it's still lurking. Only time will tell.

Chapter 1

Alice

The Accident—Christmas Eve

My family was murdered at the witching hour.

I know they were murdered, otherwise why wouldn't they have come back? Families don't just disappear. They don't just walk away from the people they love.

That night, there was nothing to make me think something bad was about to happen. No chill skating over my neck. No dark whispers riding the winter wind. No creepy premonition that everything was going to change.

We were happy. That's what I remembered most afterward.

It was Christmas Eve, my favorite night of the year. We always stayed at my aunt Mel and uncle Jack's on Christmas Eve because their house was the biggest. Every year they did a fancy, catered dinner and endless desserts, their house decked out with lights and tinsel and a huge tree with designer baubles, not the homemade ones we had on our tree. We'd go to bed late, our stomachs full, our bodies sleepy, and then, on Christmas morning, we'd roll out of bed early wearing our matching pajamas and run downstairs to open our presents together.

My parents could never afford any of the stuff Mel and Jack did. I'm not saying we were poor, just our presents were, like, pajamas and stuff, not electric ride-on cars or Apple Watches or Gucci socks.

That Christmas Eve, after dinner, somebody turned on some old dance tunes, and the adults, who by that time were hilariously drunk, had started dancing. My grandma was there, too. She'd just arrived from Florida. Mel had hired a Santa to show up for Finn, and I was wandering around snapping pictures.

I had a bit of a sore throat, so my parents decided to take us home instead of staying that night. Dad said I needed a good night's sleep. I remember walking to the car, Mom's good arm, not the one in the sling, wrapped around me. Dad was laughing at something my little sister, Ella, had said. He had a great laugh, his whole face kinda crinkling, his eyes squinting, his body shaking with joy.

Like I said, we were happy. So happy it hurts to think about now.

I stopped to catch a snowflake on my tongue. Did you know in Scotland they have 421 words for snow? A large snowflake is called a *skelt*, a fine driving snow, a *snaw-pusher*. This snow was a *flukra*, snow falling in large blobs.

"Come on, Alice!" Ella shouted. "Get in, it's freezing!"

We piled into the minivan, Ella chatting about something I no longer remember, even though now, in the darkest hours of night, I try my hardest to remember what it was. Makeup, maybe, or boys. They'd already started noticing her, even at ten, with her big blue eyes and her bubbly personality. *Ten going on sixteen,* Mom always said.

I buckled up, the taste of the snow, cold and metallic, like winter and something harder, like stone, lingering in my mouth. The clock on the dashboard said 11:47 p.m. I noticed because it was so far past my bedtime.

"Pete, do you really think—" Mom began.

"It's fine." Dad's eyes cut to the rearview window, a streetlight glinting off his glasses. "You girls buckled?"

"Yes," we chorused.

Ella was lying. Her coat was draped over her like a blanket, but I could see her seat belt. Empty. Unfastened. I glared at her, hoping she'd feel the weight of my gaze. But she didn't lift her head from under the warm nest of her hood. I didn't say anything, though. I wasn't a tattletale.

Later, I would regret that. I would torment myself with how different things could've been if I'd only spoken up.

Something fluttered in my peripheral vision. Maybe a bat? Or a bird braving the cold. I didn't think about it too much. I felt safe and secure surrounded by my family.

Snow battered the windscreen, the roads already covered. The wipers beat on max, rhythmically shoving at the white flakes. The headlights barely cut through the snow swirling around us.

I was just starting to fall asleep when the car slowed. A couple of construction barriers with a ROAD CLOSED sign were blocking the road.

"That's weird," Mom said. "I wonder what's happened."

"Maybe they're fixing some of those potholes," Dad said. "I'll turn around."

"Maybe we should . . ." Mom's voice was pinched with worry.

"This road's closed, honey."

"Pete, I really don't—"

"It's fine." Dad cut her off, a little impatient, a little annoyed. He'd been getting annoyed with her a lot more lately. He'd been getting annoyed with all of us lately. Not anything big, just little things I only noticed *after*.

That's how life breaks down when something bad happens. Those dark, sudden moments that happen without warning. This was my life before. This is my life now. The two are nothing alike.

Dad spun the minivan around and turned into Killer's Grove.

It was kind of a dumb name. Killer's Grove. I guess years ago, a serial killer claimed he'd been burying bodies there. All you had to do was mention Killer's Grove and people would go, *Oh, you mean that haunted road where all the bodies are dumped?* And you'd say, *Yeah*, even though only one body was ever found there, and that was in, like, 1970 or something. And they'd tell you one of the billions of ghost stories everybody knew.

Mostly, those stories were told in a breathless *dude you won't believe this* sort of way, and they usually started with a bunch of goths staying in Killer's Grove on Halloween while stoned off their faces. It was the sort of dead zone where stories of people going missing were common, where your phone couldn't get a good signal, and if you stood just long enough, you'd feel the cold scratch of something whispering over your skin.

Nobody ever had any specifics, really. Just that the couple of miles of road that stretched through the forest near Black Lake were haunted and had always been haunted.

My dad didn't believe in those stories, but my mom did. Maybe it was the Irish in her. She's the one who warned us about the witching hour.

Nothing good ever happens after midnight, she'd tell my sister and me. *That's when all the spirits come out of hiding. When the veil lifts between the dead and the living and the spirits travel between the worlds.*

So, yeah, the name was dumb. But still, some things stick with people. The past isn't some sandcastle that can just be wiped away by the tide.

I stared out my window. The road ahead was long and narrow. Darkness had stitched the trees together, a curtain of black. Our headlights barely cut through the white snow swirling around us like static from an old TV screen.

Ancient evergreens dusted with white pushed up over the sides of the winding road, thick branches arcing like gnarled fingers. On either side of the road was forest, miles and miles of it: northern hardwood, white pine and red oak, with jagged chasms and plunging gorges and caves. In the summer, we'd go camping, hike the cobwebbed paths, but now everything was frozen.

My parents were arguing in the front, still doing that thing they sometimes did where half their conversation was out loud and the rest was telepathic. They'd always done it, as long as I could remember. It was totally annoying. I closed my eyes and let their voices merge with the windshield wipers as sleep pulled at me.

"Do you think—" Dad began.

"No."

"Are you—"

"Tomorrow. Honestly, tonight I . . ." Mom sighed.

"I know, I get it."

"It's just, it's Christmas, and I think . . . Pete, watch out!"

My eyelids fluttered at my mom's scream.

There was a flare of something. Light? Shadow? I couldn't tell.

It all happened so fast.

Dad slammed on the brakes, and the minivan skidded, then swerved. My stomach leaped into my throat. Dad cursed, trying to correct. But the tires couldn't get any grip on the snowy pavement, and we veered off the road, clipping a tree with a bone-jarring *thwuck*. And then we were airborne, metal crunching as the car flipped.

I could hear someone screaming—was it me?—as we spun, inside a washing machine of white snow and black night. Pain ripped through my arm. The metal on the roof screeched as we landed upside down on the pavement. The minivan rocked and then, with a final sickening groan, tipped onto its side, flinging me against my window.

My head cracked against the glass. Blood filled my mouth, poured into my eyes. And then everything went black.

I don't know how long I was out, but when I came to, the only sound was the windshield wipers still going. *Swish, swish, swish.* Blood, hot and sticky, dripped down my nose, the scent like melting rust. Pain gushed over me in a hot wave. My arm was twisted in an unnatural direction.

The car had landed on its side. My side. Snow dusted my cheeks.

"Mom?" I whispered, my eyes still squeezed tightly shut.

But there was no answer. Only the gentle sound of snow falling and the hiss of the wind and the beat of the wipers.

"Dad? Ella?"

Still no answer.

I opened my eyes. I was lying on the side of the car surrounded by junk: my backpack, a box of crackers, an empty Coke can. I tried to move my head, but pain made me stop. A whimper escaped my mouth. I slit my eyes open again, turning my neck slowly despite the pain and dread and panic filling me. I expected to see Ella next to me, to see my mom and dad in the front.

I was afraid they were all dead.

But what I saw was worse.

Horror gushed in. I started to tremble. My heart hammered. Hot tears filled my eyes. I squeezed them shut, then open again. But everything was still exactly the same.

There was nobody there.

Besides me, the car was empty.

My family was gone.

In my peripheral vision, the clock ticked over: 12:01 a.m.

The witching hour had arrived.

Chapter 2

Alice

December—A Year Later

I'm taking a Jell-O shot when my dead dad walks in.

A wobble shivers across the room. A stutter, like the click of a shutter. The music's pulsing bass dims. And there he is.

He's so real—sad and disappointed as he sees the mess I've become since he disappeared. He's wearing the same clothes he wore that last night, a suit jazzed up with a Santa tie and the string of tinsel my mom wrapped around his neck when they were dancing. He's standing across the living room, a sea of teenagers stretched between us.

It isn't really him. My dad's dead. My whole family's dead. I know this because they wouldn't have left me behind. They were victims, too, although of what I don't know.

I shake my head, trying to dislodge my dad from my vision. I'm not sure why I've started seeing him lately. Why I *think* I see him. Maybe it's that time of year, the anniversary in a few weeks.

Teenagers whirl wildly across the living room. Music throbs. Rainbow strobe lights ping around the downstairs. Somebody shoves against me. The house party has gotten out of control. Maya used to invite only friends to these parties she throws in empty vacation homes around Black Lake. But that number seems to have grown lately. There must be thirty teenagers here, some I don't even recognize.

I'm right in the middle of it, but I feel totally alone.

I tug on the strapless top Maya loaned me. "Come on, Alice!" she'd pleaded. "You *have to* come to this party! It's gonna be *lit*!"

Just being here makes my stomach twist and squirm. My body feels shivery, my lungs rigid, unable to get enough air. Every nerve ending is screaming, like I'm caught in the ragged teeth of an electric fence. It's too loud, the air too hot, the smell of teenage sweat and hair products overwhelming.

I've always been overly sensitive. Mom used to call me her orchid child. As a kid, I would cry about my socks getting bunched; I'd feel sick at the overpowering smell of perfume, get upset at loud birthday parties. I could feel what others felt, even actual pain when they got hurt. My sister, Ella, broke her wrist when she was six, and I swear I actually felt her pain. I cried more than she did.

I shouldn't have come here, to this house. I feel like I've fallen through the looking glass, like the world I live in has become unfamiliar.

"I gotta get out of here," I mutter.

I flee upstairs, find an empty bathroom. I lock the door and throw the window open with adrenaline-numbed fingers, letting the cold winter air slap at my hot cheeks.

Finally, the sounds of the party are muted. Sound can be a trigger for me. I rub my fingers over the ropy scars on my forearm, taking deep breaths.

I hear a burst of laughter on the other side of the door, my friend Runy shouting—drunk or high, he's always something. "She *said* that, are you fucking kidding me?" And then more laughter.

I shut the bathroom window and splash cool water on my face. I look older than seventeen, my face pinched, mascara smudged. My mother's blue eyes stare back at me. I cut my long, marmalade-colored hair recently, slicing it into a shaggy bob, hoping to not see the ghost of my dead mom every time I looked in the mirror. But here she is.

I touch my reflection. Sometimes the absence of my family is a physical ache. I'd give anything for one more moment with them. To hear their voices. Feel the warmth of their hugs.

My eyes fall to the silver heart locket set on a musical note that hangs around my neck. My mom got it for me as an early Christmas present last year.

You have everything you need right here. She'd flipped open the tiny latch to show me the picture inside, the four of us at Mel and Jack's house for Christmas the year before, wearing matching pajamas and grinning like crazy. It wasn't diamond earrings or a pair of Nike Air Force 1s like Mel got me, but I've worn it ever since.

My fingers reach, almost without my permission, to the clasp. What's the point in wearing it? My family is gone. I unfasten it and drop it into my purse.

I use toilet paper to clean up my mascara, finger-brush my hair; then I dig one of the Ativan I swiped from my aunt Mel from the bottom of my purse and dry-swallow it. The taste it leaves is sharp, acidic.

I'm about to leave the bathroom when my phone buzzes from my purse.

It's my grandma. I hesitate, thinking about our conversation yesterday. I'm not ready to give her an answer, so I press "End."

A knock comes at the door. "Alice?"

It's Maya. I throw the door open, ready with a big, fake smile, but it slides away when I see Jinx behind her.

Jinx moved to Black Lake in October. At first, I thought she was one of the goths who'd come for Halloween with their dark clothes and black makeup, hoping to scare themselves by staying in Killer's Grove. But then she didn't leave. Lately, she and Maya have been hanging out.

I can't figure out her vibe. Usually, I can feel people's energy. Their anger or sadness or whatever. It's like a hyperawareness, I guess, or a sixth sense. If I'm not careful, people's energy can float right into mine. But not Jinx. She's like looking into Black Lake, murky, opaque.

"You okay?" Maya's brown eyes are cool and assessing.

Queen of to-do lists and high-achieving goals, Maya has a ten-year plan that freaks me out. She's the type who gets shit done. If she wants it, she makes it happen. Only Maya would find a way to make money throwing parties in empty vacation homes. And this one is perfect: massive, mostly isolated, near the lake. It's how she's saving up to pay for college. Maya's here to make money, and I'm here for . . . what? I don't even know. Oblivion, maybe.

"I'm fine," I say.

"You sure?"

"Totally. I just want to party."

I push past them and head downstairs, into the writhing bodies, the pulsing music, the steamy heat. My dead dad isn't there, and I'm not sure if I'm relieved or sad.

I grab another Jell-O shot, tossing it back as I drift from room to room. I hover outside little cliques, listening to their conversations. Harper gossiping about some mean-girl drama. Runy talking about a booze run. Devin discussing the pros and cons of the new class president.

Nobody seems to notice me. I imagine I'm invisible, like a ghost.

It's even more crowded now. I want the Ativan to kick in. The prickle of anxiety huddling at the base of my neck creeps down my spine. I don't know these people.

If I had my camera—not my iPhone, the Canon Rebel my dad splurged on for my birthday last year—maybe I could see them clearer. I could see when their muscles relax, the masks drop, the people they *really* are, the things they try to hide. But I stopped taking pictures the night my family disappeared.

I want a cigarette. Not that vaping crap. A real cigarette like my aunt Mel used to smoke, sneaking outside during family gatherings like nobody knew what she was doing. She doesn't smoke anymore. Not since she had Finn.

"Runy!" I shout over the music, miming a smoking motion. He shakes his head, eyes like saucers. Definitely high.

The girl Runy is dancing with says something to him. Her mouth moves, the word *freak* twisting her lips. She cackles loudly. Eyes turn toward her, then dart to me. Their faces change. I see it. The buzzkill. The freak. The one left behind.

I flush and turn away, pushing through the crowd.

I'm aware of all their theories, the rumors, how their stories twisted and turned, bouncing from one person to the next. It was a satanic cult. A serial killer. They were involved with a criminal gang. They were drug dealers. It was group suicide. They faked their deaths and were now in witness protection.

And then the unofficial verdict: that my father had killed my mother and Ella, hidden their bodies, then killed himself.

But that didn't answer one question: Why was I left?

I stare at the teenagers on the dance floor. Prickles scatter up the back of my neck, an eerie, sinister feeling clawing at my skin. I hate it here. The thought comes at me in a violent rush. Until I get away from Black Lake, I'll never be anything but a freak.

The Ativan is kicking in, blending with the Jell-O shots. A gentle fog winds its way through my body. I float across the room to the bay window. The world outside is velvety dark, a handful of Christmas lights dotting the black.

A sudden flash catches my attention. Someone is driving toward Killer's Grove. The headlights flicker, dark, then light, then dark again, like they are swaying. Or maybe that's just me. Something's clenching in my gut, something sharp and painful. I don't feel quite right, and it's more than the Jell-O shots or the Ativan.

And then I see a shadow, something shifting in the darkness across the street. Someone is watching the house. I press my nose to the window but can't see who it is. The streetlight is out, and their face is hidden by the darkness. But I can feel their gaze hot on my skin.

My breath becomes shallow, and then, for a flash, not even a second, I'm back in that car, the world whirling, metal crunching. And then silence. Only snow falling, the gentle murmur of the wind.

From far away, footsteps crunch over broken glass. A shadow.

Someone was out there.

I jolt back to the present, breathless, shivery with adrenaline, my heart kicking wildly despite the Ativan. What the hell was that? A memory? A daydream? A hallucination?

Outside, the shadow is moving toward the little field that leads into Killer's Grove. Fear sparks like a live wire inside me.

Someone is out there. Again.

I push myself through the living room and throw the front door open. Cold December air slaps me across my face. I jog down the porch stairs and cross the road to the frost-coated field.

I know I'm being dumb. Reckless. I should be running away, not toward this person. But I need to know. Who is it? Why are they watching me?

A hand lands on my arm. "Alice?"

I whirl. Maya, Runy, and Jinx are staring at me.

"Are you okay?" Maya asks.

The house looms behind her, a sticky, malevolent presence. Its black shadows threaten to claw me back, to push me under. Something flares in my mind. A flash of light. A hard crack. Wind raking at my face.

I twist away from Maya, launching myself toward Killer's Grove.

"Alice?" Maya's voice floats after me.

I ignore her. The distant shape of the person has almost reached Killer's Grove.

"Stop!" I shout.

And then, as they reach the tree line, they do.

She looks over her shoulder. Recognition comes in a flash. In the darkness, I can't see her face, but this isn't the first time I've felt eyes on me, seen the whisper of her shadow as it turns a corner.

"Wait!"

But she doesn't. She slips into the trees.

Once again, I'm alone in the dark. The forgotten one. The girl left behind.

The only one still here with a story to tell.

Chapter 3

Alice

I'm a sweaty, panicking mess as Maya drags me from Killer's Grove back to the house. She leaves Runy and Jinx in charge, grabs my coat, and pushes me into her car.

The radio blasts on when she starts the car. I flinch, the noise like a slap. She turns it down and pulls out of the driveway. Silence is thick between us, sticky as saltwater taffy.

The lake whooshes by, Christmas lights dotting the perimeter like a diamond necklace. A papery moon is rising, moonlight catching on the water's surface, turning it white and shivery and drawing the trees in charcoal. Gradually I relax, a weight lifting the farther we get from the party, from the house, from Killer's Grove.

"I'm sorry," Maya says, shooting a side glance at me. "I shouldn't have made you come."

"It's not your fault."

"It's too close to where it happened."

"I wanted to go." It's a lie—Maya knows I didn't want to go—but I don't want her to feel bad.

I tug at my socks, which have twisted in my shoes. The sensation makes my fingernails feel like they're peeling backward.

She glances at me. "What were you chasing, Alice?"

I close my eyes. She didn't see the person standing on the edge of Killer's Grove. I'm not sure I did, either. Like the weird vision of my dad at that party, she's just a figment of my imagination.

"What were you chasing?" Maya asks again.

"I don't know." The lie tastes rusty, like blood. I can tell from the tension in her jaw she doesn't believe me.

My phone beeps, a text from Runy.

Dude. You okay?

I don't reply. After a minute, another text.

My sister Chloe works for a true-crime podcast. She told me you can call anytime if you want to look into what happened that night.

The thought makes me feel sick. I mute my phone.

By the time we reach Maya's house, the Ativan has become a heavy hand pushing down on me. All I want to do is sleep.

Maya lives in a tiny, sixties ranch house about a half a mile from mine. Well, from where I used to live. Now I live at my aunt and uncle's house in a fancy gated development outside town. These days, my house just stands there. Quiet. Dark. Waiting. For what, I don't even know.

Maya moved here a few years ago when her mom's cleaning business took off. Before that, they lived in a trailer. Her mom worked two jobs while her dad didn't work at all. Whenever I came over, I'd hear them, Nancy and Dom, fighting over bills. Dom's kind of a loser, although I'd never tell Maya that.

We sneak in the back. It's Saturday night, and her parents think we've gone to a movie. I used to be jealous of the freedom Maya's parents gave her. Now I think independence is something you want when you're a kid, but then you grow up too fast and you wish you could give it back, regift it like a dusty bottle of wine.

Inside, the house is lit with a string of Christmas lights, flashing green, then red. Maya's older brother's door is closed. I hear Dom snoring down the dark hall. I head straight to the kitchen and grab one of his beers, crack the top, and guzzle half of it.

"Seriously?" Maya hisses. She rolls her eyes and heads to her room.

I finish the beer in great, greedy gulps even though I know I shouldn't. I need to stop drinking, stop taking Ativan with my new antidepressants, stop acting so reckless.

The call with my grandma flashes in my mind again. I push it away. Bury it. I don't want to think about it right now. I just want to forget. Just for tonight, I want to sleep.

Maya's sitting on the edge of her bed, bent over, unstrapping her heels. I feel tension coming off her, anger maybe.

"Is it okay if I stay here?" I ask.

I'm supposed to ask my aunt Mel before I stay at Maya's, but I never do. I don't know why. Sometimes I'm too good at the hate part of love. I want to hurt the people who love me on purpose. My shrink says I'm testing them, seeing if they'll really stick around. Making sure they really love me. It isn't fair, I know. Obviously, I have issues.

"You know it is." I don't have to see Maya's face to know she's annoyed. She thinks I'm not taking care of myself. Maybe I'm not.

I text Mel, then turn my phone off so she can't call me. I sit next to Maya, the metal bedsprings squealing under my weight. I drop my head onto her shoulder, my fingers playing across the scar tissue on my forearm.

"I don't understand what's going on with you, Alice," she says.

I don't know how to tell her. What will she think if she finds out I'm seeing things?

I'm suddenly so tired I can barely keep my eyes open. The silence stretches. I'm whirling and swaying, diving toward sleep, and it's pulling me in.

"You don't have to do this to yourself, you know," Maya says. "They wouldn't want you to."

"I know," I murmur.

And I do know.

I see my dad standing on the other side of that dance floor. He would want me to be happy. They all would.

Maya sighs. I feel my body sliding down to the bed. She lifts my feet, drapes the blanket over me, and then I don't say anything more. I let the warm chemical slumber pull me under.

The next morning, I wake early. Frost prickles the grass in the backyard. A thick mist hangs like a ghost over the street. The sky is gray and the house is freezing, which is probably good because a hangover is chewing at my head.

I check the clock on the wall: I have an appointment with my shrink in an hour.

I stagger out of bed, desperate to water my dehydrated brain. Maya's still asleep, sprawled on the camp bed on the floor. A soft snore bubbles from her mouth. Her feet hang off the end. I should've let her take the bed.

I step over Maya and look around for my purse. I have a moment of panic before I remember I left it in the bathroom at the house party last night.

Shit. My new antidepressants are in there. Panic fills my chest, followed by a thump of dread. I'll have to go back later.

I grab my phone and take it into the bathroom. As soon as I turn it on, notifications light the screen. Mostly from Mel.

Mel has only ever been Mel, not Aunt Mel. Same with Jack, even though he's my mom's brother. I'm not sure why; they just never asked us to call them aunt or uncle.

Living with them is so different from what my life was like with my family. Our house was always warm, filled with light and noise and mess. Mel and Jack's house is supermodern and super-stylish with too much glass and too much order. They have money. Lots of it. Jack's a property developer—he owns half the land around Black Lake—and Mel runs a successful yoga studio.

I scan Mel's texts and then shoot her a quick reply.

Soz, studying trig last night and forgot to turn phone back on. Don't worry, I won't forget shrink this morning. Will be back to yours after.

That's another thing I never do: call Mel and Jack's house *home*. Home is my house, the house where my family and I lived. Even though I haven't been back since they disappeared.

In the bathroom, I guzzle cold water straight from the tap, then shower and dress in clothes I keep at Maya's. I leave my shaggy bob to air dry, then rifle through the medicine cabinet, looking for anything, Xanax, Valium, Ativan. But there's nothing there.

When I yank the door open, Nancy is standing there. She's wearing full makeup already, dressed in a navy pantsuit, her dark hair in a neat french braid. Gold jewelry at her ears and neck glows against her smooth skin. Ready for work, even on a Sunday.

I slide past, shooting her a nervous smile. *Crap.* I hope she didn't hear me going through the medicine cabinet. She grabs me for a big hug. Nancy is all motion, all action. She loves big and laughs big.

"Hey, Sweet Pea." Nancy has called me that since I was five. "Want some cereal?"

"Yes, please."

I sit at the kitchen table as she pulls out a box of Cheerios and shakes some into a bowl. Outside the window, a deer steps through the front yard. It leaves tiny footprints in the frosted grass, each foot placed tentatively in front of the other. I watch the deer. It seems so alone, as lonely and abandoned as I am.

Nancy slides the bowl and a carton of milk onto the table.

"Thanks," I say.

Nancy pours hot water over a mug of Nespresso, and the smell of coffee fills the room. She sits across from me, and for a moment her face drops and she looks tired. Usually Nancy is so vibrant, so alive. Mom always called her a fireball. But lately—maybe since last year—she's seemed, I don't know, haggard? Stressed? Maya says she works a lot now that her cleaning company is growing.

"Your aunt called last night," she says.

"Sorry." I rub a hand over my bleary eyes. "She's so neurotic."

Nancy lifts one eyebrow.

"I know, I know." I'm such a bitch. Mel's literally the opposite of neurotic. She's calm and levelheaded, warm and protective. She's been nothing but good to me. "I'll call her back."

"I told her you were studying."

"Thanks." I don't meet her eyes. I'm guessing she doesn't know Maya steals the keys to the vacation homes her company cleans, throwing parties she charges entry for every weekend.

"When's the last time you slept, Alice?" Nancy asks. "Like, *really* slept. You look exhausted. Is everything okay?"

I know what she's seeing, because I can feel it. My eyes are fat and bloated, more red than white. My brain is fuzzy, like I'm underwater.

"I'm not sleeping great," I admit. "The anniversary . . ."

I let the sentence trail off, looking out the window at thin rays of sun trying to burn off the fog. I think about telling her I've been seeing my dad lately. That last night I chased a figment of my imagination into Killer's Grove.

But I'd just sound crazy, so I don't say anything. I don't want people to think I'm more of a freak than they already do.

She reaches across the table, squeezes my hand. "Tough times never last. Tough people do."

"I have a friend whose sister works for a true-crime podcast. I was thinking, maybe I should let them interview me, you know, for the anniversary? Maybe it would, like, renew interest, get new leads."

"Are you going to do it?"

Mel warned me from the very beginning not to talk to the media.

They will ruin you. Ruin us, she'd said. *Nothing will be off-limits for them.*

"Do you think I should?" I ask Nancy.

Nancy sips her coffee. "I think you need to take care of yourself. Get a good night's sleep. Focus on your future.

"The past"—she shakes her head—"sometimes all it does is weigh you down."

Chapter 4

Alice

I ride my bike to my shrink's office. Mel tried to convince me to get my license, but after the accident, driving a car was the last thing I wanted to do. The world's full of enough scary shit, thanks very much.

Dr. Pamela Overton's office is usually closed on the weekends, but I'm what you call an overflow patient. She was booked solid during the week, but Mel has a way of getting people to do what she wants. She's just like that, all calm and decisive. She makes a plan and people can't help but go along with it. And Mel wanted me to see a shrink.

After what I did, I kinda don't blame her.

I actually like Dr. Pam. She has a soft southern accent and white-blonde hair she twists into a neat bun. She always wears soft sweaters and floaty, colorful scarves.

I turn down Sunshine Street, where Dr. Pam's office is located. Maya thinks it's hilarious that a psychologist's practice is located on Sunshine Street. I lock my bike in the rack in front of the old redbrick building and go inside.

I sign in using the touchpad and sit in a hard plastic chair. The front door dings, and a woman enters. She's pretty, with long, espresso-colored hair pulled into a tight ponytail, sharp cheekbones, quick, dark eyes. She unzips her coat and stomps snow off sturdy biker boots. She limps across the room, her cane making loud thunks as she walks. There's something about her, a sort of restless, edgy vibe.

She jabs at the touchpad with sharp, impatient movements, then sits across from me, her good leg jiggling against the floor. I can feel her gaze, heavy on me. She's probably trying to figure out where she recognizes me from, which makes me uncomfortable. I meet her eyes defiantly.

"You okay?" I say pointedly.

Before she can respond, Dr. Pam peeks her head out of a door.

"Oh, hello, Jess." Dr. Pam motions for me to wait, drawing Jess back into her office.

I'm annoyed because I was here first, and am about to leave when Dr. Pam waves me in. *Jess* must've gone out the back.

"Apologies for the delay," Dr. Pam says.

She escorts me into her office. It's decorated like a living room, all overstuffed furniture with fluffy throw pillows, a glossy walnut desk, soft watercolors on the walls, a shelf of books, a strangely twisted bonsai tree, its growth stunted by the tiny pot.

Like me, I think. Stuck in a static life in a small town, unable to move on or move past.

Dr. Pam's made me tea, my favorite market blend, and it waits on the table in front of a low cream couch. I sink onto it, wishing I could lie down and pull one of the blankets over me.

She sits in her chair, ankles crossed, calm, patient. That's all I ever get off her, just total serenity. "How are you feeling, Alice?"

Lonely. Abandoned. Like a total freak.

"Okay," I say. "My grades are up."

I lift my mug, inhaling the cinnamon-orange scent. It's hot and sweet, just the way I like it. "Thanks for this."

She nods, waiting for me to continue. I'm not good at talking. Not anymore. But like I said, therapy is sort of nonnegotiable now.

I look down at my forearm. The gnarled *F R* stands out, ropy pink scar tissue against skin so pale I can see blue blood vessels pulsing.

It was all a big misunderstanding. I wasn't actually trying to kill myself. It happened a few weeks after I'd gone back to school. I was sitting in math class when I just sort of . . . detached. Like there was a skin separating me from everybody else. And suddenly I wasn't sitting in class.

My vision went black. The shrieking of metal on metal filled my ears. Glass cracking. Footsteps crunching. The hot metallic scent of blood in my nose. And fear. So much fear. An iron band tightened around my chest. The air had turned gooey and viscous, like peanut butter. I tried to scream, but only a strange, gurgled moan came out.

And then my eyes had snapped open and I was back in math class, everybody staring at me. I wasn't sure if I'd fallen asleep or if I'd had a flashback or what.

Later, after my next class, I went to my locker. A message was painted across it in red.

Freak.

I did pretty much what you'd expect. I ran away.

I got my bike and cycled to Killer's Grove. I sat next to the tree where our car had gouged a scar into its flesh and gouged my own scar, using a compass from my backpack to carve FREAK into my forearm.

Except I only got to *F R* before I passed out. Blood kinda grosses me out. And that's where the school principal and Mel found me, covered in blood at the side of the road.

She thought I was trying to commit suicide, but I wasn't. It's not that I don't think about dying. I think about it pretty much every day now. Cancer. Drunk driver. A wall falling on me. A gunman. My problem isn't that I'm scared to die. It's that I'm scared to live.

I guess I just wanted to release some of the pain, and that word— *FREAK*—made sense to me. Because why am I the only one left? Why are they gone and I'm still here?

That was the only time Mel brought up That Night.

"Do you want to talk about it?" she'd asked. "Tell me how you're feeling?"

I didn't know how to answer. I've learned that it's better to swallow your voice than to speak the truth.

"I know it must be so hard," Mel said. "Let me help you."

I didn't answer. Maybe silence is a sort of superpower.

Dr. Pam interrupts my thoughts. "Are you still having problems sleeping?"

"Sometimes." I hurry to add: "Better than before."

"How are the new pills working?"

Dr. Pam changed my depression meds a few weeks back because I started getting fat. I heard some of the kids at school laughing about it behind my back, so I asked to change.

"Fine," I lie.

I don't tell her how tired I've been or that I feel more anxious than ever, that my head constantly aches. And I definitely can't tell her I've started seeing my dead dad.

I need the chemical numbness of these pills. I can't go back to the place I was last year.

"You're being careful not to drink, right? No recreational drugs?"

"I don't do drugs," I say, horrified. The pills I swipe from my aunt are so I don't feel so anxious. They're totally legal, not recreational.

Dr. Pam tucks a strand of hair behind her ear. On her desk, there's a picture of a square-jawed husband, two grown children with the same soft features, intelligent eyes. They're standing on a patio overlooking a beach with palm trees. Hawaii, maybe.

My dad talked about going to Hawaii once. It was maybe a few weeks before That Night.

Maybe we should move somewhere new, he'd said to my mom. *Hawaii or, I don't know, Fiji. Somewhere tropical.*

"How's school?" Dr. Pam asks.

I laugh, but it sounds hard and bitter. "School is school."

She gives me a sympathetic smile. "That bad?"

"You have no idea. Everybody looking at me, talking about me behind my back, like I'm some sort of shit magnet."

My hand goes to the locket at my throat before I remember I took it off last night. It's in my purse, which is still at the party house.

"Experiences like yours naturally leave behind a latent fear of abandonment, especially coming up on the one-year anniversary. There's a lot of uncertainty in missing, presumed dead cases."

I make a sound at the back of my throat. The phrase *missing, presumed dead* makes me low-key furious. Like there's any doubt. The police know it. I know it. Their bodies were never found, but there was blood, hairs, clothing fibers.

They aren't missing. My family died that night in Killer's Grove.

Nobody seems to really know what happened. I was basically unconscious, so it's not like I'm much help. It's been a year, and every lead has gone cold. There are no suspects. No new information.

The case is still officially open, but that *presumed dead* part, that's the cops saying unofficially they're done looking.

The problem is, without their actual bodies, there's always this cruel little sliver of hope.

"I just wish I knew where their bodies are." The words are out before I can stop them.

"I understand," Dr. Pam says quietly. "Closure is an important piece of a complicated puzzle. We've spoken before about ambiguous loss. When we don't have all the information, we lose any sense of control, and we go to the wildest places in our minds to fill in the blanks. Closure provides us with a way to process what's happened."

"Well, there you go," I say snottily. "I can't get any closure. No wonder I feel like I'm sinking."

"Is that how you feel?"

"Sometimes."

"Closure is important in grieving, but it can mean different things to different people. Perhaps your version of closure isn't just about getting answers but in learning to feel grateful that you lived. That you can take a deep breath when you walk in the sunshine. Sometimes there's no closure, exactly, but there is what's called reconciliation, and that means integrating your new reality of life without your family there. Not just surviving but thriving. Connecting with those who love you here and now is an important part of that."

I tell her about my phone call with my grandma. "She asked me to move to Florida with her."

"That's a big step, Alice. What do you want to do?"

"I don't know. We're supposed to talk about it more when she comes up for Christmas, but . . ." I shrug.

"You don't want to leave Black Lake?"

"I do, I just . . ."

It's hard to explain. Here, I'm a freak. The girl left behind. I feel like I'm frozen in time. But . . . it's all I know. I guess I'm scared. Maybe that's why I'm seeing my dad.

"You're seeing your dad?"

I didn't realize I'd spoken out loud, but Dr. Pam's response surprises me.

"They're called grief hallucinations. Hearing your loved one's voice, catching a glimpse of them, it's part of bereavement. You aren't alone, Alice. It means you need something from him."

"Like what?"

"Like closure."

I frown. It didn't feel like a hallucination. My dad is bloody, injured. I can hear his voice clearly, like he's standing right there. "You don't understand."

"Why don't you explain it to me."

And so I do. We talk about the accident and survivor's guilt and how hard it's been and how I feel when I see my dad. The hour passes quickly until she's standing, announcing our time is up for today.

And then I'm outside. It's bitterly cold, but the sun has burned away the fog, and it's a beautiful, clear day. I call Maya while I unlock my bike.

"Hey, I left my purse at the house last night," I say when she answers.

"My house?"

"No, the party house. Any way you can bring it over to mine?"

"I can't, soz. I have to go clean up so I can get the keys back to my mom before she notices they're missing, and then we're supposed to have some family dinner or something. Meet me there?"

I swallow hard, bile edging up my throat. It's impossible to explain exactly why I don't want to go back there, the memories it rakes up, the feelings.

"Okay. Sure," I finally say.

I hang up and get on my bike, cycle through town toward the party house. I pass the café, the post office, the beach, the church with its white steeple, pedaling harder and harder until my chest burns and my lungs feel like they're about to explode, trying to outrun the memories shoving at me.

But as usual, I'm not quite fast enough.

Like tennis balls, they keep bouncing back. Dad teaching me to ride my bike, his hands strong and steady on my back. Ella crying when she tipped her ice-cream cone onto the sand. Mom laughing and sharing hers. And then another: eleven years old, the school Christmas concert in the park. I was supposed to sing "Joy to the World," and I froze. But then Dad was there, pushing his way through the crowd, his big, warm hand in mine, his rich baritone singing, so all I had to do was join in.

There's *no way* he did what they said he did. My father was a gentle man. He loved photography and the Red Sox and Greek history. He had a calm voice and a cheerful demeanor. He couldn't be a murderer. A—what do you call them?—family annihilator.

But who killed them? And why was I left?

Chapter 5

Alice

By the time I reach the party house, dark clouds have rolled in. Little slivers of light outline the clouds in shimmering gold.

The old me would've photographed it, capturing the strands of golden light, the way they twist through the gray. Photography used to be something I did with my dad. He bought me my first disposable camera, then a point-and-click, then my Canon.

It's not about the tool, it's about your mind. It's about the story you want to tell, he always said. *Photography's a multisensory experience.*

I haven't taken any pictures since the night my family went missing. At first the cops took my camera as evidence, but when they didn't find anything and returned it to me, I just put it in a box in my closet, along with my mom's laptop, which they also returned.

My phone buzzes in my pocket as I arrive, climbing off my bike and nudging the kickstand into place. It's my grandma calling. Again. And I still don't know what to say.

Mel says you're not happy, she'd said the last time we spoke. *Why don't you come live with me in Florida? You can start a new school in the New Year. Focus on your future. Graduating. Dating. Just being a normal seventeen-year-old.*

Did you know the day after tomorrow is called overmorrow? I can't even figure out what I'll be doing overmorrow, let alone next month.

But I have an idea. I text Runy, asking for his sister's number. I'm not sure I want to talk to a true-crime podcaster about my story, but I know I want that option.

Runy sends through Chloe's details. I try to psych myself up to call her, to tell my story, but immediately lose my nerve. I shove my phone back in my pocket and look up at the house, the frost-tipped grass, the tall, whispering trees. My breath hits the air in little white puffs. Killer's Grove is at my back, and yet I feel its pull, the darkness like ink soaking into my body.

My chest twists, and suddenly my vision blurs. Water rushes in my ears, rain pummeling my face, my arms. I hear a shout from very far away. Male. Fear like ice fills my veins. My heart is beating too fast. My breaths are too shallow. And then I'm shivering, my teeth cracking together.

"Alice?" Maya's brother, Dash, is standing on the porch, looking at me with a baffled expression on his face. "Are you coming in? You've been standing there, like, forever."

"Oh." Words float elusively, just out of reach. There's no water and, except for the sweat prickling under my sweater, I'm not wet.

"I . . . was on my phone." I hold up my phone as proof.

It was nothing, I tell myself. *Nothing.*

But even I know the lies we tell ourselves are the most dangerous.

I follow Dash inside. He's wearing yellow rubber gloves, cleaning up a disgusting, gloopy pink mess on the floor.

"Maya rope you in, too?" He flashes me a smile, one eyebrow arched.

I return his smile shyly. Dash is hot. And older. And I'm not the type of girl guys notice. They tend to be surprised when they talk to me, like where had I been hiding?

"Um, no, I'm just picking up something I forgot last night."

"Well if she does, make sure she pays you. You think I'm doing this shit for free?" He holds up a spray bottle. "You know how she can be. All for one and one for herself."

I hide a smile. Maya can be a little . . . self-serving. But only because she's saving money for college. That's why she charges for entry to her parties. And to be fair, nobody else has access to these empty houses.

"I think she's upstairs," Dash says.

I thank him and head for the stairs.

"Maya?"

I peek in the bathroom, but don't see my purse. I check each bedroom, but don't find her. I'm about to head downstairs when my cell phone vibrates.

"Hello?"

There's a heavy exhalation on the other end. A breathy whisper, something ominous and low layered over static. Chills scatter down the back of my neck. This isn't the first call like this I've gotten. They started a few months ago, as if someone from another world is trying to reach me.

I move to the bedroom window and split the blinds, my gaze moving left, then right, sweeping over the field and landing at the shadowy tree line of Killer's Grove.

"Hello?" I say again. "Who's this?"

I run down the stairs, throw the door open, and launch myself outside. The street's empty, not a person around.

Static crackles and then a faint whisper. My name. *Alice.* The voice is soft, female. Familiar.

"Mom?" I whisper.

Behind me, footsteps crunch over gravel. Dash has followed me outside, yellow gloves still on. He lifts his arms, questioning.

I press my ear harder to the phone. "Hello?"

There's a sound, very faint, like music. A peppery sense of urgency swells inside me. My skin prickles. I feel like I'm being watched, except nobody's around.

And then again. *Alice.* Tears spring into my eyes . . . *not safe.*

I open my mouth, but then there's a click as the connection is severed.

Disappointment curdles in my stomach. I stare at my phone, urging it to ring again. But it doesn't.

"Everything okay?" Dash asks.

"I—I . . . ," I stammer. "Yeah. Wrong number."

I'm not sure why I lie, what I'm hiding. But I feel like I shouldn't tell anybody about this. They'll think I'm crazy. Maybe I am.

It was just a wrong number. Or maybe a prank. I snake my fingers up my coat sleeve to my scars, rubbing them like a worry stone.

I wish suddenly I was a kid again. That I could run to my dad and burrow my face in his chest. Which is weird because I used to always wish I was grown up, that he would let me make my own decisions, and now here I am and all I want is to be small, flying down the slide into my dad's arms.

Back inside the house, Maya emerges from a doorway at the end of the hallway carrying a heavy-looking wooden table chair.

"Hey." She sets the chair down in the living room with a grunt. "I put your purse in my car. Can you help me bring these chairs upstairs?"

I swallow hard, glancing back at the front door. I don't want to, but I can't tell her that. "Sure."

I follow her down the stairs into a half-finished basement crammed full of old furniture and boxes and other miscellaneous junk. It's freezing, like a million degrees colder than upstairs. My breath forms an icy white cloud in front of my face.

It smells weird down here, musty and dark, like the room hasn't been let out to air for a long time. I shiver as I look around. This place is creepy as fuck. Dust and fear fill my throat. I want to get the hell out of here.

The basement is filled with junk, old gym equipment, mildewed cardboard boxes with dusty old newspapers, dried-up old paint cans, a handful of mismatching suitcases. There's a torn, black leather sectional and a coffee table that's like one of those old vintage steamer trunks.

I spot a battered violin, one string twisted and broken, poking out of an open box. I strum it, but it twangs discordantly. I used to play. Before. I wasn't any good, but Ella was. She practiced regularly, faithfully, a high achiever in hobbies and life. Me, I'm quiet, distractible, artistic. You'd think it would be my mom, the artist, who I'd take after, but it's not. I'm more like my father, easily startled, sensitive to pain, to smells and sounds, watchful, always on the outside looking in.

Maya surveys the basement with hands on her hips. "Look at all this crap. They just left it here. Just up and moved out of the country. Somebody needs to Marie Kondo the shit out of it."

She swings around, eyes glowing. "I bet there's some stuff here we could sell. You'd be surprised how much vintage shit goes for on eBay. They'll never miss it."

I bite my lip. Maya always has an angle, a way to make a buck. Ever since she got fired from that sports store last year, she's been looking for ways to make money. She never talks about it, but I know she took the fall for something dodgy her manager was up to.

"Can we just finish up here and go?" I feel a creeping desperation to get out of here, away from the oppressive darkness, the musty smell.

Maya rolls her eyes so hard her eyeballs nearly fall out of her head. "Don't be such a wuss."

"Come on . . ."

"Not all of us have a windfall coming." Maya's tone is barbed, and I flush, hurt.

I hate this about myself, how easily I blush. Did you know humans are the only animals that blush? Or maybe other animals are just better at hiding it.

Maya's my best friend, but sometimes she can be like this, her vibe just kinda off. Okay, so one day I can declare my parents dead and collect their estate or whatever, but what sort of trade-off is that?

She immediately realizes what she's said, and she grabs my hand. "OhmyGodI'msosorry." Her words tumble over each other. "That was a dick thing to say."

"It's okay." I shrug, trying to cover the hurt. "Let's see what we can find here."

We dig through boxes, pulling out random crap like chipped old plates and mugs and sweaters riddled with mothballs. There's a box of dusty stuffed animals and another of ancient chargers, tangled and useless.

"Whoa. Check this out." Maya holds up an old flip clock.

I look at it, doubtful. "Who'd want a crappy old clock?"

"Trust me. This'll be worth something." She throws the flip clock into an empty box and picks up a spotlight of some sort. She finds an outlet and plugs it in. A flash of bright white light fills the room, and suddenly I'm tumbling back there, the car swerving, metal on pavement, the splinter of glass. And then ice-cold air. Boots crunching.

"Alice?"

Maya's voice snaps me back. "Yeah?"

"Do you want this?" She holds the spotlight up.

"No, thanks." My voice comes out rusty.

She throws it into the discard pile and keeps digging. I watch as she finds a vintage record player, some patterned glassware, a couple of old board games. She moves to the old steamer trunk and yanks up the lid, reaching inside. She stares at the item in her hands, her eyes flat, a strange, overly nonchalant look she sometimes gets when she's deep in thought.

"Maya?"

She whirls, losing her grip on the item. It falls to the floor, thuds softly against the hard cement. My gaze drifts to the item she's dropped. It's a small backpack with a large daisy across the back.

I stare at it, my brain reeling, rejecting what I see.

And yet somehow, I know. This is only the beginning. The worst is yet to come.

Chapter 6

Jess

The house is navy, a two-story Craftsman. Lovely, if a bit unloved, in need of some TLC. I slow my motorcycle, wheels crackling over frost-coated gravel, and stop next to an unmarked Explorer. I flip open the compartment for the hand-operated side stand and yank the lever. It pops open near my right heel as I kill the throttle.

I unsnap my cane, get my balance, and dismount. One year today and I'm still adjusting to my limitations, to the things I can no longer do.

I hang my helmet on the handlebars, a gust of wind tugging at my hair, the icy bite almost blistering. I hunch deeper in my winter parka as I pull out my phone. I read the text from Lieutenant Galloway again, a strange, sticky feeling hitting me.

Relief. Something to distract me from the fact that the anniversary is today. What'd my shrink call it, a *traumaversary*? The events, everything that happened, everything I lost, swirling in my head.

I need to keep my head full, my hands busy, away from the amber bottle in my cupboard. It's why I'd volunteered to be on call for the weekend.

Need you to check out a house. 4200 Lakeside Court. A backpack found there has been handed into the station. May be related to the Harper case. Could be a secondary crime scene. I'll send Shane along, too.

The Harper case.

It rings a bell. Not my case, but a case like that casts a long shadow. A family went missing last Christmas. No witnesses. No ransom demands. No motive. Just an entire family, vanished with barely a trace.

I was still in the hospital at the time, learning to walk again, losing myself in pain meds, then booze, trying to escape everything that had happened.

I look around, feeling a strange sort of unease, a sense of something looming. The house is set on a private lot across the street from a small field that leads to Killer's Grove.

The dark copse of wood is smaller than when I first moved to Black Lake over a decade ago, the trees cut back, new housing developments growing faster than the old oaks. Still, Killer's Grove has a reputation. Witch gatherings, ghost sightings, and then the unexplained disappearance of the Harpers last year. People say it's haunted.

Once upon a time, I would've laughed at this. I know better than that now.

I turn my attention back to the house.

Approaching a crime scene—even a secondary one—isn't just about the evidence or the crime. It's a full-body sensory immersion. It's about the bent grass and the direction it lays, the acrid scent of gunpowder lingering in the air, the blood spatter and how a body has fallen and the stillness in the air, like a soul has just left it.

I limp up the path, feeling a brittle stab of annoyance that Shane hasn't roped off the property yet, step one of any investigation. And another stab that I've been sent Shane Townsend, our most junior detective.

Today of all days, the anniversary, I don't have the patience for it.

My nose wrinkles at the smell of old cat pee, the boxwoods lining the pathway, and I climb the steps. As I reach the door, my skin prickles, cold chills scattering along my neck. I glance over my shoulder, scan the front yard, the gravel drive, the field across the street. There's no one there, but in my peripheral vision I see the blinds in the large bay window flutter.

Another stab of annoyance. Who has Shane let inside?

My cane makes a hollow *thunk-thunk* on the hardwood floor as I enter into a sparsely furnished living room. Someone's hung Christmas lights. A sprig of mistletoe droops from an arched beam. Couches are pushed against the wall, the nut-brown hardwood flooring beneath scuffed. The ceilings are high, the walls a bland beige.

The place smells of bleach and Windex and just slightly of stale booze. Beer and something sweeter. Whiskey. My mouth waters, and for a second the urge to drink is so overwhelming that I have to close my eyes.

I fumble in my pocket and grasp my one-month chip. For a little while, alcohol became my first love, my biggest crutch, more essential than the cane I now use for my shitty leg. I grip the chip, staring down at my closed fist, the torn, ragged flesh around my nails. I can still see blood on them, still feel it. Like it's seeped into my skin.

I move into the living room, to the large bay window where someone was watching me. But there's no sign of anybody now.

"Shane?"

"Down here." Shane's voice floats out from an open door at the end of the hallway.

"Don't you want to rope off the house?"

Shane appears in the hallway, his red hair tousled, faint circles under his eyes, his clothes a little rumpled, like he was out partying late, pulled from a deep sleep early. He has a pleasant face, young, naive, with bright freckles spattered over his nose; quick, intelligent eyes; and a mouth that naturally forms an easy smile.

"Sure. I only just got here."

I peer past him. "Did you guys find anything?"

He gives me a quizzical look. "I'm on my own."

I frown. Is he lying?

He shoots me that *aw shucks* smile that charms people so easily, one of those people who's eternally happy. It's pretty rare in our line of work. I wish I could be the same.

"Shall we have a look downstairs first?" I say, stepping around him.

The stairs down to the basement are dark, dusty. I lean hard on my cane, my leg dragging.

"Watch yourself, they're a bit rickety," Shane says from behind me.

I reach the bottom and look around. It's cold and smells damp and musty. It's packed with junk: a broken running machine, mismatched suitcases, stacks of old newspapers. There's barely any floor space to walk around.

Shane bumbles his flashlight, almost dropping it. I try not to roll my eyes as I snap on gloves and suggest he follow suit. Sometimes in this job, you get a feeling, and I have that feeling now, a fissure of alarm, something tingling along my spine.

We take opposite ends of the basement, walking it slowly. The lights are on, but it's still dim, gloomy. Dust prickles my nose.

"You out partying last night?" I say, for something to fill the silence.

"Ha. No, not my scene," he says with a chuckle.

"Ah." I smirk. "Hot date."

Shane's pale skin flares red, even in the murky light. "No."

I shrug, catching the hint. I'm not one for sharing details of my personal life, either.

"Backpack was found in there." Shane points at a steamer trunk that lies on its side, lid propped open.

I get to my knees with difficulty and direct my flashlight inside. Shane keeps moving, flashlight jumping over old weights, stacks of boxes, shelves of moldy books.

My flashlight lands on something smeared across the edge of the trunk. In the thin yellow light, I know instantly what it is.

"We've got blood."

Across the room, Shane turns sharply to hurry to me, but his foot catches on a suitcase and he trips, arms outstretched, legs tangled. He and the suitcase both fall, landing on the floor with a heavy thud.

Dust poufs into the air, making me sneeze. "You all right?"

But Shane doesn't answer. He's staring at something, his expression one of horror.

I follow his gaze.

And I know I won't be focusing on the anniversary today.

Because emerging from the suitcase he just knocked over is an arm.

Chapter 7

Alice

I enter the code, letting myself into the gated development where Mel and Jack's house is. My breath comes in ragged little gasps, and not just from my crazed bike ride over here. I don't know what to think about that backpack.

I didn't get a very good look at it. Maya had immediately scooped it up and turned to leave. We kind of fought about it. I wanted to keep it, but Maya wanted to turn it in to the police. She said it's evidence. I said if it's Ella's backpack, it's mine. Maya said we didn't know it was Ella's, so it wasn't mine. Maya won. Like always. She took the backpack and drove off.

Maya's bossier than I am. Or maybe she's just more confident, I don't know. She doesn't care what people think, and she does things I would never dare to. Maybe that's what she likes about Jinx. She's got that no-fucks attitude about her, too.

I didn't wait around for the police to show up. I figure they know where to find me. They never had a problem last time.

I walk my bike up the road to Mel and Jack's house. It's set in a bend of the lake, a huge, ten-thousand-square-foot, modern monstrosity. So big that my house could probably fit in one corner.

They own other houses, too. A hunting estate in Connecticut, a beach house in the Hamptons. But I've never been to them.

I lock my bike in the side shed and walk up the front driveway. The old me would've thought living here was so cool. I used to love the movie room, wine cellar, fitness room, infinity pool, and private beach. This me, the new me, hates it. All the emptiness, what Mel calls *minimalism*, and those windows, there're so many of them—sometimes I feel like I'm on display. Mostly I hide out in my room. Alone.

I fumble in my backpack for my key. Last summer, a local woman was murdered, her body found floating in the reeds in the lake. Black Lake's pretty small, and we don't get a lot of crime. Underage drinking and DUIs, that sort of thing. But a murder, and then That Night, everybody's freaked out. Now people lock their doors, check their cars, make sure their Ring videos are on.

I overheard Jack telling Mel that houses in his new gated development over by Killer's Grove are selling like crazy. Even the slogan taps into people's fear: *Put your family's safety first.*

I unlock the door and step inside. From the massive, two-story entry I can see straight through to the kitchen, stainless steel on shiny white, out to the lake. Everywhere are clean lines, white and steel interior with little splashes of color.

"Alice, is that you?" Mel's voice floats from down the hallway.

I don't answer. Ever since That Night, I've found it hard to speak up. The words die in my throat, like it's too weak to carry the weight of my breath. I try to sneak straight up to my room, but she calls out to me again.

"Alice?"

I sigh and turn around. I find my aunt in the home gym, surrounded by a Peloton with a large monitor, a range of workout machines, a full set of weights. She's on a yoga mat in handstand scorpion pose. She's reached total Zen. Her ice-blonde, pixie-cut hair is perfectly tousled. She got it cut the same time as I did. It suits her. Brings attention to her sharp cheekbones, her big, flashing dark eyes. My four-year-old cousin, Finn, is sprawled on another mat playing on his iPad.

"Hello, sweetheart. How'd studying go?" Mel drops into downward dog and smiles warmly up at me.

Mel is all about mental health, mindfulness, wellness. I guess on the surface, she looks pretty chill, but I know a medicine cabinet full of benzos and sleepeasies that says differently.

"Fine."

Finn's face lights up when he sees me, his arms reaching out for a hug.

I squeeze him tight, kissing his neck until he giggles. "Alice!"

I low-key hate my name. At best, it makes people think I'm some lost girl falling down a rabbit hole. At worst, I mean, it has *lice* in it. Gross.

"I'm playing *Minecraft*!" Finn exclaims earnestly. "I made a roller coaster!"

"Dope. You're super good at *Minecraft*, Finn."

Mel peers at me, her eyes seeing too much. "Are you okay?"

We don't talk about it, Mel and me. I never planned for it to be that way, it just sort of happened. After the car accident, when she brought me here from the hospital, it was too hard to be around her, to see the agony frozen on her face. It hurt to see the mirror of my pain reflected in hers. The scent of her grief, so raw, like torn leaves and lightning strikes, was too much for me to take.

She only asked once and then never again. Now it's this thing stuck between us.

"I'm fine," I say.

Mel sinks onto the floor gracefully, spine straight, legs crossed. "You look tired."

That's the second time someone's said that to me today.

"So do you," I say. And she does. She looks pale and drawn, dark circles sketched beneath her eyes.

A stab of alarm jolts through me. Sometimes I worry she'll get sick again, like she did when she was pregnant. Like she did after my family disappeared.

Peripartum cardiomyopathy. A weak heart caused by pregnancy. She's fine now. She has a pacemaker, she's careful about her health. Mom told me once it was why Mel treats her body like a temple. Yoga. The home gym. The organic foods. She wants to make sure she stays alive. For Finn.

But I still worry. That she'll leave me. That I'll be all alone again.

"Are *you* okay?" I ask.

"Don't you worry about me, I'm fine." She smiles; unfolds her long, lean frame; and comes to give me a hug, rubbing my shoulder blades in small, reassuring circles. I feel myself stiffen. I want her comfort and I don't. It's like glass under my skin.

Her arm falls to her side, and she does that thing where she consciously centers her breathing, draws energy from the earth or whatever.

"I know exactly what we need." Her eyes light up. "We'll get massages! And a facial. It'll be so relax—"

"Rain check?" I cut her off. The backpack, seeing my dead dad, my conversation with my grandma, these thoughts are pressing down on me, too heavy to share. "I have to study. Thanks, though!"

I run up the stairs to my room. My bedroom is a lace and white monstrosity that Mel decorated after I moved in. She obviously has no idea who I really am, because I'm more a blackout blinds, chill-out lights kind of girl.

My long-haired gray tabby cat is asleep on my bed. Alfie is basically the only thing I have from my old life besides clothes. Alfie and a box of stuff the cops returned to me months later, after they lost hope of ever finding my family.

I change my socks—freshly washed socks are best for not bunching—and run a hand over Alfie's soft fur. He makes that funny *prr-meow* cats do when they're startled awake, then stands, arches his back, and glares at me. Alfie's kind of a dick, actually. But I love him.

I watch him walk away, feeling like I'm floating, untethered, belonging nowhere. I shake myself and stand, scoop Alfie up, and give him a kiss despite his protests. "Come on, Alfie, let's get you some food."

He follows me back downstairs to the kitchen, where I pull a can of cat food from the designer walk-in pantry. The whole kitchen is high-end, high-tech: a ginormous chef's fridge with a wine fridge, a luxury espresso machine, a Gaggenau oven, which apparently is lusted over by designers around the world but means nothing to me.

I snap the lid off the cat food and empty it into Alfie's dish. While he eats, I browse Snapchat on my phone, post a picture of Alfie eating. My fingers play over the scar tissue on my forearm as I scroll. I take a few deep breaths. That's what Dr. Pam always says to do to calm myself, to smooth out the sadness. Breathe.

But breathing doesn't always work when your chest is filled with cement.

Mel and Finn come into the kitchen, and she starts frying some venison sausage and eggs for lunch, my uncle's favorite. The smell makes my stomach twist with nausea. Eggs gross me out. Did you know Alfred Hitchcock was scared of eggs? *Blood is jolly, red,* he said, *but egg yolk is yellow, revolting.* I totally agree.

Jack enters then, immaculately dressed in a collarless shirt and navy Gucci blazer. He's dressed down for him, but obviously on his way to work. What is it with grown-ups always working on Sundays? Jack kisses me on the cheek. He's tall, lean, muscled, his red hair lightly gelled. Jack and my mom were fraternal twins. Sometimes he looks so much like her, even though he's a guy, it actually hurts. It's his eyes, I think, a vivid dark blue.

Jack checks his Rolex. He's always in a hurry, one of those guys who thinks you can only be successful if your day is planned down to the minute. He hates waste.

"You look nice." I point at his tie. "Business on Sunday?"

"No rest for the wicked," he says with a grin. "I'm doing a site visit to check on some new construction."

Mel turns to him, frowning. "You're working today? You said we'd spend time together as a family."

Jack's nostrils flare as he sits at the table, the only sign he's annoyed. "It's unavoidable. I'm meeting Nick on-site."

Mayor Nick Greene is the reason Jack gets planning permission so fast. My dad was friends with him in high school. Dad liked to joke that introducing Jack to Nick was what opened all the doors for him. Apparently, in politics and real estate, money makes things happen. They'd go hunting together, golfed together, played poker together. Until my dad died. Now it's just Jack and Nick.

Mel sets a plate in front of Jack, maybe a little too hard, then turns and leaves the room.

Jack and I exchange a look. It's unlike Mel to act out.

"Some days are still hard for her," Jack finally says.

I stare at him. It's the *for her* that really gets me. But Jack, clueless like always, doesn't seem to realize what a dick he sounds like saying that to me.

"I think she's still figuring out how to cope. You know for a long time, she used to go back to your house? She'd just sit there, like maybe one day they'd come home. I think she still goes there sometimes."

Mel returns to the kitchen, her face once again serene. She begins putting the dirty dishes into the dishwasher. Finn hugs Jack, then pokes him in the belly, making Jack laugh.

An ugly stab of jealousy twists in my stomach, tangling with the nausea from the eggy smell. And then a heavy thud of sadness. They may have their problems, but they're still a family.

We were robbed of this. My family and I.

I slip upstairs, eager to escape. Keeping my ears open, I sneak into Mel and Jack's bedroom. It's decorated in soft grays and cool whites with huge windows overlooking the lake. I go into the bathroom and open the medicine cabinet, tip a few of Mel's Ativan into my palm. I feel better just knowing I have them. That there's backup.

I hurry upstairs to my bedroom and shut the door.

An icy breeze is cutting across my room, sending loose chills that shiver down the back of my neck. I swallow hard and wrench my curtains open.

But my window is closed.

I stare outside at the breeze ruffling the black lake, the trees dancing like a marionette, the dark clouds scuttling through the sky.

Somewhere down on the beach, a shadow dips and spins, disappearing as fast as a blink. My heart hammers in my chest, and I feel sweaty and shaky all at once.

I close my eyes, mind again flashing to that backpack. What does it mean?

When I open my eyes, there's nothing there. Just the empty beach, a sweep of storm-dulled sand, a gnarled tree stump.

But my breath has gone raspy in my chest. It feels like something is wrong. Like something very bad is about to happen. Again.

Chapter 8

Laura

It all starts with the milk.

I mean, obviously milk doesn't have much to do with what happened next, but when I think back, when I sit down to write this diary, that's the thing I land on. That hot August day, and the milk.

This is my chance, I guess. To get it all out. But I keep sitting here, staring up at the dark skylights in the attic studio Pete built me, thinking about the milk my brother, Jack, wanted me to get that day.

I close my eyes and I'm back there, and as I remember, it spools across the insides of my eyelids, like it's happening now.

It's early when the text message pings onto my phone.

It's from a number I don't recognize, so at first I ignore it. I'm in the bathroom with Ella, who's showering while I test her on her Spanish vocab. It's the first day back to school, but Ella is an overachiever. She throws her heart and soul into everything, the school play, softball, Spanish. She likes to be the best, and only the best will do.

Pete calls out to me from the hall. "Is Ella almost ready? We need to get going."

Pete drops Ella at the elementary school, then takes Alice with him to the high school, where he teaches history.

"Ella, time to get out." I brush my hair off my sweaty forehead, my colorful bracelets jingling.

My phone vibrates from the pocket of my floaty peasant skirt.

I know what you did.

My heart jumps into my throat, the bathroom contracting around me. My legs turn to rubber, and I drop to the toilet seat.

"I'm washing my hair," Ella says.

"Hurry, Dad's waiting." I take a deep breath, trying not to let my fear show.

Pete pops his head in.

"Sorry, she's still washing her hair," I say.

I know what he's thinking. He's been cleaning up the breakfast bowls, putting away the cereal, and wiping down the counters while I've been sitting here on my ass.

He doesn't say it—my husband isn't the type to get angry. But I feel his annoyance. Pete hates being late.

The shower turns off. I grab a fresh towel, toss it over the shower curtain, phone still in hand. It must be a wrong number, I decide.

"Mo-om," Ella whines. "I need to get out."

"Sorry. Leaving now."

My eyes are still on my phone as I step into the hall. I bump into Alice as I'm deleting the text. She's bleary-eyed, exhausted. Hormones at sixteen are a bitch, and Alice is more sensitive than most. She is my orchid child, a girl with an eggshell heart, fragile and prone to breakage.

I wish I could protect her from the world. She soaks up emotions like a washcloth, sadness and pain, but also beauty and joy. As a child, she got overwhelmed by bright lights and scratchy clothes, by strong smells and unexpected changes. She clung to me when I dropped her off at school or took her to the playground. Unlike Ella, my confident little diva.

"Morning, sunshine." I run a hand over Alice's tousled hair.

She grunts something indecipherable. I catch Pete's eyes, and we share a grin. Parenthood is a crafty bastard. You think you're finally getting the hang of it and then everything shifts and you're shit at it all over again.

My phone pings again, causing my heartbeat to ramp up. But this text is from my brother, Jack.

Grab some milk on the way into work, yeah?

That's it. A demand more than a question. So very Jack.

Pete raises one eyebrow as he slides his arms into his corduroy blazer.

"Do you have an administrative-assistant emergency?" he jokes.

He doesn't mean it in a cruel way, but I stiffen, offended, and he can tell.

"Jack wants me to pick up some milk," I say. "He has a big meeting today. Some shareholders, I guess."

I lace up my sandals, then go into the kitchen. I pour myself a glass of orange juice, but I've just brushed my teeth, and the taste it leaves in my mouth is bitter.

Lately, since I lost the art studio and stopped painting, if I'm honest, I've felt a little lost. And okay, maybe angry, too. Sometimes I wonder if I have a single notable thing about me. Artist, wife, mother. I look at Alice and Ella, and of course I love them, but I also wonder if this is all I am? Sometimes I daydream about becoming someone more exciting, more . . . just more.

It hasn't helped, being forced to accept a job working for my twin brother. There's failure and then there's rock-bottom failure, and then there's being rescued by the rich, successful guy you shared a womb with. Even our house is owned by Jack. We'd probably be living in a moldy two-bedroom apartment if Jack hadn't given us such a good deal on rent. It's generous and fortunate and really, really humiliating.

"I'm sorry." Pete comes up behind me, wrapping strong arms around me. "I was just joking. I didn't mean anything by it."

"I know." I lean into him. "I love you."

"Love you, too."

My phone pings again.

"Sounds like Jack really wants that milk."

"Gotta run." I kiss him goodbye, even though it's ridiculous to rush off for milk.

But this is my life now. Jack pays me a good wage, and Pete and I need the money. Now that I have a real salary, we've finally caught up on our bills. Our student loans are almost paid off. We have health insurance. Life insurance. Soon we'll be able to start saving properly. Retirement, 401(k), vacations, maybe even buy our own place.

I call a quick goodbye to the girls and rush out the door. At the grocery store, I go to the milk aisle, but I don't know what milk Jack wants or how much. Exasperated, I pull my phone out to text him and see another message.

I'm watching you.

My gaze darts down the aisle, the elderly lady bent over cheese, a dad with his toddler looking at yogurt. My palms are sweaty, my stomach twisting.

"Laura? Laura O'Brien."

The use of my maiden name behind me is confusing. I whirl around.

"Theo Moriarty!" A surprised smile spreads over my face. "Oh my God, how are you?"

"Damn, Laur, I can't believe it's you!"

Theo's grinning from ear to ear. He shakes my hand, like we didn't spend a year of our lives together in college. A year in which we were wholly consumed with each other, physically, mentally, emotionally. A year in which my best friend Mel, now Jack's wife, worried I'd "lost" myself. Looking back, maybe she was right.

Our relationship was passionate, the kind of unfettered intensity only a first love has. Where you become subsumed in it, two people folding into one entity. It was like I was hypnotized by him. He could get me to do things I never dreamed I'd be willing to do. Only later did I see that not all of it was good.

I can't stop staring at him. Theo Moriarty is still magnetic, amiable. Still good-looking in that edgy, almost dangerous way. His black hair is longish, a little tousled, hanging into bright blue eyes. Even now, in his forties, his body is sculpted, his chest broad.

He's wearing a light black jacket, dark jeans, and a dark T-shirt, even though it's a million degrees outside. It reminds me he has a darker side, too, the tortured, angst-ridden hero. The artist in him coming out, I suppose.

Back in college, he played guitar in a band. He loved Radiohead, Smashing Pumpkins, Pixies, sure, but also Ani DiFranco and The Posies. I wonder if he still plays.

"Wow, how long has it been?" he says. "Twenty years?"

"That long?" I brush a strand of hair from my forehead, aware I haven't dyed the gray from the red in months. Years? Who knows anymore. Sometimes I still feel like that teenage girl, just buried inside a middle-aged woman with a sagging body.

Theo and I broke up midway through sophomore year in college. Some relationships just aren't meant to be. After all that had happened, I needed to walk away, to move on. And I did. We never spoke again.

Until today.

We talk about what we've been up to since the last time we spoke: marriage and kids for me, two divorces and a work-based accident that broke his back. About his music that went the same way as my painting (the trash). About failed dreams and hopes.

As we talk, the years fall away right there in the dairy aisle. I need to get to work, and yet something holds me here.

"So what brings you to Black Lake?" I finally ask.

He flashes me that mischievous grin I remember so well. "The lake."

He draws the word out long enough for me to die of embarrassment. My cheeks burn. Of course that's why he's here. The lake is the only reason people come.

"I'm meeting a buddy for a few days of fishing. He works over there." He waves at the sports store across the street, his eyes twinkling.

I don't know why I do it. Inviting my ex out for a drink is a little brash. Maybe it's something about the past, the nostalgia it brings, draping over me like a wintertime fog. The reminder of youth, of all the optimism and excitement you feel when you're young, before family and marriage and responsibility change you.

But as I grab the milk, I ask, figuring it's just one drink. What harm could that do?

Chapter 9

Jess

The house is officially a crime scene.

Shane and I call it in, rope it off, then go outside to wait.

The sky is heavy, bloated with snow clouds. In a few weeks, it will be Christmas, thick banks of fluffy snow on the ground. But right now, everything just feels dark and gray.

A patrol car pulls up, two uniformed officers I vaguely know getting out.

"Want to get them canvassing?" I suggest to Shane. "There were no signs of forced entry, no weapon found, and no neighbors to get video surveillance from, but maybe someone saw something."

Shane snaps his fingers. "On it."

While he's talking to the cops, I scan the front yard. My eyes land on someone out in the field across the street. The one leading to Killer's Grove.

It's a man. He's of average height with thick, dark hair flopping over his forehead, a neatly trimmed beard, black-framed glasses. He's wearing a suit and a black peacoat, the hem flapping in the breeze.

Something cool and sticky slides down my spine. There's something about him. Something . . . unsettling.

Later, when I find out who the man is, this feeling will make sense. But right now, I only vaguely recognize it, the whisper of something on my neck, a faint buzzing at the edges of my brain.

I turn away from him, watch as Shane talks to the other cops. Pressure builds in my ears, blood rushing in my head. I limp over to my motorcycle, open the saddlebag, and grab a bottle of water. It's ice-cold sliding down my throat, a sharp snap that focuses me.

Something cold touches my hand. I jump and whirl around.

"Oh, it's you." I smile softly when I recognize the person. "You scared me."

"Sorry." Shane comes up behind me, shooting me a funny look. He doesn't see her. Nobody does. "You're very jumpy today."

I shake my head, trying to clear it. "Um, catch me up on that backpack."

Shane pulls a notepad from his pocket. "According to Maya, the girl who brought it in, she was here with her brother and a friend. They were cleaning up after a party they had last night when she noticed the trunk was open and peeked inside, saw the backpack. She recognized it and brought it in."

"How'd she get inside?"

"She stole the key from her mom, who owns The Merry Maid."

"The cleaning company?"

"Yep. Her mother is Nancy Shepherd. She and her husband, Dom, run the company, so they have the keys to a lot of places in Black Lake now."

"Especially since that new gated community went in just up the road."

"Exactly."

"Is this house a rental?" I ask.

"Unclear. I chatted with a lady out walking her dog before you got here, and she says it's been sitting empty for a while. Last she knew, it was up for sale after the owners moved to England a few years back. I'll check the property tax records and find out who owns it now."

"I take it Nancy Shepherd didn't know her daughter was throwing a party here."

Shane laughs. His laugh reminds me again how young he is. Not so much older than someone who might have been at this party. "Like parents ever know."

"Tell me about the case."

Shane scans my face. I wonder how much he knows, if he's aware of my own gruesome history?

Last year, when the Harpers disappeared, I was still a mess. My husband gone. My daughter gone. My family fractured, splintered like a piece of wood that's been cleaved in half by lightning. I could barely get myself out of bed most days, let alone pay attention to somebody else's tragedy.

I tried to talk to Mac recently, drove up to his new place. But in the end, I couldn't do it. And Isla, Isla is gone, too, although I still see her on occasion.

"We received a call from an off-duty paramedic who'd driven past the wreckage of their car by the side of the road." Shane is still talking. I force myself to bring my attention back, to focus on him.

"He found a teenage girl wandering along the road a few hundred feet away, clearly in shock."

"That's right," I say, remembering now. "She was the only one who was ever found."

"Yep. Alice Harper. She said they were heading home after a family Christmas gathering at the house of their uncle, Jack O'Brien."

"The property developer?"

"Yep. Liu and I worked the case hard. In the weeks and months after they disappeared, we had more than a thousand tips, conducted over a hundred interviews, took over four thousand photographs, and followed up on multiple 'sightings,' but nothing panned out. No witnesses; no fingerprints; no real, useful evidence; no suspects; no motives. No bodies. The FBI was brought in, but they didn't find anything, either. It was like they'd just *poof*, magically disappeared."

As he speaks, I glance over Shane's shoulder at the field. But the man, whoever he was, is no longer there.

"Any theories?"

"Liu liked the husband for the disappearances," Shane replies. "He thought that Peter Harper killed his family, hid their bodies, then killed himself. He'd been suspended from his job as a history teacher at the high school the week before. He came in drunk, falling all over the place. Cussing at one of the teachers. A week later, the whole family except Alice disappeared."

It isn't a bad theory. Family annihilators are, for all intents and purposes, loving husbands and good fathers, often seen as successful, stand-up citizens. They often see their family as a symbol of their own success, so when they fail—getting fired from a job, for example—the family members are the ones who pay.

"Got a history of domestic disturbance calls from the family?"

Shane shakes his head. "No, but a lot of abused women never call in their husband."

"True. Could've been battered wife syndrome. He hit her one too many times and she snapped, killed him."

"Or he took it one step too far and killed her and the rest of the family."

"Did *you* think he did it?" I ask Shane.

"If the body in that suitcase is Pete Harper, then it blows that theory out of the water. But at the time, it seemed plausible."

"What did Alice say?"

"She claimed to have no clear memory before or after the accident."

"Do you believe her?"

Shane bites his cheek. "I don't not believe her."

It isn't the same thing, and he knows it.

"But why leave one daughter behind?" I say.

Wheels hit gravel, and we turn. A CSI truck pulls into the driveway, "Jingle Bells" blasting from the speakers before the engine cuts and

Khandi Dawson gets out dressed in a white forensic suit, a paper mask hanging off one ear. She grins when she sees me, hazel eyes sparkling.

"Jess! Hey, girl, it's been ages!" she exclaims, dimples flashing. She hugs me tightly. "You look amazing! Hold on. Let me get my kit."

She returns a moment later with a box of tools, still smiling. Khandi is friendly, cheerful, with a strangely optimistic outlook considering her line of work. She has smooth russet-brown skin, a twinkling nose ring, and long, cinnamon-colored twists pulled into a jaunty ponytail. She wears a dark choker with a tiny black heart.

Khandi moved to Black Lake with her husband, like I did a decade ago, looking for a quieter life, a more peaceful life. The type of life we thought a small town could give us to raise a family. We used to meet for drinks after work occasionally. Before.

"How are you?"

"Good. Can't complain." I introduce her to Shane, and they shake hands.

"How's the leg?" she asks.

"Better." I tap my cane against my shoe. "I'll be running marathons before I know it."

She laughs because it's obviously not true. My leg will never be good enough for running again. But I've started swimming, and in the summer I'll try rowing. It's therapeutic, and it helps offset my other hobby, which is baking.

"So, tell me what we've got," Khandi says.

We fill her in, pulling on crime-scene booties before heading inside. They make a quiet shuffling noise as I limp across the hardwood, my cane thudding as I follow them into the basement.

Downstairs, Shane points to the large, graphite-colored suitcase that has tipped onto its back. The soft-bodied outer shell has torn, or maybe the zipper has broken, exposing the mostly decomposed arm of the body inside.

I snap on a pair of gloves. The arm has a coat on, black, matted in dried body fluids, but the hand is pale and still, a shocking white against the dark hardwood.

Khandi extracts her tools as I awkwardly get onto my knees. I flick my flashlight over the suitcase. As you'd expect, there's staining at the bottom, dried body fluid and flecks of mud, as well as bits of twigs and clumps of dried dirt on the suitcase wheels. But I don't see any signs of blood.

"Whoever it is, they were dead before they were put in the suitcase," I say, "and probably moved, possibly pulled through Killer's Grove to this house in the suitcase. The Harpers went missing near Christmas, right? It would've been impossible to bury a body. The ground would be too frozen for digging. The victim in that suitcase is clearly male. But if it's Pete Harper, where's the mother and other daughter?"

It's a hypothetical question, and I don't expect a reply. Neither Shane nor Khandi gives one.

Khandi kneels next to me and flips the suitcase lid open, releasing a musky, stale scent. We stare down at the mostly skeletonized remains inside. The victim is wearing blue jeans and a black puffer coat. His hair has partially fallen out, strands of brown clinging to the scalp.

She plucks out a battered leather wallet from under the body and hands it to Shane, who's gone a little pale. He flips it open, reads the driver's license.

"Looks like we found Peter Harper."

I stare at the body for a long moment. "Something isn't right."

I bend closer, pointing my flashlight right through the open eye sockets. One side of the skull has collapsed. Before or after death? And there, at the back, is one small hole.

"A bullet wound." I look up at Shane. "Nobody shoots themselves in the head and puts themselves in a suitcase. This was murder. Pete Harper didn't do this."

I get to my feet, tapping my fingertips against the handle of my cane, try to grab the slippery thought that's darting around my head.

"Do you have that picture of Pete Harper?" I ask Shane.

"We got it off Alice's Instagram. Let me see if I can find it."

He taps at his phone, opens Alice's Instagram page, then hands it to me. I stare at the picture of the Harpers smiling in front of a Christmas tree last year. My mouth drains of all moisture when my eyes land on Pete Harper.

I recognize him.

Faintly collegiate, black-framed glasses, floppy brown hair. It's the guy who was watching me from across the road earlier. Except now that feeling I had—the tap of cool, sticky fingers down my spine, the unsettling whisper on the back of my neck, the faint buzzing at the edges of my mind—it makes sense.

Because he wasn't really there.

"This isn't the man in the suitcase." I hold up the phone, tapping the picture. "Pete's wearing a suit with tinsel around his neck."

We look down at the man in the suitcase. "This guy is wearing jeans and a puffer coat. Unless somebody undressed and then redressed him, this isn't Pete Harper."

"If this isn't Pete, then he could've been the killer after all," Shane says, his face grim.

And that's when I know.

Somewhere, out in Killer's Grove, Pete Harper is dead. But did he kill his family and hide them first?

And who the hell is inside this suitcase?

Chapter 10

Jess

My dad appears on my doorstep late Sunday night, as I'm getting home from the crime scene. No call. No notice. Just a worn backpack and a big grin, his whiskey-colored eyes, same as mine, sparking with a million unsaid words.

"Sorry I'm late, Bug." He still calls me by my childhood nickname, like I'm six instead of thirty-six. "I meant to be here by midday, but there was an accident on the I-85."

I give him a quick hug, his smell, woodsmoke and coffee and a faint hint of Old Spice, evoking childhood memories.

"No problem." I don't want to talk about it, to be honest, and I tell him so.

We order Chinese food, barely saying a word between us. My dad isn't the talkative type, and for once I'm glad. Eventually I go to bed, falling into a restless, uneasy sleep.

Monday morning, I rise before the sun and leave a note on the kitchen table, telling him where I'll be.

It's cold and gray in the graveyard. Isla's hand grasps mine tightly as we stare at the grave at our feet. That weird, anxious energy thrums inside me, like black fingers curling beneath my skin.

As a detective, a paramedic before that, I've spent years around death. But it didn't prepare me for grief.

"Somebody weeded it." I dig a toe into the bare ground by the headstone. It's hard, prickly with frost.

Isla gives me a funny look. I suppose weeds aren't something eight-year-olds think about.

I notice something nestled at the base of the granite headstone, a small heart-shaped stone, and bend to pick it up. Pain shoots through my leg. The heart is smooth, its surface blank. I'm pretty sure I know who left it here.

Isla plucks the heart out of my palm, rubbing it between her thumbs. "What do you think heaven's like, Mommy?" she asks.

"Oh, Isla . . ." My chest clutches, my throat closing.

Isla drops the heart stone back on the headstone, seeming to know I can't speak. She flicks a messy blonde braid over one shoulder and skips after a leaf that's whirling by, blown by the icy morning breeze.

Before I can call her back, I hear gravel crunching behind me.

"You were up early," my dad calls as he strides across the frost-tipped grass.

He's carrying a Starbucks cup in each hand, the lines around his mouth pronounced, his back hunched in his wool coat. His ears poke out from beneath an old tweed flat cap my mom gave him years ago, ears that earned him the nickname Q-bear, instead of Quinn.

He looks old, I realize. Isn't it strange when you realize your parents are getting old? Maybe parents age us as much as we age them.

He thrusts a cup at me, and I thank him.

"I let it pass me by yesterday," I say. "The anniversary. I didn't want to think about it."

"Sometimes it's easier that way."

"Yeah."

"Wow." He whistles, taking in the view. "Sure is pretty up here."

I follow his gaze across the graveyard, the gravestones like teeth biting at the sky, down the sloping hill to the dark waters of Black Lake.

Beyond that, the islands that dot the lake's surface, the town curled along its shore.

Pretty can be an illusion, though. A perfectly pleasing deception. My eyes dart to the frost-coated pine forest of Killer's Grove, where the Harpers went missing last year.

Dad studies me. "You look like shit. That job of yours is giving you wrinkles."

"Gee, thanks." I try not to roll my eyes, to revert back to the teenager I once was. "Being a detective isn't exactly all sunshine and roses, as I'm sure you remember."

"I know, Bug." He drapes an arm around my shoulders, our breath puffing white into the frigid air. "Why don't you quit?"

"I can't."

"Transfer? You could move back to New York or, hell, to Atlanta, with me. It's warmer there."

"I have a case."

He hesitates, then: "I'm worried about you, Jess."

I want to tell him I'm feeling better now. Rehab. Counseling. I bake in the evenings, swim in the mornings. I'm doing okay. But just then my phone rings. Lieutenant Galloway, who took over after Rivero got promoted and moved to Boston last month. I'm late for work, a meeting about the Harper case. I press "End."

"What exactly is it you want here?" Dad asks.

I glance at Isla, who's inspecting a nearby headstone, and I suddenly yearn for the smoky burn of whiskey, the black beast of my addiction stirring. A list of regrets scrawls across my brain. Perhaps, like Sylvia Plath, I desire the things that will destroy me in the end.

I look again at Killer's Grove. Ominous clouds skitter like whispers, dark over the tree line. I think of Pete Harper, how he'd hovered there in the hulking shadow of the forest. And then I think of my last case, the case that nearly broke me, solved under an oppressive, brutal sun.

"I want to help them," I say. "The victims. I'm their voice when they no longer have one."

I became a detective because I wanted to create order in an otherwise unorderly world. I've dedicated my career to bringing closure to those left behind. But balancing empathy and horrific crime is a battlefield, and I'm a soldier who can't put down her sword. Now, I think, maybe I'm not supposed to. I want to find the truth for the dead. That's all any of us want, after all. The truth.

"Solving more cases isn't going to make you feel any better," Dad says. "Trying to save the world, it's a compulsion, same as drinking."

A sharp breeze whips my long, dark hair around my face. I wince at the chill.

"I appreciate you coming here." I change the subject. "Your support . . ."

"It's okay, Bug." He clears his throat. "I know I wasn't around much when you were younger. I . . . regret that. But I'm here now."

I look at my dad, surprised. We Lamberts are not an expressive bunch. A cold drop of fear squirms in my gut.

"I wish I could help you," he continues. "The thing is, you can't move forward if you're standing still. That's the honest truth."

Somewhere in the distance, the sound of an ambulance drifts by, ghostly and distant. I glance down at Isla, who's come up beside me, beautiful now as she was in life.

Then I look down at her grave, embedded like a shipwreck in the ocean floor.

Isla Elizabeth Lambert

Age 8

Always with us

And I miss her all over again.

◆ ◆ ◆

Dad and I make vague plans for dinner later; then I head to work. I pull into my space at the front of the police station, hurry along the sidewalk, cane thudding against the icy pavement. I press my ID to the door, wait for the familiar buzz.

The bullpen looks the same as always, different mug shots, same crimes, a mess of files stacked haphazardly on the desks, drab blinds. The air is stale, too warm, thick with the scent of burned coffee.

Roll call has begun. I try to sneak in without anybody noticing, sliding in behind my old partner, Will Casey.

"How's the case?" he whispers.

"It's weird, isn't it?" I whisper back. "Shane leading? Why aren't y—"

But I don't get a chance to finish.

"Lambert, good of you to join us!" Lieutenant Brooke Galloway calls.

The sound of Galloway's voice ignites a frisson in my belly. When she first took over for Rivero, I was a little relieved. Finally, another woman on the team. She seemed smart, pragmatic. A decorated naval officer, she'd moved into policing and was one of the youngest female lieutenants in the country. She was known for being persistent, tough, black-and-white as a checkerboard. I thought we would be allies. I was wrong.

I think she'd fire me if she could, but she's already down one detective since Bill Liu's getting chemo, plus Shane's pretty green. Not that we have a lot of crime around here—mostly prowlers, burglaries, low-level stuff—but I pull my weight.

My stomach cramps with nerves as heads swivel, like I'm a kid who's been marked as the unpopular one. I catch a couple of side glances. I know what they say behind my back. I hate it. The looks of pity. The snide comments. I just want to get on with the job.

"Listen up . . . ," she continues.

Will shoots me a reassuring smile as Galloway goes over outstanding cases, incidents, suspects. When she's finished, I head to my desk, which is shoved up against the wall near her office. When I first started, I had a view from the window, but now I'm stuck here. I suspect Galloway's keeping an eye on me.

Galloway calls my name on the way to her office.

"Shut the door," she tells me. "Sit."

I do as she asks. My good leg jiggles, a restless habit. She sits across from me. The room feels crowded, like she's taking up all the air, all the space.

"I read the police report on your accident last year," she says. "It's different from what some of the officers said."

I frown. I've never read it.

"You'd been drinking."

I want to tell her it was only one drink, but it's no excuse. I know that.

"There was no proper investigation. No urine, no bloods taken. Just a rainy day, a random deer, and an old man who was a less-than-reliable witness. And word on the street is, now you think you can see dead people? Can you tell the future, too?"

She lifts a sleeve and extends one arm across the desk. "Read my palm, then. Tell me what it says."

I stare at her. I can't see the future. I don't read tarot cards or crystal balls or palms. I have no control of this *thing* that happens to me. It's a gift, or maybe a curse. All I know is sometimes the dead appear to me. Sometimes they talk. Sometimes I know things that are inexplicable.

But it isn't exact or precise. I don't even know if they're real or just a heightened perception I have.

When I don't answer, Galloway sits back, pushes her inky-black curls off her forehead. For a second, I glimpse a scar near her temple. She smooths the hair back in place. Cops don't hide scars they're proud of getting on the job.

"Some people say your last case is confirmation of your 'powers.'" She puts the word in air quotes. "But I worry. And I can't have one dysfunctional cop fucking it up for everybody else. Understand?"

It's a warning. I understand that. So I nod.

Galloway stands abruptly, throws the door open. "Townsend!"

Shane hurries into the office, that easy smile on his face. "Heya, Lieutenant."

He moves to shut the door, but Galloway stops him. "Leave it. This won't take long. We got the labs back. Blood on that backpack matches Ella Harper."

She pulls a school picture of a teenage girl from a folder. "This is Alice Harper. She was there yesterday when Maya found the backpack."

"She was there?" I say, surprised.

Galloway nods.

I study the picture. *Holy shit.* It's the girl who was at my shrink yesterday. She's cut her hair, looks a little more . . . strung-out or something, but it's definitely her.

"She was the only one left behind." Galloway hands us another picture, this one of the backpack. Black with a daisy, the white center now a deep, rusty red, a small badge near the bottom that I can't quite make out. "And now we know that backpack belonged to Ella Harper. Someone stashed it in that basement. The body, well, we'll know what the connection is soon enough. But Alice Harper, she's our only witness. You guys have got yourself a case. I want Shane leading this one."

Shane's eyes widen, his ears flaring bright red.

"Wait . . ." I blink. I'm far more experienced than Shane. "That isn't right."

"Are you telling me how to do my job, Detective?" Galloway asks stonily.

"No . . ."

"Shane worked the case last year. And I'm not sure you being in charge is such a good idea. After all, it's not so long ago you were talking to your daughter's ghost, isn't that right?"

Outside the office, the bullpen goes quiet. My face flames hot.

Galloway's eyes are flinty. She's testing me. Thinking I can't be trusted. I grind my molars. So this is how she wants to play it. Fine. Fucking fine.

"I want the case cleared by Christmas," Galloway continues. "The mayor's a personal friend of Jack O'Brien, Laura Harper's brother, and they want it solved. Yesterday."

Seriously? Christmas is only a few weeks away. And assigning me a new partner on an old case while making me the junior? It just doesn't make sense. But I give a tight smile and limp out of her office.

I don't stop at my desk. I keep going, down the hall, to the bathroom, into a cubicle. I lock the door and sit on the toilet, stomach burning. I hear three sharp knocks on the bathroom door, then Will's voice as he steps inside.

"Hey, old girl. You all right?"

I flush the toilet and wipe my eyes before opening the cubicle.

"You shouldn't be in here, Will."

I twist the hot-water tap, thrust my hands under. Will looks back at me from behind black-framed glasses, his skin glistening pink in the fluorescent lights.

"What Galloway said was unprofessional."

I sigh. "Maybe she's right, Will. Our last case, I was . . . distracted."

I turn the tap off, dry my hands. I'm still a mess. I barely sleep at night. I have a constant restlessness inside me. I did my time in rehab and still I crave a drink.

"I get it," I say. "Having a preoccupied detective on a case is the last thing a lieutenant wants."

"Especially a new one who wants to make her mark," Will says dryly.

"Maybe I shouldn't be here."

Will is the only one who knows the extent of everything. That I still see Isla, even now.

Grief hallucinations, my shrink calls them. Except it isn't only Isla I see.

"You're a good detective, Jess. Trust your instincts. And don't let Galloway get in your head."

Chapter 11

Alice

School is total hell. Rumors are flying. People are whispering. I can feel their wide-eyed stares. I'm not exactly popular, but people know me. The price of infamy, I guess.

Monday and Tuesday pass in a blur. Maya and I don't talk about what we found. We don't actually *know* what we found.

When Spanish ends Wednesday afternoon, I grab my backpack and head to my locker. The hall smells of cafeteria lasagna. Nausea claws at my stomach. Somebody's locker creaks open, a sound that makes me shudder. Sharp staccato laughter hits me between my eyes. My head pulses.

"Hey, guurl!" Runy falls in next to me.

I flinch. Why's he talking so loud? One arm is looped around Taylor, a pretty sophomore I've literally heard one teacher describe as "American as apple pie," which is dumb because apple pie was actually invented in England.

"Dude, I was, like, *soo* hungover after Maya's party!"

Runy grins at me from under a tawny flop of hair hanging in his brown eyes. He'd actually be kind of cute if he'd stop doing all the drugs.

"It was lit." Taylor giggles. "Remember when Brad stripped and dove into the lake? It was *totally* extra!"

I unlock my locker. I have trig next. A test I never studied for. It doesn't matter. Math is my best subject. I like that there's a right and wrong answer, nothing subjective about it. And I'm good at tests. I'm that weird kid at the back of the class doodling cats and seeming tuned out, but who knows all the answers. Sometimes I get a few wrong on purpose, just so people don't look too hard at me.

"I waited for you guys. Thought you might come back," Runy says.

I shake my head. "I couldn't."

Something sparks in his eyes. Runy's dad died when we were in junior high. He'd battled schizophrenia for a long time, but the voices found him. He killed himself and another guy at the UPS Store where he worked.

It's taken Runy a while to shrug off who he used to be in relation to that. He started smoking pot, creating this new image, a stoner dude always up for a good time.

I get it. I know what it's like to want to step outside your own skin. To be a freak. Sometimes you just don't want to be yourself anymore.

"Is it true?" Taylor lowers her voice. "Did you find the body?"

I recoil like I've been hit.

"Dude!" Runy glares at her.

Taylor blinks. "I just wanted to know if she—"

"Fuck. Off." Runy's eyes glow.

"Wait. What body?" I pluck at Taylor's sweater to stop her from huffing away. "What are you talking about?"

"The house we were partying at on Saturday? The cops found a body in the basement."

I'm speechless. That isn't what Maya and I found.

"Who told you that?"

"My uncle's a detective. I heard him tell my mom."

I have a sudden weird feeling, like I'm balanced on a cliff, about to be pushed over the edge.

"Get outta here," Runy snaps.

Taylor huffs away, but I hear what she mutters.

Freak.

"Ignore her," Runy tells me.

"We found a backpack, not a body." It feels important he knows that. I shove my trig book into my bag with numb fingers. "It looked like my sister's backpack."

"Shit. Really?"

"Yeah. It went missing the night of the accident."

"You still don't remember?"

That's what I told everybody. At the time. It was an easy excuse. The truth is, I remember *everything.*

I just don't want to.

"Maya took the backpack to the cops." I avoid his question. "They must've searched the house. I thought the detectives would come and interview me or something, but I haven't heard anything."

"So they found a body with your sister's backpack. You don't think . . ."

"They would've told me, though. Right?" My voice sounds weird. Like it's been pinched somewhere in my throat. "If it was one of them, they would've told me?"

We stare at each other, but Runy has no response.

Loud laughter comes from down the hall. It's Maya and Jinx, holding hands now. Maya towers over Jinx, tall and slender in her pink hoodie and ripped jeans. Jinx is wearing some sort of black lacy corset with a leather skirt, her hair spiked with a glossy gel. She has, like, six earrings in one ear. I never got my ears pierced. The thought of a needle stabbing my ear . . . I shiver.

Runy follows my gaze. "You okay?"

I'm still mad at Maya for not letting me look inside that backpack. I didn't even *really* get to look at it. Maybe I was wrong about it. Maybe it was just some regular old backpack. I have a similar one at home. Mom got them from Walmart; it's not like they're unique or anything.

The bell rings, saving me from answering Runy. He says goodbye and rushes off. But instead of going to class, I duck into the bathroom.

My throat feels like a giant ball of metal is lodged in it. I lock myself in a stall, feeling sick. What does the body in the basement mean?

I don't know why I bothered coming in today. Last night, I couldn't sleep. I couldn't shake the sight of that backpack lying there in the basement, the sense that something was coming.

Since the accident, I've kept my memories safe, buried deep inside. But now it feels like they're stirring, eating their way to the surface.

Did you know that over 600,000 people are reported missing every year in America? And how many of those turn up dead?

Last night, after looking up that fact, I curled up in bed, scared to be awake but scared to sleep. Lately I've been having these crazy, vivid dreams. Of That Night. When I wake, my clothes are soaked, my covers tossed on the floor. Reality is like an icy slap in the face. Then the loss sinks in, crushing and raw, and all I can do is cry.

Eventually I took one of the Ativan I'd stolen from Mel. When I'd finally drifted into an uneasy sleep, my dreams were worse than usual. I was in the woods, running, branches snagging in my hair, ripping at my skin. And then I burst through the trees and there was our car, lying on its side. And lit by the headlights . . .

The image pushes up against the inside of my skull, but I bat it away. The dust of bad memories is usually best left alone, unswept, untidied. A nice layer of dirt to cover it. But it's like someone's dragged a fingertip through it, revealing more than I want. I know what happened. I know what I saw that night.

But sometimes it feels hard to separate what's real from what isn't.

◆　◆　◆

I leave school.

By the time I get to Mel and Jack's, it's snowing. Inside, the house looks like somebody vomited up Christmas. A giant tree with white lights and silver tinsel fills the living room. Fir branches are scattered around, fairy lights draped all over, white stars hanging in every window.

"Mel?"

Silence.

I unravel my scarf, yank off my gloves and coat. There's the faint whiff of something I can't quite identify. Something sweet and floral. And then a heavier scent. Cigarette smoke. Except neither Mel nor Jack smokes. I circle the downstairs, but nobody's home.

Most of the yoga classes Mel teaches are early or late, so I wonder where she is. A flicker of anxiety sparks in my stomach. I'm overreacting, being irrational. But I don't know how to control this fear and dread that's coexisted inside me ever since my family went missing. The fear that maybe my aunt, uncle, and cousin have disappeared, too.

That I've been left behind again.

I grab my phone with sweaty palms, about to call Mel. My eyes land on Runy's sister's number.

I looked up her podcast. It's called *The Darkest Night*. Last year they investigated the twenty-three-year-old disappearance of this high school girl. They found her body, hidden all those years under the patio of the school janitor's house. Now he's serving life in prison.

I imagine calling Chloe; then I imagine upsetting Mel and Jack. I grab my purse and take out an Ativan, looking between my phone in one hand and the pill in the other.

The truth is, finding that backpack has raked up memories I don't want.

I think of everything that happened after the accident. The search, the media chaos, the talk-show chatter, the invasive news reports and my parents' deepest secrets dug up, an investigation that found no evidence as to where they were. And then the theory that my dad had killed them, then himself.

I can't go through that again.

I delete Chloe's number and swallow the Ativan.

In the kitchen, I pour milk over a bowl of Whoppers and eat it like cereal, staring out the window at the black lake, a dull smudge blurred by the falling snow. Alfie winds around my legs.

Soon numbness settles over me, like I've been coated in glue. My limbs are thick and sticky, my brain dull. I ride my Ativan wave up the stairs, trailing my fingertips over the pictures lining the wall. They follow me like ghosts, their eyes on me. The pictures are of their family and mine. Mel and my mom. My mom and Jack. Jack and my dad. Finn, Ella, me.

My mom was Jack's twin sister, but she was Mel's best friend. They were friends in college before Mel ever met Jack.

Dr. Pam's words circle through my mind. *Closure can mean different things to different people. Perhaps your version isn't just about getting answers, but in learning to feel grateful that you lived.*

It's shrinky bullshit. There's no way to thrive when I don't know where they are and why I'm still here.

When I reach the landing, I notice something red, a splash of scarlet against the pale carpet. I pick it up. It looks like a petal of some sort, crumpled and broken, like it's been stuck to someone's shoe and carried inside. My gaze jerks up. Is someone here?

My palms have started sweating. And then I notice something else. That subtle, light scent, sweet and floral. I breathe it in. Lilacs and vanilla. My mom's body lotion.

"Mom?" I whisper.

I swallow hard, my throat dry, and notice that Finn's door is cracked. I jam the petal into my pocket and push the door open. Finn is starfished across his bed, his arms thrown over his head.

I frown, confused. I thought Finn was at day care. If he's home, where the hell is Mel? And why is he asleep? Finn's four. He doesn't nap anymore.

From somewhere far away, I hear my phone ring, but it sounds weird. Like it's echoing in a tin can. The shadows shimmer and shift. A strange, low-level buzzing starts at the corners of my brain. Something catches in my peripheral vision.

It's Mel. She looks different, wild and disheveled, her pale silk top filthy, streaked with something. Dirt? Her hair is wet, her mascara smudged, eyes feral as a cat's.

"What are you doing?" Her voice is low-pitched, barbed.

"I . . . I . . ." I don't understand what's happening.

I turn back to Finn, but he's no longer there. In his place is a little girl. Long blonde braids and a pink Hello Kitty satin bow headband.

I've seen her before. The night of the accident.

I remember waking in the car, snow falling on my face. My arm was broken. Blood dripped down my head, its sharp, metallic scent filling my nose. I became aware of a presence, and when I turned my head, I saw a little girl, maybe seven or eight, next to me in the car.

She raised one hand to her lips. "Shh."

Outside the car, footsteps crunched over broken glass. Someone was out there.

Now the little girl sits on Finn's bed.

What do you want from me? I try to say, except no words come out.

Her mouth moves around a single word that somehow doesn't come out but echoes in my ears.

Run!

My heart is an engine in my chest, and the room tilts dangerously. I stagger out of the room into the hallway.

Something dark trails across the oatmeal-colored carpet. Muddy footsteps. Cold air gushes from under my bedroom door. I slam it open with my palms. It's even colder in here. Not normal cold, but the kind of cold that wraps around you like seaweed. And there's a smell, too. Of something rotting, decaying. Like the dead rat covered in maggots I once found in Ella's toy box.

I gasp.

My dad is sitting on my bed. His face is streaked with blood, his skin loosely draped on his skull.

A sob wrenches from my mouth. "Dad?"

"Why haven't you found us?" His eyes are so black, they look like holes.

There's a roaring in my head. The bedroom stutters, like a camera's lens taking a photograph.

My dad stands and takes a step toward me. And another.

A fresh drop of blood rolls down his face. It hovers on his chin, then falls, slow motion, and lands on the carpet at his feet.

That's when I start screaming.

Chapter 12

Jess

I'm having breakfast with my dad when the text from Shane comes in.

The dentals from the body don't match anyone in NamUs, the National Missing and Unidentified Persons System. It was always a long shot. There's no national database for dental records, and a medical examiner needs a PTB—presumed to be—before they can identify a person.

In other words, we need something to compare them to.

Still, it's a blow. It means that deadline of Christmas is looking less and less likely.

I tell my dad, who's scraping Marmite over his toast. In the background, an old Christmas song plays on the radio.

"Now that we know the blood on the backpack matches Ella Harper's, we've focused the investigation on the Harpers' disappearance last year," I say. "We know the body in the suitcase is linked to that. We just need an ID now."

I make a face as he licks Marmite off his fingers.

"How do you eat that stuff?"

"It's delicious. You should try it."

"I have. It's motor oil flavored with soy sauce. On bread."

He grins and pops a large bite of toast into his mouth. "You got anybody to compare the dentals to?"

"Unfortunately, no." I shake my head. "And the dude had no dental work done. Whoever he was, he took good care of his teeth."

I glance at the clock. I need to get going if I have any chance of swimming this morning. "We've been working our way through follow-up interviews with witnesses from the Harper case, but no mention of a man who's gone missing. It's slow going."

We interviewed the teenagers at the party and Maya's parents, Nancy and Dom Shepherd, who own the company in charge of cleaning the house where the body was found. We also interviewed the paramedic who found Alice, as well as Clarissa O'Brien, Alice's grandmother, who'd been staying with Jack and Melanie O'Brien the night the Harpers disappeared. But we didn't learn anything new.

"People forget pretty fast," Dad says, chewing his Marmite toast. "Life moves on."

"We did catch a break with Jack O'Brien. His lawyer told us to back off Alice and Melanie, but Jack set up a meeting with us at nine a.m. Friday morning." I take my bowl into the kitchen and drop a kiss onto my dad's balding head, a funny role reversal from when I was a child. "I really need to get going."

"It's fine, Bug. Been there, remember?" He grins wryly, twenty-five years as a detective shining in his whiskey-colored eyes. "Look, I gotta get home anyway. Think I'm going to head back to Atlanta tonight. There are some things I need to take care of."

"I'm sorry I haven't been around much while you've been here," I say, pulling on my boots and grabbing my backpack of swimming gear. "Let's meet for dinner tonight. I want to see you before you go."

I also want to ask him what's going on. I get the sense he isn't telling me something.

My dad and I have gotten closer lately, but we have a complicated relationship. With my mom it was easy, effortless, but my dad, I spent most of my childhood being mad at him. First, he was physically distant in the military, then mentally distant as a cop. And then there was the drinking. It always felt like he cared more about the victims than his own family. Now I get it, but then, to a kid, it made as much sense as quantum mechanics.

"Shall we say Sammy's, six p.m.?"

Dad looks doubtful. "A bar? Are you sure you want to meet there?"

I'm a recovering addict, which makes a bar the worst place to go. But I know Dad loves Sammy's fried chicken, and I say so.

"It's the best I've tasted," he admits with a grin. "Okay, if you're sure."

The good thing about my dad is he doesn't baby me. He lets me deal with things my way. I grab my cane from its spot on the coatrack and turn to go.

"Hey," he calls after me. "You better decorate this house for Christmas."

I laugh and head outside. As if.

By the time I've swum laps for an hour, the weather has turned, thick gray clouds spitting tiny white flakes, the ground slippery with ice. When I pull into my parking space at the police station, a couple of news crews are setting up. A reporter leaps forward as I dismount, shouting questions. A light pops. I feel a spark of anger that they've seen me, my awkwardness, how clumsy I still am. I unsnap my cane and turn away, cheeks burning, and hurry inside to where Shane is waiting.

"Morning, Jess. Here." He thrusts a paper cup at me. "Will said you take a skinny latte."

"Thanks. You see the press setting up?"

We look out from reception at the reporters filling the parking lot. Neither of us is inclined to get to our desks.

"Yeah. I've scheduled a press conference for tonight."

He sounds glum, and I chuckle. "You'll be fine."

Shane looks about eighteen in his wrinkled navy shirt, his faded jeans, and dark jacket. He's tall and gangly, all elbows and knees. If he isn't careful, the media will eat him alive.

I don't mind training, I just don't like it being sprung on me this way, as a punishment, a way to say, *I'm watching you.* Especially with such a big case. I could have gotten on board with Will leading, but Shane? But I figure I can solve this case whether I'm lead or Shane is. When you know how to handle a rookie, they don't slow you down.

"So, what's your plan, boss?" I'm not trying to be a bitch, but the stunned look on Shane's face makes me feel like one.

I clear my throat. "Pro tip. Don't get distracted by pointless shit. Focus. Act like you're in charge. Even if you don't feel like you are, fake it till you make it, yeah?"

"Yeah."

I watch as a news reporter fluffs her hair, swipes makeup under her eyes. A cameraman counts down with his fingers as she plants a smile on her face.

"Put a rush on a specialist postmortem, then ask the medical examiner to put together a DNA profile. We need to find out who that body is and how it's linked to Ella Harper." I cast a glance over his clothes. "This case is a headline grabber. Appearances are important. Get a tie."

I shift the weight in my leg to ease some pressure. "I wonder how long that suitcase was there. It's hard to believe a teenager would bring a suitcase with a body into the house, but I've seen crazier things. Maybe someone snuck it in."

Shane thinks for a moment. "There was a circle of dust around the suitcase. It had been there awhile."

"So we can presume the body was put in that suitcase around the time he died. Someone who had access to that house. Maybe the CSIs will find Laura's and Ella's bodies somewhere in the house as well."

"The body being found so close to Ella Harper's backpack means something."

"Agreed."

"Maybe Pete Harper killed whoever's inside," he theorizes.

"And then threw his own ID in there?"

"Could've been an accident. It slipped, fell in. Pete had been drinking more. Maybe he was just clumsy."

I'm not convinced, and I say so. In general, I don't believe in accidents.

"There were rumors Laura was having an affair," Shane tells me. "Their marriage was already rocky after her business went bust, plus his drinking. That's a lot of pressure on a marriage. He catches her having an affair, kills the guy, then his whole family."

I lift an eyebrow. "Laura was having an affair?"

"Nothing concrete, just rumors down at the bar."

It's only as we start talking about the case that I notice Shane's face relax. Rookie nerves are a bitch. I remember them myself.

I catch something in my peripheral vision and turn to see Pete Harper standing across the station's parking lot, staring in my direction.

Shane follows my gaze. "What is it?"

I drag my gaze back to Shane. That restless feeling is burning in me, like I've stuck my finger in an electrical socket. "I want to look at the original scene where the car accident happened. Can you send me the coordinates?"

"Sure. I'll send you the original report, too."

"Thanks."

I turn to go as Shane calls after me. "See you at the press conference."

"I'll be there. Don't forget to get a tie, Shane. And maybe an iron."

I get on my motorcycle and follow the coordinates Shane sent me to Killer's Grove. Some places have a feeling to them. A creeping, cold feeling. A sort of prickling along your spine. A tightening of your scalp.

I feel it the moment I enter Killer's Grove. I cut the engine as that cold, slithering feeling coats my arms and legs. A wave of dread, like vertigo, hollows out my stomach.

I unsnap my helmet, use my cane to climb off, and look around. I'm a little surprised there aren't any news crews here yet, but it won't be long. A body possibly linked to a family that went missing a year ago, the reporters will be salivating.

A weird type of cold skates over my scalp, the type of cold that goes deep into your bones. I can hear something, too. A faint humming. Familiar. Troubling. It makes the hairs on my arms bristle.

I can't really put my finger on what makes Killer's Grove so creepy. Maybe it's the light, the way it falls between the trees, the corners and edges too dark, the shadows restless, shifting. Or maybe it's the air, which feels wrong, like it's been replaced with something else, something heavier, making it hard to catch my breath. Or this weird sense of isolation, like I'm the only person in the world right now.

Or maybe it's none of that, only the stories people tell that leave their imprint on this place.

Hundreds of years ago, this land was considered cursed by the Native Americans. Now it's a place parents use as a boogeyman cautionary tale. Rumors veer between stories of it being a serial killer's dumping ground to it being haunted. I read a few years ago a trucker spotted a child floating like mist along the side of the road here, but when he stopped to help, the child disappeared. And there have been reports of a woman wailing in the dead of night, but nobody can ever find her. Plus there's Alice Harper's family, who disappeared on Christmas Eve, never to be seen again.

Most myths grow from a seed of truth, but sometimes they're fertilized with lies. And the more time passes, the blurrier the line between fact and fiction becomes.

Snowflakes fall softly, turning everything white. The trees are thick with it, their boughs pushing up over the road, forming a dense canopy. Farther into the forest, there are dangerous chasms and plunging gorges.

Plenty of places to hide a body.

After a moment, I hear an engine, and a truck pulls alongside me. A man peers out from the driver's-side window. Craggy face, shaggy hair, eyebrows that need a trim.

"You all right there?" he calls.

"I'm good," I say.

"You broke down?"

"No, just looking around."

"Lost?"

I pause to take the old man in again. Curious and helpful or suspicious and weird?

"You shouldn't be here." His thick eyebrows pull down. "It ain't safe. You know this road is haunted, right? Bad things happen here. Everybody knows it."

"I'll be fine, thanks."

He eyes me for a long minute, then tips his head. "You be careful now."

He rolls his window up and puts the truck in drive. I make a note of his license plate in my phone—just in case—and watch him leave. A gust of wind lifts my hair. I shiver, gripping my cane a little tighter.

I limp along the road in the direction the Harpers' car was traveling, eventually stepping into the dense brush at the side of the road. I lean heavily on my cane, eyes scanning, not sure what exactly I'm looking for. The ground has become slippery with snow, and the cold has gotten into my leg. Usually the pain is manageable, but right now it's a bottomless ache. I dig my knuckles into the muscle as I walk.

The bottoms of my jeans quickly become soaked. I tug my parka up higher and keep going. It's about fifteen minutes before the trees abruptly end and I reach a field. On the other side of the field is the house where we found the body.

I glance over my shoulder at Killer's Grove. The road isn't too far behind me. It wouldn't have been difficult to drag a suitcase from there to this house.

Next to me, I see Isla moving in and out of the trees. Her laughter tinkles on the breeze, faint, delicate, bringing a heavy dose of nostalgia.

Everywhere around me is now gauzy with snow, but there's something here, something I can't explain. Something intangible, ethereal. It isn't physical, it's more abstract than that, sliding up my spine. I can feel it, but I can't see it.

The old man's words float back to me.

Bad things happen here. Everybody knows it.

Chapter 13

Laura

August

I wake to the smell of coffee and Pete kissing me gently on the lips. I groan and peer up at him, bleary-eyed. My head is thumping from the three mai tais I had last night, my first hangover in I don't know how long.

Last night I met Theo at the Garden Shed, a cute gastropub by the River Rothay. I chose it because it was far enough out of town that nobody would recognize me. Not that I was doing anything wrong, but I wouldn't want people getting the wrong idea if they saw me with a man who wasn't my husband.

"Must've been a good night out with the girls." Pete sets the coffee and two ibuprofen on the bedside table.

I flinch, like he's slapped me with my lie. Some lies have a vibration; they tingle in the air like electricity. They get all tangled and it's hard to unpick the truth from the fiction.

"How are Mel and Nancy?" he asks.

"Good."

"I'm glad you got to go out. I know things have been hard since the studio shut down."

I sit up and reach for my coffee, feeling like the world's worst person. He's right, I have been a little blue. My life is nearly halfway over. Probably. And what have I accomplished?

Even though I never filed for bankruptcy, I lost my art studio. I simply couldn't afford the lease, so I didn't renew. I stopped painting, canceled my social media accounts. I wasn't bringing in enough money to contribute to our family to begin with, but after the pandemic, it really all fell apart. Nobody wants to buy art during a cost-of-living crisis.

Closing the doors that final time was the hardest thing I've ever done. Pete told me I didn't have to quit, but he was wrong. The thing about dreams falling apart in the present is that you lose the future you associated with those dreams. You lose the you who you thought you'd be. I have extraordinary dreams and an ordinary talent and there's an insurmountable gap between the two. I had to do something that I had a chance of succeeding at. Or at least, not failing at.

"No matter what happens, I'm here. I've got you," he told me.

Looking at Pete now reminds me of how good he is, loyal and kind and trustworthy. I feel bad for lying because I *am* happy. It's my own failures that make me sad. I don't know why I have this ridiculous need for validation in my life.

I groan and shove the ibuprofen into my mouth, wash them down with coffee. Pete smiles, that familiar twinkle in his eye. He thinks it's funny that I have a hangover like I'm twenty-one and still in college.

"I'm gonna get to work." My husband is a creature of habit. Saturday mornings are reserved for grading papers.

"Mm-kay," I murmur.

Pete leaves and I close my eyes, let my mind drift back to last night with Theo.

I was running a little late, thanks to a last-minute typo in an important document for Jack. When I parked at the bar, I caught sight of Theo on the phone near the river. He looked angry, his mouth shouting, even though I couldn't hear his words.

I almost left, but Theo caught sight of me. He held up a finger for me to wait just as a text pinged onto my phone.

You better watch your back, Laura.

I gasped. Whoever was texting me knew my name. It wasn't a mistake I could brush off. This was personal. I looked around the parking lot but couldn't see anybody.

I blocked the number just as my car door opened, Theo grinning at me. "You look amazing."

I glanced down at the colorful rainbow bracelets I'd slipped on my wrists, my lacy boho skirt and sleeveless white blouse with the hem tied at my waist. I'd taken a little extra time with my appearance, mascara, eyeliner, a shimmery lipstick. I'd even bought a touch-up stick to cover my grays, let my long auburn waves hang loose around my shoulders. I looked nice. Not twenty-one nice, but nice enough.

"Thanks."

I got out of the car, determined to ignore the creepy texts. The air was warm, balmy. Theo guided me inside to an intimate corner table. I was aware of the heat from his palm on the bare skin of my arm, the scent of his aftershave, like wood chips and lemongrass.

One drink, I told myself. *It's just one drink.*

Of course I didn't have one drink. I had three. And then we went for a walk along the river under the moonlight, ending up at a hollowed-out old tree just beyond the end of the path.

"Funny how life turns out, isn't it?" he said, grinning at me with that old light in his eye. "Sometimes you end up back where you started."

"Oh, I don't know." I ran my fingertips over the gnarled tree. "We learn things along the way, I think. Carry the past into the future. Even this tree has rings showing where it's been."

Theo's hand came up to cover mine, but I slipped away, headed back to the pub. After a brief pause, he followed.

"Mom, can we make pancakes?" Ella's shout from the kitchen interrupts my thoughts.

I roll onto my back and stare at the ceiling. The girls love pancakes on Saturday mornings. And I love making them. But right now all I can think about is the mess they'll make and how much my head hurts.

"Pllleasssse!" Alice chimes in.

I smile, resigned. It is a tradition, after all. And family traditions are important to me.

Our parents divorced when Jack and I were small, our dad abandoning us on our mother's front doorstep one chilly winter's morning when we were six years old, each of us gripping a cup of hot chocolate. We never saw him again.

I always swore I would be around for my kids. I would have all those little traditions that make a family. Matching pajamas at Christmas. Pancakes on the weekend. Barbecues and bonfires and movie nights.

You don't have a family, you build one. They aren't a given, they're a gift, shaped like clay in the hands of an artist and forged in the fires of sleepless nights and high temperatures, of broken-down cars and missed bills.

No matter the disappointments in my life, this family I've built is more important to me than anything.

"Chocolate chip pancakes coming right up!"

I get up, pull on sweats. I'm just coming out of the bathroom when I hear a key in the front door.

"Hello?" Mel's voice floats up the stairs. She and Jack both have spare keys, just as we have keys to theirs.

I hurry downstairs and greet Mel. Mel and I met in college when we were assigned the same dorm freshman year. At first, I was enamored by her confidence, her designer clothes, her shiny black Mustang. I envied her calm, her poise, and loved that she was a thoughtful and intelligent conversationalist with a quick laugh. But as we became closer, I recognized a kindred spirit, too.

Even though Mel grew up rich and I grew up poor, we both knew what it was like to have a parent abandon you. How it always felt like no one had your back. How standing up for yourself became an act of self-preservation.

I give Mel a hug. "Hey, how are you? I didn't expect to see you today."

"I was in the neighborhood. Thought I'd bring doughnuts." She smiles and lifts a bag of doughnuts from Gail's, the bakery in town.

"The kids will love it," I lie.

They won't. They'd prefer pancakes and family time. But I won't hurt Mel's feelings by telling her that. She's here and she's smiling, and that's a win.

Ever since her heart problems, Mel's been quieter. More serious. An extreme diet. Organic food. No alcohol. Yoga and meditation every day. All good, of course, but a little over-the-top. Her way of fighting back. Mel has never taken shit lying down. She goes after what she wants, she fixes problems, finds solutions. When she's threatened, she doesn't hesitate to strike back. But this isn't an enemy she can fight out in the open. I think the truth of that wears her down a bit.

My phone pings as I lead Mel into the kitchen, a panicked text from Rose, my brother's assistant, asking if I've seen some contract or other. I reply, telling her where the contract is.

Almost immediately, Rose answers, Next time maybe you should leave the contracts in the file where they belong.

I roll my eyes, and Mel asks what's up. I lie again and say it's Jack about work.

Rose is infatuated with Jack, which plays out in her snippy attitude toward me. But I don't want Mel knowing that. Rose is annoying, but I wouldn't want her to lose her job.

My phone pings again. A new number, one I don't recognize.

I saw you do it. I told you I'd be watching.

Chapter 14

Jess

I'm in Killer's Grove, no more than a few hundred yards from the road, when my phone pings. Service has returned, however briefly.

Shane's sent through an email with a digital copy of the crime report attached. I skimmed the original report at the station the other day but haven't had time to properly read it, so I lean against a tree, hooking my cane over one arm as I take some weight off my leg, and read it now.

Peter, Laura, Alice, and Ella Harper were on their way home from a family Christmas celebration at the house of Laura's brother, Jack O'Brien. Alice told the detective that their normal route home was blocked by a ROAD CLOSED barricade, even though no work was scheduled for that night. The family had turned around and cut through Killer's Grove. She said they'd been traveling on the road for about five minutes when there was a flash of light and the minivan skidded on the icy road. It hit something and launched into the air.

At 12:49 a.m., an off-duty paramedic on his way home from a shift spotted the minivan. It was lying on its side, pointing west on the eastbound side of the road. The off-duty paramedic found Alice a little ways up the road, in shock. He called 911, but while they waited, she told him that she'd heard a beeping in the car, like a fire alarm when its battery is dying. She thought something was wrong with the minivan and had wanted to run, but someone was with her—a young girl who told her to stay quiet.

A tingle of adrenaline hits my spine as I read, a million bees swirling under my skin. Because the girl Alice said was in the car with her was about seven or eight, blue eyes, a pink satin Hello Kitty headband perched on messy blonde braids.

I hear a twig snap behind me and whirl.

"Isla." Twin emotions of guilt and relief spiral through me.

"Hi, Mommy."

"*You* were with Alice Harper," I say. "Why?"

"I didn't want her to die."

"The others? They're dead?"

Isla just stares at me, her face sad. A frigid wind bites at my face. Snow falls in little flurries, faster now.

"Are the others dead?" I press.

Isla still doesn't answer.

I don't know why, exactly, I still see Isla. My shrink says as long as I know she isn't really here, it's fine to talk to her. But she's wrong. Isla *is* here. She's as real to me as Shane or Will or my estranged husband, Mac. I've accepted that. She's real *to me*, and that's what I need right now. But is she real to Alice, too?

I stare out at the snow-blanketed forest, feeling unbalanced. I take a deep breath. I need to talk to Alice Harper. I turn to leave, but Isla calls out.

"Mommy!"

The sound of my daughter's voice, barbed, jagged, drags me back to the night she died, memories making my mouth go dry and sticky. The icy river water swirling around my cheeks. My leg stuck fast in the truck's mangled window. My blood watering the mud. The crack of thunder reverberating in my bones. And then ice-cold arms dragging me to the road.

Isla was eight years old when she died. She looks exactly the same now, standing in the gauzy light of Killer's Grove, wearing her blue-and-white dress, her pink Hello Kitty headband. The gap where her two front teeth fell out is still there.

I was in the hospital for nearly a week before Mac told me she died in the accident. I blamed myself, of course. I'd had a drink before I drove. One, but that was all it took. It was almost inconsequential that I'd hit a deer. I turned to booze, blocked Mac out, drove him away.

An ache blossoms in me. A yearning. For a long time after Mac left, I would call him. Not to talk or anything, just to hear him breathing down the line. I don't do that anymore. But it doesn't mean I don't want to.

I feel that familiar fire scratching at the back of my throat, and I yearn desperately for a drink, the hot fire of just one whiskey to bury this feeling.

"One little drink." It's a trick I learned in rehab. I used to say, *One little drink won't hurt.* Now I say, *One little drink could send me back to where I was.*

I think of what my dad said. *You can't move forward if you're standing still.*

I do honestly believe what I told him. That I've been left here for a reason. I help them. I'm their voice when they no longer have one. There's a connection here, a reason Alice saw Isla.

I've helped them before, those left behind. Maybe I can help Alice and her family, too.

So I squeeze my one-month chip, the edges pressing into my palm, and I carry on. Everything is temporary, love and pain. Soon, like everything else, this will crest and pass, just like an ocean wave.

Something prickles the skin at the back of my neck. There's a presence in the forest. Something heavy and dark. I can feel it moving closer to me in the dim light. Ominous clouds skitter like whispers, snow falling in little flurries. My body is alight, tingles tapping up and down my spine.

A snap behind me. The rustle of bushes. A man is walking toward me, maybe fifty feet away. It's the same man I saw in the field across from the house the day we found the body. His thick, dark hair bristles in the wind. He's wearing a dark suit, a tie with smiling Santas. A string of silver tinsel is wrapped around his neck.

Pete Harper.

My head, it's like it's filling with sand, an electric feeling washing over me, as if I've stuck my finger in an electrical socket.

"Where are they, Pete?" I raise my voice over the rising wind and the swirling snow. "Did you kill them?"

Pete keeps walking through the forest, passing me. He doesn't even look at me, doesn't seem to know I'm here.

"He wants to find them." It's Isla speaking from behind me. But when I turn, she isn't there. And neither is Pete Harper.

I'm alone in Killer's Grove.

There aren't even footprints in the snow to prove they were ever here.

◆ ◆ ◆

I should head back to the police station to help Shane prepare for the press conference. The journalists are circling like sharks. They're going to eat him alive.

Instead, I pull up the address where Alice Harper now lives with her aunt and uncle. White flakes swirl around the streetlamps, pinging against my exposed cheeks. I'm grateful I had the foresight to switch to all-season tires last weekend. The weather's getting worse.

The O'Briens live in one of the luxury houses in a new, private, gated development set on a curve of Black Lake, all shimmering glass and blocky steel fixtures with an infinity pool overlooking a private beach. I have to pass through a gate in order to even get in, but flashing my badge at a sleek Jag that's pulling out as I arrive seems to do the trick.

I park in the half-moon drive, kill the engine, and unsnap my helmet. From here, I can see inside their glass house. The kitchen is all white, sleek handle-less cupboards and designer appliances. The living room, similarly designed in white, has a minimalist feel to it. It's like a show house, something for pretty people to brag about.

The walkway up to the front porch is pocked with footprints. Somebody is home.

An oversize Christmas wreath hangs on the front door. I ring the doorbell. It flies open almost instantly, a too-thin, frazzled-looking woman wearing yoga pants and a long-sleeve workout top standing in the doorway. The Christmassy scents of spiced candles and gingerbread cookies float into the chill night air.

"Melanie O'Brien?" I hold up my badge, smiling politely.

She stares at me, her face blanching very white, her eyes blinking rapidly as her mouth hangs open.

"What are you . . . why are you here?" She sounds out of breath. I wonder if she's just run down the stairs. Or if I've frightened her. People don't exactly love seeing a cop on their front doorstep.

"I'm Detective Jess Lambert. There's nothing to worry about," I assure her. "Is your niece, Alice Harper, home from school yet?"

Melanie's eyes darken. She's about to shut the door in my face, so I start talking.

"I thought I'd pop by and chat with Alice. I know we're all eager to solve her family's disappearance, and I have some questions—"

"About the body over by Killer's Grove?"

I'm not surprised it's leaked already. It's a juicy story. A missing family. A teenage girl left behind. A body found with items that disappeared when the family did.

"Yes."

"Is it them?"

"I'm afraid we have no details about identification at this time. Could I speak with—"

But I don't have a chance to finish.

Because a sudden scream rips through the air.

Chapter 15

Alice

I am frozen as my bloodied dad staggers toward me.

He has one hand extended, staring at me from eyes so black, so sunken, they look like holes in his head. Crimson blood glistens on his face. It drips onto the carpet, leaving large black splotches. The air around me has turned to ice. My breath fogs, my teeth clatter. The ground feels unstable under my feet, like I'm standing in quicksand.

And then the room does a weird sort of wobble. I blink and my dad is gone. The carpet doesn't have any bloody splotches. It's just a normal bedroom, my bedsheets tousled, my shoes kicked across the floor, my books and homework scattered across the desk.

I am panting, my heart roaring.

Mel bursts into my bedroom.

"Are you okay?" She scans me, runs a hand over my hair. "I heard you scream! What happened? Are you hurt?"

I stare at her stupidly. What *did* happen? I don't understand it myself. My aunt isn't even wearing the same clothes as a few minutes ago.

Tears fill my eyes. Mel's face softens with compassion, and she wraps her bony arms around me, pulling me close. I feel her collarbones press against mine. She smells of lunch—pinot grigio—and the peppermint mouthwash she's used to cover it up. I know, like me, she's been struggling, but it's too much. Her scent will drown me.

What the hell is wrong with me?

The words are like a siren blaring in my head.

A gentle thudding sound drags my attention away from her. A woman is limping down the hallway, her cane clunking on the carpet. She's slim with eyes the strange ambery-gold of a lion's, sharp cheekbones, and dark hair escaping from beneath a maroon woolen hat.

It's the woman from my shrink's office yesterday. From the look on her face, she recognizes me, too.

Her eyes dart behind me, scanning my bedroom, but whatever she's looking for isn't there. Her mouth tightens. I wonder what she expected to find. A man in a *Scream* mask holding me at knifepoint? A Chucky doll that had slashed me to pieces?

"Alice Harper?" Her voice is calm, neutral.

I nod, suddenly mortified. I scrub at the tears on my cheeks.

"I'm Detective Jess Lambert. Is everything okay?"

I look between Mel's concerned face and Detective Lambert's curious one, and I know I can't tell them the truth. I can't tell Detective Lambert what's happening to me, these hallucinations or visions or whatever they are. She'll think I'm crazy. A freak.

A cold, floaty feeling hits me. I need to sit down. I slump onto the edge of my bed.

"I had a . . . nightmare," I say.

The detective watches me for a moment, then says, "I'd like to ask you a few questions about the night your family went missing."

"No," Melanie replies firmly. "Alice is upset. As I told you, any questions should go through our lawyers."

Irritation fizzes in me. "Is that why I haven't heard from them? Nobody's told me anything!"

"Alice, I'm trying to protect you—"

"Really, this will only take a minute," the detective interjects.

I straighten my shoulders. I have a right to know. "I'll talk to you."

Just then, the sound of Finn crying floats down the hall. Mel looks torn.

"It's fine." I grit my teeth to cover my impatience. "Finn needs you."

What I want to say is *Stop acting like you're my mother.*

I try not to notice the hurt roll across her face. After a second, Mel nods and slips from the room.

I pull my knees into my chest and wrap my arms around them. Detective Lambert adjusts her weight, leaning on her cane as she watches me carefully. "That was some nightmare, hey?"

I nod, an ugly, gray panic tightening my chest.

"I used to have nightmares like that. Sometimes they felt so . . . *real*, you know? I'd wake up, and it was almost confusing."

I don't answer, but she continues anyway.

"There's a word for it. It's called hypnagogia. It's a moment between sleep and waking when reality is just a bit . . . warped. It happens when we're very sleep-deprived. Or traumatized. It can feel hard to tell the difference between what's real and what isn't."

The thought hits me hard, like suddenly bashing on a piano. Could it be as simple as that? I'm traumatized and, like a horse, I fell asleep standing up? That maybe all I need is a good night's sleep? "That's exactly what it's like."

Detective Lambert pins me with her golden gaze. "Except, once you're awake, you *can* tell the difference. Right?"

I pull my knees tighter to my chest and nod.

Detective Lambert points next to me with her cane. "Mind if I sit? My leg . . ."

"Sure." I move over a little, and her weight dips the mattress. She pulls her bad leg in with her hand and leans her cane against the bed, making that groaning sound old people make when their joints are stiff, even though she doesn't look *that* old. I want to ask her what happened to her leg, but I think it might be rude, so I stay quiet.

"Alice, are you okay to talk about the night your family went missing?"

Hot tears spring into my eyes. I hate talking about it. Hate raking over those memories.

"Because of the body?" I ask.

She doesn't look surprised that I know. Things don't stay secret for long in a town like Black Lake. "I heard it at school."

"Oh. Well, yes. About the body we found."

My head is reeling, and I feel like I'm going to fall over, even though I'm already sitting. I press my forehead into my knees, closing my eyes.

It's over.

"Is it one of them?" I ask. "My family?"

"No. It doesn't appear to be."

My eyes pop open. I should've known. It's never going to be over. "Who is it?"

"We're still working on identifying the body."

Melanie slips back into my bedroom, this time with Finn clinging to her leg, cheeks flushed, eyes damp. He lets go of her leg, moving toward me, but Mel pulls him back.

"Not now, Finn," Mel whispers. "Alice is busy."

Finn scowls and folds his arms over his chest.

"He's not feeling well today," she explains to the detective. "I'll take him downstairs." She turns to me. "Are you sure you're okay, Alice? You don't have to do anything you don't want to."

"It's fine."

"Okay." Her eyes dart between us. "Let me know if you need anything."

She hovers outside the door for a second, then disappears downstairs.

I turn to Detective Lambert. "So if it isn't anybody in my family, why are you here?"

She digs her phone out of her pocket, taps the screen, and hands it to me. "Do you recognize this item?"

I'd tried to convince myself it wasn't really hers. That there were a million backpacks like this. That I hadn't seen it well enough before

Maya took it away. But I feel the bottom fall out of my world as the worst thing is confirmed.

The picture is undoubtedly of Ella's backpack, black, with a large white daisy on the front. The daisy is saturated with something dark, the color of blackened rust. Blood. I know it instantly. At the very bottom of the left side is a small GirlzRule badge, the same badge Ella's friends all had sewn on at the beginning of the year.

"Yes," I whisper. Nausea swirls in my stomach. "It's my sister's backpack."

"Can you walk me through finding it in the basement?"

I flash back to Maya pulling it out of the trunk all casual, like it wasn't even a surprise. "Maya found it inside a steamer trunk. She was looking for . . ." I hesitate, not sure if I should tell her. "Things to sell. I mean, nobody lives there, the stuff is abandoned, so she thought, I mean, we thought—"

"Relax, Alice." She cuts me off. "You're not in trouble."

"It was just . . . suddenly in her hands."

She tilts her head, curious. "Did Maya know it was there?"

"What? No! I . . . I don't think so." I shake my head, a sandpaper fist squeezing my heart. "I swear, we didn't see a body. We would've told you that."

"I'm sure you would've." The detective gives me a small, reassuring smile.

She used to be pretty, I think. Maybe when she was younger. Now her eyes are too serious. Her body is filled with too much pent-up energy. I feel it vibrating off her, like she's teetering on the edge of a diving board, ready to jump. It unfurls in me, this feeling. A tightness in my chest, a driving need to . . . what?

This sixth sense I get about people means I can read their energy, their emotions. Their lies. It's like reading braille, something you learn and become aware of. I can feel a sadness behind Detective Jess Lambert's smile. Until her face shifts. A mask drops. And then . . . nothing. She's closed herself off.

"Are you reopening their case?" I ask.

"It was never closed; we just haven't had any new evidence."

I look out my window at the swirl of snowflakes fluttering against a Q-tip-white sky. "Well, you have new evidence now."

But I don't know if it makes me feel better or worse.

Chapter 16

Alice

"Did Ella have the backpack with her the night your family disappeared?" Detective Lambert asks me.

"Yeah. We both did. We were supposed to spend the night at my aunt and uncle's. My family, we always stayed there on Christmas Eve. It was like a tradition. But I had a sore throat, and Ella didn't want to stay without me."

"So you weren't supposed to go home that night?"

"No. My parents were kind of arguing about it, and then my dad said we'd all leave, that he'd bring us back in the morning."

A frown pins her mouth down. "Bring you back? Just you and Ella? Did he not plan on staying?"

"I don't know." I pause. "Actually, now that I think about it, my parents didn't pack a bag. Maybe they weren't planning on staying? But that doesn't make sense. We always stayed on Christmas Eve."

"Did you tell anybody this? After the accident?"

I think for a second. "I don't know, it didn't seem important."

"What happened to your backpack?"

"The police gave it back to me. They looked through it and stuff, but there was nothing inside, really. Just clothes, my toothbrush." I shrug.

She taps the handle of her cane, deep in thought. I flinch at the sound. She stops, sets the cane against the bed.

"You found my sister's backpack with a body. What does it mean?" I ask. "Did this person kill my family?"

"The truth is, I don't know what any of it means yet. It's still too early to say. But I will investigate if there's a connection."

"They're dead, aren't they?" I stare at a damp spot on my jeans. My throat feels clogged with tears, like I've swallowed marbles.

"I . . ." She hesitates, and in that hesitation I hear everything I don't want to hear. "I don't know."

I suddenly feel overwhelmingly tired, the Ativan wrapping itself around me. My arms and legs are floaty, weightless as a feather. My brain has gone gluey.

She's just another cop, just like the other ones, empty words and broken promises. This unknowing will never end.

Detective Lambert massages her knuckles into her left leg. "The police report says you were with someone. A little girl."

I stare at her, open-mouthed. After the accident, I told the detective about the girl who'd been in the car with me. He thought I was just dreaming.

"I guess she wasn't really there."

"You guess?"

"I mean . . . the detective said there was no evidence anybody else had been there. And no reason why a *kid* would've been there. And nobody believed me."

"I believe you, Alice. Will you tell me everything you remember?"

"It's kind of fuzzy," I admit. "When I woke up, it was snowing. The car was on its side. The first thing I remember is the pain. My arm was broken, and my head was bleeding. And then I heard this beeping sound. Kinda like when a fire alarm battery's dying, you know?"

"That chirping?"

"Yeah. I thought something was wrong with the car. I was going to get out, but she told me to stay quiet. I think I passed out after that."

I jump up and cross to my window, shove the curtain open wider. Outside, I can just see the lake. Snow hurries past, making it look like it's steaming. The bare boughs of the trees outside my window are stark against the white-gray sky. My reflection is pale, dark circles under my eyes.

"I know what you're thinking, that I just dreamed her. Maybe I did." I shake my head. "The next time I woke up, she told me to run, and I did."

The tears I've been holding back spill over, scalding my cheeks, an ugly gray guilt blooming in my chest. I brace myself for it. *Everything happens for a reason* or *It'll get easier* or some other stupid platitude people always say. They're all bullshit. It doesn't get easier.

But Detective Lambert doesn't say any of them. She uses her cane to stand and crosses the room so she's directly in front of me. "I know what it's like to lose someone you love. I promise you, Alice, I will do everything in my power to find your family."

I study her face. I see a map of pain there. And something else, a kind of stoicism, an iron will to just keep going, to not collapse into sadness. She's the type to move forward, never back. I wish I could do the same.

Maybe she isn't like the other detectives after all.

"You lost someone, too." It's a statement, not a question.

She nods. "My daughter."

"Is that why you see the shrink?"

She smiles sadly. "Yes."

The look of resigned guilt on her face says she blames herself.

You know all about guilt, don't you, Alice?

My head snaps up at the sound of the voice. But there's nobody except the detective and me here.

One thing I've learned is that guilt and grief are just flip sides of the same coin. And here's the ugly truth: they make you into a different person. When my family was here, I was part of a whole. I could be selfish and it didn't really matter. They propped me up, made up for my weaknesses.

Now I'm just me. Alone. And it feels harsher and brighter at the same time, like everything I do matters now because I don't have anybody to back me up. I'm more aware of people now. More sensitive to their pain. I've always been sensitive—to loud sounds and bright lights, to strange textures and strong tastes—but now I have a deeper understanding of emotions, too.

Right now, for example, I can feel the detective's pain, bulky and black. The scent of it comes off her in hot waves, smelling bitter and wild, like burned coffee and split wood. The scent of her sadness is wild and green, like dying grass. I want to photograph her, to capture the lines of it in her face, her eyes.

Detective Lambert sits again on the mattress. "I lost her last year. Sunday was the anniversary."

"Close to when my family disappeared."

Something tight and surprised flickers over her face. "I suppose so."

The heating kicks on, a low drone. I close my eyes. My head feels like it will float away. And then, abruptly, I'm back there. The dark forest, the yellow headlights beaming into the swirling snow, the cold slap of it against my face. I'm running through the icy forest, branches clawing at my face, snagging on my clothes.

I went back. After I ran away. I never told them that.

"Alice."

My eyes jerk open.

"Are you okay?"

"Yeah."

I hear a scratch at the door and pull it open. Alfie saunters in. He rubs himself against Detective Lambert's legs, purring.

"I can't believe him. He hates everybody. Except me," I add.

She bends to pick him up. He nuzzles her chin. I shake my head. Traitor. She plucks a piece of fur out of her mouth and sets him on the bed. "Were your parents fighting before they disappeared?"

I scowl. "Last year the detectives were, like, obsessed with that. They thought my dad killed my mom. Do you, too?"

"It's often the case, unfortunately," she says honestly, "but it's too early for me to say. Other than rumors, there's no evidence. Of anything." She touches my knee. "I need you to be prepared for whatever I find. I'll follow the evidence, and I *will* investigate with an open mind, but sometimes the answers we get aren't the ones we want."

I'm a little surprised by her honesty. Usually grown-ups just try to hide things, like teenagers are dumb or something. I take a deep breath. "She was mad at him for what happened at school."

"Getting fired?"

"He wasn't *fired*. Everybody said that, but he was just suspended. My dad never had a drinking *problem*. He just drank *sometimes*. The school was looking into it."

"That must've been hard for you."

"It was embarrassing," I admit. "Everybody was talking about it."

"Did you know why he went to work drunk?"

I look away, face burning. "No."

She changes tack. "Your dad was driving the night they disappeared. Was he drinking?"

"No."

"Were any of the adults fighting? Any arguments you remember?"

"No." Frustration leaks into my voice. "It wasn't like that. It was a family Christmas gathering. We were dancing and laughing. We were *happy*."

The detective leans closer, her amber eyes serious. "Alice, can you tell me, from the beginning, what happened that night?"

So I do. I tell her what happened. My version of it, anyway. That's all the truth is. A version you choose to tell.

". . . and then I ran into the forest, and that's where that guy found me."

I've started to sweat, my armpits slippery. That phrase *sweating like a pig* pops into my head, even though it's biologically inaccurate. Pigs are born without sweat glands. They literally can't sweat.

"He found you in the forest?"

"No, I mean"—I shake my head, flustered—"by the side of the road, I think. I don't remember very clearly."

The detective looks at me for a long moment. "But something happened, didn't it? Something you're not telling me."

I stare at her, not sure how to answer. Sometimes we tuck our secrets into that tiny little space between words, the weight of them turning us into liars. Sometimes the truth isn't good for anybody.

"What happened to your family, Alice? Where are they?"

This time, I tell her the truth. "I don't know."

After Detective Lambert leaves my room, I lie down and let the Ativan carry me away. Alfie is on the pillow next to me, his body wrapped around my head, like a hat.

I hear the detective in the hallway, speaking to Mel. I can't tell what they're saying, just their tone. Mel is pissed, getting all overprotective and annoying. I'd bet my left boob she's telling the detective to talk to her hotshot lawyer.

I stare at my ceiling, the smooth white nothingness of it. I didn't really see my dad, I tell myself. It was hypnagogia, like the detective said. I hallucinated while I was drifting off to sleep.

Mel knocks softly. When she enters, she has a large mug of hot chocolate. She sets it on my bedside table, chattering away about Finn and Christmas shopping and what we'll do when my grandma arrives. I sit up, reach for the hot chocolate. I know she really just wants to find out what the detective and I talked about.

I tell her they found a body with Ella's backpack, but it isn't anybody in our family.

"What does it mean?" she asks, her brow furrowed, confused.

"I don't know." I lie back down, roll over so I'm facing the wall.

She rubs my back, her palm hot through my sweater. "Are you okay?"

"Yes."

I want her to leave. She's giving off those *need me* vibes, and I just can't deal. I don't want a different mother; I want *my* mother. I don't want Mel's stupid home-cooked meals and hot chocolate and lace curtains. I just want my family back.

Finally she leaves, shutting my door with a quiet click. I stare out the window, feeling like someone has carved my insides out. A crow streaks past, a black smudge. It caws angrily. Crows get a bad rap for bringing bad luck, but they're actually, like, supersmart. As smart as a seven-year-old.

I feel like I'm going crazy, my memories bleeding into my nightmares. I think about that creepy, staticky phone call, and I think about seeing my dad at Maya's party and his words to me earlier.

Why haven't you found us, Alice?

I think of my sister's backpack found with that body. How do the pieces fit together?

My grandma is right. I need to get out of Black Lake. I need to try to move on. Until I do, I'll never be anything but a freak. The girl left behind. But something inside me is frozen. I can't leave until I know what happened to my family.

I can't bear the thought of doing a true-crime podcast about my family's disappearance. Of going against Mel and Jack's wishes so publicly. But until I know why they're gone and I'm still here, I'll never be able to move on. I can't move into the future if I don't deal with the past.

Suddenly I know exactly what to do.

Chapter 17

Jess

Shane calls as I'm leaving Alice's house. I check the time and realize it's after 5:00 p.m.

I swear under my breath. I need to head back before the press conference starts. I press "End." It's probably best not to tell anybody about my little chat with Alice, a witness, without the lead detective's knowledge. Or that Melanie O'Brien threatened to call not only her lawyers but my boss on me.

My mind is on Alice as I climb on my motorcycle. She's a clever girl, perceptive, sensitive, astute. But I don't think she's telling the whole truth. She said her dad wasn't drinking that night, and yet they were at a Christmas party. I find that unlikely, especially given he had a drinking problem. As an alcoholic, I can recognize the signs. Either Alice didn't realize it or was covering for him.

And then saying the paramedic had found her in the forest, when she was found by the road. Is the girl hiding something or playing some sort of game?

I pull a worn notebook from my backpack, the one Liu kept for the investigation. Every detective has their own notebook, one where they record anything that seems strange or odd, gut feelings and theories that don't have enough basis to make it into the formal report. I yank one glove off and flip through the pages, brushing away falling snow as I scan the messy scrawl.

The facts of the case are simple enough. On Christmas Eve, the Harper family was heading home from the O'Briens'. Two hours after leaving, Alice Harper was found injured and in shock by the side of the road, the minivan wrecked nearby, her family missing.

A search for the Harper family began shortly after. The winter conditions were terrible, and any footprints had long since been covered by snow, but police set out a search area in Killer's Grove. Rescue crews and search parties reported having difficulty moving through the dense foliage in the snowstorm. They found nothing except Ella's and Pete Harper's blood in a frozen pool by the side of the road and Laura's inside the car. Enough to lead detectives to believe they were dead.

The Harpers' house was searched the next morning. Police found nothing out of the ordinary. A load of laundry still sat in the washing machine. Dishes sat on a drying rack in the kitchen. Luminol revealed no semen, no blood in the girls' beds, so sexual grooming or assault appeared unlikely.

The minivan, once processed, revealed no strange DNA or foreign hairs. There was no evidence another car had been involved in the accident, although trace evidence of milfoil—which Google tells me is a feathery, fast-spreading plant found in water—was found in the trunk.

A week after they went missing, police, partnering with the FBI, conducted a second ground and air search using tracking dogs and cadaver dogs. Divers were sent into the lake using sonar, pole cameras, underwater drones.

Nothing was ever found. The Harpers had simply vanished. Over the last year, the case had gone cold and, once Detective Bill Liu left for chemo, neglected and abandoned.

These are the facts, but not the feel of the case. When I'm on a case, I get what I call the "aura." It's something intangible, almost indescribable. It's a sensation, a chemical rush that hovers over my brain, creating some sort of magnetic field. Once I feel that, I know I'm on the right track. But I'm not there yet.

I flip to the last page in Liu's notebook. In the margins he's written: *Possible DV?* Domestic violence. And then: *Laura/Pete arguing—Ciao Bella mgr.* And at the bottom, circled twice: *car beeping? Dream?*

A copy of the evidence log of items found around the car is folded in the back of the notebook. I flatten it against my motorcycle seat. A cigarette butt, a tennis ball, pieces of ripped paper, a thread of string, a dirty strip of linen, presumed to be the sling from Laura's arm. Nothing that could issue a beep or an alarm.

I check the time on my phone. I'll miss the press conference, but I have one more thing I need to do before I meet my dad tonight.

Detective Bill Liu lives in a pale-yellow-and-brown split-level house that crouches over a two-car garage. His wife, Gina, leads me through a dated but tidy living room to a den with a giant TV and a crackling fireplace. Bill is now twenty pounds lighter and completely bald, his cheeks and chin sagging. He sits, legs up, in an overstuffed armchair, watching *Stranger Things* with his teenage daughter, Taytum.

"How've you been?" I ask as I sit opposite.

He rubs his bald head and chuckles. "I've been better, but I think I'm on the mend. How have *you* been?"

He gives me a long look, like he's peering into my soul. I hate when people do this, bring up all I lost without really bringing it up.

"I'm okay," I say brusquely. "Good to be back to work."

"Yeah. I'm counting down. Hope to be back in a few weeks."

I try not to look surprised. He doesn't seem well enough to go back to work, but I know how it can be the thing tethering you to life.

Bill asks Taytum if we can have a few minutes alone, then says, "I wondered when you'd come by."

"You heard about the body found with Ella Harper's backpack?"

"Yep. Can't help but hope the two are connected and you solve this one. I hate that it's still hanging over me. The one that got away, you know?"

"Sure. Do you think they're still out there?"

"The Harpers? Oh, they're out there, they just aren't alive. That's my professional opinion, by the way. The crime scene was cleared up, the bodies, if that's what they were, moved. Any sign of them in the house?"

"The CSIs are still going through it, but the dogs haven't found anything, so I'm thinking if they're dead, they aren't there."

"A lot of places to hide a body in those woods. All those chasms and caves. We looked, the FBI looked, but maybe we missed something."

"Maybe they were picked up, taken somewhere else, killed somewhere else."

"There were no sightings, no evidence that's how it played out."

"Shane said you liked Pete Harper for it."

Bill draws a knitted blanket from the back of his chair over his lap as Gina enters again. She sets some kind of green smoothie along with about six different pills on the coffee table.

"Time for your meds, my love," she says cheerfully.

Bill looks embarrassed as he drops the pills in his mouth and takes a slug of smoothie. I look away. I don't know if it's a cop thing or just a human thing, but it's hard letting others see you when you're at your most vulnerable. I think maybe that fear of vulnerability sometimes leads you to hurt others, the way I've hurt Mac. And yet, how to fix it? Loving yourself despite your flaws and past mistakes is a tough lesson to learn.

"What were we talking about?" Bill asks when Gina's left.

"Pete Harper."

"Ah. That's right. We looked at a lot of theories. Abduction, voluntary disappearance, murder. The possibility they'd left on foot and frozen to death. We had a lot of armchair detectives and crazy conspiracy theories to contend with, if you remember, like that a ghost had pushed them into a wormhole, shit like that."

He shifts in his seat, rolling his eyes. "Some people are bonkers. But like I said, there was no sign they'd up and left. Not voluntarily. We checked airlines, rental car counters, watched their bank accounts and credit cards, but there were no charges and no cash withdrawals. None at all. So we knew they hadn't left to start a new life somewhere. Their wallets and cell phones were missing, but we searched their phone records and never found any unexplainable calls. Pete Harper killing his family and hiding the bodies before killing himself was the best theory we had."

"Sure, but that comes with holes in it, too."

"You mean Alice Harper."

"Yeah. Why kill your family, but leave one daughter behind?" I ask.

And that's exactly it. Alice Harper was left. If it weren't for her, it might've been an open-and-shut case. But it isn't. I can't help thinking there's something more going on here.

"Maybe it was an accident. Alice got away before he could do it."

I shake my head. "I don't buy it. If she got away by accident, why wouldn't she tell anybody?"

He shrugs. "'When you hear hoofbeats, think horses, not zebras.'"

I frown. "What?"

"You ever hear of Occam's razor?"

"Yeah. The simplest solution is almost always the best."

"Well there you go. Maybe Alice didn't see anything. Maybe she regained consciousness when he was running after the little one or his wife. Maybe she just got lucky."

It's a lot of maybes. I don't like maybes. "Did you get the sense she was hiding something like that?"

"No," he admits. "I was never sure if she was telling the full truth, but I'm not sure it could've been something like her own father's guilt. Why hide that if he'd tried to kill her?"

"Exactly. I can't get my head around it," I say. "What about the beeping sound you wrote about in your notes? Any idea what that was?"

Bill tells me the same thing Alice did, that it sounded like what a fire alarm battery makes when it's dying.

"We didn't find anything around that could make the noise she says she heard in the car," he says. "We checked with the manufacturer to see if any car parts could make that sound, but that came back negative. It had to have been outside the car."

Bill stands, crosses slowly to the fireplace, and puts his hands out, soaking up the heat. "Alice Harper wasn't exactly a reliable witness. She was injured. Traumatized. We eventually concluded she hadn't really heard it, just like she didn't really see a child sitting in the car with her. Maybe she dreamed it."

"Or maybe somebody else was there," I say. "Just like she said."

Bill levels watery brown eyes at me. "Why would a kid be at a car crash scene in the middle of a snowstorm at that time of night?"

"I'm not talking about that. I'm talking about a killer. Someone who caused the accident, then killed them."

The fireplace crackles, a piece of wood spitting. Bill rubs his hands together over the flames. "We don't know exactly what happened that night, but there was no evidence of that. After a few weeks, Shane and I, and the FBI, we all concluded that the most likely scenario was that Pete killed them."

He ticks the reasons off on one hand. "Laura Harper's medical records showed she dislocated her shoulder shortly before going missing. A nurse who treated her said she had bruises all over, not consistent with a fall on wet pavement, as she'd claimed. A restaurant manager where they regularly went said he'd seen them arguing. Pete had been drinking more the last few months; he'd shown up drunk to school, verbally abusing his coworkers. Plus, there was Laura's art studio, which had folded just a few months before. That would have created some stress."

I nod, staring at the dancing flames.

Bill watches me carefully, his gaze too heavy, too intense. "The first anniversary is approaching. The media will be all over this. Will you be able to handle it?"

I stiffen. Bill, like the rest of my colleagues, has heard about me. The rumors are still swirling. I'm crazy. Broken. Haunted.

Maybe I am. But I'm still here.

I flash a big, fake grin. "Haven't you heard? Shane's leading on this one."

Bill can't hide his surprise. "Shane? Damn. Poor kid."

"Why?"

"Don't you know?"

"I guess not."

"Shane's little sister went missing when he was a kid. They were outside, playing, and somebody took her. She was never found. It's why he became a cop. His dad, too. Working the Harper case last year was hard on him, but he was the first one in every morning and the last one out every night. He has the makings of a fine detective."

"I agree." Maybe I haven't given Shane enough credit. He's been working his own personal cold case longer than I've been a detective.

I stand, thrust a hand out to shake Bill's. "I've taken enough of your family time. Thanks for talking to me. I can see myself out."

I call goodbye to Gina and Taytum and step outside. Snow is falling gently, kissing my cheeks with feathered fingers. The air has a snap to it, my breath turning to mist in front of my face. Isla is standing by my bike. She looks like she's hidden in a snow globe, one more shake and she'll disappear forever.

"What do you think?" she asks.

I fold my cane, slide it into my backpack, and clip my helmet on. "I think maybe Bill Liu focused too much attention on Pete Harper and not enough on looking for possible other suspects."

The truth is, the simple answer often turns out to be the correct one. But my gut tells me nothing about this case is simple.

Chapter 18

Jess

I pop the clutch and roar out of Bill's sleepy neighborhood on my motorcycle, heading back into town.

Sammy's Bar is set in Black Lake's historic downtown, next to a yoga studio and across from a pretty clapboard church and a dead-end street that leads to a sandy beach. I brake, wheels crunching over gravel, and slide my motorcycle into my old parking space. When was I last here? August, maybe. Before rehab, definitely. The sun was out, every day an oppressive heat like a smack to the face. The neon sign has been fixed, the roof is cluttered with snow, but other than that, it looks mostly the same.

I yank the lever for the side stand, snap my cane out, and climb off the motorcycle. The icy gravel is slippery, so I'm careful as I walk, more precise with my movements. My leg is cramping, an ache so deep I wonder if I'll ever shake it. I stare up at the bar, my mouth watering.

"You shouldn't go in there," Isla says.

She's just behind me, but I feel her presence, feel the chill of her in my hands, ice trickling down the back of my neck, an uncomfortable pressure in my head.

"I know, baby. But I'm strong now. Stronger. I can do this."

I turn and she is there, my beautiful daughter. But Isla isn't looking at me. She's staring over my shoulder past Sammy's, a strange expression on her face.

"Go home, Mommy."

Music pulses as someone exits the bar. It's a couple, young, midtwenties, out for a date. Second or maybe third date. I can see it in the way they look at each other, how she slides her hand into his butt pocket, how he gently tucks her scarf around her throat. I scan the dark behind them, the yoga studio, the clapboard church. A little farther away is a bakery, a tea shop. A handful of people bustle along the darkened street, hurrying to get home, out of the chilly winter night.

When I turn around, Isla is gone, and I'm alone once again. I push through the bar's heavy front door, trying not to drag my bad leg as I make my way inside. The place is an assault on the senses: the sweet, heady scent of whiskey, of stale beer and old cigarettes, of body odor and old men all being absorbed into the cracked vinyl booths.

Behind the bar, Sammy waves at me, his face lighting with a surprised smile. He's an aging hippie with wild gray hair and a full-on wizard beard. I return his wave, then scan the half-empty bar.

My dad's waiting at a table near the back, his thick woolen scarf and old tweed flat cap on the booth beside him. I limp across the bar to him.

"Hey, Bug." Dad stands, gives me a hug. His hugs have gotten tighter, I've noticed. Like he's worried I'll slip away.

A busty waitress with soft, kind eyes comes over, a new one I've never met before.

"Back again, Quinn?" she asks.

Dad grins sheepishly and tells me he was here yesterday for lunch as well. We both order Diet Cokes and plates of fried chicken with fries. My stomach rumbles.

"You know Mac's in town?" Dad says when the waitress has left. "I saw him at Java Jane earlier."

My eyebrows hike. I flash back to seeing the heart stone on Isla's grave. "It makes sense. The anniversary."

"You think you'll meet up?"

My dad loved Mac. Loved us together. I think he's felt our separation as much as we have. He looks at me, his whiskey-colored eyes filled with hope.

"I don't know, Dad." I don't want to break his heart, but the shame and guilt I feel about the accident has erected a barrier between my husband and me, too thick to penetrate. For me, at least.

The waitress leaves tall, sweating glasses of Diet Coke on the table. I take a long sip and change the subject.

"Christmas is coming up. What are your plans?"

"Why, you inviting me round?" Dad grins.

"You know you're always welcome." I don't tell him I'll probably work. The thought of sitting at home, the pull of the whiskey, the memories, the loneliness, it's too much.

"Actually, I wanted to talk to you about something."

"What's that?"

"I'm thinking of moving to Seattle."

"What?" I'm shocked. "Why?"

"You know Riley moved there a few years ago."

My fun-loving, outgoing baby sister is a free spirit who's spent most of her life traveling. She worked on a cruise ship for years but settled in Seattle with her boyfriend when the pandemic hit. They have an adorable little boy I haven't even met in person yet.

"Something doesn't feel right," he says. "Something with Zeke. I don't think they're getting along very well, but she won't leave him."

I take a sip of Diet Coke. "Is that really any of our business?"

Dad scowls. "It is if he's hurting her."

"Is he?"

"I don't know," he admits.

"Is that what's been bugging you?"

"You noticed, huh?"

"Jeez, Dad, give me some credit. I'm a detective."

He chuckles. "Yeah, it's been on my mind. I don't want to move too far from you."

"I'll be okay," I say, even though I don't know if it's true. My dad and my job have been the only constants in my life the last year. Dad visits every other month or so; he calls every week. He's been supportive when I've needed it but leaves me alone when I need that. I'm not sure what I'd do if he were all the way across the country.

"It sounds like Riley needs you right now."

"Nothing's decided. I'm just . . . thinking."

The waitress arrives with our fried chicken, and we dig in. The bar fills up around us. A couple of cops I know enter. Their voices drift over to me, followed by laughter.

Shane . . . spilled water . . . reamed him!

I cringe. I should've gone. Should've prepared him. It sounds like he didn't do such a great job in front of those reporters. I glance over my shoulder at the door, hoping Shane doesn't show up.

I tell my dad about the case as we eat, about Alice, that I hope to bring her some closure.

"How horrible to be the only one left," I say around a mouthful of chicken. "To think your father has killed your whole family. Honestly, I'm finding it hard to believe Pete Harper did it. It doesn't fit. I mean—" I pause, thinking. "It does, actually, but something's off. Maybe it's the body. Without an ID, it's just this huge missing puzzle piece. We don't know what it means yet. But also, Alice being left behind, it must mean something."

"Poor girl."

"She's so young. Only a teenager."

I dig out my phone and tap into Instagram, call up the picture Shane showed me on Alice's Instagram, the Harper family all squished together in front of a Christmas tree, a happy, smiling unit, Christmas baubles and twinkling lights sparkling around them.

Alice looks so much like her mother, the long, marmalade-colored hair, those bright blue eyes. How different she seems from the girl I met earlier, with her messy, tangled bob; her glassy eyes; the pain stamped between her brows.

She reminds me of . . . well, me. The way grief can weigh on you, how it imprints on your bones like a graveyard etching, revealing itself in pieces over time. She's lost her family. The same as I have.

"They're such a normal-looking family." I slide my phone across the table, and my dad peers down at the picture.

"I never knew you to be surprised at how vile humans can be." Dad pops a fry into his mouth. "Humans kill indiscriminately every day. Their family. Their loved ones. Strangers. We kill for greed and for love. We kill for power and for hate. We have and always will have the capacity to be the very worst of our imagination. This family, they aren't any different from a thousand others."

"Maybe. But this case *feels* different."

He hands me back my phone, and I look again at the photo. Something snags my gaze. I zoom in, scanning every detail. Whatever is niggling at the edges of my brain flares again, then slides away. I'm about to put the phone away when it snaps into place.

A familiar face.

He's just off to the edge of the picture, his face a little blurry, gazing at something off-screen. But I know exactly who it is.

My partner. My friend. Detective Will Casey.

Will was at the O'Briens' Christmas party the night the Harpers disappeared.

"You okay?" Dad's voice floats at me from across the table.

"I . . ." I'm not sure how to reply. "Yeah."

I shove my phone into my pocket, mind spinning. We finish our dinner, talking of casual things, a leaky faucet I need to fix, my little sister's upcoming birthday, her baby's newest tooth.

When we finish, Dad insists on paying the bill, then says he has to hit the road. I tell him I'm going to stay for a bit longer. I want to look through Liu's notes again, try to pull together a timeline. Truthfully, I want to figure out how Will fits into this case. And maybe, just maybe, I'm hoping he'll show up so I can ask him in person.

"You sure you're gonna stay here?" Dad asks as he hugs me goodbye.

"I'm assuming you aren't just talking about Sammy's?" I joke.

He laughs. "I'm talking about staying in Black Lake."

"I think I'm where I need to be right now."

Dad kisses my forehead. "All right, Bug. Just remember, no one on God's green earth can make you happy. They can make you a cup of coffee or make your bed or make you a bowl of soup, but they can't make you happy. And neither can solving more cases. Don't let it become a compulsion."

"I won't."

"And for God's sake, at least put up a tree. It's Christmas! You need some cheer in your life!"

When he's gone, I settle into the booth, nursing my Diet Coke as I make notes in Liu's notebook. I get lost in my work and lose track of time. The bar is packed now, a cacophony of noise. I decide it's time to go home.

There's something I need to do, something I do every night. Part of my routine.

I gather my things and limp toward the door, but before I reach it, Will enters.

And he isn't alone.

I inhale a sharp whoosh of breath, my heart ricocheting off my ribs. I can barely breathe.

Mac, my estranged husband, stands only a few feet away. I stare at him like someone who's been lost in the desert. His blond hair has grown a little, curling softly over his ears. He's shaved his beard, every angle of his face painted in sharp relief. His blue eyes soften as he catches sight of me. For a moment, we just stare at each other, the bar disappearing around us.

The yearning I feel is so intense it's physical, a fist squeezing my chest, a longing for then, for before.

I miss you. I need you. I love you.

The words tumble through my head, all true, but followed by one overshadowing truth.

I killed our daughter.

Somewhere in the distance, I hear the familiar sweet sound of Isla's laughter, and then my phone rings, breaking the spell I'm under, leaving me torn between confronting Will, talking to Mac, or answering my phone.

In the end, I do none of them. I brush past without a word and head outside. The freezing air hits my lungs like a scalpel. The ground is slippery. I pick my way across the snowy parking lot, away from Mac. Away from everything that was. Isla's death clipped the fragile thread that held us together.

My phone rings again. It's Shane. This time, I answer. "Hey, sorry I couldn't make it to the press conf—"

Shane cuts me off. "You won't believe this. The owner of the property where we found the body? It's Jack O'Brien, Alice Harper's uncle."

Chapter 19

Jess

Jack O'Brien owns the property where we found the body.

Shane's words slide down my neck, landing in my belly like lead as I stare into the darkness behind Sammy's. My phone, pressed to my ear, is cold, my bare hands already half-numb.

"So Alice's uncle owns the house where we found Ella's bloody backpack and a body," I say.

"He bought it and the surrounding land last year, before the Harpers went missing," Shane says. "He plans to extend the gated community he's been building over by Killer's Grove, but it's been tied up getting planning permission."

"Hell of a coincidence." My voice is heavy with sarcasm.

"For sure."

It's stopped snowing now, the clouds scuttling across an iron-gray sky, dancing over a yellow moon curved as sharp as a scythe.

"Do you wanna . . . ," Shane begins, hesitant.

"Spit it out, Shane."

"Meet me at Jack O'Brien's office tomorrow morning?"

"I'll be there."

At home, I pull my motorcycle up to the curb and sit for a moment, engine going. The automatic timer has kicked on, the lights releasing a homey warm glow. But inside, it's cold and empty, a brooding silhouette forever altered by Isla's death.

I think of what it would be like if Mac were still here. The fire dancing in the grate. The smell of something comforting cooking, a roast or a casserole. How he'd set down his book when I walked in. *How was your day?* he'd ask, and he'd take me in his arms, and all the darkness of my job would melt away.

I shake the regrets off and pinch the remote control attached under my seat. The garage opens, and I pull inside.

The house bullies me with its silence. After seeing Will and Mac at the pub, I feel unsettled, badly in need of a drink. Of course they know each other, but I didn't know they were drinking buddies. It makes me uncomfortable. I'm not exactly sure why.

I go directly to the kitchen for my routine.

The thing I do, I *need* to do, every night.

Some recovering alcoholics turn to religion, some to exercise, but we all have something. This is what I do to remind myself.

I pour two fingers of Jack Daniel's into an old plastic Snoopy cup, Isla's favorite. Over time, one of Snoopy's ears and part of an eye have been scratched off. It looks like he's winking.

I swirl the booze, let the sugary scent of vanilla and oak rise up to greet me. I imagine the soothing burn, feel the tightness in my throat. Only a thin piece of plastic separates me from my past, from who I was.

I open my phone, scroll through my pictures to one of Mac, Isla, and me at Disneyland the year before the accident. We're all wearing Mickey Mouse ears.

You're worthless. A killer. They deserved better than you.

Sometimes the whiskey is cruel.

"One little drink." My gaze slides again to the picture.

This is what you lose.

I stand there, inhaling and exhaling. Then I toss the whiskey down the sink.

I put some Christmas songs on and pull out ingredients for ginger-bread Santa cookies. I eat a Cup Noodles as I mix and sift and stir. The scent of sugar and spices floats through the house, the music moving from familiar Christmas songs to weirder ones by pop stars I've never heard of.

My love affair with baking began shortly after rehab. Will picked me up with a container of cookies his wife, Shelby, had baked. That night, I got home from seeing Mac and I cried on the floor while eating them. They tasted like heaven, like nostalgia and hope. I decided to make them myself. I baked and baked and ate and ate.

My love affair with swimming began soon after.

I mix red and white buttercream frosting and decorate my Santa cookies, then leave them on the counter and move into the living room. I flick on the gas fire and lie down on the couch, prop my bad leg on a cushion. It's been a long day, and it's throbbing, an insistent, dull ache.

I stare at the flickering flames, steering my mind in a different direction. Something I can't figure out: Why didn't Pete Harper speak to me?

I'm pinned by a horrible realization. Maybe the dead won't speak to me anymore.

Giving the dead a voice doesn't absolve me of what happened to Isla. But maybe that's what I've been hoping. That solving this case, and the next one, and the one after that will turn me into someone who deserved the family she had. Can I ever be that person?

I'm drifting off, weighted by invisible anchors. I dream something is beeping, the warning sound of a dying battery.

The temperature in the room dips, ice trickling down my spine. An uncomfortable pressure builds, somewhere between my ears. The air has turned dense, pounding at my skull. *Beep. Beep. Beep.* The fine hairs on the back of my neck rise as I jerk awake.

The doorbell is ringing.

I expect Isla to be here, but she isn't. I've been seeing her less lately. My shrink has theories. I'm healing. Letting go. Allowing my mind to explore the possibility of a life without her. Things I'm supposed to do. But seeing Isla, knowing she exists, if only in my mind, maybe I don't want to lose that.

The doorbell goes again. I scoop my cane off the floor and yank the door open.

"Mac," I breathe.

My estranged husband looks a little unkempt, a lot drunk. His eyes are red and bleary, stubble bristling his jaw.

"You stopped calling," he slurs. The scent of whiskey is sharp on his breath.

They say 80 percent of marriages end after the death of a child, but I'd say that figure is higher when one is directly responsible for the child's death. For so long afterward, I wasn't able to face Mac. My shame was a physical thing. I'm still haunted by Isla, but I'm trying to focus on the future, too.

"Why are you here?"

His hands reach up, scrubbing at the webbed reds of his eyes. "For the anniversary."

I look over his shoulder at the snowy road. I can't send him back out in this.

"Why don't you come inside?"

Mac follows me into the living room, swaying a little before slumping onto the couch. I bring him a glass of water and a gingerbread cookie on a plate.

He lifts one eyebrow. "Cute." The old Jess never baked so much as a chocolate chip cookie. "How are you?"

"Good."

The lie sits between us, a jagged crack too deep to fill. The problem with lies is they leave debris—debris that eventually needs to be swept up.

Silence expands and stretches. I sneak my knuckles into my thigh, trying to release the pain. I have a sudden sense of déjà vu, like I'm sitting inside a memory, the present and the past, dread and longing.

"Where are you staying?"

"My parents'." He eats the cookie in a few quick bites.

Mac's parents don't speak to me anymore. I'm not sure if they're too caught up in their own grief or if they still blame me, but it doesn't matter. I blame myself enough for all of us.

"Oh."

My one-word reply sounds stiff, awkward. Is it really possible that only a little over a year ago, we were a couple? He knew me deeply, intimately, like his finger could trace me like braille. Like I was a road he'd memorized, rutted and uneven. And now we are like strangers.

Mac and I met at a bar in Boston. I was meeting my sister, who introduced him to me, waggling one eyebrow suggestively behind a curved palm. He was tall and lean, this long-limbed guy with shaggy blond hair and a wide, white-toothed smile. He looked like a hippie, not a law student, with his scuffed Converse and his beaded leather bracelet. It turned out his niece had made it for him, which I found endearing.

What do you call it when you find someone you've been waiting for your whole life? Love at first sight? I'm not sure I believe in that, but there was something about Mac that made me want him to stay. Not just that night, but every night. It was like finding my way home.

I wanted to be the reason for that smile, wanted to live in his blue eyes. He was funny and smart and *hot*. Very hot. We couldn't keep our hands off each other. A defense attorney and a cop, we had all the cards stacked against us, but we made it work. Until Isla died.

"Why were you with Will?" I sit in the armchair, leaning my cane against my knee.

"Ran into him in town. He mentioned you'd been demoted for this new case." Mac studies me. "Do you want to talk about it?"

This is something I used to do when a case got sticky: talk it through with Mac, unraveling the threads that had knotted in my head.

"All right." I adjust in the armchair and tell him about the Harper case. "Why would a family in perfect health, with no crazy debts and no reason to run, walk away from their entire life, but leave their teenage daughter behind?"

"They wouldn't," he says immediately.

"So they're dead."

"Most likely. Have you found a connection to the body in the suitcase and the backpack?"

"Nothing concrete. But the blood on the backpack is Ella Harper's. The house where we found the body and the backpack is owned by Jack O'Brien, her uncle, and it's walking distance from Killer's Grove, where the Harpers went missing."

Mac leans forward, elbows on knees. "Enemies?"

"Pete and Laura were active in the community. Laura volunteered by painting with underprivileged kids. Pete was a member of a local photography club. They had good credit history, not even an outstanding parking ticket between them. They were well liked with literally no enemies."

"Well, that can't be true," Mac counters. "Nobody has *no* enemies. There has to be somebody out there who had something against one or both of them. Even if they loved them, too. It's possible to feel love and hate at the same time."

My mouth goes sticky. I want to ask: *Is that how you feel?* But I don't.

Mac pokes a finger onto his empty plate, gathering the cookie crumbs.

"There were rumors Laura Harper was having an affair. Never confirmed in any interviews, though. If it's true, it makes the theory that Pete did it more compelling, but it still doesn't explain why he'd leave one daughter alive and not the other."

Mac thinks about that. "You know I went to Black Lake High with Pete?"

My eyebrows lift. "Seriously?"

"He was a couple of years below me, so I didn't know him well. Pete was one of the smart kids, a little shy, chess club, band club. But he had a sense of humor, which gives you an edge in high school. People liked him. I wouldn't pick him for a family annihilator."

"He fits. A loving husband, a good father, not known to criminal justice or mental health service, seen publicly as successful and well liked. And if there was an affair, possibly even a family breakup, that's the most common cause of family murders."

"True. Self-righteous killers hold the mother responsible for the breakdown of the family. Maybe he found out about the affair. Maybe she was going to leave him. I just . . . I don't know. The Pete I remember was just a nice, normal guy."

"Even nice guys can turn into family annihilators," I point out. "You never know with some people."

"But you don't think he did it."

I sigh, rub my thigh. "I guess I don't want to tell a girl who lost her family that her father's the one responsible."

"You're protecting her."

"Maybe."

Again, silence stretches between us, the flames dancing in the shadows. But this time it feels warm and comfortable, like chicken soup on a wintry day.

"If I'd stayed, would we have worked things out?" Mac's voice is low and ragged, like he's swallowed coal and the sound is filtering through the jagged edges. "Would we still be together?"

Mac's words stab ice picks into every raw nerve. And then he's at my knee, hands grasping mine. His eyes, the color of sea glass, are rimmed with red, glistening with unshed tears. The booze on his breath smells sweet. I want to lick his lips.

"It wasn't your fault, Mac. I pushed you away. I went . . . insane. I think I still am."

"You can go insane. What happened, it isn't fair. You can cry and scream and go completely crazy. You have the right to do that. We both do. Just come back. All right? Just come back to me."

His face is a constellation of emotion, but the truth about grief: it makes you selfish. My pain felt bigger than his. It still does.

"Maybe, one day, we can find a way of surviving without her," Mac says. "Together."

I drop my forehead to his, tears welling in my eyes.

Our left hands are entwined, wedding rings pressed together. I've never taken mine off, not once. Has he?

"I don't deserve you," I whisper.

"Let me be the judge of that."

And then his mouth is on mine, his hands in my hair. He smells of lemongrass and whiskey and heat and I want him, *God* I want him. Our bodies are like forgotten shipwrecks on the ocean floor, rising to the surface to be exposed to the harsh white sun once more.

Chapter 20

Laura

September

I'm late to work. Again. Jack had me pick up milk and now I have to deal with Rose being annoyed about it, like I get preferential treatment, which I don't.

You'd think since my brother owns the company and all I'm doing is filing and typing, that he'd take it easy on me. But he doesn't. Jack can be an asshole about work stuff. He takes it all so very seriously. Which, I guess, is probably how he's made himself so successful. Unlike me. I don't take anything seriously. Well, except my art studio. I threw everything into it and look how that turned out.

When our dad left, I became the loose cannon while Jack became the stoic, responsible one. He was doing a paper route by the time he was thirteen, while I'd already started smoking and taking vodka shots. At sixteen, Jack was busy selling pot out of the gym lockers, while I was busy stealing pot from him and getting high with my friends. In high school, they called Jack Mr. Business. He's still Mr. Business, only now he sells property, not drugs.

"Nice of you to come in today," Rose snips.

"Sorry I'm late. I got milk, *aaannnnddd* I brought a coffee with extra sugar and a pastry just for you, Rose," I say brightly as I set the pastry and coffee on her desk.

Rose is on Atkins. Rose has no self-control. Rose reaches for the pastry, and I don't even bother to hide my smirk.

Jack strides out of his office, on his way to his next meeting.

"Morning, girls," he calls cheerfully.

Girls? Sometimes I loathe my brother.

I turn my computer on with a sigh and check my phone as I wait. I've received a few more weird texts over the last few weeks, and now I'm nervous whenever my phone pings. I block the numbers, but the texts just come in from new ones. I've thought about telling Pete, but I'm worried he'll find out I met up with Theo. I'm sure whoever is texting has seen me with him. Not that Pete would be mad, he'd just wonder why I hid it.

The day inches by, seconds turning into minutes, minutes into hours. There's nothing interesting about organizing Jack's meetings, scheduling appointments, typing up client contracts.

At noon on the dot, I grab my things, jog down the stairs, and head up the block to my Tuesday yoga class, which Mel teaches. I change and hurry into the fitness room. Mel's already there, and she greets me with a smile.

I unroll my mat and get into a comfortable position, using the class as an opportunity to shake off the unsettled anxiety from those weird texts, the guilt from lying to Pete, the sadness of having my art studio fail, the irritation of working a dead-end job for my brother.

I breathe in through my nose, filling my belly with air, then exhale, forcing myself to relax. Just as class is beginning, an older woman rushes in. It's my neighbor Mrs. McCormack, who sometimes babysits the girls when Pete and I go out for date night. I lift a hand, and she nods at me as she ties her long silver hair in a ponytail.

Mel is a wonderful yoga teacher. She guides us expertly through the warm-up, then into our different poses, finishing up in child's pose. I feel more grounded after. No one's out to kill me. I'm just being paranoid. It's probably just a prank. One of Alice's or Ella's friends being stupid, not realizing how terrifying something like this can be. Kids their age would absolutely know how to get around me blocking all the numbers. I'm sure there's an app for that.

After class finishes, Mel chats with the other students, her face calm and poised. But I can see a stiffness in her, a tension. Ever since she got ill, those literal life-and-death thoughts have clawed at her. She tries to hide it, and mostly she does. But not from me.

I help her carry her yoga mat out to the car.

"You okay?" I ask. "You seem quiet."

"Do I?" She tilts her head.

"What's wrong? Is it your heart?" I ask quickly.

She laughs. "No. My heart's fine. Quit worrying about me! Finn was up a lot last night. Preschool's taking it out of him, and lately he's been like Satan. I think he's overtired. And you know he never wants Jack, just me." She stifles a yawn. "Honestly, I'm fine."

I remember how it was with the girls, how they'd get overtired, have those wide, crazed eyes. How they'd be hyper and excited, then turn weepy and angry. How impossible sleep seemed.

"Okay, phew. You almost gave *me* a heart attack," I joke.

Mel groans but laughs. "Too soon!"

I throw her yoga mat in the back of her car and give her a hug. We say goodbye; then I set out for the lake, settling on a park bench to eat my chicken sandwich. I'm just taking a massive bite when Theo appears.

"Hey, you." He gives me that grin, his eyes sparkling, and my stomach flips.

"Mmm," I say, chewing fast so I can speak. Heat climbs up my neck. "Hey, Theo."

I feel stupid reacting this way. I love my husband. I wouldn't risk the life I've built with Pete. But at my age, it's nice to feel beautiful. Special.

"Okay if I sit?"

"Sure."

He sits next to me, tells me he's gotten a job as a plasterer at Jack's new property development.

"When I saw you, I was actually interviewing for the job," he admits. "I didn't say anything because I knew Jack O'Brien was your brother, and I didn't want you thinking I was using you to get the job."

I think that's sweet and I tell him so. We watch as a boat motors by, a shirtless man at the wheel. Mrs. McCormack comes into view, carrying a paper bag of groceries. She lifts a hand in greeting but then notices Theo. Her eyes flick between us before she hurries away.

"Do you ever talk to Cody?" I ask after a minute. His name in my mouth is cut glass.

Theo seems surprised. Cody. The reason we broke up. The reason I walked away. Without even being around, Cody became too large a presence for either of us to ignore.

"I . . . well, yes, I see him regularly." Theo takes a long swig of Coke.

I wait. I wanted to ask when I first saw him in the grocery store, wanted to confront it, this terrible thing I knew. About Theo. About what happened. Something I still feel awful about.

It was spring, junior year, and we'd been dating about nine months. I'd spent the night at Theo's apartment off campus, as I'd been doing more often. His place was clean, food always in the fridge, the heating always available. He had money, obviously. I didn't.

Theo walked me to my first class, Critical Issues in Contemporary Art, but on the way, we stopped at his friend Cody's apartment. He said he needed to drop something off. Cody was a drummer in Theo's band, so I figured it was music-related.

I liked Cody. He was a nice guy, talkative, young with sharp, ratlike features, a splash of freckles, a gap between his front teeth. He wasn't in college like the rest of us, but he often hung around, and I saw him whenever they played a gig.

I had a full day of classes, then a shift at the café where I worked. I remember being rushed off my feet bringing fancy cakes and cappuccinos to kids spending their parents' money. After work, I cut across the main intersection, heading back to Theo's, when I caught sight of flashing lights.

An ambulance was sitting in front of Cody's building.

"What happened?" I asked a girl standing out front. She was about my age, another student.

"I think some guy OD'd," she said, eyes wide. "I heard they found a paper bag full of drugs in his apartment."

A loud slam came from the building's front doors. Two paramedics rushed out, somebody on a stretcher. It was only an instant, the briefest flash as they hurried to the ambulance, but I saw who it was.

Cody.

Bile rose up my throat. The paper bag Theo had delivered, what had been inside?

Something was niggling at the back of my mind. A realization. How did Theo afford his nice apartment? His designer clothes, his new car? All those people who stopped by his apartment, were they friends, as I'd always assumed?

Like me, Theo's student loans barely covered tuition, let alone books or food or rent. But I worked to pay for those things. Theo didn't.

I refused to believe Theo dealt hard drugs. We smoked pot together, and Theo even dealt sometimes to close friends. But that wouldn't cause someone to OD, would it?

It turned out I was wrong. Because it wasn't pot inside that package, but oxy.

I broke up with Theo after that. I was furious. I felt betrayed. Cody might die because of him. I felt guilty by association.

"He was in a coma for a few weeks," Theo says now. "But he's doing okay."

His sentence trails off, and he looks out over the lake.

"That's good, right?" I say.

"Yeah. I mean . . ." He sighs. "Honestly? There was some brain damage. He's in what's called a minimally conscious state. He's awake but can't really communicate. His sister cares for him, but she's been trying to get him into a care home lately. It's getting too much for her. I send her a check every month. To help out, you know . . ."

"Oh my God!" I exclaim. "I had no idea."

Guilt overwhelms me. It wasn't my fault, but I still feel responsible. Like I could've prevented it, even though I know that isn't true.

Theo touches my hand. "But he's alive, that's what's important."

"I wish there was something I could do."

There's a beat of silence, and Theo meets my eyes.

"Maybe there is."

Chapter 21

Alice

Melanie offers to call me in sick to school on Thursday, but I have something I want to do after, so I tell her no thanks.

She's making porridge for Finn when I come into the kitchen. I grab a glass of water and swallow my antidepressant. My head is pounding, my mouth thick and cottony. I feel like I could go back to bed and sleep for a year.

My stomach is swirly, so I skip breakfast and yank my hat and coat on as I call out to Mel that I'll be at yearbook club after school. It's a total lie, but I don't even want to think about what she'd do if I were late getting back. She's already worried enough about me as it is.

It's cold outside, but the snow has stopped, and the roads have been cleared. My breath turns into white clouds as I pedal to school. I make it through third period, then do my trig test. It's easy, but I make sure to miss two questions so I don't get any extra attention from a perfect score. I mean, it's not that I'm disliked or bullied or anything, just that, other than Maya, I'm mostly ignored, and that's how I like it. It's better than being called a freak.

Before my family disappeared, I was sort of an unknown. Now everyone knows me, but not for the right reasons.

Maya is gone at lunchtime, helping drama club set up for their production of *Scrooge* in a few days. I sit at the back of the cafeteria by myself, picking at today's abomination—"brain pizza," which is basically a lumpy beige square with fleshy white strips of mozzarella glued together like neurons and something green that could be spinach. Or mold. Tough call.

I jump when a lunch tray clatters onto the table next to me. It's Jinx. As usual, she's dressed all in black with purple-black lipstick, black eyeliner and mascara, and a choker necklace that's a battlefield of spikes.

Maybe Jinx's vibe is angsty. But no, I decide, that isn't quite right. She's definitely not sad, with her Cheshire cat grin. She takes a giant bite of whatever gloop—meatloaf?—is on her plate, eyes fixed on me.

"Where's Maya?"

I shrug and pick at a blob of mozzarella.

"You know an English teacher at this school was murdered by a serial killer?"

I blink. "Seriously? When?"

"Like, ten years ago. I read about it before we moved here." Jinx's mouth moves around her meatloaf. *Schlmt, schlmt, schlmt.* Making a sound while eating is called *klut*. It's like knives in my ears.

"You know that creepy forest—Killer's Grove? She was walking home through there, and somebody shot her in the back of the head. Cut both of her arms off, too. Now she wanders through the forest, looking for her arms and all the pieces of her brain. It's one of the ghost stories in Killer's Grove I read about."

"Whatever."

But Jinx laughs, and for some reason, it makes me laugh, too.

"Is that true?" I ask.

"Google says it is."

I wonder what else she's googled, if she knows about me.

"I looked you up," she says, as if she's read my mind. She leans closer and whispers, "Actually, Maya told me all about it. That you talk to ghosts now."

My face goes hot, and a ringing begins somewhere in my brain. "Maya said that?"

She nods.

I stand quickly, ready to get out of there, but Jinx touches my hand. "Don't go. I shouldn't have said anything. I think it's cool."

"It's not *cool*," I snap, but I sit back down, resume picking at my brain pizza.

She chews another bite of meatloaf. "I'm sorry about your family."

"Thanks."

"Was Maya close to them?"

"We grew up together, so I guess. Why?"

Jinx shrugs. "She still seems pretty torn up about it. About your mom especially. I wondered if they were close."

I stare at Jinx, baffled. I never got the sense Maya even liked my mom, let alone grieved her.

"Why'd you move to Black Lake?" I change the subject.

A shadow crosses Jinx's face. She looks down at her legs stretched out under the table. She has a run in her tights, all the way from the top of her boots to her skirt hem. "My parents divorced. Mom got me, and we moved here."

"Lucky you."

"It isn't too bad." She grins. "It fits my vibe."

And for some reason, that gets us both laughing again for, like, no reason, and it feels good and clean and normal.

Danny and Kevin, two popular jocks on the football team, pass our table.

"Freaks," I hear Danny mutter.

This shuts me up fast, but Jinx just laughs harder, her teeth very white against her purple-black lips.

"Oh, come on." She nudges me with her toe. "You gotta have a sense of humor or you can't survive in a place like this."

"Doesn't it bother you?"

"What, being called a freak? Whatever, man. Everybody feels like a freak sometimes. Even those dickheads."

I stare at her.

"I'm going to my house after school," I blurt. "I mean, the house I used to live in with my family. Before they disappeared."

Jinx arches one eyebrow and shoves the last bite of meatloaf into her mouth. "Let's go now."

"Now?" There's still half a day of school left.

"Yeah. Now." Jinx grabs her tray and marches off. It kinda feels like I have no choice but to follow. So I do.

I push my bike through town toward the park. Jinx walks next to me, her cheeks and nose bright red from the cold. She obviously isn't from here; she isn't dressed warm enough for a Black Lake winter. I take my scarf off and hand it to her.

"Thanks." She winds it around her neck and hunches deeper into the soft material.

The park is empty, just a long stretch of white snow that crunches under our feet. Jinx pulls a wrinkled joint and a lighter from her pocket and veers toward the gazebo.

I lean my bike against the side, and we sit on the bench inside. Jinx lights up, takes a deep drag.

"Want some?" She hands the joint to me.

I hesitate. I've never done drugs before. I mean, besides prescribed ones.

Jinx shrugs, pulls the joint away. But I reach for it. I don't want her to think I'm scared. And I want to try. To numb everything going on inside me.

The joint tastes like burned paper, and my lips and throat feel like they've caught fire. I break out in a coughing fit that Jinx finds hilarious. Tears stream down my cheeks, but I'm laughing, too.

Jinx plucks the joint out of my hand. The pot hits me almost instantly. It makes me a little giddy. Soon I'm sweating like a micro-waved cucumber. My eyelids feel like they're weighted with kettlebells. I am a sloth. I cannot move.

"Did you know sloths can't fart?" I tell Jinx.

"What the fuck?" She splutters with laughter behind a haze of smoke.

"The methane in their digestive system gets absorbed into their blood."

Jinx is howling now. "That is totally useless information!"

"They can also hold their breath for forty minutes. That's how lazy they are."

"How do you know that?"

I shrug. "I read things, and they just stick in my brain. What's your real name?"

"How do you know it isn't really Jinx?"

"Is it?"

"Ha. No. It's Summer."

"Seriously?"

"Why do you think I go by Jinx?"

I crack up.

Jinx tells me about her life as a military brat, moving from country to country, the cool rigidity of Berlin, the cosmopolitan vibe of London, the hot passion of Buenos Aires. I tell her about life in Black Lake, how suffocating it's felt since my family disappeared, my upcoming decision on leaving. She has this way of listening that makes me feel like I'm the most fascinating person in the world.

"I think Summer fits you," I blurt.

"Yeah?"

"You're a cheerful goth." The words come out more accusing than I mean for them to. But it's true. Despite her spiky choker and her black makeup, Jinx's vibe is sunny. And I realize that all this time, her vibe has been colored by my own jealousy.

Jinx grins and takes another hit. "Life's too short to be mad. You almost died, you should know."

I sit back and think about that.

My brain feels like it's folding in half. Time passes. Stars die and oceans evaporate. Children are born. Glaciers melt. I am high as fuck. We are laughing like lunatics; I can't remember why. My mind feels numb and empty. I'm not thinking about my family or worried about being a freak or whether I should leave Black Lake. Nothing.

Jinx is talking about this pastry thing called an empanada, and my mouth is watering when suddenly I see something in my peripheral vision. A movement. A shadow. I jump up, looking around wildly. Jinx thinks this is the funniest thing ever.

"You're tripping sack, girl." She stubs the joint out, laughing hysterically. "It's the weed. Come on, let's go check out your house."

I still feel eyes on me, prickling up and down my neck, but I grab my bike, and we head across the snow-covered field. Nothing feels funny anymore. Now I feel jumpy, like I have Pop Rocks bursting under my skin. But Jinx is right. I have to go home. I have to go back there, just to see. To check.

If there's something about my mom and dad I don't know, secrets they kept, maybe it's there, in our old home.

If I can find something, anything to tell me where their bodies are, maybe these grief hallucinations or hypnagogia or whatever the hell is happening to me will stop. Maybe I won't be such a freak. If I can find some answers, maybe I'll be able to leave Black Lake.

We round the last corner and there's my house, a typical New England Colonial, three bedrooms with dingy white paint and navy shutters. It's a little outdated, tired, the paint peeling, the shutters cracked. The lawn is overgrown. But for a second I see how it *was*: Ella's and my bikes thrown haphazardly onto the front lawn, the swing set out back creaking as Ella pumps her feet. Alfie sitting in an apple tree that drops ripe fruit onto the shed my dad built with his own hands, watching, like me.

I used to compare our house to Jack and Mel's. Their place is so *expensive.* They could afford all the designer things I thought were so important. I always felt a little embarrassed, but now I see everything differently. My house looks like what it is: a family home. And it makes my heart ache.

"Is that Killer's Grove?" Jinx asks, pointing past my house to where the pavement stops and the street dead-ends, the trees blanketed with snow.

A shiver scatters down my spine. "Yeah."

It isn't really called Killer's Grove, obviously, but if there's another name for it, I don't know it. My whole life, people have been scared of it.

"When I was a kid, me and all the neighborhood kids used to dare each other to go in. It was, like, a rite of passage or something."

"Did you do it?"

"Yeah. I was ten years old. You can't run away from a dare when you're ten or you look like a scaredy-cat."

I remember walking into the trees, palms slick with sweat, grass-stained knees knocking together. That feeling, it was like I'd just been swallowed. The sun had disappeared, blotted out by the dark shadows of the tall, tightly knit trees. My heart thrummed wildly in my throat, my feet kicking up dust from the dirt road as I walked. But I kept going, deeper into Killer's Grove.

The dare said I had to stay in Killer's Grove for two minutes, so I started counting. One Mississippi, two Mississippi. But soon I lost count. Killer's Grove was different than I'd expected. Light filtered in from the trees, casting god rays all around. The green was a deeper shade than I'd ever seen. The sound of a river babbled in the distance.

The forest floor was a carpet of purple bluebells stretching deep into the woods.

"What happened?" Jinx's voice brings me back to the present.

"Nothing," I say.

It's both a lie and the truth. I walked out of Killer's Grove a few minutes later. But that was the day I realized beautiful things can grow in the darkest places.

Jinx and I cross the street. My dad's ancient Honda is still parked in the drive. The cops never found anything useful inside. I run a finger over its frosted surface, scoring a line along the side.

I unzip the outer pocket of my backpack, fishing around for the keys I still keep there, the cute little *Alice in Wonderland* figurine dangling from a key chain. My dad always wanted to leave a spare in one of those decorative rocks, but my mom wouldn't allow it, even though she was the one always forgetting her keys.

Mom could be a little airy fairy, which was her best and her worst trait. She'd forget to take us to soccer practice because she'd get caught up baking chocolate chip cookies. Or she'd get distracted painting and forget we needed groceries.

My mom was a free-spirited artist, quieter than my uncle Jack but just as magnetic. My dad always said she had charisma, a golden ambience, that she had a genius for friendship. People were drawn to her. They *liked* her because she liked them.

But, like many artists, she never "made it." She started working for my uncle Jack last year after her art studio closed down. She never said it out loud, but I always got the feeling she was sad about that. That she felt like a failure.

She used to keep a diary in the bedside table next to her side of the bed. Maybe it's still there.

A shadow flickers in my peripheral vision. I rock back on my heels, scanning the neighborhood, the snowy road. There's a subtle movement in my old babysitter Mrs. McCormack's curtains across the street. Is she watching? I'm still high, I tell myself. I'm just being paranoid.

"I can't find my keys!" I call out to Jinx, frustrated.

Jinx has climbed the stairs, and she points at the front door, which I now see is cracked open a little ways. "Maybe you won't need them."

She pushes it with the toe of her boot, and it creaks open.

Chapter 22

Alice

Someone's in my house.

My mouth goes dry, breath sticking to my ribs. My mind feels like a tornado.

I wave at Jinx to stop, but she ignores me and walks straight in. All I can do is follow.

My house is like a time capsule. A time capsule that's been tussled with a busy hand. It looks like it's been ransacked. Books have been pulled off the shelves, drawers left hanging open, cupboards disturbed, letters and papers scattered around. There's some sort of powder dusting just about every surface. I feel a flash of anger that the cops left it like this. Except it looks more violent than a regular search. Maybe it wasn't the cops at all.

Last year's Christmas tree is still up, but it's now just a shriveled skeleton. Dry and brittle pine needles are scattered across the floor, along with hand-painted Christmas decorations and cheap plastic baubles. One of the stockings hanging on the fireplace has fallen onto the hearth. There's something missing, and it takes me a minute to figure it out: the orchid my mom had on the mantel. It's gone. Did she move it? Or did someone take it?

I move on, through the kitchen where two wineglasses and a couple of plates sit on the drying rack, back to the living room, where my gaze snags on the painting of my family my mom hung on the wall. It always surprises me how much I look like my mother. I lift a hand to the tips of my hair. Even with my blunt-cut, messy bob, I still have her eyes, her jaw, the shape of her mouth.

In the painting, the four of us stand on a patch of bright autumn leaves, the lake stretching behind us to the setting sun. Mom, Dad, and I are to the left, and we're all smiling indulgently down at Ella, who's done something silly for attention, as she usually did.

And then I am crying, hot tears burning my cheeks. My family home is swollen with memories, ghosts swirling, clamoring for my attention. Mom and Dad and Ella and me decorating our gingerbread house on Christmas Eve and then promptly eating it, crumbs and icing scattering in our haste. Holding Ella's small hand as we roller-skate down the street in the summer. My funny little sister, ten going on sixteen, feisty, stubborn, silly, annoying.

I remember when my parents brought her home. I was completely unbothered at first, this mewling pink blob. But then she started walking and talking. She made me laugh, mimicked me, followed me around. When she cried, I was the one who could soothe her. She looked at me like I'd hung the moon. I'd never been loved the way Ella loved me. Not even by Mom and Dad.

I've always been fearful of so much, all the emotions churning inside me, overthinking anything and everything. But watching Ella, I felt strong. Safe. And now she isn't here and I feel unsteady and alone.

Suddenly, a creak comes from above. My gaze shoots to Jinx, panic unfurling in my chest. Someone's up there.

Jinx moves toward the stairs. I hiss at her to stop, but she ignores me. Again. She seems to do that a lot. It's annoying.

After a second's hesitation, I follow her up the stairs.

We look through my bedroom, then Ella's, but they're only filled with more memories. The painting of an orchid my mom did hanging over my bed. The doll perched against Ella's pillow.

I pick up the doll. Her blue eyes blink open. I remember when Ella turned three, I saved up all my money and bought it for her birthday. I'm not sure why, but she named her Lisa. It was a knockoff, cheap, but when you sat her up, her eyes opened, and when you laid her down, her eyes closed. Ella thought that was cool, but by the time she was five, she'd put Lisa on a shelf, too babyish for her bed. I'm surprised to find her propped against Ella's pillow like this.

I think of Ella when she was small, one arm hooked around the doll. I think of her playing the violin, her stuffed animals a captive audience. The Rubik's Cube she was trying to teach me. The Uno cards still sitting on my desk, one Wild card missing.

I think sometimes memories hide inside us. Like ghosts, we barely notice them until we look directly at them. Being here, it reminds me of all I had.

Of all I lost.

Memories hurt. At least if they're good enough. I guess I've been blocking them out, but only because the pain is so bad.

There's that sound again. A creak. It's coming from my parents' room. My pulse kicks, but Jinx goes straight down the hall and pushes the door open.

Both of us stare in shock at what we see.

Maya is bent over the bedside table on my dad's side. She whirls around when we enter, her face breaking into a relieved smile. "Oh, there you are."

"What the fuck are you doing here?" Jinx folds her arms over her chest, scowling.

I'm surprised by the animosity in her voice. Yesterday they were holding hands.

"Alice told me she was coming here to find her mom's diary."

Jinx turns to me. "Is that what you're looking for?"

"Yes," I say slowly. I don't actually remember telling Maya that, but we did talk on the phone last night. I think. I was pretty out of it from the Ativan.

"How did you get in?" I ask her.

"I used my mom's spare."

I frown. Did I know they had a spare key?

"I haven't found a diary, Alice. Sorry. I did find this, though." She points at something by the side of my father's bed. Jinx and I move to see what it is.

It looks like a couple of broken sticks, but it's only when I take a step closer that I recognize what it is.

I hear the shouts again, angry words, a horrible crash, the sound of wood cracking, the chair splintering. Seeing it now reminds me of my own secret. The one I never want to share.

"It's nothing," I lie. "Ella fell off the chair. My dad was going to fix it."

"What's upstairs?" Jinx asks. "I saw a cord hanging in the hall. Is there an attic?"

"It's my mom's painting studio."

"Maybe it's in there."

Jinx and Maya follow me into the hall. I grab the cord and pull the attic stairs down. A bare light bulb clicks on, a soft orange. Shadows scatter over the exposed steps, following us as we climb.

The attic was my mother's sanctuary. Converted by my dad when she decided to close down her art studio in town. He cleared out all the old boxes and cotton-thick spiderwebs, painted the sloped walls a bright white, and installed skylights on either side. Shards of light streak inside, gray and dirty. Paint-splattered tarps are scattered on the old floorboards; pots of paint and dried-up old brushes clutter her work desk.

This is where I feel my mom the most. Even now, I can faintly smell the scent of her body lotion: lilacs and vanilla.

Before she closed her studio in town, she painted pretty landscapes with abstract blobs of color and occasionally portraits, people emerging like ghosts from the curve of her fingertips. Once the studio shut down, she didn't paint as much, like it was too painful a reminder.

I move around the studio, looking at the paint-splattered easel, the dusty tarp thrown over the floorboards.

I feel an icy finger tapping down my spine, and there's a sound. I run to the steps and peer down, catching sight of someone rounding the corner downstairs, blonde hair, blue-and-white dress, and then my vision wobbles, and all around me it's black, shards of light breaking the periphery, a sound like rushing water filling my head.

"You all right?" Jinx asks.

And snap, like that, I'm back, my heart revving, my legs shivery. I swallow hard. Jinx and Maya are both giving me concerned looks.

"Yeah." I push past them. "I'll check the desk. Look behind the canvas paintings, the wooden easel, in the boxes of paint. Anywhere she could've hidden a diary."

We split up, searching the small attic space. I shuffle through the desk's drawers, through charcoal sketches and cups filled with paintbrushes. We don't find anything.

I examine each of the paintings. I riffle through a stack of canvas paintings leaning against one wall: Black Lake at sunset, the sea on a brilliant summer's morning, a cool autumn day in Killer's Grove, a river of fog winding through a deep chasm.

At the back is a new painting, one I've never seen before. It's different from my mom's usual abstract paintings but still distinctly her style. It's a self-portrait, Mom's face emerging from a whirl of black and vivid red. I pull the painting out. It's heavy. Large. I take a painting of Ella and me off the wall and awkwardly hang the self-portrait in its place. Jinx, Maya, and I examine it.

"That's dope AF," Jinx says. "It's total chaos."

"It's angry," Maya says.

"No." Jinx tilts her head. "It's sadness."

"Come on." Maya turns to head down the stairs. "Let's check your dad's office. Maybe the diary's there."

Jinx follows her, but I stay. When they're gone, I slide open the middle drawer in my mom's desk. I stick my pinkie nail into the edge and lift out the false bottom. I saw my mom the day she snuck upstairs with a handful of wine corks and a drill, saying she had work to do. She hadn't painted for months by then, and why would you need wine corks for painting?

So I followed her. That's just the type of person I am. Watchful. Observant. That ability to slip through the cracks has helped me in photography. I always get the best candid shots, the genuine, unposed moments. You have to be quick to catch people before they notice. That's what I'm good at.

I slipped up the steps on silent feet and watched as my mother built a false bottom inside her desk drawer. She used the corks as supports, gluing them into the corners of the drawer. As soon as she wasn't around, I looked. I am the cat called curiosity; of course I looked. But it was empty.

This time, however, when I use a small metal hook to wedge the thin piece of wood up, it isn't empty. No diary, but there are two other items.

An envelope addressed to someone called Theo Moriarty.

And a handful of pictures.

My head feels all floaty and weird as I stare at the first picture, like a balloon that will drift away into space. Or not space. It would only take an hour to drive to space, so it would have to be farther than that. Maybe Mars. Or Neptune.

The picture is of Ella and me at her school play last year, in front of the *Alice in Wonderland* poster featuring Ella's face. We have our arms wrapped around each other, grinning wildly. But just a little behind us is another girl photobombing the picture. She has cat ears on, and her face is painted into the huge grin of the Cheshire cat, her fingertips pressed together in the shape of a heart.

My heart thrashes wildly as I stare at the girl in the picture. Seven or eight years old. Blonde hair. Bright-blue eyes.

No Hello Kitty headband, but I recognize her just the same.

Isla. The girl I've been seeing.

"You remember me now, don't you?" Isla speaks from behind me.

"You were in the school play with Ella," I say.

"Yep."

"You're dead. It was all over the news." Connections are forming in my head, my gut twisting with nausea. "What do you want from me?"

I see Ella crying in her bedroom after the school announced Isla's death. She saw a counselor after, but it hit her hard. I cried with Ella more than once.

My vision narrows, and my chest seizes. I can't catch my breath. I feel like I'm on the verge of having a panic attack. Because now I have to admit it. I'm seeing a dead girl.

"Alice?" Jinx's voice drifts up the stairs.

I shove everything in my pocket and take a deep, steadying breath, then hurry downstairs to Jinx and Maya to finish searching for Mom's diary.

It's only later, as I'm letting myself into Mel and Jack's house, that I remember I never found the keys to *my* house. They weren't in my backpack. And it's then the thought crosses my mind: How did Maya really get inside my house? Because I'm sure her mom never had a spare key.

Which means Maya is lying.

Chapter 23

Jess

It's early, still dark outside when I wake.

The bed beside me is empty, the sound of the shower running in the bathroom.

Mac.

I get dressed, grab my cane, slam some things into a backpack, and leave before he gets out.

Some ghosts haunt us long after we think they're gone. Like William Faulkner said, *The past is never dead. It's not even past.*

I swim laps for an hour, then roughly dry my hair and hurry into a morning that is bleached gray, clouds swollen with impending snow. I arrive at Jack O'Brien's glass-and-steel office to see Shane waiting out front.

He's fresh-faced, eager-looking, a constellation of freckles standing out on his nose. Today he's wearing a tie, black slacks. At least he's learning. Getting reamed at the press conference probably taught him more than I could.

We exchange awkward good mornings. Neither of us mentions the press conference.

We head through the revolving doors of O'Brien Group Development into a bright, soaring lobby, white walls, lots of glass. A thin, dark-haired beauty greets us from behind a mahogany desk. Shane tells her we have an appointment with Jack O'Brien, and she shows us to a waiting area, heels clicking against polished concrete. We sit in egg-shaped chairs. I rest my cane at my side.

"We've got the sniffer dogs at the property today," Shane says. "Khandi also found what she thinks is part of a fingernail and a partial fingerprint on the suitcase's zipper. It's running through AFIS now."

The Automated Fingerprint Identification System uses a computer to match fingerprints, although it doesn't work as well with partials.

A minute of silence passes. "I'm sorry about your sister," I say.

"I'm sorry about your daughter." Shane looks down at his hands. "I work her case every night. My sister. Hoping to find a new lead, something that was overlooked. How can someone just be there one minute, then not there the next, you know?"

"I do know, yeah."

"My family fell apart after Kiera went missing. My mom had a heart attack a few years later. My dad became obsessed with her case. He got sick a few years back, so I took over for him."

I think of Shane's rumpled clothes, the dark circles under his eyes, how he always looks like he's been up late. Partying, I'd assumed. What would that be like, I wonder, looking for someone you don't know is dead or alive? That tiny kernel of hope in the face of that cruel gut instinct.

"I can't even imagine," I murmur.

Shane looks at me, eyes sad as a poet's. "I think you can."

Maybe he's right. My daughter is dead, but I'm still chasing her ghost. Still looking for her, even though I know she isn't here.

"Look, there's Jack O'Brien." I nod to the tall, fit man with wavy auburn hair exiting the elevator.

He's talking to another man, a city council member I recognize. Jack shakes his hand goodbye, then crosses to the receptionist. He touches a palm to her waist, whispering something in her ear. Her eyelashes flutter as his breath dusts her ear.

I see it then: they're sleeping together.

He straightens, catches sight of us. "Detectives!"

Jack is classically handsome with high cheekbones, a straight nose, full lips. His suit is expensive, shiny black Italian loafers, a navy silk tie. He is smiling, all charm and charisma, his teeth very white.

"Fuck me, he's a redheaded George Clooney," Shane mutters under his breath.

I smother a laugh. I remember someone once saying charisma is power that can make others drink the Kool-Aid. Jack O'Brien is the type to make others drink the Kool-Aid. His success isn't just because of his good looks, but his ability to get people to like him, trust him. It's made him one of the richest property developers in the state.

Jack shakes our hands in turn. He smells slightly of cedarwood.

"Thanks for coming," he says, as if he's the one who reached out to interview us.

For some people, every interaction is about power, control. I've learned the only way to win with people like this is to give in.

"Happy to help," I say, ignoring the crush of his fingers on mine.

He leads us to the elevator, which whisks us to a top-floor conference room laid for serving coffee. Steam wafts from a steel pot in the middle of a glass table, sleek and modern and important. A snow-white orchid sits next to it.

No lawyer. Encouraging. A series of black-and-white photographs of steel skyscrapers, smooth and sleek against a nighttime sky, lines the room.

"Pete took those," Jack says. "He was very talented. Coffee?"

We nod, and he pours into delicate white china as we sit in plush leather chairs.

"Are you reopening my sister's case?" he asks.

"It was never closed, sir," Shane says.

"So the mayor tells me. And yet you haven't found them."

"We're working on it. Sir." Shane's tone is firm, and I'm glad. It takes a strong person not to be intimidated by a man like this. "We have a few more questions. I'm sure you're aware we found a body in a house near Killer's Grove on Monday."

"I did hear something, but I'm afraid I've been in back-to-back meetings every day this week."

"The owner of the house," Shane says, "is you."

Jack's eyes widen. He's off-balanced by this but recovers quickly. His face hardens. This is a man who built himself from nothing to a net worth most people could only ever dream about. He's clever. Shrewd. Calculating. I wonder how honest he'll really be.

"Is it . . . ?"

"We're still working on identifying the body, but we don't think it's any of the Harpers."

"Then why . . . ?"

"We found Ella's backpack near the body. We're investigating a connection."

Sadness darkens Jack's features. "Ella. Do you know what happened to her?"

"We don't have those answers yet, Mr. O'Brien," Shane says. "We wanted to speak to you again to see if there's anything else you remember, any new thoughts or information that's come to your attention."

Jack sips his coffee, gaze thoughtful. "You know, there was one thing. I didn't think about it until recently, but it was . . . strange."

He glances up as a pale, hollow-cheeked woman who looks more like a librarian than a personal assistant slips in, replacing the coffee with a fresh steel pot.

"Thanks, Rose." He returns his attention to us. "Maybe a few months before she went missing, I saw Laura with one of my guys. It was strange because the builders wouldn't usually know anybody in the office. There's no point where their jobs would intersect. But she seemed to know him. Theo Moriarty was his name."

"Do you think they were having an affair?" I ask.

Jack laughs. "No way. Laura and Pete were like this." He twists his pointer and middle finger around each other.

Interesting. Rumors usually stem from a kernel of truth. So who thought Laura had been having an affair?

"No, it looked like they were arguing."

"Do you know how we can get in touch with Theo?" Shane asks.

"No idea. He quit before Laura disappeared. My assistant can give exact dates."

"The family Christmas gathering at your house, did Laura or Pete seem . . . unusual? Were they fighting?"

"No."

"You and your wife were at the hospital when they went missing, correct?" Shane asks.

"That's right. Mel was having chest pains."

"What time was that?"

Jack looks exasperated. "As both my wife and I have told you, Mel went up to check on our son, Finn, shortly before Pete and Laura left, and she fell asleep with him. That was around midnight. After they left, I went to my office to catch up on emails. My mother was staying with us, and she went to bed at eleven. Mel started having chest pains around two a.m., so I took her to the hospital. And no, you can't check the house alarm data. We didn't set it that night. We didn't want my mother to accidentally set it off if she opened a door or anything."

I hear a gentle shushing sound and turn. The personal assistant has been listening to our conversation. She drops her gaze and exits quickly.

Jack checks his watch and stands. "Now, if you don't mind, I have a meeting to get to."

We follow him out of the conference room.

"I'll leave you with my assistant. Rose, can you confirm when Theo Moriarty picked up his final paycheck?"

Rose taps her computer as Jack shakes our hands and leaves. She confirms that Theo Moriarty collected his final paycheck on December ninth, a few weeks before the Harpers disappeared. She prints out the résumé they have on file for Theo and hands it to me with a polite smile. I expect her to say something, but she quickly turns away.

Shane and I walk back to the elevators with more questions than answers.

"We need to find out more about Theo Moriarty," I say.

"Let's call everyone on that résumé," Shane says.

"Detectives?" Rose is behind us, her eyes worried little brown caves. "I thought you should know, Theo Moriarty picked up his last paycheck, but it was never cashed."

Shane and I exchange a look.

"And there's something else . . ." She looks over her shoulder. "It isn't exactly true what Jack said. Laura and Pete *were* having problems."

"What makes you say that?" I ask.

"I heard her on the phone a few times, snippets of angry conversations."

"Was she speaking with Pete?"

"I . . . think so?" Rose looks flustered. "Laura was usually quite sunny, upbeat. But the last month or so she became, I don't know . . . withdrawn. Jumpy. Maybe the month before they went missing, Pete came in to surprise her for lunch. She got really annoyed and told him to leave." Rose looks embarrassed. "It was shortly after that I noticed bruises on Laura's belly. She was reaching for a file, and her sweater rode up. And then she came in wearing a cast on one arm."

"You think he hurt her?" Shane asks.

"Maybe?" Rose glances over her shoulder again. "I think Laura needed money. I heard her and Jack arguing about it."

"When was this?"

"Maybe the summer before they disappeared? I came into work a bit early, and they were in his office. Jack sounded angry, and Laura was crying. It sounded like Laura had asked him for a raise and he said no. I didn't want them to think I was eavesdropping, so I left."

"Did you talk to her about it?"

"No!" Rose wrings her hands, looking horrified. "Anyway. I should get back to work."

"There was nothing to suggest Pete and Laura were struggling financially," Shane says as we head to the elevator. "Their finances were modest, but they'd paid their bills on time, their car was paid off, they had no credit card debt."

"I thought Laura's art business had folded."

"It did, but she didn't go bankrupt. She just closed everything down."

I think about that. What would make someone voluntarily close their business down? "It's interesting Theo Moriarty picked up his last paycheck but never cashed it."

"Maybe we've found out who our body is," Shane says.

"Let's find out who this Theo is and get dental records to compare to our body."

"On it." Shane makes a note in his phone.

"What about the house? Were their mortgage payments on time?"

"They didn't own the house. Jack did. Still does."

"*Jack* owns their house?" I say, surprised. I'd missed that in the file somehow.

"Yeah. They'd rented from him for over a decade."

I shake my head. "Anything to do with money is bad when it comes to family. Especially if they can't pay it back."

"We looked at that angle. The Harpers always paid their rent on time, which was good for Jack; he gave them cheap rent, which was good for them."

The elevator dings, and we step inside.

"So Laura asked Jack for money *and* she had bruises on her body and a dislocated shoulder before she disappeared. I don't like that Jack didn't tell us any of this," I say.

"Should we bring him into the station?"

"What do you think?"

Shane ponders this. "He'll lawyer up. Rich guys like him, it's all about appearances. He wouldn't want anybody thinking he's being officially questioned about this case. Maybe I'll take a crack at him on my own. Mano a mano."

I roll my eyes and laugh as we step outside. Freezing wind bites at my neck. "You know that means hand to hand, right?"

"Oh." Shane laughs, too. "What's man to man?"

"Hombre a hombre. Jesus. Didn't you take Spanish in school?"

"Sure, but I didn't really pay attention."

"Busy paying attention to girls?" I tease.

"Actually, I'm gay."

"Oh, shit, sorry."

He shakes his head, faux disapproving, as the elevator slides open. "And here I thought you were a detective."

I laugh. "Let me try again. Busy paying attention to boys?"

I smile, and he smiles back, that easy, likable smile, and I *do* like him. Maybe we'll make it as partners after all.

"Pretty much. But I'm paying attention now, and it feels like Jack O'Brien is hiding something."

I tell Shane I'm going to stop by the Harpers' on the off chance there's something about Theo Moriarty the CSIs missed last year. I grab the key from evidence and fifteen minutes later step inside the Harpers' house.

It's cold, dusty. The Christmas tree looks sad and lonely, surrounded by dead pine needles and fallen baubles. But I can see what the house used to be. Much-loved suede sofas, tasteful vintage lamps, one wall painted aubergine, Laura's paintings and family pictures scattered around. There are PlayStation games, a shelf with well-read books. It was lived in, a family home.

Now there are just shadows drawn in charcoal. Ghosts whirl like moths, mouths twisted in silent howls.

There is nothing obvious downstairs, but upstairs I see a set of stairs has been pulled down, leading to the attic. Left open by the CSIs? I know from my research that Jack O'Brien has kept the house, ostensibly for Alice when she turns eighteen, but has anybody been here since the Harpers disappeared?

I climb the stairs, a high-pitched buzzing beginning in my ears. The fine hairs on the backs of my arms stand on end, a cold breeze dusting my cheeks.

"Hello?" My throat is bone dry.

The man on the other side of the attic studio doesn't acknowledge me. He's staring at a painting on the wall. I skirt the room until I can see his face.

It's Pete Harper.

He's dead. A ghost. I know that. I wait for him to speak, to tell me what he wants. But no words pass his lips. He doesn't seem to know I'm even here.

I follow his gaze. The painting is different from the others, which are soft, abstract. Lovers walking a moonlit path, a misty autumn morning.

This is a self-portrait. Laura's face is clear, but the rest of her disappears in a whirl of red and black. It's like she's emerging from the darkness or, no, being *ripped* from it. The expression on her face is distinct. Despair. Self-hatred.

"What did you do, Laura?" I murmur.

The wooden frame is cracked, a narrow fissure at the bottom. I lift it off the wall, but it's heavier than I expect and tips out of my hands, thudding hard against the floor. The crack widens.

Pete Harper continues looking at the painting. I flip it over, my fingertips following the split in the wood. I ease my nails into the crack and pull at the thick cardboard back. It snaps easily away.

Something falls to the ground with a thunk.

It's a bundle of cash. Followed by another. And another. I peer behind the cardboard, looking for more.

Taped inside the false back is a small, thuggish-looking gun.

Chapter 24

Laura

September

Theo's idea is simple but brilliant. Overbilling customers is the world's easiest way to skim a tiny bit of money off the top of a very full pot, he said. Nobody would ever notice.

I said no. Obviously.

The thought of scamming my brother made me *very* uncomfortable. He can be an asshole, but he's still my brother.

Still, I can't stop thinking about Cody. I feel terrible. Sick with guilt and regret and shame because I got to walk away from it all, go on with my life, fall in love, have two beautiful children, and Cody got to do none of that. I am ashamed.

And now, Theo tells me, Cody's needs are becoming too much for his sister. She's been saving for a good care home, but it's slow going with all the health bills. I want to help, but how?

I think about it for a few days, and then I have the solution. I'll ask Jack for a raise. I figure any extra money I earn, I can send to Cody's sister.

But Jack says no.

"Laura, Laura, Laura." He tuts and gives me that look, that one he so often has, like he's so tired. Of me, of the mess I've made of my life, of rescuing me. "I've tried to help you, really I have. But there's only so much I can do. We all have to work for things in this life."

"You don't think I work?" Angry tears burn in my eyes. "You patronizing fuck, I worked my ass off on my art studio and it *still* failed."

"It didn't fail, you gave up. That was a choice. You can't be mad about that."

Gave up? Is that what he thinks? Everything I did was for my family, so we could have more money, more security, a better future.

"I tried, Jack. *I tried!* You have so much, and you can't even give me a raise?" I've started crying, and that makes me even angrier. "Don't think I won't tell Mel you've been cheating on her with that little dish down at the reception desk."

Jack's mouth twists into an ugly sneer. "You're such an idiot, Laura. I know things about you, too. And anyway, Mel already knows. She wants the same thing as me. To raise a healthy, happy child with two parents. Finn's only little. The last thing he needs is his parents going through a messy divorce the way hers did. Mel isn't going anywhere."

He turns and storms out of the office, leaving me alone with my fury and resentment and humiliation. I wonder what exactly he thinks he knows about me. And then I remember the texts. Has Jack been sending them?

I consider the idea but can't think of a single reason why he would. Except power. Jack always has to have power over people. He always has some agenda. Nobody makes me feel as small as my big, strong, successful brother. He sweeps everyone and everything up in his path.

He has so much. So much! What's a tiny extra little 10 percent?

But Jack has worked hard to build his business. He's been more than generous giving me a job. What right do I have to steal from him?

I argue with myself, my internal voices clamoring to be heard. All day I listen to these voices, thinking. Thinking. And as the day goes by, I hear one voice dominating the others.

I've failed at a lot of things lately, my art studio, not being able to paint anymore, Pete and I feel like balloons drifting farther and farther away from each other, my daughters are growing up, forging their own lives. They don't even need me anymore.

But at least I can make one thing right. I can help Cody. Jack will never miss such a tiny amount. And I'll be doing it for a good reason.

I take a deep, steadying breath and text Theo.

I'm in.

◆ ◆ ◆

Pete and I are sitting down for date night at our favorite Italian restaurant when the text message pings onto my phone.

Nobody listens to lying bitches. Sometimes they get their tongue cut out.

It's been nearly a week since the last text. Maybe that's why this one shocks me so much. Or maybe it's the explicit threat it contains.

"You okay?" Pete asks.

He's shed his corduroy blazer and is wearing a light-blue button-down with the sleeves pushed up to his elbows. He looks handsome and smart and safe, and I want to lean into him, to let him hold me and tell me everything's going to be okay.

I block the number and delete the text, forcing a smile. "It's Nancy," I lie. "She's been stressed since this business with Maya."

Nancy is Alice's friend Maya's mom. She's my closest friend, besides Mel. The two are very different, Mel poised and calm and contained while Nancy is loud and lovable, all movement and motion with a huge, colorful laugh like a rose bursting into bloom. They don't always get along. Nancy has no filter, and Mel can be overly touchy. Especially lately.

"What happened with Maya?" Pete asks.

"She got fired from her job at the sports store. There was a break-in, a bunch of stuff was stolen. Expensive jerseys, tennis shoes, *guns*."

"Guns? Jesus."

"Yeah. They questioned everybody, but it looks like it might've been one of the managers. In the end, the store fired a bunch of them, including Maya. For a while Nancy was worried they were going to press charges, but it looks like they didn't, thank goodness. No evidence."

"Poor Nancy."

"I'm glad Alice and Ella haven't gotten involved in anything like that."

Pete smiles. "Our kids are pretty great."

He leans across the table and kisses my lips. The kiss isn't rushed, and I find myself letting it go on. I've missed this. We get so caught up with juggling parenting, work, bills, all the life admin that comes with middle age and having a family, that sometimes we forget to take a moment for each other.

"What was that for?" I say, smiling.

"I love you."

"I love you, too." I slip my phone into my purse, determined not to let those texts ruin our night.

Except . . .

I can't stop thinking about them. For the first time ever, I feel like date night drags on a little too long. I'm distracted, my mind whirling from Jack to Mel to Theo to Cody.

"What's wrong?" Pete asks. Again.

His lips are stained a dark ruby from the three glasses of wine he's already drunk. I'd be lying if I said I wasn't concerned with the amount of alcohol he's started consuming. Pete isn't an angry drunk or anything; it's just so much lately.

I stare at my husband's face, the man I've loved my entire adult life, and I want so much to explain. *I'm a failure. A wreck. But I'm going to make it right. You'll be proud of me, I swear.*

"Nothing. In fact, everything's perfectly right."

Later, when he suggests a drink at Sammy's after dinner, I claim a headache and ask to go home.

"I'm worried about the girls," I say, and it isn't a lie.

They begged to stay on their own tonight, and we agreed, although Mrs. McCormack said she'd pop in to check on them. It's a compromise I'm not entirely comfortable with, but mothers have to start releasing their children at some stage, as Pete likes to remind me.

I take a slice of tiramisu to-go for Mrs. McCormack, and we head home, walking the long way along the lake. I half listen as Pete tells me about some drama among the teachers about how classrooms should be run. It sounds stressful, like the teachers are about to break out into a war over it, and I wonder if that's why Pete's been drinking more.

Mrs. McCormack's lights are still on when we get home. "I'm going to run this tiramisu over," I tell Pete.

He kisses me and heads inside. He'll probably just grab a bottle of wine and pass out on the couch watching TV.

Mrs. McCormack opens her door, peering at me from behind large-framed glasses, a bottle of bug spray in a gloved hand. "Hello, dear. Come in, come in."

She waves me inside, and I follow her into a small conservatory at the back of the house. The room is glorious, filled with colorful orchids bursting into bloom, firecracker red and sunset orange, twilight blue and jewel pink. A small water fountain tinkles peacefully in the corner.

I hand her the tiramisu. "I wanted to thank you for checking on the girls tonight."

Her face brightens as she takes it. "Thank you! And it's no trouble. If my daughter were still around, I'd check on her, too."

"I never knew you had a daughter. Where does she live?"

"Oh." Her smile is sad, heavy with memories. She turns away, delicately spraying an orchid's petals. "She passed away a long time ago."

"I'm sorry. That must've been hard."

"It was. But of course, time is a cruel lieutenant." She spritzes another orchid. "We sometimes can't choose what happens to us. All we can do is choose what we do with it. That, and avoid toxic forces in our lives."

She lifts her eyes to mine. "My daughter, she wasn't good at that. She was a tender girl, my Bethany. Got herself a cruel man who crushed her and then killed her. Sometimes people aren't who they say they are." She gently thumbs a purple petal and sprays it. "I always think we must be cautious of the company we keep. The world is hard on soft things. Don't you agree?"

I think of Alice, my desire to protect my sensitive girl. "Yes. I do."

She plucks a shriveled leaf from a stem and hands it to me. It takes me a minute to see a tiny green bug blending into the leaf.

"Some of the most poisonous things," she says, "come in the most clever disguises."

When I get home, Pete's dozing in front of the TV, empty wineglass tipping against his chest. I'm about to wake him when my phone vibrates. It's a text from Jack reminding me to get milk for work on Monday.

Whole milk this time! None of that 2% nonsense.

"Fucking milk!" I hiss under my breath.

I turn on my heel and go straight upstairs to my art studio, grab my laptop, and google *how to set up a business*.

It's a fairly straightforward process and within a few minutes, I've registered a business with the Secretary of the Commonwealth in the state of Massachusetts. I call it DIY Building Supply Ltd., nice and generic. Nobody at Jack's property development company will ever think to investigate who actually owns it. Then I design a logo and invoices that I'll send to Jack's company. I open a free Dropbox account, upload the files to the cloud, and delete everything I've just done, including my browser history.

I regularly send out customer contracts, so it'll be easy to email those customers fake invoices requesting payment for fake admin and local tax fees. They'll pay the fees directly into Jack's company account. I'll invoice Jack's company that exact amount from DIY Building Supply Ltd. And Jack's company will pay into a bank account I'll open tomorrow for myself. Every month Jack's company books will balance. A company as big as Jack's, with money constantly moving around, nobody will ever find out. At least not for a while. And I'm not planning on doing it for long.

I think of Jack's face when he refused to give me a raise. *Laura, Laura, Laura . . . you're such an idiot.*

I've always been a quick learner. It's one thing my teachers always told my mom when I was a kid. I'm creative and proactive and productive. One thing I am *not* is an idiot.

I want that money, and I'm going to get it. Jack can go fuck himself.

Chapter 25

Alice

It's Saturday night, and I'm alone in my room.

I'm staring at my phone, Maya's number on the screen. I want to ask her if she took my keys, but I know I won't. I haven't used them in, like, a year; I probably just misplaced them.

Anyway, Maya's busy. Her mom grounded her for stealing clients' keys from her office. There will be no parties for the foreseeable future. She's pissed. And now Maya has to have *family time*, like that's such a bad thing. Dash is home from college for the weekend, and Dom is sober, according to Maya's earlier text. She has no idea how lucky she is. Thinking of them all together fills me with longing.

I lie on my bed listening to Lizzy McAlpine. Alfie is curled up in a ball on my fuzzy slippers. His tail twitches, like I'm the one who's done something wrong.

The house is quiet. Jack has left on his annual hunting trip. Finn's in bed. I don't know where Mel is.

My phone buzzes, an unidentified number. Journalists, TV shows, podcasts, they've been calling me, waiting for me at school every day since news of the body broke. Mel tells me not to talk to them.

They'll spin everything you say, she warned me. *Just one wrong word and it could ruin everything. Your reputation. Mine. Jack's business.*

The sound has disturbed Alfie. He stands and stretches. I scoop him into my arms, press my face into his silky fur. He gives me a disgusted look and squirms, then saunters away as soon as I release him.

She's right. At least, that's what I thought. But now I've started thinking about that podcast, and maybe I *should've* called Runy's sister. Maybe I'd have more luck finding out the truth.

My phone buzzes again. This time I snatch it up. Static blasts into my ear.

"Hello?"

The static continues.

I'm about to hang up when I think I hear it. My name.

Alice.

I press the phone to my ear, heart slamming against my ribs. There's something there, far away. Music, maybe. A series of beeps. And then a click as the connection drops.

It was nothing. A wrong number or a pocket dial. I throw the phone on my bed and flop onto my back, anger burning hot and bright in my stomach.

Getting through this week after the body was found has been pretty brutal. I'm exhausted, jumpy.

I feel like I did after my family disappeared. Like my blood is flowing too close to my skin. Like my nerve endings are sparking like live wires inside my body.

I think about calling Jinx, asking her to come over, to bring some weed. We could get high and I could numb these feelings. Except I don't want that anymore. I want to know what happened to my family. I want to think about them, I want to remember.

I open my closet and lift out the box where I've hidden the things I found in my mom's desk.

First, the envelope with THEO MORIARTY typed across the front. Inside is a paycheck from my uncle's company, O'Brien Group Development. There are numbers scrawled at the bottom of the paper in my mom's familiar slanted scribble. A password, maybe, or a bank account number?

I set the paycheck aside and grab a notebook from my desk, start writing a list of clues. I'm writing so fast, my arm moving in swift, jerky motions, that my elbow hits my purse, balanced on my bedside table. It tips, spilling everything onto the floor, my phone, my cherry ChapStick, the pills I stole from Mel. The necklace my mother got me pools on the carpet. I lift it, the chain cool to my touch. I wedge my fingernail inside the locket's tiny latch and flip it open.

My family stares up at me from above the musical note, all smiles, no idea what the future would bring. I never should've taken it off.

I pinch the clasp and fasten the chain around my neck.

You have everything you need right here, Mom had said.

I return to my list. Why does Mom have Theo Moriarty's paycheck? I write this down, my pen a black scrawl on bright white.

Next: the pictures. I slide the one of Ella and me, Isla flashing the heart symbol in the background, into my backpack so I don't lose it and flick through the others. Bile fills my throat. Even seeing them a second time, the shock is still raw.

Because these pictures are of my mother.

She's standing in her bra and underwear, bruises like black stones marking a dark path over her fair skin. The pictures are from different angles, capturing bruises that trail down her rib cage, around her waist, up to her neck. She holds one arm cradled against her chest, her eyes hollow, red rimmed.

"Poor Mom," I whisper.

"Where'd she get those bruises?" Isla says from somewhere behind me.

A flicker in my mind. My dad? No. I immediately push that thought away.

"Aren't you tired of feeling like this?" Isla asks.

I ignore her and slide out the laptop nestled at the bottom of the box. It was my mother's, returned to me after the police found nothing interesting on it. I open the lid, but of course the battery's dead. I dig in the box and find the battery, plug it in, and power it up.

The laptop is password protected, but Mom never hid it from us. I type in *sunshinefamily* and the laptop opens. I spend a few minutes going through her files and folders, scanning her photos and most recent documents. But there's nothing that stands out. I slam the lid shut. If the cops didn't find anything, why would I think I will?

I glance again at the pictures of my bruised mom, Theo Moriarty's paycheck. I should give them to Detective Lambert, but last time the detectives were so sure my dad did it. Detective Liu had made his mind up before he'd even finished talking to me. When he finally asked me if my mom was having an affair, I knew it was over.

I pace the room. My brain feels dull. I can't land on anything of value. Alfie hops up on the bed and stretches out on my pillow. For a second, I think about curling up next to him, sliding under the cozy covers, and going to sleep. It would be so much easier to just give up. On life. On the future. It would be so simple.

Death would be easy. It's living that's hard.

But I know I won't sleep. And there's been enough sitting around. I need to rejoin the living, I need to reclaim what happened That Night.

Somebody real killed my family. A flesh-and-blood person hid their bodies. And I'm going to find out who.

I peer out my curtain at the white street below, snow flurries swirling in the black night. My blood is buzzing, or maybe it's my bedroom light. I hear it, like a mosquito in my ear, and then I hear a crash from downstairs, glass shattering.

I yank my door open and run out into the hall. I peer over the banister, but the entryway is empty. I slip downstairs on bare feet. There's a sound. The living room. I inch forward, heart punching at my ribs, and peek around the corner.

Mel is sitting on the couch in semidarkness. She isn't moving. Isn't doing anything, actually. Not reading or watching TV. She's just sitting there staring into space, her shiny Louboutins, the ones I've always coveted, propped on the coffee table next to a wineglass. Liquid drips down the shattered widescreen television, glass from a fractured wine bottle across the floor.

I step into the room slowly. "Are you okay, Mel?"

She turns to me. Her eyes are bloodshot and puffy. When she finally speaks, I can tell she's been drinking. She's not supposed to with her pacemaker, but I've smelled it on her more often lately.

"No," she says. "No, I'm not. But thanks for checking."

"Is Finn okay?"

"Finn's fine."

My eyes dart around the room. "Should I call Jack?"

She gives a hard, angry laugh. "No. I definitely don't want you to call him."

"I'm sure he'd come back from his hunting trip . . ."

"You think he's gone on a hunting trip?" She laughs again, a hard sound. "You're more naive than I thought."

I swallow hard, remembering Jack the night of the Christmas party.

The music had gotten loud, everybody laughing and chatting. The adults were drunk, merry. They'd started dancing. I'd gotten my camera out, the Canon from my father, and was snapping pictures, candid, unposed shots.

Candid shots show moments in time. They're so different from posed shots, which are carefully planned and crafted. I feel like they aren't real that way. So many things are unreliable in life, they disappear, shift, change, like the sea reshapes the sand. I like finding those pure moments, the way a person's expression can be so interesting when they don't know someone is watching. It makes it more honest.

I slipped through the room, snapping pictures of Finn with the Santa Claus Mel had hired and his cute, curly-haired elf; my parents, who were doing a silly boogie in front of the Christmas tree with Grandma and Will and Shelby, Mel's business partner. And then later, next to a table piled with desserts, Mom and Mel talking, heads bent close. Mom's face was tilted toward the camera, Mel had a plate of cookies in one hand, the other on Mom's arm. *Click, click.*

I wandered through the downstairs rooms and found Ella, who'd snuck off to the bathroom to put on her new Bobbi Brown makeup. I snapped pictures of her until she screeched at me to stop.

I was returning to the living room when I heard female laughter coming from down the hall. I followed the sound to the den, and there was Jack whispering something in the curly-haired elf's ear, one hand low on her back. I backed away, embarrassed to have caught them.

I loved my silly, narcissistic uncle, but sometimes Jack could be a dick.

"I was just chatting with Nancy." Mel's voice jolts me back to the present. "She said you're thinking about talking to a podcaster." Mel's mouth twists, like I've just served her poop.

I flash back to telling Nancy about *The Darkest Night.* Not that I was going to do it, just that it was something interesting to think about.

"Be careful what you say." Isla's voice floats somewhere over my shoulder. A warning.

"No, of course not," I lie. "My friend's sister is a podcaster, that's all."

"Jack would be very disappointed if you did. So would I."

Mel stands, stepping into a little puddle of moonlight. For the first time, I notice she has blood down her white silk blouse, the pearl buttons glowing in the creamy light. I can see a pool of blood forming on the white carpet under her injured hand.

Mel takes a step toward me.

My heart starts hammering. I feel that weird disorientation again, the one I felt when I hallucinated her in Finn's room.

"Mel?"

Mel looks down, notices her hand is bleeding. Her whole face crumbles, and she sinks onto the couch, like she's lost her bones. She folds over and starts crying.

"I'm sorry," she sobs. "I didn't mean to scare you."

I sit on the couch next to her. "It's okay. I wasn't scared."

Another lie. But it isn't her fault. It's my stupid brain, seeing things that don't exist, seeing ghosts, people who haunt me, even now.

She sniffs and wipes her eyes. "I've tried so hard to move on, but the police opening this new investigation . . . it's just bringing back memories, you know? And it hurts. That's why I didn't want you talking to that podcaster. Digging up the past never helps anything. I need to focus on Finn. On the life I have now. I have to move on. We *both* do. But it's *so hard*."

Sometimes my pain is so big and raw, I can't see anything else. I guess I've been ignoring the fact that my mom was Mel's best friend. That Mel is hurting, too. Sadness—no, not sadness, *anguish*—comes off my aunt like an oversprayed perfume.

We sit there in silence. Not touching. Not speaking. Just quietly grieving together. It feels . . . nice. Kinda soft and woolly. It's impossible to explain to others how much it hurts. But Mel gets it.

For the first time in a long time, our loss is a fragile string connecting us.

"I miss them," she whispers.

I slide my hand into hers.

I do, too.

Chapter 26

Jess

Someone has strung Christmas lights around the police station. Inside, a Christmas tree fills the entryway, a pink plastic doughnut haloing the top. I bought it for Rivero, our old lieutenant, a few years back.

I jab my ID against the door and let myself into the bullpen. On the far side of the room, my old partner, Will Casey, is at his desk. He's staring intently at his computer screen, a cup of coffee in hand, but he looks up as I enter and follows me to my desk, settling a butt cheek onto the edge.

"You've been avoiding me," he says.

"No," I say. "Well, yeah."

He laughs, his large belly jiggling a little, his face flushed pink.

"But it isn't your fault," I add.

He raises an eyebrow. "It's not you, it's me? That old chestnut?"

I can't help laughing. "In this case, it's true."

"Want to tell me why?"

I lean my cane against my desk and sit, digging my knuckles into my aching thigh. "All right. You were at the Christmas party the night the Harpers disappeared."

"That's right," he confirms. "That's why I can't be on the case. Potential conflict of interest."

God. Now it makes sense why he wasn't assigned to the case.

"What, you thought I was hiding it?"

"I mean, yeah, a little," I say honestly. "Coming into this case midway through, I feel like I'm only getting half the picture. I didn't realize you weren't assigned the Harper case with me because you were at the O'Briens' Christmas party—that it was because it could be seen as a conflict of interest. I just wondered if you were hiding the fact you were there from me."

He's shaking his head, but I keep talking. "I know now you weren't, but in the moment, yeah, I thought you might be." I glance at him. "Honestly, I thought Galloway was trying to punish me by putting me with Shane. It didn't occur to me she had a real reason for keeping you off the case."

"So you added two and two and got five."

I'm mortified; I try to cover it with a wry chuckle. "Yeah. You know me. Sometimes I get too caught up in my own head."

I go a little insane.

I hear Mac's words again.

You can go insane . . . just come back.

"Shane isn't so bad, is he?" Will asks. "I've worked with him before, and he's good."

"He's *really* good," I agree. "You know he works his missing sister's case at night, after work?"

"Shit, I didn't know."

We fall into a comfortable silence; then I say, "I'm sorry, Will."

"No need to apologize, old girl. I would've wondered, too." Will pokes my shoulder and grins. "I just would've asked you about it. Want to know why Shelby and I were at the O'Briens' Christmas party?"

I nod. My job. This case. Helping the dead. I need to focus on that. "You know I do."

"Shelby co-owns the yoga studio with Melanie O'Brien—you know the one over by Sammy's? Mel invited us to their Christmas party. I think she felt bad for us, since we don't have any other family around."

"Did anything stand out that night, anything weird or unusual?"

Will rubs a hand over his pink, balding head. "Man, I've gone over and over that night in my head a million times. I just can't think of anything. Jack was pretty drunk, flirting with the elf, which was pissing Mel off. She was already stressed out because Finn hated the Santa she'd hired, but she wanted pictures with them together. Alice and Laura were sniping at each other, I don't know what about, so don't even ask. Teen drama, I guess. Laura was pretty drunk. Pete less so, but still drunk. Just normal family drama, you know?"

"So you were all drunk?"

"Very. Shelby and I walked home, and it was a looong walk." He laughs. "Oh, except Clarissa, Jack and Laura's mother. She was sober. But she went up to bed around eleven p.m. or so."

"Hmm. Alice said nobody was drunk."

Will raises his eyebrows. "Not sure why she said that."

Neither am I. But it makes me wonder what else she's lied about.

"So Pete drove even though he'd been drinking?" I ask.

Will pushes his glasses up his nose. "I guess. We'd already left by then. Honestly, I thought they were spending the night. The girls came with their backpacks, and they were talking about it."

"Alice had a sore throat," I murmur. "She wanted to go home."

Or was it something else that made them leave?

I glance over my shoulder at Lieutenant Galloway's closed office door. She's on the phone, arms gesturing, like she's angry, which she probably is.

I tell Will about the cash and the compact .22 LR revolver I found hidden in Laura Harper's painting, a gun often used for concealed carry.

"No shit! Ballistics running the gun?"

"Yeah. It'll be a few days. No idea where the cash came from, but we're combing through the Harpers' finances again."

I fiddle with the top of my cane. "You know the weird thing? In her initial interview, Alice Harper said there was a girl in the car with her when she woke up."

"A girl?"

I nod. "Seven or eight. Messy blonde braids. A Hello Kitty headband."

Will looks confused.

"Isla. She saw Isla. But why? What is Alice Harper's connection to Isla?"

"Is that why this case matters so much to you?" Will asks carefully.

"What? No." I'm flustered by the insinuation that I'm letting my personal life get in the way of my professional one. Again.

"Don't let your guilt be an obstacle that gets in the way of what you want, Jess."

"I'm not!" I press my fingers into my temple. "I see him, Will. Pete Harper."

"You do?"

"Yeah, but . . . he doesn't speak to me. I don't know why. I can't figure out how he connects to the body in the suitcase. How Isla connects to Alice. How Jack connects to all of it. None of it makes sense."

"The worst thing a detective can do is make the case about themselves. Maybe Isla is connected to Alice because this is the case she thinks you need. Don't make it personal."

"I just want to help them," I say.

Will studies me for a long moment. "Maybe you should ask yourself whose wounds you're trying to heal by solving this case, Jess, theirs or yours."

I blink but don't get a chance to reply because Shane lopes into the bullpen, waving a report at me. His hair is slightly damp, his face freshly shaved. He's wearing jeans with a blazer and tie.

"Lambert. Townsend," Lieutenant Galloway barks from her office.

Good luck, Will mouths as I grab my cane.

Shane and I hurry into Galloway's office, shutting the door behind us.

"I was just on the phone with the FBI, and they want to get involved in this case," Galloway says.

"What? No!" My protest is instinctual. No cop likes the FBI swooping in and taking over a case.

"They were involved in the search for the Harpers last year," Galloway points out. "I'm inclined to say yes. We just don't have enough manpower for a massive investigation. They can help."

"We don't even know for sure if the cases are linked!"

She gives me a withering glare. "We have Ella Harper's blood on her missing backpack with an unidentified body. You don't think they're linked?"

I grind my teeth. Of course they're linked, but I don't want the FBI stealing this case. Galloway must see something in my face because she backs off with a sigh befitting a teenager. "We'll give it a week. See what we find. Then I'm calling them in."

She levels her gaze at Shane. "Catch me up."

"Right. I'm waiting for a call back from Jack O'Brien again. I've also tried to schedule an interview with Alice, but Melanie O'Brien told me to go through her lawyer. Melanie's her legal guardian, so I'm organizing that now. We've finished interviewing the kids who were at the party, including Maya, who found the backpack."

"We've also checked security video from the nearest neighbors, but nobody saw anything unusual, and there's nothing on the security videos," I add.

"Have the dogs or the search team found anything yet?" Galloway asks.

"Nothing." Shane darts a look at me. "We may need to expand our search."

"Do we have an ID on the body in the suitcase?"

"The specialist postmortem examination is scheduled for tomorrow," I say. "Khandi's working on dental records for Theo Moriarty, the man we suspect is in the suitcase. We should know more soon."

"I just got a preliminary report from Khandi this morning." Shane taps the report he's set on the table. "We got a bullet. The head shot was a through and through. It's likely what killed him. But he was also shot in the shoulder, and that bullet's been recovered."

"Okay, let's hope the gun you found in the painting is a match," Galloway says.

"Khandi's running the partial fingerprint found on the suitcase's zipper through AFIS, but so far there aren't any matches. When we get DNA from that fingernail, she'll run it through CODIS. There was also trace evidence on the suitcase and the victim's coat of a plant called milfoil."

Milfoil. I riffle through the files in my head. Where have I seen that recently?

My mind is whirling, so I don't notice when Galloway dismisses us.

"Lambert," she snaps.

I look up. Galloway is glaring at me. "What the fuck are you waiting for, a hug?"

I flush and jump up, hurry after Shane. My phone's already in my hands, Google open.

Milfoil. *A submerged plant with feather-like whorled leaves.*

"Aha." I snap my fingers, making Shane turn to look at me. "I know where I recognize this from. We need to talk to Khandi."

He follows me up the stairs to Khandi's lab. We find her bent over a microscope. Today she's wearing a new choker, one with a tiny skull and crossbones.

"Yesss! Just the detectives I wanted to see!" Khandi's fist pumps the air, her long, cinnamon-colored twists swinging.

"Wait, Khandi." I hold up a hand. "I have a question for you. Milfoil. Your report says you found it on our victim?"

"That's right. Bucketloads of it. Like he was bathing in the stuff."

"Like he was submerged?"

"Possibly. I found it on his clothes, his hair, even his shoes."

I turn to Shane. "Milfoil was found in the trunk of Laura Harper's minivan. I read it in the case file."

"He must've been in their car," he says.

"Maybe Laura or Pete Harper were with him when he died. Maybe at the lake somewhere."

"Nuh-uh." Khandi's nose ring winks as she shakes her head. "Not Black Lake. The city spends about ten grand a year to have a contractor treat the lake with an herbicide that kills milfoil and keeps it scenic and open for fishing. But milfoil is found in some of the rivers around this area."

It comes to me like a punch to the stomach. "The River Rothay."

My mind is humming; my skin feels tight. I hear the crack of my car hitting the deer. Isla's long, jagged shriek. The dizzying feel of the truck flipping. The dark face of the sky, the river, hungry and urgent, as it filled the cab.

These are the moments I most crave a drink. I swallow past a dusty throat. Shane gives me a questioning look, but I shake my head. Some things hurt too much to explain.

"Can I tell you what I got now?" Khandi's voice breaks into my thoughts.

"Yes. Sorry."

"We have a match on Suitcase Man based on the dental records you had sent over," she says. "You guys were right, it's Theo Moriarty."

My heartbeat thumps, that sense of the clock ticking, ratcheting up.

Shane turns to me. "Well, there's no question now. The missing Harpers and the body in the suitcase are definitely connected."

"And we have exactly one week to figure out how."

Chapter 27

Alice

Monday morning and everybody seems to have forgotten about the body found in the basement of the house where we partied just last weekend. They've forgotten about me.

One of the cheerleaders had a party on Friday, and somebody drove a car into the lake, Runy tells me as we walk toward my AP History class. So that's the big gossip now.

I try not to care that nobody invited me. They think because I'm weird it doesn't hurt when I'm left out. But it does.

In the wild, animals that are different, that have the wrong markings or the wrong color, they're shunned, cut off by their group, making them exposed and vulnerable. These animals usually die. Or they're killed.

Sometimes that's how I feel. Like I'm too different. Like I won't survive.

It's a dark thought, and I wonder if maybe I shouldn't have canceled my appointment with Dr. Pam yesterday. But I couldn't face it. I stayed in bed reading for most of the day, a book of useless facts Jack bought me.

Knowledge is power, he likes to say.

I actually love it. Did you know a caterpillar has four thousand muscles? And that blue whales' arteries are so big, a fully grown person could swim through them?

Runy and I round a corner and spot Jinx and Maya. I lift a hand to wave, but they don't notice. They're too busy speaking to each other in furious whispers.

I feel that throb again, a quivering desperation. Like I'm being left out.

Runy heads off to Spanish, calling hello to Maya and Jinx as he passes. They glance up and catch sight of me. Something flashes on Maya's face. Shock. Dismay.

Confused and mortified, I duck into my classroom. I sit at the back and bend to yank up my socks, which are bunching in the toes of my boots, making my skin crawl all over. After a minute, Jinx comes in. She looks flushed, embarrassed. She slides into the seat next to me.

Our teacher hasn't arrived yet, so students are sitting on desks, chatting loudly. A girl near me is chewing gum, popping loud, obnoxious bubbles. Someone else is tapping a pen over and over, the sound grating at my ears.

"Everything okay?" I ask Jinx.

For a minute, she doesn't look at me. Something's wrong, but I don't know what. Then she lifts her eyes, and what I see there takes my breath away. Anger. At me?

"Maya's the one you should be talking to, not me," she says.

Mr. McCafferty enters, and everybody scuttles to their seats. He's a crotchety old man with ear hair and a bulbous nose. He tosses his battered briefcase on his desk and pulls out a stack of papers—our essays on how the Spanish-American War affected foreign policy. There are groans as he moves around the class handing them out.

He drops mine onto my desk. "Your essay was one of the finest I've seen. Well done, Alice."

Blood rushes to my face as everybody turns to look. I feel their collective eye roll, their disdain. This is why I hate doing too well. The attention is like fire ants under my skin.

"Right." Mr. McCafferty unsnaps a red whiteboard pen and writes a quote on the board. "The past is in the past: True or false?"

Devin, at the front of the room, raises her hand. "False. The more you know about the past, the better prepared you are for the future."

"Theodore Roosevelt," Mr. McCafferty says, writing it on the board. "Good."

"But Abraham Lincoln said to walk slowly but never look backward," Jinx argues.

"Raise your hand, please, Miss Lee," Mr. McCafferty reprimands her.

Jinx smirks. "Which one?"

The class laughs, and Mr. McCafferty glares. The class begins discussing the merits of moving forward versus looking back, of the past weighing us down or shedding it like a skin and moving on.

I'm jotting notes when a weird buzzing fills my brain. That distinctive wobble shivers across the room. The lights start to hum, and a horrible pressure fills my head.

I blink, and there's a man sitting on Jinx's desk.

This isn't real, I know that. But the ground under my shoes, the seat under my butt, the wooden desk under my fingers, it all feels real. I need to wake up. *Wake up.*

This man is not my dad. He has a scruffy beard. Deep-set blue eyes. He is covered in blood, a hole in his shoulder, dark and oozing. Weirdly, this makes me think of spiderwebs. We need a spiderweb to bandage it, like they used to do in ancient Greece.

Or we could try the first aid kit, the rational side of my brain screams.

Rational? still another part screams. *Nothing about this is fucking rational!*

The man's head turns so he's facing me.

Half of his head has been blown off, shards of white bone and fleshy chunks of writhing pink where his brain used to be. Blood drips down his face, shimmering like black oil in the fluorescent lights. He skewers me with an angry glare, his one eye a glistening, dark pool.

I am frozen, lashed to my chair, my heart pounding so wildly, I've gone tingly all over. I know him. I know this man.

I hear a scream. Several seconds pass before I realize it's my own.

I clamp my mouth shut as thirty teenage faces swivel to mine.

I try to stand, but my feet are tangled in the legs of my desk. My arms windmill, and the desk flips, taking me with it. I land hard on my side, legs trapped. Nervous giggles ripple around the room.

"Freak," someone mutters.

"Miss Harper . . ."

My classmates have become meaningless shapes, jabbering, meaningless sounds. Voices rumble, pencils clatter, fabric swishes, whispers shush. They get louder and louder. It's too much for me.

I cover my ears as Jinx stands over me. Her lips are moving, but I can't hear what she's saying over the other sounds splintering in my ears.

And then a loud crack breaks through the noise. Mr. McCafferty slamming a paperweight against his desk.

"That's enough!" he roars.

There's that hard wobble again; the lights dim and then brighten. The bloody man is gone.

Jinx helps me to my feet. I am beet red, mortified, as everybody just stares.

I can't do this.

I grab my coat and backpack and run out of the room, down the hall, bashing through the doors and bursting outside.

It's started to snow, the sky the color of ash. I unlock my bike with shaking fingers and start pedaling frantically. I have to get out of here. I don't know what's wrong with me.

I'm so scared and so sad and so alone, and all I want is to be close to my family, to feel less lonely, so I head for Killer's Grove, to the place I last saw them.

The cold bites at my exposed cheeks, my nose. It burns my eyes, tears rolling down my cheeks as I pedal.

I stick to the roads, which have been cleared of snow. I quickly reach the lake. The water is blacker than usual in the creeping winter light, a chill breeze rustling its surface like rumpled silk. I blow through a stop sign, veer right, the house we partied at last weekend appearing in my peripheral vision.

I stop, watching as officers in high-vis jackets move around the yard, parting the bushes, digging in the garden. Dogs strain against their leashes, noses pressed to the ground.

"I wonder if they've found anything," Isla says from behind me.

I don't turn around, but I hear her laugh. The sound sends ice trickling down my neck. She's not real, but something about the way she's laughing feels cruel.

"At least they're looking." Isla's voice has turned accusing. "You aren't. Not hard enough, anyway."

I'm trying, I think.

"Then where are they?"

"I don't know!" I snap out loud.

A cop turns at the sound of my voice. I get back on my bike and pedal hard until I reach Killer's Grove.

It's darker under the cover of the trees, like they're huddling closer together. The road is an empty ribbon of white unfurling in front of me. I drop my bike to the side of the road by the pine tree with the gash in the bark.

A gust of wind lifts fresh snow off the ground, swirling it around, wrapping icy tendrils over me. I yank my gloves off, run my fingertips over the ridges of the tree's scar, then to the scar on my forearm.

Freak.

I pull out my phone to google a name: *Theo Moriarty.*

The name on the paycheck.

Service here is crap. It takes forever for my search results to load, but it all comes back like a slap to the face.

I'd woken to the sound of angry voices. I heard Mom from behind their door, "Pete, no!" then the crack of wood as it splintered. The low, dull thud of something smacking the wall. And then Dad stumbling out of their room, storming downstairs.

I followed Mom up to the attic and found her hunched on a chair, looking pale and tired.

"Who was he?" I asked her. "That guy I saw you with?"

"I don't know who you mean."

"I saw you go into his house."

"Oh, Alice." She shook her head. "Sweetie, it isn't what it looks like."

"Who is he?"

"Someone I used to know."

"What does that even mean, Mom?"

She sighed, rubbed her hands over her arms. "I knew him in college."

"Knew him or knew *him?"*

"We were together a long time ago, yes, but it isn't that way now. It's . . . complicated."

"Affairs always are." My voice was acerbic.

"You have to trust me on this. Theo was . . . helping me with something."

Theo. That was his name.

Theo Moriarty.

Finally my search results load. Instagram. Facebook. A couple of random business sites.

And then, on page two, a news article.

Theo Moriarty, a contractor and builder from Boston, had been reported missing by his wife last December when he failed to return home after a job one weekend. He had a history of drug dealing, he'd served time for burglary, assault, embezzlement. Nobody looked very hard and, unsurprisingly, he was never found.

There's a small, grainy picture of Theo Moriarty. I squint and pull my phone closer to my face.

It's the man who was sitting on Jinx's desk in my classroom.

The memory of him, his head blown off, settles on me like Jell-O. I start to shake. My whole body. Even my teeth chatter. I slide down to the ground, my back against the tree.

My phone rings. I answer it, but all I hear is static. "Hello?"

I check my phone, heart revving, hands tingling. One bar.

"Hello?" The static continues, followed by a breathy whisper.

I hang up, but the phone immediately rings again.

This time, the display says it's my grandma. I punch at the phone. "Grandma!"

"Alice, what's wrong?" she says.

I dissolve into sobs I can't seem to control. Panic unfurls in my chest. I can barely breathe.

"He's dead!" I wail.

"What? Who . . ."

Isla stands across from me. She shakes her head, like she's disappointed in me. I drop my head to my knees, my face numb with cold.

"Alice, who . . ." Grandma's voice cuts out, and then she's back. ". . . you there?"

"Grandma?" Still only one bar.

"Are you okay?"

"Yeah. I . . ."

A hollow, fuzzy sound comes down the line. Grandma doesn't answer. My phone beeps. Shit. It's lost service.

I shove my phone in my pocket and scrub my eyes with my sleeve. I pull the pictures of my poor bruised mom from my backpack and hold up a lighter to the first one. It blackens and curls, the flame a hypnotizing blue-orange.

I touch the flame to the next picture. And the next. Mom's bruises melt away, disappearing into ash that I cover, like my lies, with snow, the white once again pristine.

Like it never happened.

This secret is safe, at least. Secrets, I've learned, are dangerous. Like caterpillars bursting out of their self-made coffins as butterflies, changed, transformed, secrets can turn into lies. And once they fly out into the world, there's no way to get them back. If anybody sees these pictures, they'll think my dad hurt her. But it can't be true. We were happy. Broken and happy, like bits of beautiful, shattered glass.

Overhead, a branch cracks from the weight of the snow. I pull my camera out of my backpack. The urge to take pictures is strong, and I'm done resisting it.

I snap pictures of the tree, the way the gash cuts across it; the snow, how it piles on the dead tree branches; the woods, shards of muddy light scattering between the boughs. I keep walking, documenting, photographing.

The camera lens is an unwavering eye, the pictures appearing on the screen bathed in a strange, ghostly light, cast in the shadow of everything that happened. I follow the line of the path where I ran, snapping pictures, little witnesses to everything I see. Eyes are unreliable. So is memory. But photographs capture everything. Maybe they're the only truth I'll ever have.

Eventually I reach a snowy chasm, deep and craggy, trees prickling its jagged edges. It isn't massive, just a narrow cleft in the earth's surface, maybe a few hundred feet long.

I turn around, return the way I came until I burst through the foliage and reach the road. I stop and stare at it, memories rising in me like steam off a field.

He didn't hear me at first. Didn't see me staggering through the trees to him. But from where I hovered at the edge of the forest, I could see my dad illuminated in the car's headlights.

He was bent over something. Or someone? A body lying there on the cold pavement beneath him. His back was hunched and shaking, an awful sound coming from him.

I opened my mouth to say his name—*Dad!*—but a twig cracked under my foot.

Dad whirled, eyes landing on me. And in his face I saw everything. A frenzy of rage and resentment and fury carved by jagged shadows and blurred by snow.

He lifted one hand. In it was something black, menacing. And a scream wrenched out of him. "Run! You're next!"

I staggered back, almost falling, scrambled to regain balance. And then I turned and ran. Back into the black forest, branches slapping at me, my eyes blinded by snow.

I don't let myself think about it very often. What it means. *You're next.*

Somewhere in my peripheral vision, there's a flash of messy blonde braids. A childish giggle. Isla.

"Wait!" I fling myself after her, back into the snow-draped forest. She keeps moving, pulling away from me. I speed up, panting, my arms pumping as I try to catch up. "Isla!"

She stops, turns to face me, her body half-hidden in the shadow of a tree. A sudden rushing fills my head, water roaring, like I'm under a waterfall. Pressure fills my head, so crushing that I cover my ears, bending at the waist.

"What do you want from me?" I scream.

And then I'm standing in the middle of a black road, icy rain splattering my face. Lightning flashes, and I briefly see trees bowing low, a fast-moving river. A shadow moves, just out of reach.

And then it's dark once again.

"You don't want the answers to your questions, Alice." Isla's voice echoes over the rushing water in my head.

"What do you mean?"

The rushing suddenly disappears, replaced by the heavy thud of footsteps. I whirl.

Standing behind me is Detective Jess Lambert, watching me with those bright amber eyes.

"Who are you talking to, Alice?"

I look around me.

But Isla is gone once again.

Chapter 28

Jess

Alice looks like she's drowning. I know because I've been there, too.

I've brought her to Black Lake's British tearoom. It's set in a Tudor-style building, Bea's Teas, written in curly white cursive across the front. Inside, it's cozy with painted ceiling beams, dark hardwood floors, faded vintage chairs, twinkling Christmas lights. Red stockings hang from a fireplace, a small, decorated Christmas tree in the corner. Wham! is singing about last Christmas.

I was on my way to the River Rothay when I spotted Alice running into Killer's Grove. I almost didn't stop. Theo Moriarty's body having milfoil on it, possibly from the River Rothay, has made me uneasy. I needed to go there, to pick through these confusing facts. But then I thought I heard someone shouting Isla's name.

I order Alice a chamomile tea, thinking it will be better than giving her caffeine. The girl looks keyed up enough as it is. The waitress sets the tea and a little pot of sugar on the table. Alice curls around the steaming mug like she wishes she could climb inside it. Her hands shake as she lifts it to her lips. The liquid shivers, a bit splashing onto the saucer.

The Christmas lights twinkle in the hazy warmth, catching a sheen of sweat on Alice's face and turning her waxy and gray, more lost than I've ever seen someone. A girl shipwrecked from another planet. Dark, puffy circles under her eyes. Lips raw and chapped. She looks so faded, so tired she could nearly blend into the cold, wintry snow outside.

Alice has texted her aunt Mel, and now we're waiting for her to arrive. It's busy, lunchtime, and we're lucky to get a table. The sounds of china and cutlery tinkle around us. I dip a teaspoon into the sugar bowl, stir it into my coffee as the waitress sets a massive slice of chocolate cake topped with ice cream, whipped cream, and crushed peppermint in front of Alice.

Alice stuffs a giant bite into her mouth. Her cheeks poof out like a chipmunk. I stare at the cake, wondering how they get it so fluffy. My cakes are always so dense.

"Want some?" Alice asks around her mouthful of cake.

"No thanks."

My phone buzzes. It's Mac. Again.

I think about the other night, but I don't know what it means. I don't know what to tell him. The truth is, I don't know if I'll ever get to the point where I can simply accept his love. His forgiveness. I want to, I really do. If I could snap my fingers, I would find my way home to him. But it isn't that easy. Because you can't *tell* people you're good, that they can trust you and you won't hurt them. You have to show them.

Mac is kind, compassionate, and loyal. He believes there's honor in defending people who would otherwise have nobody to stick up for them. He goes for a two-mile run every morning. He would live on tacos if he had the choice. He likes the windows open when he's sleeping and he always wanted a dog, a big, smiling golden retriever. He doesn't deserve any of the pain I've caused.

I press "End" and slide my phone back into my pocket. I yearn for a drink, my throat bone-dry. I tightly grasp my one-month chip in my pocket, letting it bite into my palm.

"Did you know that clouds aren't actually light and fluffy at all?" Alice says, shoving another bite of cake into her mouth. "One cloud can weigh over a million pounds. The water's super dense, that's why it weighs so much."

"How's that possible?"

"The air below the cloud is heavier, so the cloud can still float."

"Huh."

Alice is unlike anyone I've ever met before: sweet but shrewd and highly perceptive, clever but breathtakingly naive, young but with eyes that are old beyond her years. Part of me thinks she's as innocent as Bambi, but the other part thinks she's playing me like a fiddle.

At the root of it all, however, is a girl lost in the chasm of grief and tragedy. In her I see something I found in myself. Strength. This girl is a survivor.

On the other side of the café, somebody drops a plate, glass shattering. Alice startles, hands lifting to cover her ears like it physically hurts. She sees me looking and blushes, drops her hands. She looks so young, her face pale, her upturned nose sprinkled with freckles.

"Sometimes I'm, like, really sensitive to things," she says. "Like sounds and smells."

"I'm the same way," I admit.

"Especially socks," we say at the same time. Our eyes meet, and we laugh. There aren't a lot of people who understand the torture of loose socks.

"Some people call me a freak," Alice says.

Pity squirts through me, like someone's stepped on a ketchup packet. After everything she's been through, having to deal with cruel peers. It sucks.

"I'm sorry. That must hurt."

"It does." Alice's face crumples, and I feel a physical pang in my heart at everything she's going through. I know and I understand. I wish I could tell her how to move through it, but I have no answer for that. You just do. You surrender to the unfairness and the despair, and then you hope the people who love you will be able to pull you back again. It's the only thing you can do.

"Alice, I know we've spoken before, but would you mind if I ask you a few more questions?"

I shouldn't question her. She's a minor and there is no lawyer around, nor her legal guardian. But we're just talking, and I can keep it informal. A chat over tea and cake.

"Off-the-record, of course."

"Okay."

I leave my notebook in my pocket and keep my hands loose on the table. "Before your family disappeared, had you all been to the River Rothay?"

"What, like in the summer?"

"No, within a month or so of that night."

She frowns. "In the winter? No. Not that I remember."

So it must've just been Laura or Pete. Or both.

"Do you know who Theo Moriarty is?"

I see a flicker on her face. Recognition. I hold my breath. We need to find out exactly how the Harpers are connected to Theo Moriarty. If, as Jack O'Brien said, Laura wouldn't have necessarily known him through work, how did they meet? Was Pete connected to Theo?

Alice seems to consider something. She sets her fork down, reaches for her backpack. She pulls out an envelope and slides it across the table to me.

"I found this in my mom's desk. She had a false bottom in her desk drawer. She used to hide her diary there."

Like she hid the bundles of cash.

I lift open the envelope and slide out a piece of paper. It's a paycheck from O'Brien Group Development for Theo Moriarty from last year. December first. The one Rose said hadn't been cashed. There are numbers scrawled on the bottom.

Laura must've taken Theo's paycheck. Which confirms what Jack said. Laura and Theo Moriarty knew each other. But why would she have taken his last paycheck?

"It isn't there anymore. The diary. I checked." Alice seems dreamy, half-asleep. She closes her eyes, and for a second I wonder if she's fallen asleep.

I tap her elbow. "Alice, have you been taking any drugs?"

Her eyes pop open, horrified. "What? No, I swear!"

"Drugs can cause a lot of problems," I tell her. "Even pharmaceutical ones. Like hallucinations, memory problems, anxiety."

"That's what you think, isn't it?" she says accusingly. "That I hallucinated That Night in Killer's Grove. I'm crazy. I'm just a druggy freak!"

"Trust me, that's not what I think. I just know drugs can—"

"I'm not taking drugs, okay?" she snaps, standing abruptly. She unzips her backpack and yanks out her scarf, ready to storm off, but something shakes loose, flutters to the table.

A picture. It settles on my hand like a whimsical butterfly. I lift the picture with numb fingers, feeling suddenly like the oxygen I'm breathing is made of something more volatile than air.

"That's Isla." I point at the picture.

Alice shrugs. "Yeah."

"That's my daughter. My daughter who died last year. Did you know her?"

Alice's eyes widen. "Isla was your daughter?"

"Yes. How did *you* know her?"

She swallows hard, teeth burrowing into her lower lip, tearing at a dry piece of skin. A new song starts up, "Rockin' Around the Christmas Tree." It jangles discordantly in my head.

Finally, Alice sets her bag back on the table and drops into her seat.

"I didn't really. But my sister, Ella, was in a school play with her. Do you remember? *Alice in Wonderland.* It was the summer before last."

I think of all those after-school practices for the school play. Isla loved it, loved dressing up and being on the stage and delivering her lines. Mac was in charge of stuff like that. I was always working. I regret that now, regret that I didn't spend more time with her when I had the chance.

"They never hung out or anything," she continues. "Isla was a few years younger than Ella."

I rub my leg, staring at her, trying to see beneath her skin, to tell if she's lying. I don't know why, but Isla has chosen this girl. Because she's innocent?

Or because she isn't?

"Why do you have this picture?"

Alice frowns. "Not to be rude, but it's a picture of us, Ella and me. My mom took it, and Ella always loved it."

She's right. I hate that she's right. Isla isn't the focus at all.

I lift the picture. "This is who you saw the night of the accident?"

Alice flushes and looks away. "I thought . . . but she wasn't really there."

I can see it in her face; she won't admit it. She's afraid of being different, afraid of being a freak. I don't know why she's seeing Isla, only that Isla is drawing a line between Alice and me, connecting us in ways I haven't quite figured out yet.

Alice drops her chin into one hand, as if she's so tired that her neck can't hold it up anymore. "Do you think people can ever be free of the past?"

"Speaking with some authority on the matter, no. I think we carry the past with us like turtles with their shells, taking it wherever we go." I pause, letting something settle on me, burrow into me. "But . . . maybe that isn't a bad thing."

Alice looks down at her hands, and then her eyelids flutter. It's like she falls asleep for half a second right in front of me, her chin dropping, her mouth relaxing. And then she's back, her eyes widening. The tendons in her neck tighten, and panic and fear flare across her pale face.

"Alice?" I touch her hand, alarmed.

"I went back. That Night." Her eyes are unfocused, like part of her is still there, back in the forest the night her family went missing.

I lean forward, waiting for her to go on.

"I ran away, but I went back. That's when I heard it."

She went back? Alice never mentioned that in her original statement. She said she couldn't remember anything until the paramedic found her.

"What did you hear?" I keep my voice soft, neutral, afraid of disrupting this dreamy, truthful state she's in.

"My dad. He was crying."

"What was he doing?"

"He was by the side of the road, bent over something. He heard me, and he turned around." Her breathing has increased, her chest rising and falling faster. "There was . . . something in his hand. Something dark. He shouted at me. I was so scared. I ran away."

She presses her lips together, Christmas lights reflecting in her wide, glossy eyes. "It was only a few seconds later that I heard a gunshot."

Chapter 29

Jess

I straighten, surprised. "You heard a gunshot?"

This *definitely* wasn't in the case files.

I think back to the revolver I found behind Laura's painting. There were no gunshot casings found by the road, which could point to a revolver. A revolver doesn't eject casings, although whoever fired a gun that did could have collected them. The snowstorm would have erased any gunshot residue, any evidence that a gun had been fired.

Could somebody have used the gun on the Harpers, then hidden it at their house? Seems unlikely. Or maybe it wasn't the gun used at all. Maybe Laura had it for a different reason, and there was a second gun out there.

Neither Laura nor Pete had a gun permit, although that doesn't mean they couldn't acquire one illegally. There are more guns than people in the United States, more than enough for every person in the country to have one. It's nothing to go to any sporting goods store or gun show or hell, buy it from some random guy off the street. Guns are stolen from homes, from shops, from cars, from manufacturing sites. There's no shortage of them around.

"Yes." Alice's response is swift and certain.

"You never said this before."

Alice looks shamefaced. "I didn't think they would believe me. They didn't believe I saw a girl. They thought I was crazy."

So somebody *was* shot. But who? Did Pete shoot whoever he was crouched over? Or did someone shoot him?

"How many shots?"

"Just one."

Theo Moriarty was shot twice.

It doesn't match.

Alice's eyes land on mine. "Everybody thinks my dad did it."

"Did he?"

"*No.*" She presses her palms into her eyes. "I don't know."

Alice folds over, sobs shaking her entire body. I push myself up with my cane, go around the table, and slip into the chair beside her, wrap both arms around her. I can't imagine the pain she's in. How awful to think your own father could take your entire family away from you.

It's been a long time since I've held somebody, offering comfort like this. The weight of her is different than Isla, but she still has that feel to her, fragile, like I'm holding eggshells. Her grief, how much must it weigh?

The thing about grief is that the reality is different from what you think it will be. There's pain inside you that's worse than you ever imagined. It can't be fixed, only carried. But after a while, maybe months, maybe years, maybe one day you realize that pain you're carrying, it isn't a burden, it's a gift. The bigger the pain, the bigger the love. Isn't that what grief is, love persisting?

But while you're in it, you need someone to hold you, to keep you from crawling into the hole that's been blown in your life. I hadn't allowed myself that, and I wish I had. So that's what I do now. I hold Alice as the sounds of the café swirl around us, as prying eyes peer beneath heavy hands. Until eventually she straightens and wipes her damp cheeks.

"I'm sorry I didn't tell you the truth." Her voice is raw. "At first, when I was in the hospital, I thought you guys would find my family, and I didn't want him to get in trouble. But then more time went by and you didn't find them, and it was too late to tell the truth. I didn't want you thinking he did it. He *couldn't* have done it."

I've known a lot of people who've believed the same thing about someone they love, only to one day be proven wrong.

"You said your dad shouted at you. What did he shout?"

Alice's gaze slides away. "I don't know."

She's lying. I can feel it, the sideslipping twist to her voice, the bouncing eyeballs, like Ping-Pong balls. I just can't put my finger on why.

Pete Harper is still everybody's prime suspect. A possible family annihilator, bloated with self-righteous anger after learning his wife was having an affair. Maybe he held her responsible for the breakdown in the family, took out the kids in a mercy killing, made her watch, killed her, then himself.

"They *were* drinking that night," Alice continues. "All the grown-ups were. Even my dad, who'd promised he wouldn't. I think my mom was annoyed because he'd been drinking more than usual."

"Do you know why?"

"No. It wasn't sudden or anything. Just gradually he started drinking more on weekends and then on weekdays, too. Then one day he went into work drunk. He shouted at one of the other teachers. He got suspended, but it kinda took everyone by surprise."

It's amazing the things you can hide from people, I think. *Even the people who know you best.*

"I need to ask you something that might make you a bit uncomfortable, okay, Alice?"

She nods, her gaze drifting out the window.

"Were either of your parents having an affair?"

"No. They wouldn't do that."

Her voice is flat, wooden. There's that sense again, like she isn't telling the truth. Like she's playing with me. Tug-of-war or tying a noose around my neck?

What exactly does Alice Harper know?

I lean closer. "I promise you, I'm going to find out the truth, okay?"

She lifts wide blue eyes to mine and nods.

"But to do that," I continue, "I need you to tell me the truth. And, to be honest, Alice, I kind of get the feeling you aren't."

Alice remains mute, her jaw set. Silence floats between us, stubbornness coming off her like an elbow to the throat. I wait, hoping she'll speak, but then the door bursts open, the bell jingling brightly, and Melanie O'Brien enters.

She's wearing a white bobble hat and a knee-length white wool jacket, a red cashmere scarf wrapped around her throat like a gash. She's perfectly made up, her cheeks flushed with that cold-girl-makeup look people talk about, but her face is hard, sharpened by old trauma and not enough food. The woman could do with a hamburger or two.

"Alice!" She drops to her knees next to Alice, her features softening. I have to give her credit; she loves her niece.

"Are you okay?"

"I'm fine," Alice assures her. "I'm sorry, I didn't mean to worry you. Were you at the hospital?"

"Yes, but everything's all good." Melanie sets her hat on the table, smooths her stylish pixie-cut blonde hair.

"Mel had a checkup to make sure her pacemaker's working," Alice tells me.

Melanie frowns, obviously uncomfortable with her niece divulging private medical information. "I'm fine. Nothing to worry about."

Relief flashes across Alice's face. I really feel for her. She's lost her whole family; the last thing she needs is to lose her aunt, too.

"Now, for you, young lady, I've made an emergency appointment with Dr. Overton." Melanie turns to me. "Alice, can you give us a minute?"

Alice's gaze flicks between us. She grabs her backpack and leaves without another word. On the overhead speakers, "Feliz Navidad" begins playing, the cheerful beat filling the space between Melanie and me.

"You." She sits, turning a fierce gaze on me. "I don't know if I should thank you for helping Alice or sue you for trying to speak to her without our lawyer present."

She sighs. "I guess I'll start by saying thank you. Alice has been . . . troubled since her family disappeared. She's in therapy, of course . . ." Her words trail off, and she stares out the window at Alice, who's tapping at her phone.

"While you're here, is it okay if I ask a few questions?" I say.

"I told your partner to speak to my lawyer."

"We can do that, of course. I just thought it might be easier on everybody involved to get these questions out of the way. You're aware, I'm sure, that we found Ella's backpack with the body over by Killer's Grove?"

"Yes, I heard."

"We just want to get answers. For Alice."

I wait as she wrestles with herself. "Fine. Ask me whatever you want, just leave Alice alone. She needs a chance to heal. To move on."

"Do you have any idea why they disappeared?"

"I don't know. Honestly, I don't."

"Laura was your best friend, correct?" I find it hard to believe she knew nothing about Laura's inner struggles and worries, but then we're all experts at hiding pieces of ourselves, the pieces we don't find pretty enough to display. Maybe that's what Laura did, hid the pieces of herself she didn't want others to see.

"Yes. We met in college. We were friends from the start." Her lips curl up, softening the sharp planes of her face. "Laura, she had this smile. Everybody loved her. She was just so accepting. Once she loved you, her loyalty was forever. She used to volunteer with this charity helping kids who'd gone through traumatic experiences paint. She was generous and warm. I don't know anybody who'd want to hurt her."

"And Pete?"

"Everybody loved him, too. He was quieter than Laura. Calm. Steady. They fell in love like falling into water. It was just so natural for them. No drama. They were just . . . it."

"Where were you when they went missing?"

Melanie sighs, her frustration clear. "Can't you read the police report?"

"I have. I want to hear it from you."

"I was with my son, Finn. He'd woken up crying. It was late, so I laid down with him, and I ended up falling asleep. When I woke a few hours later, my chest hurt. I couldn't get back to sleep, so I went to Jack. He took me to the hospital."

It tracks with what Jack said. "Just one final question. Who was Theo Moriarty?"

"Theo." She gives a small, derisive laugh. "Why are you asking about him?"

I pull the pay slip Alice gave me from my pocket and slide it to her. "He worked for your husband's company shortly before the Harpers went missing. Who was he?"

"Theo was Laura's boyfriend before she met Pete."

I blink, surprised. "Did Pete know this?"

"I don't think so. She never said."

"I've heard rumors of an affair."

Her eyes widen, and she shakes her head. "No way. Neither of them would've cheated. I can tell you that for sure."

"Why was Theo in Black Lake?"

"I think he found out her brother had made it big-time. Laura, of course, thought it was just chance. She always gave people the benefit of the doubt. She started spending time with Theo again, nothing suspicious, just lunchtime picnics, but it worried me. Even in college, Theo was bad news. Drugs, assault, a total loser. At first Laura didn't see it. She was charmed by him. But you know how it goes. The shine eventually faded and they broke up." Her voice breaks and she clears her throat, her eyes shimmering with tears.

"But she loved Theo once?"

Melanie dabs at her eyes with a tissue. "Back then, yes. But it wasn't like she pined for him after they split. She said it was better to move forward than to stay stuck in the past. We can't rewrite history."

"Is that what you've done?"

"I'm trying."

"And what about Jack?"

"What about him?"

"He and Laura fought before she disappeared. About money. How's he dealing with that?"

Melanie's white teeth grasp her bottom lip, worrying the red skin. I wait, holding my breath, because I can feel it. She's holding something back.

Melanie draws in a ragged breath, again glancing outside at Alice. "You should talk to my husband, Detective."

"And what would I ask him?"

Melanie stands, taps one long fingernail, painted bloodred to match her scarf, on the wooden table. "You would ask him about the money that went missing from his company. The money Laura and Theo stole from him."

I sit back, a puzzle piece clunking into place. The cash I found in Laura's paintings.

Before I have time to ask anything else, Melanie sweeps out of the café.

I throw a twenty on the table and grab my cane, hurry after her out onto the snowy street. But it's too late. She's already too far down the road, one arm wrapped around Alice's shoulders.

I turn, heading back to my motorcycle, when I see someone standing just across the road staring at me.

Shane.

He's caught me talking to Alice and Melanie behind his back.

And he looks furious.

Chapter 30

Laura

September

I'm running late, as always. I've left work early for Ella's soccer game, but I need to stop by Theo's house to check on him first. He hasn't been to work for two weeks, and he hasn't been answering my texts. I have to talk to him about the money that's building up in my account. I need Cody's sister's bank details so I can transfer it to her.

I call Mel.

"Hey, are you free?" I ask. "Can you go to Ella's soccer game for a bit? I'm running late. If someone isn't there, she'll do The Hump."

Mel cracks up. "The Hump" is this thing Ella does where she rages, then sulks, then goes borderline hysterical about something. Pete says he thinks one day her head will start spinning around and we'll have to call a priest.

"Just think what she'll be like when she's a teenager!" Mel says.

"God help us all!" I joke.

Alice has always been so quiet. She's watchful. The kind of girl who reads a room like a map, who spends a lot of time in her head, picking away at her thoughts like a knot she wants to unravel. Not Ella. She stands out, makes noise, gets attention.

"No problem," Mel says. "I'll bring Finn, and we'll have a picnic."

"You're a legend. Thanks, Mel."

I hang up and plug the address I found in our company database earlier today into Google Maps and head to Theo's. I pull up in front of a small, run-down cottage situated on the main street.

I get out and stare up the road. The shop where my art studio was is just two blocks away. Without really thinking about it, my feet start moving in that direction.

It's still warm outside, although most of the tourists have left by this time of year. The air is ripe with the scent of freshly baked bread, the bakery half a block away. When I reach the vacant shop where my art studio used to be, I stop. It's just a barren, black hole with empty walls, broken shelves, crumbling plasterboard now. No paint-splattered tarps. No canvases hung with pride.

I run my fingertips over the FOR RENT sign in the window. Ten years ago, when I first opened my art studio, the world seemed full of possibilities. Now it feels like a series of dead ends and bad choices. Sometimes I wish I could just start over.

I think of what Pete said to me the day I walked out of here that final time.

No matter what happens, I'm here. I've got you.

I take a deep breath. I have a consistent paycheck. We've paid off most of our bills. We're almost financially free. Jack's right about one thing, at least. I can't be mad about a choice I made.

I turn my back on the empty shop and return to Theo's. The September sun beats down on my scalp, dust shimmering in the still, hot air. As I pass my minivan, I notice something on the dashboard. It's a piece of paper.

My pulse kicks. What the hell?

The paper isn't on my windshield. It's actually *inside* my car.

I wrench the door open—did I leave it unlocked?—and snatch the note. On it there's a crude drawing of a hangman with a message written in a glittery gold pen: *Traitors gonna swing, bitch.*

I'm shaking, I realize. I never leave the car unlocked. How the hell did they get in?

I should tell Pete. Or the police. But it could lead them back to Jack's company, to what I've done. I can't risk that.

I shove it deep into my pocket. Later I will tear it into tiny pieces and flush it down the toilet.

I cross the street and knock on Theo's door, calling his name. There's no answer. I cup my palm around my eyes, trying to peer inside, but the sun is too strong.

"Theo?"

Nothing.

I push through the weeds at the side of the house. The back door wrenches open with a squeal.

"What are you doing here?" Theo stands in the shadows of the house, arms over his chest.

"I . . ." I'm thrown by how angry he seems. "I was worried about you."

"I've had COVID."

I take a step closer. Even from here, Theo looks wiped out, his face haggard and grim. For the first time, I really see how much he's aged since college. I wonder if he ever looks at me and thinks the same.

"I need Cody's sister's account details."

Theo steps into the light, and I see one of his eyes is black, dried blood crusted around swollen purple skin. There are abrasions and dark bruises on his arms, a bandage wrapped around his left hand.

I gasp. "Theo, what happened?"

"It's nothing." He looks at his hand. "I . . . fell down the stairs."

"You fell down the stairs?"

"Yeah. COVID messed with me. I fainted and fell. Scuffed myself up pretty bad."

"Wow. Sounds like a rough few weeks."

"Yeah. But bad news. I caught up with Cody's sister, and she's worried about any money being transferred and leaving a paper trail. If she's ever audited she'd have to pay taxes on it, so she said thanks but no thanks."

"What? That's ridiculous!" I'm stunned. Who turns down money?

"Yeah."

"Well, what about if we just give her cash? Nobody can track cash."

"That's true." He looks thoughtful. "Give me a few days to organize it, okay?"

"Sure."

"You're a good person, Laura O'Brien."

A rush of warmth unspools over me. I don't even correct him when he uses my maiden name. He steps closer to me, the purple skin under his eye glistening in the harsh sun.

"That looks sore." I reach up to touch his cheek.

"Laura." Theo captures my hand, brings it to his lips. A shiver runs down my spine at the intensity in his eyes.

There's a rustle behind me, something moving in the bushes. I glance over my shoulder, my skin prickling in the warm afternoon sun. But there's no one there.

"Come inside."

I close my eyes, and all of it rushes into the black space that's been eating at me. The failure of my art studio. How sad I've felt by its loss. How hard it is being someone you're not, accepting handouts from a brother you barely know anymore.

I nod and follow Theo through the door. He pulls it shut behind him. We stare at each other, the shadows pooling in the dips and curves of our bodies. Suddenly, his lips are on mine, my jaw, my neck, his breath in my ear. We are a tangle of flesh, our hands grasping at each other, thrusting under clothes to bare skin.

And then I hear Pete's voice in my mind. *No matter what happens, I'm here. I've got you.*

"I can't." I love my husband. What am I doing? "I've gotta . . . I'm sorry . . ."

I run out of the house, pushing through the bushes and hurrying to my car. But as I start the engine, I look back. And that's when it hits me.

Theo's house doesn't have stairs.

I get all the way to Ella's game, cheering her on, sitting between Pete and Mel on the bleachers, when a thought occurs to me. Something Mel said at brunch a few days ago. She'd mentioned seeing Theo in town, reminiscing about what a creep he was, how he'd been responsible for Cody Leily's overdose when we were in college.

Thank goodness Cody was all right, she'd said.

I remember being surprised. I wouldn't call being in a minimally conscious state okay at all.

Unless he wasn't.

I tell Pete I'm going to the bathroom. The public toilets smell of ripe, hot urine, poop smeared across the cubicle I stand in. Which is fitting, considering what I read when I google Cody Leily's name.

Cody Leily is the owner of an indie production company in Boston, Leily's Records. There's a small photo of him on the About page. It's been over twenty years, but I recognize him instantly. The ratlike features, the freckles, the gap between his front teeth.

Cody Leily isn't ill. Theo never needed money for a care home.

The realization is intense and brutal.

All this time, Theo's been feeding me a bunch of bullshit.

Chapter 31

Jess

Shane has gone to Boston to speak to the BPD detectives about Theo Moriarty.

The past two days, ever since he caught me speaking to Alice and Melanie, he's been weird with me. I'm sure by the looks Galloway has been shooting me, she suspects something is up, but Shane obviously hasn't told her anything, otherwise I'd be in far more trouble.

I wanted to explain that I wasn't intentionally trying to speak to her behind his back, but I knew I could've texted him anytime. I should've. And I *did* talk to her behind his back last week. The anger and hurt on his face made me shiver.

"Do you think this is some way to prove yourself?" Shane asked, voice tight and hurt. "To make yourself look better? It isn't a competition. We're *partners*, for Christ's sake!"

"I know!"

"Then what were you doing?"

"I was driving through Killer's Grove when I saw Alice running."

"Why the hell were you even in Killer's Grove?"

I didn't answer. I couldn't. Because I had been driving through Killer's Grove to get to the River Rothay, to the place where Isla died. And that was something I couldn't bring myself to talk about.

Shane had tired of waiting for me to answer and turned to leave.

"Shane, wait." I reached out to stop him. "Melanie told me Laura Harper was stealing money from Jack's company. I think that's where the cash came from."

"So Laura was embezzling money from her brother, and he found out."

"Money's a big motivation for murder."

"True. Money and greed are two of the biggest motivations for violence."

"And love. There's a fine line between love and hate. Sometimes people confuse the two."

I told him then that Alice had admitted going back to the scene, seeing Pete crouched over someone. How she'd heard a gunshot.

Shane cursed. "That confirms everything we've been saying all along. Pete Harper killed them."

I shook my head. He was jumping to conclusions. "She didn't witness it; she just heard a shot. There could've been somebody nearby, or maybe the person on the ground fought back. We don't know for sure. We need her to give an official statement."

"Will she?"

"I doubt Melanie will let her without her lawyer. There's something else."

I told him that Theo Moriarty and Laura Harper had dated in college, that they worked together for Jack's company, and that Alice had found Theo's paycheck in a false bottom of Laura's desk.

"Maybe she picked it up to make it look like he'd left town," he said.

I pulled the paycheck out of my pocket. "It looks like a bank account number is written at the bottom."

"Why don't you track down the bank account and go through their finances?" Shane's eyes had gone hard. He was testing me.

"Sure, no problem." I hated how eager I was to make it up to him, to prove I was a team player, that I hadn't been trying to steal the case from him.

"I don't like that Jack didn't tell us any of that when we spoke to him," Shane said. "What else is he hiding?"

"We should bring him in. Talk to him again."

"He's on a hunting trip at his property in Connecticut."

"He's left town while we're conducting a murder investigation? That doesn't look good."

"No, it doesn't," he admitted. "I'll try to get him back here."

Shane turned to leave but stopped, tilted his chin in my direction. He wanted to say something, but even then he was uncertain. "Don't take this the wrong way, but we never exactly cleared Alice as a suspect. You looked awful cozy in there with her."

"I w-wasn't . . . ," I spluttered.

"Liu always thought she was hiding something. Might want to remember that. Not get so . . . emotionally invested."

"She had no motive to kill her family."

"Not that we know." He turned to leave but again stopped. "Look, I know you like working alone. I know you think I'm too young and too inexperienced, but this is how it is. We've been assigned to this case, to each other. We only have a week before it gets kicked off to the FBI. Maybe we should just make the best of it while we have it."

The words hung between us, bright and hot and acerbic as a burning match, and then he turned and strode away.

Now, I pull my motorcycle onto the gravel at the edge of the River Rothay. I yank the side stand's lever and climb off clumsily. I drape my helmet over the handlebars, still thinking of my conversation with Shane.

Part of me wonders if he's right. Have I become too emotionally invested? Have I lost my impartiality? I want to solve this case because of Alice. *For* Alice. Because I know what it's like to lose your family, to have no way back to the life you used to know.

But the other part of me thinks, to hell with him. I'm good at my job. Not just because I can read a witness, a suspect, a scene, or even because Isla tells me things others might not know. I'm good at my job because I care. And I won't stop caring. I want the truth for the victim, and I will get it.

The problem is, who exactly is the victim here? Things in this case are less and less what they seem.

I limp along the river walk. Someone has salted the pavement, but the ground is still slippery with snow. I feel unbalanced and grip my cane tighter. Ice is crusted along the river's edge. A freezing gust of wind lifts fresh snow off the trees, swirls it around. I continue until the paved walkway disappears, turning to muddy slush.

I think about the crime report, the milfoil found on Theo Moriarty's clothes. Was he in this river? But why pull him out, then, just to hide his body?

After a few minutes, I reach the embankment where my truck went off the road. My whole body is vibrating, my muscles bunched under my winter clothes.

I'm one of those people who thinks best when moving, otherwise I'm too high-strung, too tense. Even before my life fell apart, I was restless like this. Mac was the opposite, calm and peaceful. It was one of the things I loved about him, how his stillness could seep into my soul, calm my wild, restless being.

I look out across the river, the night that is coming in. Snow has gathered in between the rocks. The water is roaring just beyond my toes, rushing fast, just like it did the night I crashed.

My throat burns, that familiar fire. I want a drink more than I have since I got out of rehab. First I drank to numb the pain; then I drank because I didn't want to live anymore. But now I've found a way past it, clawed myself back up to the edge of that cliff. I can't fall back down it again.

"One little drink," I mutter to myself.

Galloway's words come back to me.

There was no proper investigation. No urine, no bloods taken, no witnesses. Just a rainy day, a random deer, and an old man who was a less-than-reliable witness.

An old man.

This confuses me. I don't remember a lot about the accident, to be fair. After the crack of the truck hitting the deer, it flipped, landing on the muddy riverbank. I'd blacked out. When I came to, the pain in my leg was worse than anything I'd ever felt. But it wasn't a man's voice I heard.

It was a woman's voice.

We have to move her, she was saying.

Where's Isla? I wanted to ask, but I couldn't open my eyes. I was diving under a black fog wrapping itself around me.

And then Isla's thin arms were tugging at me—ice-cold but solid and reassuring. I screamed as pain ripped through me.

Mama, please! Isla's voice was urgent, scared.

Her voice in my ears was clear, a fine thread pulling me toward consciousness. And then I was on the riverbank, a few feet from the truck, rain battering my head, my skin, until finally, mercifully, blackness descended again.

I stare at the swift-moving water, letting its roar fill my head. That's when I feel it: that needle-fine vibration. It starts in my temples and creeps down my arms to my knees, deep into my bones.

"Hi, Mommy." Isla is standing next to me, her blonde braids moving gently in the icy wind.

"Hi, baby." I smile and touch her cheek with my gloved hand. "I miss you."

"I miss you, too."

I lean my forehead against my daughter's, feel the soft brush of her blonde hair against my cheek, smell the strawberry scent of her shampoo. She feels *real* to me. As real as the mud under my feet.

"Isla." I pull away, study her face. "Who was there that night? Who found us?"

But she doesn't answer.

Something is forming, a wisp of a thought. I dial Mac's number, Isla sitting on the rock beside me. He answers on the first ring, Christmas music floating gently through the speaker. I wonder where he is, who he's with, then cut off the thought.

"The night Isla died, who found me?" I burst out.

There's a beat of silence.

"Mac?"

"Um . . . it was an elderly guy. Calvin Stevens."

"Not a woman?"

Another beat of silence.

"No," he says slowly. "But initially Calvin said there was a woman there. He said she flagged him down and told him you'd hit a deer."

"Who investigated?"

"It was Bill Liu."

My heart jumps straight into my throat. "*Liu* investigated?"

"Yeah. It's in the accident report."

No wonder Liu had seemed to look at me so intently when we spoke the other day. He saw the state I was in.

"What happened to the woman?"

"She didn't exist. It turned out Calvin Stevens had a touch of dementia. He wasn't even supposed to be driving. Liu wasn't able to confirm most of his statement."

I stare out at the thrashing river. "I need to talk to him."

"Babe, I already did. He's not a reliable witness."

I pause, surprised. "You spoke to him?"

I hear Mac exhale down the phone and imagine his face, the way a muscle in his jaw twitches when he's debating his words. "Something didn't feel right. When Liu let slip who the guy was, I tracked him down. But Liu was right, he wasn't reliable. The woman he thought was there? He said she was Boudica."

"Who the hell is Boudica?"

"You know, the ancient Celtic queen. Led an uprising against the Roman army."

He says it like I should know, but history was never my best subject.

"Long red hair, always had a spear in her hand?" He continues. "Jess, why are you asking this?"

Before I can answer, call waiting beeps through.

"Mac, I gotta go."

"Jess, wait—"

I switch over to Khandi on the other line.

"Heya, Jess!" She sounds ridiculously cheerful compared to the turmoil whipping in my head. "You with Shane? I got the ballistics report for you guys, but I can't seem to get through to him."

"Umm . . . yeah." I make a calculated decision and lie. I need to know what's in that report. I'll call Shane with the update myself. "What's it say?"

"So, striations from the bullet we found in Theo Moriarty match the gun you found in Laura Harper's painting, but this is where it gets interesting. The gun was registered as stolen from a sports store the summer before the Harpers went missing." Khandi's voice has increased with excitement. "And I did a little digging. Want to know who worked there at the time of the robbery?"

"Who?"

"Maya Shepherd. The girl who found the backpack."

"Alice's best friend?"

"Yep. I have a friend who's a serious marathoner, so she shops at the sports store a lot, and she told me there were rumors going around that the manager was in deep with, get this, a drug dealer."

"Theo Moriarty."

"No names, but possibly. She said everybody thought he'd roped in a few of the teens who worked there, including Maya, to carry out the robbery. But no evidence was ever found, so no charges were ever filed."

"Maybe Maya stole the gun from the sports store, and Laura stole the gun from her."

"Maybe Laura killed Theo, then hid the gun in her painting."

"Or maybe Pete killed him and hid the gun."

"Or anybody in that house, really. They all had access."

"It's a lot of maybes," I say.

Alice.

The thought hits me like a bullet. Could she have learned her mother was having an affair with Theo, stolen the gun from her best friend, and killed him?

"Okay, thanks, Khandi."

We arrange to get dinner after the case has finished before hanging up, even though I know I won't follow through. I'm not very good company anymore. I can't celebrate a friend's husband getting promoted or sympathize when their nanny leaves or bring myself to give two shits when their child only gets into their second-choice school.

I stare out over the river, trying to wrangle the thoughts pinging around my mind. Bill Liu. The milfoil on Theo Moriarty's clothes. The cash. Maya Shepherd and the ill-fated gun. Boudica, the red-haired woman.

Red hair.

But there are a million red-haired women. And the timing doesn't match. My accident happened nearly a month before the Harpers disappeared. It makes no sense for Laura Harper to have been there that night.

I think of what Will told me. *The worst thing a detective can do is make the case about themselves. Don't make it personal.*

And here I am doing exactly that.

I huff, disgusted with myself, and dial Shane's number. He doesn't answer, so I hang up, making a mental note to call back later. And then I return to my motorcycle and head back to town.

Chapter 32

Laura

October

Theo is waiting in front of the office on Monday morning with a cinnamon latte. A peace offering, I gather, as we haven't spoken since that kiss at his house a few weeks back. He's been texting me, but I've been ignoring him.

I should've known he was lying about Cody. That he had some angle. How had I let him weasel his way into my life again? I should've listened to Mrs. McCormack. Some of the most poisonous things come in disguise.

At first, I thought I would put a stop to everything. But then I saw the figure in my new bank account. The memory of my empty art studio floated back to me.

Everything I do seems to fail. Even trying to help Cody had been a mistake. But it doesn't have to be that way. There's so much money. More than enough to open my own art studio again. Hire a marketing manager. Actually make it a success this time. I can come up with something to explain the money to Pete. A long-lost relative or that I won the lottery.

It's not like I can put it all back. Anyway, I'm good at this. And I won't lie, it feels fucking amazing. I finally understand Jack's obsessive dedication to building his company. Why he's worked so hard.

It isn't the money. Or, at least, not *only* the money. It's the success. The accomplishment. The validation. Isn't that what money is, a symbol of all that?

Theo begins pacing. He looks twitchy, like he hasn't slept. "Cody had a fall."

"Oh. Is he okay?" I keep my voice neutral.

"Yeah, but his sister needs that money."

"Keep your voice down." I pull Theo away from the rotating doors and down a little alley.

"I've found a care home that'll take him," Theo continues, "but we'll have to set up a regular payment plan."

"I don't know. I think we should press pause on this, Theo."

Panic flares in his eyes. I wonder why he's been lying to me. What he wants this money for. But I push the thought aside because it doesn't matter. He isn't getting it.

"Jack's assistant, Rose, almost caught me. I need to lay low for a bit."

"You can't back out now," Theo says, and it sounds like a warning, not a plea. "You can't do that to Cody's sister."

"Of course not. We'll get Cody that spot in the care home. Just give me a few weeks until Rose backs off. Then I'll start it up again."

I turn to leave, but Theo's fingers snake out, grasping my forearm, digging into my flesh like talons.

"You better not back out," he says again. This time, it's definitely a warning.

I shake him off. "Get your hands off me."

I storm away. But not before I notice my brother peering around the corner into the alley.

A few days later, when I get to work, Rose is riffling through my drawers.

"I'm looking for Mr. and Mrs. Chapman's contract," she says. "Did you forget to file it?"

Fear flaps in my chest. Christ. Talk about a lie becoming the truth. I've taken all my invoices for DIY Building Supply home, but what if I missed one? I can't let Rose find anything suspicious.

"Here, let me look."

I nudge Rose aside and flick through papers on my desk, then pull open a drawer. The contract is there, buried under a pile I haven't yet filed. "Here. Chapman." I give Rose a big smile. "Sorry about that."

She doesn't smile back. Just stares at me with her small, pale face, then whirls back over to her desk.

It's only when I sit down that I notice my hands are shaking.

Later, Mel calls, asking if I want to meet for lunch. The day has been tedious and slow. File. Type. Schedule meetings. Repeat. I jump at the chance to get out.

I walk to the Boathouse Café, which overlooks the lake and a small dock. The trees along the street are bursting into a riot of red and orange and yellow. It's chilly, a brisk October breeze skidding over the velvet-black lake. I'm glad I dug out my winter coat, a knee-length suede with luxurious, soft faux fur around the wrists and neck. Mel bought it for me for Christmas a few years ago, a gift I resisted but absolutely love.

The café is quiet, the summer tourists now gone. Mel greets me with a kiss on the cheek. "Love your coat."

"Love my bestie who gave it to me."

We share a smile as we slide into a window seat.

"Nancy's on her way, too," Mel says.

"Oh, good!" I say. "I haven't seen her in ages!"

I try to remember when the last time was. A month ago, at least. Nancy was going through a crisis. She'd called me sobbing. Maya had been brought in for questioning about a break-in at the sports store where she worked. I'd gone right over.

"I called a friend who's a lawyer," Nancy had said, eyes raw and red as we sat with coffees in the kitchen. "She told me their next step will be to get a warrant to search our house. If they find anything, they'll press charges. Maya could go to jail!"

"But she didn't do it, right?" I said.

"I want to think she didn't, but honestly? I don't know." Nancy gave a shaky little laugh. "It's weird. When your kids are young, you know everything about them. Who their friends are. What they like. What they don't like. They can't hide anything. Maya couldn't even play hide-and-seek without giggling and giving herself away. But now, she's older. She's pulling away. It feels like she's stepped behind a veil and I can't see her as clearly as I used to."

Nancy got up, opened a cupboard beneath the sink, and pulled out a bottle of whiskey hidden behind the cleaning products.

"I have to hide it from Dom." Nancy looked more exhausted than I'd ever seen her. "I think we need something stronger than coffee."

She poured healthy shots into our coffees and took a swig. "It doesn't help that I'm always working. I have to leave everything to Dom, and he's not exactly reliable.

"Maybe we can only ever know pieces of each other," she continued. "Even of those we love *so much*."

She lowered her head to her hands and just sobbed then, and my heart broke for my friend.

Nancy's phone rang, and she wiped her eyes. "Sorry, I need to take this."

She was gone a long time. I eventually decided to go to the bathroom and head home.

Maya's room was the first door I passed on the way to the bathroom. The door was open a crack. I don't know what made me do it, but I stepped inside. The smell of old laundry and feet and strawberry ChapStick hit me like a slap. My eyes skated around, adjusting to the dim light, taking in the typical chaos of a teenager's room. The sliding door to the closet was wedged open with a bundle of clothes. I slid the door open farther with my toe.

Inside was a large suitcase, the lid open. Sports jerseys and hoodies and designer tennis shoes spilled out, the tags still attached. And nestled amid the clothes was something that made every nerve ending stand on edge.

A gun.

My whole body went rigid. I thought about Nancy sobbing with worry and Maya getting arrested, and I wanted to help. So I scooped it all into the suitcase, zipped it up, and wheeled it out to my minivan.

"She's had a hard time with Maya," Mel says now. "I thought she could use a break."

"Yeah. She told me Maya was the fall guy for the manager at the sports store stealing stuff."

"I don't know about that."

"You think Maya did it?"

"Maybe? But Nancy wouldn't see it, would she? Maya's her kid. Parents never see their kids' flaws."

"I'm sure she'd know if Maya did something like that."

Mel laughs, but it's flinty, hard. "Well, you of all people know how blind love can be."

I stiffen. "What's that supposed to mean?"

"Uh, *Theo*?" Mel sets her menu down. "I saw him, you know. A few weeks ago."

"I did, too." I force myself to sound casual. "He's working as a plasterer for Jack."

"*What?*"

"Don't worry, he didn't ask me to help him get the job or anything."

Mel never liked Theo. She thought he was too sleek, too pretentious. That he was showy and grandiose. But that was what made him so intoxicating at the time. A shy, insecure girl getting the attention of someone as confident and self-assured as Theo was a dream come true.

Theo just thought Mel was a stone-cold bitch.

"Just be careful," Mel says. "You're too trusting, Laura, and Theo Moriarty is scum."

"You always said that."

"And I still believe it. Trust me. I worked with him. I should know."

I scan my memories, trying to remember when they worked together. "What are you talking about?"

Mel sips her water. "Sometimes I hooked him up with a friend I knew."

"Hooked him up? You mean . . . with drugs?"

Mel shrugs.

I stare at her. "Wait. So that time you slashed Mandy Parsons's tires for her 'fake' report about you dealing"—I put the word *fake* in air quotes—"it was true all along?"

"I couldn't let her get away with saying that. And it *wasn't* true. I just . . . facilitated their connection."

"So it was true."

"It was a long time ago. It doesn't matter now. I'm out of that world."

I rub my forehead, my mind spinning. "Jesus, Mel . . . why? You never needed money."

Mel rolls her eyes. "Not everything is about money."

Spoken like a true rich person. If you don't have it, *everything* is about money.

"We all want to feel like we're good at something. Like we're worth something. I was good at it, so I did it."

Mel is still talking, but I've stopped listening. Because outside, I see somebody I recognize. She's half-hidden behind a tree, her arms crossed, eyes darting around like she's waiting for something. And then another familiar person strides into view.

"I have to use the bathroom," I announce.

I hurry out of the restaurant, down the stairs, to the back of the building. I peer around the corner at the dock.

I can just about hear their voices. What I can't figure out is how the hell Maya knows Theo.

"I don't have it," I hear her saying.

Theo replies, too low for me to hear, but I can make out *Mikey* and *manager* and *sell*. Whatever it is, it makes Maya mad.

"I got fired, you prick! There's nothing else! My mom took it."

Theo says something unintelligible.

"Yeah, even that. She didn't want the cops finding it."

Awareness trickles in, slow, and then all at once, like a slap to the face. Maya stole the stuff from the sports store to sell with Theo. Mikey, I remember now from Nancy, was the manager of the sports store. I remember the first day I saw Theo, he'd mentioned meeting a man who worked there. He must've roped them into another of his sleazy cons.

Theo grabs Maya's arm, like he grabbed mine earlier. Maya shakes him off.

"I'm out," she calls over her shoulder as she walks away.

I duck back behind the building and hurry inside, thinking of the gun still in my minivan. I'd burned the jerseys, donated the shoes, but the gun was more difficult to get rid of. I couldn't keep it in the house around the girls, so I'd wrapped it in a blanket and hidden it in the back.

I won't need it, I tell myself. Still. Maybe it's time to move it to the front of my car. And it's definitely time to come up with plan B.

Trust isn't like a library book. You can't borrow it and then give it back. At least you shouldn't be able to.

I'm not stupid enough to trust Theo a third time.

Chapter 33

Alice

I don't go back to school the rest of the week.

I can't face Maya or Jinx or Runy. I can't face the Christmas sweaters and the jingly music and the excited vibe of anticipation everybody will have. Only a few more days and school will be out for Christmas vacation, but so what? Maybe that means something for everybody else, but not me.

Every day I head to Killer's Grove. I can't forget the look on poor Detective Lambert's face when she saw that picture with Ella and me, Isla flashing the heart symbol in the background.

I can still feel the moment. How I couldn't breathe. Like I'd forgotten how to. I've lost my family, but she's lost her daughter.

So I wander the frozen forest, looking for Isla, looking for Theo, for my dad. But the ghosts that haunt me are silent.

I don't believe in ghosts, but my mom did. She was always superstitious. *It's not the dead you should be scared of, it's the living,* she used to say. But I think bad things can imprint on the air, like a stamp on paper. Even when the thing that made the impression is gone, you can still feel it, the sensation of it. At least I can.

They aren't real, I know that. Isla, Theo, my dad. They're all dead, reflections of my own guilt, my own grief. I guess I just hope that if

I can find out what happened to my family, maybe they'll disappear. Maybe I won't be a freak.

I can't move on until then. And why should I? What would you do if your whole family just disappeared? If you knew in your bones that they were dead, but you couldn't prove it? You have two choices when something like that happens: move on or find them. And I'm going to find them. Even if doing so means I learn something horrible.

Back at Mel and Jack's, I pull the folded piece of notebook paper listing my evidence out of my pocket. Something wrinkled and dark flutters to the floor. I scoop it up. It's the petal I found in the hall last week, crunchy and broken, barely recognizable now. I rub my fingers together, and it crumbles to ash, scattering at my feet.

I flatten the paper on my bed, letting my eyes trail down my list. The photos of my mom, which I burned but still exist in my mind, Theo Moriarty's uncashed paycheck, the numbers on the bottom.

I saw them together, my mom and Theo.

It was a warm fall day, and I was late for Ella's soccer game. I'd gotten distracted taking pictures of the trees as their leaves started to change. I cut through town, desperate not to be late, when I saw her.

She was knocking on the door to an unfamiliar house. Black Lake is pretty small, and I'd never seen her there, so I stopped my bike and watched as she snuck into the backyard. Then I followed.

I saw the way he looked at her, his lips, the way he pressed them to her hand, how she said his name, *Theo*, a breathy sigh. I lifted my camera, snapped a picture.

I didn't even go to Ella's soccer game that day. I was so angry. I looked at that picture over and over. I veered from fury to fear. I eventually deleted it, not wanting proof of what I'd seen, then raged because I'd deleted it. I lashed out. At her. At Ella. Even my dad. I never got to explain. Never got to tell her the truth behind my anger.

I think the things that really shape us are the things we don't say, not the things we do. Not the lies but the truths we hide, buried between the letters in our words.

I'm hungry, so I take a break and go downstairs, make myself a grilled cheese sandwich. The house is too quiet, too empty. Mel's taken Finn on a Christmas train ride, and Jack's working. As usual. I take my sandwich upstairs. Alfie immediately jumps onto the bed, nose twitching. I throw him a piece of melted cheese, but he turns his nose up, tail flicking.

My phone pings, an email from school notifying me I have math homework.

It gives me an idea. I wipe my greasy fingers on my jeans and pull out Mom's laptop. I checked everywhere except her email.

I sit cross-legged on the floor, laptop open, and navigate to Gmail. Alfie strolls over, batting at my necklace. I push him away, distracted, exasperated. Mom's account has been logged out. I don't know the password. I try *sunshinefamily*, then Ella's birthday, then mine and my dad's, but they don't work, either. Gmail notifies me I have one more attempt before it locks me out.

I think for a second, then remember something my dad showed me once when I forgot the password to my online bank account. I open Chrome's settings and go into the password manager. I scroll through the different applications and find my mom's Google account and click the eye, revealing her password.

Harpers1!

I type it into Gmail, and I'm in.

A lot of Mom's emails from last year have been read, but any since July, when the cops gave the laptop back, are bolded. Most are junk. Reduce inflammation with this magic cream nonsense. But one isn't junk. And it was sent just a few days ago.

The email is from Black Lake Credit Union. It says Final Notice in the subject line. I click into it.

Turns out a payment is due for a safe-deposit box my mom took out right before she disappeared.

I'm staring at the laptop with my mouth literally hanging open when I hear Isla's voice. "She was hiding things."

"From who?"

"You know who."

"Dad?"

"They're dead because of you."

"No," I whisper.

"You know I'm right. It's your fault they were fighting."

I think of hearing my parents arguing in their bedroom, cracking my door open as their voices split the night.

It's never been enough for you, has it, Laura? Dad slurred, drunk again. *This life we've built. The life we've made as a family. Who is it, Laura? Who are you fucking?*

And then my mom's voice. *Pete, no!*

Crash. The sound of wood splintering.

Did he hit her with the chair? Or push her into it? I'll never know. All I know is the things I heard and what I saw the next morning: the chair shattered into kindling on the floor.

Isla's right. They *were* fighting because of me. Because even though I deleted the picture, I told Dad I'd seen Mom with Theo Moriarty.

He started sleeping on the couch. They didn't speak, and when they did, it was like feral cats scratching at each other.

Eventually things got better. Within a few weeks, they acted as if everything was fine again. I thought maybe they'd be okay.

Until the day Mom went to the hospital with a dislocated shoulder. She told him she'd slipped on the wet pavement while out drinking with Mel. I knew it was a lie.

Everything was fucked after that.

"You should've kept your mouth shut," Isla says.

She's right. It's better to watch. To listen and observe. To collect information like a chipmunk collects nuts. Because the truth hurts.

Now I swallow my voice. I don't speak up. I learned my lesson the hard way.

Sometimes a lie is the kindest truth you can tell.

"Go away," I tell Isla. And she does.

I write down the name and address of the bank on my notepad. I'm going to find out what my mom kept hidden in that safe-deposit box. But first I need a key.

I check my box of things, rummage through my drawers, my desk, tip out my purse, and look through every pocket. No key. I need to go back to my house. Maybe my mom left a key for her safe-deposit box somewhere there.

A banging comes from downstairs, urgent, demanding. I hurry down the stairs and throw open the door.

On the front porch isn't just one person, but two. My grandma and Jinx.

Both start speaking at the same time.

Blood . . . phone . . . Maya . . . questioning . . .

Their words roll and twist around each other. "Wait, what?"

"I wanted to make sure you were okay!" Grandma pulls me tight against her chest. She smells clean, of shampoo and coconut soap, and it's comforting in a way I haven't felt in a long time. "You were talking about blood and then you didn't call me back, and I haven't been able to get through to anybody. I've been so worried!"

"Oh, crap, I'm sorry, Grandma. I lost service when I was talking to you, and then I forgot to call you back."

"But you're okay?" She holds me back, assessing me.

"I'm fine. I promise."

"Okay. Okay, good." She releases a long breath and turns to Jinx. "This young lady is quite insistent that she speak to you immediately."

Jinx strides inside, pacing back and forth in the living room. She runs a hand through her gelled hair. Her eyes are pinched.

I follow her but stand back. Too much is coming off her at once. *Anxiety.* The scent of burning metal. *Fear.* Vanilla. *Confusion.* Rotting vegetables. Sometimes I feel like all my skin has come off, like I have no protection from other people's emotions. Jinx's hit me hard now.

"The police have taken Maya in for questioning!" she blurts.

I feel like she's punched me in the face. "What?"

Jinx's mascara has smudged under her eyes, making them look black and wide, like a crazed raccoon. "Yeah. And I think I know why."

She takes a deep breath, the chains on her choker rattling. "It's why we were fighting on Monday. I was at her house a few days ago and I found something weird. It was a phone but, like, not a smartphone. It was old and cheap. I was curious, so I opened it, and there were these texts to someone called Laura. Your mom. They were horrible. Bullying, abusive texts. I found the phone with this."

She holds up a key chain, an *Alice in Wonderland* figurine dangling next to a shiny silver key.

I snatch the key chain. "My house key! Why did Maya have it?"

"She took it."

"Wait. Maya stole Alice's key?" Grandma says. "Why?"

"And why was she texting my mom?" I add.

"She said she was trying to scare her. Your mom took something that belonged to her. Maya was looking for it. I don't know what, she wouldn't say, but Maya was afraid your mom would go to the police with it."

I flash back to one afternoon shortly before Mom went missing. Maya and I had been doing homework in my room when Mom came in. Maya had seemed angry and left abruptly. When I followed her down the stairs, I saw Mom and her whispering furiously to each other; then Maya stormed off. When I asked Maya about it later, she brushed it off, said she had her period and was just in a bad mood.

"I told Maya she needed to tell you the truth," Jinx says. "She was going to tell you on Monday after school, but you left, and now the police have taken her to the station."

My grandma and I stare at each other. A cold, sticky feeling is sliding down my neck. Neither of us says what we're thinking out loud.

But Jinx does.

"Do you think Maya had something to do with your family going missing?"

Chapter 34

Laura

November

I spread the cash on the floor in the attic. There are piles and piles of it. More than I ever dreamed I'd touch.

The rest has been transferred to a new bank account in the Caymans. Easy enough to open online. I moved it a few times to various websites. Online gambling sites, casinos, PayPal. It's well hidden.

My phone rings, reminding me I have one thing still to figure out. Theo. I've given him some cash to keep him quiet, but he's started texting me, stopping me outside work. He's even driven past my house.

But *Theo* betrayed *me*. Fool me once and all that. As far as I'm concerned, this money is mine now.

I have to convince him I'm done. That there's no more money.

When I answer, Theo immediately begins spinning his lies about Cody needing a care home. I tell him there's only a few grand but I'll give it to him next week.

"No. I'll come by your house to get it." Theo's voice is hard, and it's then I realize: he knows I'm not giving him that money.

"I'll meet you," I say quickly. He can't come to my home. "Tomorrow night by the hollowed-out tree near the Garden Shed."

I hear voices downstairs. Pete's back from taking the girls Christmas shopping.

"Tomorrow night," I say again, then hang up.

I slide the bundles of cash into my desk, snapping the false bottom back into place. My phone pings. I think it's Theo, but it isn't. It's another one of those creepy texts.

I haven't forgotten about you. You better keep your mouth shut.

A thought hits me cold and fast. Has it been Theo all along? Trying to threaten me, unsettle me? I think back to the end of summer, to when I first started receiving these text messages. Theo just happened to show up the very same day.

But . . . why? What would have been his motive back then? Or now?

My fingers hover over the screen. Keep my mouth shut about what?

I wait, but there's no response. I finally give up and go downstairs.

In the kitchen, Pete is pouring himself a glass of wine. I stare at him, rage filling me.

"What?" He's defiant.

"What do you mean, what?" I snap.

Pete's drinking has officially gotten out of hand. He knows it. I know it. Even the school knows it, now that he showed up drunk, shouting abuse at another teacher, and got himself suspended. We had our biggest fight ever after that, a fight that morphed from his drinking to him accusing me of cheating.

"It's never been enough for you, has it, Laura?" he'd slurred, drunk again. "This life we've built. The life we've made as a family. Who is it, Laura? Who are you fucking?"

I was horrified. I wanted to tell him the truth. The frightening texts, embezzling money from my brother, Theo. But how? I'd made so many mistakes. I couldn't bear him thinking the same thing as Jack: *Poor, useless Laura, always needing bailed out.*

I would fix this. I'd make it right, and then we'd be in a better position than we'd ever been.

Furious at my silence, Pete spun around, trying to storm out of our bedroom, but one of his feet had caught on a wooden chair. "Pete, no!"

It was too late. Pete landed with a crash, the chair splintering like kindling.

"Ella went to Katie's house for the afternoon," Pete says now. "Alice is upstairs with Maya. They have a school project."

I want to tell him I would never cheat, but he turns his back to me.

"I'll be in the shed working on some photos."

I rub my forehead. We'll talk later. Before tonight. I've organized a double date with Mel and Jack at a new karaoke joint in Black Lake, a throwback to our college days. We've all been busy with Thanksgiving last week and now the chaos of December coming up. It'll be the first time we've gotten together in a while.

I go upstairs, knocking gently on Alice's door. "Hi, girls."

"Hey, Mom," Alice says.

Maya stares at me, an unexpected animosity hardening her features. I step back, surprised, as she grabs her things, mutters something to Alice, and brushes past me.

Alice looks confused. I'm confused, too.

"Maya?" I hurry after her.

She's almost at the front door when something falls out of her backpack. "You dropped . . ."

I reach for it but freeze. On the floor is a glittery gold pen.

Traitors gonna swing, bitch.

I stand slowly. Maya tries to snatch the pen, but I pull it away.

"It's you?" I whisper. "The note in my car, those texts. Why?"

"You stole my shit," she hisses.

My mind is spinning. The stolen tennis shoes and jerseys. The gun. Theo.

"Did Theo put you up to this?" I ask. "I saw you with him."

Her eyes flare. "What? No."

I look at Maya, this girl I've known since she was five years old.

You better keep your mouth shut.

She's scared. But not of Theo. Of me.

She thinks I'll turn her in.

I open my mouth to tell her I would never do that. I wanted to protect her. It's Theo who's dangerous. But something else entirely comes out.

"Who is Theo working for?"

That night, Mrs. McCormack comes over to watch the girls while Pete and I go out. It's too late and too dark to leave them home alone. Mrs. McCormack and I have grown closer the last few months, going to yoga together, drinks in the evenings.

I've told her some of the troubles Pete and I have been having, although of course not all of them, and when we go to leave, Mrs. McCormack hugs me and whispers in my ear, "If every chapter had a happy ending, we'd have no reason to start the next one."

Pete and I head into town, walking slowly even though the wind is flexing its muscle, stirring the uneasy clouds. A storm is brewing.

We reach the lake, which stretches like black velvet before us, the restaurant in the distance. We talk as we walk, fingers twined together.

I tell him I've been feeling like a failure since I lost the art studio—a truth—and that the guy Alice saw me with was one of Jack's employees, that I'd been asked to check on him, as he'd had COVID—a partial lie. He apologizes for drinking so much, for getting himself suspended from work, and swears he'll do better.

"Come here." He pulls me against him as we reach the restaurant. I press my body along the length of him, grateful we're no longer arguing. Pete is the love of my life; it physically hurts when we're angry with each other.

Mel and Jack are already seated when we arrive. The restaurant is an overpriced seafood place with excellent food and a gorgeous view. The conversation flows. Mel doesn't drink and Pete promises to keep it light, but somehow we still manage to finish two bottles of wine before we head to the karaoke bar.

The place is bumping, with a full-size stage, a wall of videos, fancy lighting, and a sound system.

"I can't get up there and sing!" Mel gasps.

She looks stunning, all lithe and graceful in a low-cut, silky cream blouse and leather pants, her body toned, her hair sleek, her skin glowing with health.

"Sure you can, it's just like in college!" I have to shout over the music.

"I was drunk in college!"

"Come on, first round's on us," I say.

Jack raises an eyebrow. He always gets the drinks, but I have money now. Okay, maybe it *was* Jack's money, but it's mine now.

Pete and I grab the drinks, taking them to a table Mel and Jack have chosen near the back. Pete's hand on my lower back is warm. I lean into him, enjoying this feeling, the heat, the electricity.

We start with shots and move on to mai tais, Diet Coke for Mel. I get up to sing "Don't Stop Believin'"; then Mel belts out "Like a Virgin." When it's Jack's turn, he tosses back a shot of tequila and sings a hilarious version of "I Want It That Way" by the Backstreet Boys.

Mel moves closer to the stage to cheer Jack on, and everyone in the bar is laughing hysterically. I watch my brother capture the audience. Jack has always had that ability to charm people. It's the same power Theo had over me. But Jack is one of the good guys.

Suddenly I realize the easiest way to stop Theo's threats. It's so simple, it's almost dumb.

All I need to do is tell Jack the truth.

Except what Maya told me earlier is still niggling at me. The person Theo is working for. There *is* an alternative. Am I brave enough to do it?

"Hey." Pete's voice nudges into my thoughts. He's back from the bathroom, except I can tell from his breath he was actually at the bar. I don't want to ruin the night, so I don't say anything.

Pete reaches a hand under the table to my knee. My heart skips a beat at his touch. Maybe it's the alcohol or the way he's looking at me. I lean forward and kiss him. He tastes of lime and salt and tequila.

"Do you know how lucky I am?" Pete murmurs.

"Not as lucky as I am."

And it's true. After my dad left, I thought I would never be worth anything to anybody. But then I met Pete.

Jack actually set us up. He vaguely knew Pete, who was school friends with Nick Greene. Nick came from a political family and had high hopes of getting into office one day. I knew that Jack had set us up in order to get access to Nick. Or maybe I'm being cynical. It's pretty Machiavellian to set your sister up with a man you hope will open doors for you. But I know Jack. He loves me, but there's always an end goal in mind.

It never bothered me because I got Pete out of the deal. This wonderful, uncomplicated, loyal man who fills every space inside me. Who's given me a family, our two amazing girls, a kind of love that is both my compass and my map.

The bar is heaving, music swelling, but I feel it all disappear as our kiss deepens, Pete's tongue dancing over mine.

"Get a room!" Mel shouts as she and Jack return.

Pete and I pull apart, giggling like teens in a dark cinema.

We talk about college, about the gigs we used to go to, the music we listened to. Jack leaves, returning with three tequila shots, another Diet Coke, and a bottle of Dom. The old me would've rolled my eyes. He's showing off, I'd think. But now I just smile and let the bubbles fizz on my tongue. My big brother, just four minutes older, likes taking care of people. Flashing money around is his love language.

Pete excuses himself to go to the bathroom. He's gone a long time. Mel goes back onstage, belts out another song, leaving Jack and me alone at the table.

"I know, Laura," he says after a few minutes.

"Know what?"

"Rose found one of your invoices. DIY Building Supply?"

Everything seems to fade, the music, the people. My breath hardens in my throat.

"You don't think I know everything that goes on in my business?" Jack's eyes blaze. "I followed the accounts. I know they belong to you."

"Jack . . ." I want to apologize, but it's not like it was a fluke. I did this on purpose.

And then I don't have to because somebody trips over a nearby chair, crashing into our table and sending drinks flying. I jump up, legs splattered with booze, and see Pete scramble to his feet, eyes glassy, a sheen of sweat on his upper lip.

"Come on, buddy, let's get you outside." Jack guides Pete to the door just as Mel reappears. He doesn't look back at me.

Outside, Pete promptly vomits on a bush. I'm mortified. We're not college kids anymore.

"Maybe we should go home."

"Nooo," Pete slurs.

"I don't think you're in any state to be out right now," Jack says.

"Why don't you get him home, babe?" Mel says, ever the problem solver. "I'll stay with Laura."

Jack shrugs. "Sure. I have an early-morning meeting anyway."

Anger flickers across Mel's face, but she recovers quickly.

I know I shouldn't leave Pete like this, but I'm so annoyed, and Mel seems so eager to carry on, and honestly, I don't want the night to end. So I give in.

Jack helps Pete to a waiting taxi. As they drive off, Mel lights a cigarette.

"Mel! Is that even allowed with your pacemaker?"

"Ehh." She hands me the cigarette, and I take a drag, coughing a little as I do. It's been a long time since those heady college days.

"When did you start smoking again?"

"Oh, right about the time Jack started fucking his secretary."

"Shit."

Poor Mel. She's worried not just about her health but her husband, too.

"Yep."

"I'm sorry. Jack's a jackass."

It's what we called Jack in college. She would laugh and say, *Yeah, but he's my jackass.* She doesn't laugh now.

Mel and I finish the cigarette; then she grabs my hand and drags me inside. We order more drinks, then move onto the dance floor. Strange men hit on us and we laugh in their faces, so hard our stomachs hurt. We throw back shots and we smoke cigarettes and we dance like we're young and free.

When the night ends, we walk back to my house to wait while Mel calls a taxi. Wind tosses my hair around my face, whipping at my cheekbones. A rumble of thunder cracks in the distance and rain pings off my face. The storm is here.

We turn into my driveway, talking about Christmas, setting a date to go shopping, when someone steps out from behind my minivan.

Theo.

And he has a gun leveled at Mel's head.

Chapter 35

Jess

I hang up my cell phone, my skin tingling, thoughts racing.

I stare at the seven tiny grinning elves someone has hung on the edge of my cubicle, a feeling sweeping over me, the aura of the case humming and fizzing. That sensation, like fine gravel collecting under my skin. Like a chemical rush. Like an itch. Telling me I'm on the right track.

I dial Shane's number. He doesn't answer. I leave a message. "Just got a call back from Logan Hills Credit Union in Boston. That's where the bank account number on Theo Moriarty's paycheck was from. It's for"—I check the Post-it note I've stuck to my desk—"DIY Building Supply Ltd. And the owner of that account is none other than Laura Harper. She had a bank account no one knew about. The manager's sending me over financial statements, but I think we're onto something here. Call me."

I press "End," then text him the same information, adding that I'll be at Black Lake Hospital if he needs me.

Outside, the day is gray, the color of ash. Snow dribbles from the sky, landing on my parka like dandruff. The pavement is icy in spots, slippery. I carefully make my way to my motorcycle, pull my helmet on, and hit the throttle.

Fifteen minutes later, I'm walking into the local hospital. The smell of antiseptic and artificial fragrance hits me like a slap, making me feel faintly nauseous. Too much on my mind and too little sleep, a week's worth of restless nights digging in their claws.

The ER is busy. Crowded. A kid has spilled something sticky near a poorly decorated Christmas tree. A janitor swipes murky gray water over it, wetting the tree skirting.

I push my way through the crowd and tell the receptionist I have an appointment with Dr. Sarika Patel, the doctor who treated Laura's dislocated shoulder. I sit in a hard plastic chair to wait. I'm overtired, jittery and twitchy, my foot jiggling against the floor.

My phone vibrates. It's Mac. I stare at my phone until it goes to voice mail.

Dr. Patel approaches, apologizing for the wait. She's tall, slim, intense, with serious dark eyes and dark hair pulled into a severe bun. She takes me to a small waiting room and shuts the door, blocking out the insistent beep of an alarm going off somewhere down the hall.

We sit across from each other.

"How can I help you, Detective?" Her accent is sharp, precise. A hint of British in the Indian.

"You treated a woman called Laura Harper last year. December."

"Yes. December first," she says. "I checked her file."

"Can you tell me your impressions of that meeting? You thought she was possibly a victim of domestic abuse?"

"We flagged that, correct. My colleague was interviewed by one of your detectives shortly after she went missing."

"Was that Detective Bill Liu?"

"I believe so."

"Only your colleague was interviewed? Not you?"

"I was back in India at the time."

"So you didn't speak to him?"

"No. Detective Liu spoke with Sheri Lin, the nurse who treated Mrs. Harper. I believe she expressed her concerns about possible domestic violence to Detective Liu. This was due to Mrs. Harper's extensive bruising and her dislocated shoulder."

I note her rigid posture, the tilt of her chin. "But you didn't agree with that assessment."

She folds her long, slim fingers together on her lap and inhales. "Certainly all the signs were there. The bruising was in the areas that could indicate abuse: neck, chest, abdomen. Often in these cases, the victim claims to have been clumsy or *just had a fall.* They have bruises inflicted in places where the injuries won't show. This was all true for Laura Harper."

I wait for the *but.*

"But Laura did not appear to be afraid or nervous around her husband in any way. There were no signs of previous abuse or any old fractures or prior wounds. Honestly, I didn't believe her story about falling on wet pavement, but I also didn't feel that Pete Harper had hurt her."

"Was there any proof of this?"

"Just my gut feeling. Laura Harper left without being discharged, which was certainly another flag. But when I saw them walking by, she was leaning against him. Open. Trusting. She wasn't afraid of him."

"Did Laura mention anything hinting they were planning on leaving?"

"No, nothing."

"So you saw no indication there was tension between them? Any reason to believe he might have been behind their disappearance?"

"No, but . . ." She weighs her next words carefully. "One thing this job has taught me is that good people are capable of doing very bad things. Did it look like he was abusing her? Not in my view. But that doesn't mean he wasn't. It also doesn't mean he wouldn't kill her. People kill for all sorts of reasons, as I'm sure you know."

She glances at her watch and stands. "If that's all, Detective?"

"Just one more question. Can you confirm Melanie O'Brien came into the emergency room in the early hours of December twenty-fifth last year?"

"I'll do my best."

I follow her back out to the front where she whispers with a receptionist, presumably about patient confidentiality. In the end, she tells me Melanie checked in just after 3:00 a.m. but declines to tell me any more, which is fine. I only needed confirmation.

"Thanks for your time, Doctor." I shake her hand and leave, having learned two important things.

One, Melanie O'Brien was admitted to the hospital with chest pain that night. And two, something that aligns with my gut instinct: Pete Harper hadn't beaten Laura Harper.

My phone pings in my pocket. This time it's an email. The bank manager has sent through statements from DIY Building Supply Ltd., confirming what Mel told me.

Laura Harper was embezzling money from her brother's business.

How we missed this the first time is anybody's guess. Not enough manpower, not enough money, the lead detective becoming ill, the case going cold.

I forward the email to Shane, and my phone starts ringing almost immediately.

"You're at the hospital?" Shane asks.

I hesitate, then both of us speak at once.

Shane: "Sorry, I got back late last night from Boston and haven't had a chance to . . ."

Me: "Sorry, I couldn't get in touch with you, so I thought I should . . ."

We laugh awkwardly. "You go," I say.

"I just saw your email. The bank statements. Jesus. Listen." He lowers his voice. "Jack O'Brien's voluntarily showed up to the station. He's here right now with his lawyer. Shall we have a crack at him?"

I grin. "I'm on my way."

◆ ◆ ◆

When I arrive at the police station, at least half a dozen reporters are gathered out front. Shane released the identity of the body yesterday, although not Theo Moriarty's connection to the Harpers. But that hasn't stopped them from doing their own digging.

An industrious journalist from Boston broke the news that Laura Harper—O'Brien at the time—and Theo Moriarty dated in college. There's some speculation that it was a love triangle, that Laura Harper had gone back to her ex, that Pete had killed Theo, then his wife and daughter. Others speculate that Laura got caught up with Theo's drug-dealing associates. That she and her family were killed by the powerful mob boss he was rumored to work for.

I push past the yowling reporters and swipe my ID badge. In the bullpen, Will calls out a greeting, a paper plate with a slice of red-and-white Christmas cake balanced in one hand. I wave as I hurry to the interview room.

Shane's already there, sitting across from Jack O'Brien. He's wearing a navy suit and a tie, shiny black shoes. His hair is gelled into place, and a pair of black glasses frames his eyes. It suits him.

Next to Jack is his lawyer, a bloated middle-aged man with rosacea and a bulbous nose. Tom O'Connell, one of the most high-profile lawyers in the state.

I slide into the seat next to Shane, and he introduces me, surreptitiously tapping a folder sitting on the desk, indicating he's printed out the financial statements.

Jack again goes over when he last saw the Harpers. "I didn't realize Pete was so drunk. Or that Laura had been having an affair with Theo."

He looks genuinely distraught, and his lawyer whispers something in his ear.

"Where'd you hear Laura was having an affair?" Shane asks.

"I believe it was Rose who mentioned it."

"Your assistant?"

"Yes."

Shane lifts an eyebrow. "Your assistant told you your sister was cheating on her husband?"

Jack looks away, his eyes and the faint, mottled flush crawling up his neck giving him away. He's basically just admitted to pillow talk with one of his mistresses.

"Yes," he says, quieter now.

"Did you know Laura and Pete were having financial difficulty?"

"Sure, that's why she closed down her art studio. I wanted to help, so I gave her a job. And then she came to me asking for a raise . . ." Jack rubs a hand over bleary, exhausted eyes.

"Did you give it to her?"

Jack hangs his head. "No."

"Did you kill your sister?" I ask. I'm trying to unsettle him, to catch him off guard, and it works.

Jack's head jerks up. "What? No!"

O'Connell's eyes flare. "Don't say anything else," he says to Jack; then he turns the full force of his lizard eyes on me. "We came here to help, not to be accused. My client wants the truth as much as you do. That was his *family* who disappeared."

I tap the folder. "But Laura was stealing from you."

Jack holds my eyes. "I know."

I sit back. *That* I hadn't expected.

"That's enough," O'Connell snaps, standing. "Jack, let's go."

Jack puts a hand out. "No, they need the truth. Yes, I found out Laura was stealing from me. Rose had suspicions and came to me with an invoice, and when I looked into it, I tracked the company back to her. I confronted her about it. Laura promised to pay back every cent."

"Did she?"

"She disappeared before she ever got the chance."

"So you never got your money?"

"No, but that's exactly it. Why would I hurt Laura? First of all, I loved my sister. For all her flaws, and all of mine, we were family. But she was planning to pay me back. Now that she's gone, I'll never see any of that money."

Chapter 36

Laura

November

I never planned to drive. Not this drunk. And yet Theo tells me to get in the driver's seat, Mel in the passenger's seat.

He wants the money, but there's no way I'm bringing him into my house, where my husband and children are sleeping.

"It's in the hollow tree by the Garden Shed," I tell him. "I'll take you there, just leave Melanie out of this."

"Like I'm falling for that." He slides in behind us, the gun still pointed at Mel's head.

Mel is pale. I will never forgive myself if she has a heart attack right now because of me.

I start the engine and back out of the driveway. My hands are in a death grip on the steering wheel, adrenaline roaring in my veins. The heavens let loose as the lights of Black Lake fade behind us, rain sluicing off the windshield, the wipers beating frantically to keep up.

"Theo, please," I plead. "We can figure this out."

"This is your own fucking fault," he snaps. "You should've just given me the money."

"I know who beat you up," I say, my words tangling in their hurry to get out. Adrenaline and booze fight for control in my body. "Who you're working for. You're in debt to Ronny DeLuca, and now that you don't have the money, you're in trouble."

Ronny DeLuca is a mob boss in Boston. I'd never heard of him, but Maya had a lot to say about him, rumors her manager at the sports store, an old friend of Theo's, had spilled.

"You were running drugs for DeLuca in Boston," I say. "Then a chunk of it was stolen by a competitor. That's when you made the plan to get me involved. I have a rich brother; you thought it would be easy stealing money from him."

"It was."

"Wait, you stole money from Jack?" Mel interjects.

We both ignore her.

"And now, I'm guessing DeLuca's after you." I glance in the rearview mirror. Something flickers in Theo's eyes. Fear. My stomach clenches. "If you don't get it, you're a dead man. But we don't have enough to pay off your debt. Not yet. Give me some time and I can get it."

"I don't need all of it. Just enough to get a fake ID. To get myself set up far away from here. I know you have enough for that."

I grip the steering wheel, slowing the car as I hit a curve. "You know if you run, DeLuca will find you. You'll spend the rest of your life looking over your shoulder. I can help you get all of it. I swear I will."

"Help me like hiding money and lying to me?" he spits bitterly. "No thanks."

"You shouldn't have lied to me about Cody!"

"What are you guys talking about?" Mel asks.

"Not that it's any of your business," Theo says, "but Laura here's been running a scam on her brother."

Mel looks at me. "Is that true?"

I don't answer, but Theo points the gun at me. "Tell her."

So I do. I admit the whole thing, from emailing clients with fabricated tax fees to setting up my own business to invoicing Jack's company. How it had started out as a way to help Cody, who Theo said needed a care home.

Mel groans. "I knew you were up to something! You were manipulating Laura so you could steal from Jack."

Theo catches my eyes in the rearview mirror. "I never wanted you to get hurt, but I need that money. I'm getting the hell out of here."

A gust of wind pushes at the minivan, rattling the windows and pushing at the doors. I grip the steering wheel harder, my knuckles turning white. Along the road, trees bow low, swaying like they're drunk in the edgy, blustery dark. A flash of lightning illuminates the river. It's rising rapidly, thrashing angry and violent to our right.

I glance at Mel, the gun still leveled at her head. "Between Mel and me, we can get you that money."

I glance at Theo in the back seat, his face in shadow. He's quiet for a long moment.

"Just keep driving," he finally says. And I know I'm out of options.

A crack of lightning floods the road with a burst of light. Rain whips the windshield, pouring from the sky. We had a hotter than usual summer, less than usual rain in the fall. But this storm is making up for it. The sudden torrent is expected to bring floods, rivers overflowing, the lake rising, roads made impassable.

I pass the Garden Shed, which is now dark, the lot empty, and pull into a lay-by a couple hundred feet before a curve in the road. The minivan bumps over potholes, my tires crackling ominously over gravel. I flick my headlights off, plunging us into darkness.

If anybody comes around that bend in the road, they will see us. I can flag them down. But the road stays empty. Quiet.

Theo pushes open his door. "Come on."

"Leave Mel here," I plead again. "I swear I'll take you to the money, just leave her here."

Theo leans forward, digging the muzzle hard into Mel's throat. She inhales sharply.

"Maybe if that money is really where you say it is, if you aren't the lying bitch I think you are, maybe I'll let her go. But for now, get out of the fucking car."

I thrust my door open, shoulders tense. Lightning cracks in the matte-black sky. I grab the gun from underneath my seat and slide it into the waistband of my pants.

Mel and I walk side by side along the river walk that parallels the edge of the river, Theo behind us with the gun and a flashlight. The light bounces over the ground, exposing the roaring water muscling the riverbank, swirling like ink.

The paved walkway ends, turning into slippery mud. I pull my coat up higher, but the icy wind still knocks the air out of my lungs. Rain pummels me, plastering my hair to my face. Melanie is shivering, her arms wrapped tightly around her body.

The walk to the hollowed-out tree ends too quickly.

"Get it out!" Theo shouts over the rain.

He presses the gun to Melanie's head. She squeezes her eyes shut, her teeth chattering. Mel isn't one to cry. She's rational, calm in a crisis. But right now she's terrified, sobbing openly.

I bend, reach into the empty space at the bottom of the tree. My fingers close around a handful of mud and leaves.

It's like everything moves in slow motion. I fling the mud at Theo, shouting at Mel to run. Theo flinches, his hands coming up to protect his eyes. I yank the gun out of my waistband. He sees it, suddenly understanding what's happened.

His gun rises, but not quick enough.

Chapter 37

Alice

I just can't believe that Maya had anything to do with my family going missing. First of all, Maya? No way. I know her better than that. Second of all, why would she have taken Ella's backpack to the cops if she were involved? It doesn't make sense.

These thoughts spin through my mind all night and the next day, until Jinx calls to tell me that Maya's been released. It turns out the reason she was fired from the sports store was because she stole a gun. A gun! She left it in her bedroom, I guess, and my mom stole the gun from her.

And that's the gun that killed Theo Moriarty.

"Maya saw your mom put all her shit in her car. She realized she'd taken the gun, too," Jinx tells me when I answer my phone. "She'd seen her with Theo Moriarty once and thought they were in on it together, so she started texting her, trying to scare her so she wouldn't go to the cops about where she got it."

It's stupid and irrational, which I'd never think of Maya as being. But I also know that fear can make people do dumb things.

I don't know how I feel. Betrayed. Angry. Sad. I'm not sure I can ever forgive her.

I take my last Ativan and lie on my bed, staring at my ceiling until it kicks in, carrying me away on a medicated cloud. It doesn't matter. I can get more pills. And more after that. I can take all the pills I want. Maybe I should. I don't have to be here, don't have to be the one who survived.

I hear Grandma's voice from down the hall. She's talking to Mel. They're making plans. Plans to make me leave or plans to make me stay. Whatever.

Alfie hops onto the bed. I pull him onto my chest. He purrs happily, his body vibrating against mine.

There's a smell coming off him, strong and distinct. I pull him closer and sniff his neck, his back. Alfie meows and tries to wiggle away. It's lilacs and vanilla. The smell of my mother's body lotion.

Tears fill my eyes, the longing so fierce it's like a kick to the throat.

I stare at Alfie and he stares back, his big green eyes blinking slowly.

I know my cat is not my mom. I'm not crazy. But I can't explain why he smells of her now.

There's nothing else to do but lie back, Alfie on my chest, and inhale the scent of my mother. Maybe sometimes there is no answer. All you can do is enjoy a brief glimpse of happiness.

Alfie bats at the necklace pooled in the hollow of my throat. I laugh. The sound echoes back at me from a great distance. I move the chain, the locket with its musical note dancing. He bats at it again.

I hold the necklace in my hand. Something is rolling around in my head, like soap on a Slip 'N Slide. The musical note. It never struck me as strange before because I played the violin, but for the first time I wonder . . .

I never loved the violin and my mom wasn't a musician. So why did she choose a musical note?

My door clicks and Grandma enters. She closes the door and sits on the edge of my bed, her weight dipping the mattress.

I love my grandma. She's so calm, so easy to be with, relaxed and undemanding. She never speaks up. Never contradicts. Others just kind of steamroll right over her.

"I spoke to Mel," she begins, her voice tentative. "She thinks maybe Florida would be a good move for you."

Of course Mel made the decision.

"Sweetie, I had no idea how bad it's been for you." Her eyes land on my forearm, glossy and damp. Her fingers move from her prim navy skirt to my arm, butterfly soft, against the scar tissue, like she's spelling it out. *F R E A K.*

I sit up, Alfie sliding off me, and wrap my arms around her. "It's not your fault, Grandma."

She shakes her head, gray-blonde bob swinging. "I should've fought harder for you to come live with me."

"What do you mean?"

"I wanted you to. I hope you know that. I thought with everything that had happened, and then Mel in the hospital with her own health problems, that you should live with me. But Mel said it was better to keep your routine, the same school, same friends." She blinks hard, eyes red. "You'd lost so much, and I thought she was right, you needed some consistency in your life. But maybe we were wrong. Maybe you *needed* to start over."

I stare at her. For just a moment, I wish she wasn't easy. That she'd had an opinion, a backbone. Because another word for *easy* is *pushover*.

Mel said I should stay, and so I did. Then Mel said I should go, so I will. Everybody else makes the decisions, for Grandma and for me. She never speaks up. She's spent her life swallowing her voice, shuttering her truths.

Just like I've done, I realize.

"Please say you'll come to Florida with me," Grandma says. "We can make a life for you there. Away from Black Lake."

I thought if I could find something, their bodies, or proof they were dead, or just something that explained what happened, that the hallucinations and the ghosts would go away. But that's never going to happen. No matter how far I run, what state I live in, I'll always just be me. Alice. A freak. The girl who was left behind.

"Okay," I say.

"Okay?"

"Okay. I want to leave. Tomorrow. Or whenever. Just get me out of here."

Grandma touches my cheek. "I think it's for the best."

"I know."

"Why don't you get some rest? I'll arrange everything with Mel."

I nod. I don't want to make her sad anymore.

Grandma leaves and I close my eyes. The chemical wave carries me along. I'm floating, riding on feathers that drift on a warm wind. I think I sleep. My phone beeps a text. It's from Maya. She wants to explain. I turn it on silent and go back to sleep.

When I wake, it's late. Dark. Snow drifts past my window. There's a beeping, somewhere so faint, so muffled, I barely hear it at first. It stops, then starts again.

I've heard that sound before.

I throw my legs over the side of the bed and press my ear to the door. Something is coming at me, a thread pulling at the edges of my mind.

I hear something behind me and turn. It's my dad sitting on my bed. Crimson blood seeps down the side of his head. He stares at me, his eyes dark holes in his head.

Am I dreaming? Hallucinating?

Fear squeezes my chest, my heart roaring. But this time I don't run. I need to know what he's trying to tell me.

His voice comes from very far away, like I have cotton balls stuffed in my ears. "Why haven't you found us, Alice?"

"I don't know how to." Tears scald my cheeks.

The room does that weird wobble, like the lens of a camera closing, then opening, and suddenly I'm not here, in my room in Mel's house.

I'm at home, in the backyard shed under the old apple tree that my dad turned into a darkroom.

Dad was developing a roll of photos we'd taken on a hike the day before, showing me how to cut the film off the cassette and load it onto a reel. How to carefully place it in the film tank and add in the developer mix. How to rinse and soak and hang it.

I see us standing shoulder to shoulder, the occasional thud of ripe apples hitting the roof, watching the lines on the pictures emerge as if by magic, a shadow picture hidden in the black and gray.

"The beauty of photography," Dad says, "is that you can capture anything you feel is important. And with the right timing, the right color, and the right creativity, it's powerful enough to not only take you back in time, but to also bring back those same feelings."

He clips a picture onto the washing line and looks at it. "But the problem is, we only ever see part of the story. Every picture is both a truth and a lie because it doesn't give any context. We see what we want to see."

The scene in front of me wavers, a mirage shimmering.

"Don't go," I plead. "Don't leave. Tell me where they are."

But it's too late. Dad is gone, and I'm back in my room at Mel's house.

I force myself to get up, my limbs gummy and thick. I slide my closet door open and pull my camera from my backpack. I flick through the pictures: candids of Finn with Santa and his elf, my parents dancing with Will and Shelby and Grandma. Mom and Mel in the kitchen, their heads bent close.

What screams at me loudest are the missing pictures. Jack with the curly-haired elf. Mom with Theo. The pictures of Mom's body covered in black bruises.

Pictures are a witness to something, but like my dad said, they aren't the whole story. They're just a snapshot, one where you don't know the bigger picture.

Maybe that's all we ever know of the people we love, a tiny sliver of who they really are.

I move again through the photo gallery, slower this time. Something snags in my gaze. I go back, squint at the screen. Mel has a plate of cookies in one hand. Mom's head is tilted, her gaze serious, landing somewhere over Mel's shoulder. There's something off about her expression, but I can't put my finger on it.

Next up are two shots of my dad dancing with Shelby. In the first, their grins split their faces, Dad showing her a hilarious version of the tango. But in the second, Dad's gazing over Shelby's shoulder. His smile has dropped, his expression, I don't know . . . resolved. Like he's made a decision about something.

I close my eyes, try to re-create the room that night. To see what he was looking at. Something flickers deep in my mind. What is it? My eyes pop open.

He was looking at my mom.

I press the back arrow and pull up the picture of Mom and Mel at the dessert table. Mom's left arm is in a sling. She was at the left side of the room, gazing just out of shot, to her right. Forward: Dad was at the center of the room, looking . . .

At her.

They were looking at each other.

Something had passed between them, the way they used to have those unspoken conversations that would drive me crazy.

A thought forms. The thing I've refused to acknowledge.

Maybe all this time I've been wrong. Maybe Dad really did kill Mom and Ella.

Chapter 38

Laura

December

The next morning, I wake with a start. My mouth is dry, cottony. I taste something unfamiliar in my mouth. Blood. I try to move, but blinding pain sears through me.

My shoulder.

I think I'm going to vomit. Adrenaline surges, and my eyes pop open. With the light comes awareness. Memories of last night fall into my head like flakes of ash.

I wanted to leave Theo there, but Mel wouldn't allow it. "Someone *will* find him, and they'll see what's happened to him. The cops would open a murder investigation. It's too risky."

"What about the river?" I suggested.

"They'd still find him. Maybe not tomorrow or the next day, but they will."

I couldn't believe we were discussing ways to get rid of my former boyfriend's body. It felt surreal. How was Mel thinking so calmly? I was still in shock. I kept telling myself it was all a nightmare.

We eventually put Theo in the suitcase I still had in my minivan. Mel told me about a new property Jack had bought over by Killer's

Grove. He planned to extend his property development site, she told me, but first he needed to finish the current property development, and that could take years.

"They'll never find the body. Jack hires a junk removal company that takes everything inside the house to the dump."

We wrangled the suitcase with Theo's body into the back of my minivan, then circled around to look for Theo's gun.

I was crying, every breath ripping out of me in panicked chunks. My legs were like rubber as I staggered over the slippery boulders. I felt dizzy, the rain pummeling my head, blurring my vision.

That's when I slipped. My feet flew out from underneath me, and I smashed against the sharp edges of the rocks. I bounced, my body flopping like a rag doll until I landed in the mud. I knew instantly I'd hurt my shoulder. Seriously.

When I finally got home, the adrenaline was wearing off and the pain kicking in. I pinched one of Pete's old Vicodin from a root canal a few years ago, but it's completely worn off now.

When I look down at my body, I see it's covered in bruises, gnarly purple splotches and bloody lacerations splattered over my arms and legs.

Pete appears in the doorway, a coffee in hand. "You got in late," he teases. "You look worse than I was last night."

I don't move. I squeeze my eyes shut and try to breathe through my teeth so it doesn't hurt as bad. Pete mistakes my silence for anger.

"I'm sorry," he finally says. "I drank too much. I . . . I've been doing it a lot lately, and I know there's no excuse. It's just become a . . . a habit. A crutch. But I'm going to stop, I swear."

He sets the coffee on my bedside table and sits next to me. I scream as pain jolts through my arm.

Alarm flares in his eyes, and he jumps back. "Shit, Laur, are you okay?"

"I fell." I'm breathing heavily. "Outside the bar. I was drunk, and I slipped and fell. I think I've done something to my shoulder."

"We should get you to the hospital."

"No!"

Pete frowns. "Are you sure?"

My saliva is thick. It's hard to swallow. Hard to focus. I can't stop myself.

I bend over the edge of the bed and vomit onto the floor.

There's no arguing with Pete. He's taking me to the hospital.

When he leaves to grab my shoes and coat, I text Mel and tell her my falling-outside-the-bar story.

Don't answer any of their questions, she replies. And act normal.

Pete tells the girls I had a fall and need to have a doctor check me out. I can see their worried faces peering out of the living room at me.

He drops by Mrs. McCormack's and asks her to keep an eye on them, telling her I've fallen and hurt my shoulder. She's on her front porch looking in my direction when I slip into the car. Even from this distance, I can see her face is disapproving. I know what she's thinking: that Pete's done this. That he's an abuser. I don't have the energy to even raise my hand and assure her that he isn't.

The torrential rain from last night still hasn't eased. The world is slate gray, streetlights reflecting in pools of water that stand on the street.

At the hospital, I find out what Mel meant.

Don't answer any of their questions

Their questions quickly become pointed. They think Pete is abusing me.

Pete keeps a tender arm on my knee, baffled by the nurse's cold-eyed glares. I'm in so much pain I can barely think. I lean against Pete, hoping to absorb some of his composure.

They separate us, calling me back to a small cubicle in the ER while insisting Pete stays in the waiting room. They question me carefully, discreetly. I notice my fingernails are ragged, mud wedged under the nails. One has torn completely off. The nail bed is bleeding. The nurse doesn't believe my injuries came from a simple fall on wet pavement. The lacerations tell a different story. I'm glad Pete doesn't hear.

I'm given some painkillers and sent for an X-ray. I return to my cubicle and wait some more. I can't stop thinking about Theo. The shots. The way his body jolted. The black blood oozing from him. Folding his body into that suitcase.

Theo betrayed me, but he doesn't deserve to be dead.

I can't stand it. The guilt ravages me.

I am a murderer.

A tall, severe-looking woman in a pristine lab coat enters, informing me my X-ray shows I have a dislocated shoulder. She gives me more painkillers. Stronger ones. The same severe-looking woman returns. The pain when she sets the shoulder is blinding. I nearly pass out, but the relief is instant.

She tells me I need another X-ray to make sure the bone is fully in place, so I wait some more. When the door next opens, it's another woman. She introduces herself as a social worker with the hospital.

"My husband is not beating me," I assure her.

She doesn't believe me.

I don't care about the X-ray or even the painkillers. I need to get out of here before something slips.

After the social worker leaves, I sneak out of the room.

Chapter 39

Alice

Once the thought hits me, it's like I can't shake it, a boot wedged into a crack, flooding light onto the sliver of thought that's been crouching in the dark.

Maybe he *did* kill them. Maybe Mom stole that gun from Maya to protect herself from him. Maybe he found it, took the gun, and shot her and Ella, hid their bodies, then killed himself.

The horrible truth: it's been there all along. I've just been fighting it.

I think of my dad that night, bent over something crumpled on the ground. The expression on his face when he saw me was so fierce, so . . . *angry*, so . . . sad?

Except why kill Ella and not me? He could've come after me. I had a head injury, a broken arm. I didn't get far. He could've found me. I would've come to him if he'd called. But he didn't.

That shout: Did he want to kill me? Or *warn* me?

I think of Mom, her head bent close to Mel's at the Christmas party, her eyes gazing across the room at my dad.

Had Mel known?

I need to ask her. I twist my door open but hesitate. It's late. Mel will be asleep now, tucked up with her lavender face mask and her earplugs.

But no, I hear someone moving around downstairs. I slip into the hallway and peer over the banister.

Downstairs, Mel is fully dressed, winter layers on. She glances over her shoulder, like she's worried someone might be watching, then bends and ties her boots. A second later, she slips out the front door. Something nags at me, a thought, subtle and slippery. It darts into my mind, then disappears.

I glance at my phone. It's late.

I shiver, thinking of That Night. The witching hour.

Nothing good ever happens after midnight.

I should leave Mel to her nightly wanderings. I should go to bed.

But I don't listen to myself. Instead, I grab my coat and hat, shove my feet into my boots, propelling myself downstairs and out the back door. The icy air slices through me like a razor, sobering me up, wiping away some of the effects of the Ativan. I grab my bike from the side shed. By the time I get out front, Mel's car is already pulling away.

The snow stretches around me like a perfect white canvas. I get on my bike, forcing my leaden feet to move. That nagging thought still pokes at me, harder now but still blurry.

I lose Mel almost immediately around a bend in the road, but it doesn't matter.

Mel's been tracking me on my phone since my little episode in Killer's Grove. But I track her, too.

I stop on the icy shoulder and drag out my phone. I open the Find My Friends app and tap Mel's name.

Somehow, I'm not surprised by what I see.

Chapter 40

Jess

Back out in the bullpen, Shane follows me to my desk. He runs a hand through his red hair, making it stand on end. He looks glum.

"We had to let Jack go," I say, giving him an awkward pat on the back. "There was nothing to hold him on."

"I know. What a douche, though. Imagine being more worried about your money than someone you supposedly loved being missing, possibly dead."

"If he did it, we'll find out. He won't get away with it."

Shane pulls out his phone, checks the time. "We have a meeting with Galloway in five minutes. You coming?"

"Yup."

"Hey, wait." His eyes pop as he stares at his phone. "Just got Theo Moriarty's autopsy report."

"What's it say?"

Shane's eyes scan his phone. "Let me print it out. I'll see you in the meeting room."

I grab a cup of coffee for myself and Shane and head into the meeting room. It's getting late. Someone's ordered pizza, and my stomach grumbles, but I ignore it.

I sit at the far corner of the conference table. Shane hustles in behind me. As the lead detective, he sits at the head of the table. He has a laptop and a handful of loose papers. I slide the coffee across to Shane.

Thank you, he mouths.

Khandi enters, as well as Stan Symonds and Alec West, midlevel detectives who've been pulled in to try to clear the case in time. Last is Lieutenant Galloway. My gut cramps with nerves when she sits next to me. Her face is already crumpled in a scowl. I clench and unclench my fists, my leg jiggling.

Shane jumps right in. "I spoke with Theo Moriarty's wife yesterday. She has an alibi and has definitely been in Boston all year. She isn't our killer. I also spoke with BPD, and it turns out Theo has quite the rap sheet. Fraud. Larceny. Burglary. Even assault. More recently, he was running drugs for a local mob boss called Ronny DeLuca. Any of those guys he worked with could've wanted him dead."

"But you don't think that's the case," Galloway states.

"Honestly?" Shane's gaze flicks to mine. "I still like Pete Harper for all this. However, Jess found some compelling evidence this morning that shows Laura Harper embezzled funds from Jack O'Brien's company. So Jack O'Brien's high on my list again."

"If Theo and Laura were working together," Symonds says, "things could've gone sour fast. Maybe she killed him."

"Or Pete killed him," Shane argues. "He finds out Laura's having an affair with her old college boyfriend. He kills Theo in a jealous rage, hides his body. But Laura finds out, confronts him. They argue on the way home from the Christmas party. Somehow it leads to the accident, and that's when he snaps. A self-righteous family annihilation. He killed Laura and Ella, then dragged their bodies into the woods."

"Those woods were searched extensively," Galloway interjects.

Shane shrugs. "A lot of places to hide bodies out there."

I remember thinking the same thing.

"Except there's no evidence Laura was having an affair," I say, "*or* that Pete had ever hurt her. Dr. Patel, who treated Laura's dislocated shoulder, said Laura exhibited no signs of being afraid or nervous around Pete," I say. "And there were no signs of previous abuse, old fractures or wounds."

"Laura left the hospital without being discharged," Shane counters. "And Dr. Patel didn't believe Laura was being truthful about falling on wet pavement."

Frustration bubbles under my tongue. "You're still not accounting for Alice. Why didn't he kill her, then?"

"It was an accident leaving her alive. He didn't know she'd escaped into the forest."

"What'd Dr. Arquette's autopsy report say?" Galloway cuts into our squabbling.

"We're bringing in a forensic anthropologist to help establish the exact time and cause of death, but obviously that could take a while." Shane taps the report on the table. "What we have from Dr. Arquette is preliminary."

Dr. Arquette is one of the best medical examiners in the country. He moved to Black Lake a few years ago from Seattle, where he was well respected in his field. He's extremely precise, scientific, methodical in his methods, but even he has his limitations. Apparently bones are one of them.

"Dr. Arquette says that Moriarty was shot once in the chest—that's the bullet we recovered—and once in the head," Shane says. "However, the gunshot wound to the head isn't what caused the damage to his skull. His head was crushed by something. A fall, maybe, or he was hit by something."

"So somebody hit him over the head, incapacitated him, then shot him?" My hands have gone to my thigh, kneading at the ache that's settled there.

"Impossible to tell which happened first, due to the advanced state of decomp. He could've been shot and then hit on the head, or hit by a car or a bus and then shot, or vice versa, for all we know. Dr. Arquette did say the bullet left a pretty small hole, like from the revolver in

Laura's painting, although we don't have confirmation on that. But it's the hit that caused the skull to cave in."

I feel a sudden jolt at his words, a creeping realization dawning on me. I glance at Khandi, whose eyes have gone wide.

"The ballistics report . . . ," I begin, then stop.

"What ballistics report?" Shane's voice has hardened.

All eyes in the room swivel to me. My cheeks blaze. I forgot to tell Shane about the ballistics report after Khandi called me. Last night I went home, did my whiskey routine, and spent the night baking, working hard not to think about Mac or Isla.

I clear my throat. "It's my fault. Khandi called yesterday to tell us that the bullet recovered in Theo's body matched the gun hidden in Laura Harper's painting. I tried to call you, but . . ."

"I'm sorry, Shane." Khandi bites her lip, worried. "I did cc you on the email, but I should've called you, too."

Shane's jaw spasms, betraying his annoyance. The tension is as thick as leather. "I haven't had a chance to check my email today. It isn't your fault, Khandi."

I bristle, taking the implication to be that it's mine. I open my mouth to snap back, but Galloway speaks up, trying to get us back on track. "So Laura killed Theo?"

"Maybe," Khandi says, eyes lighting up. "But here's the interesting thing."

She tells them what she told me: that the gun had been stolen from Black Lake Sporting Goods the summer before the Harpers went missing.

"I did some digging, and it turns out that Maya Shepherd, Alice Harper's best friend, was fired from that store after a robbery that was assumed to be an inside job."

"Maya Shepherd. Shit." Shane rubs his forehead. "Have we been looking in the wrong place the whole time?"

I'm about to say something when there's a shift in the air. An electric buzzing starts inside my skull, pressure building in my head. And then a sound, a beeping, like a dying fire alarm battery.

It's the same sound Alice said she heard that night in the car.

Someone's saying my name, but I don't answer because there's Isla, sitting in the chair to my right. When she speaks, her voice is urgent.

"You have to hurry, Mommy. You don't have much time."

And then, abruptly, she disappears.

When I look up, the room is emptying. West throws a look over his shoulder at me, like I've lost my mind.

"Let's go, guys," Shane says. "We've got four days to solve this. Clock is ticking."

I grab my cane and get to my feet, look around for Isla. That sound, what did it mean?

I limp back to my desk.

"Lambert!"

Behind me, Galloway's sliding her coat on. "Come with me."

I follow her out to a small courtyard at the back of the station, expecting her to light into me. Maybe she'll fire me. I probably deserve it.

Galloway pulls out a vape, presses the button, and takes a long drag. A rich, luscious scent fills the courtyard.

"Is that butter?" I ask, surprised.

She shrugs, a small smile tugging at her lips. "You found my weakness. Can't eat it 'cause my cholesterol's too high, so I vape it." Galloway's breath fogs in the cold air. "You know, Rivero warned me about you. *She's too damaged for this job* were his exact words. You don't listen to orders, don't play well with others, get too emotionally invested."

I lean on my cane, releasing some of the pressure in my bad leg. "Yeah, sounds like something a misogynist would say."

Galloway laughs. Actually laughs! "Exactly what I thought. Hard enough being a woman in a male-dominated job."

She takes another drag, exhaling in a long whoosh, bangs lifting off her forehead. Again, for the briefest second, I catch a glimpse of the scar near her temple. She sees me looking and taps the scar.

"That there? I got involved with a bad group of people in high school. I ran away. Lived on the streets for a while. I refused to tell my parents what was going on. I was too proud. A woman beat me up for my last tampon, can you believe it? She almost killed me. It was a wake-up call. A friendly doctor contacted my parents, and they took care of me until I was back on my feet again."

She lets her bangs fall back. "Look, I'm your boss in there, but I'm saying this as a friend out here. Woman to woman. Being a detective is about teamwork. You can't do it on your own, Lambert. Not this job. Not life. We need people."

She takes another buttery hit on her vape, closes her eyes as she lets the taste linger on her tongue. "Now. You've got four days before I call the FBI in for help and you guys lose this case. Two if you take the weekend off. What are you going to do about it?"

I don't have a chance to answer because Khandi bursts into the courtyard, her cinnamon-colored twists flying. "Lieutenant! I've got something."

"Let's have it."

"The DNA from that fingernail we found on Theo's body? It isn't from Maya Shepherd."

Chapter 41

Alice

It's late, and the road is slick with snow. My hands and feet have gone numb as I pedal. The snow blurs my vision.

I skid to a stop at the fork in the road: straight to go the longer way through town or right to cut through Killer's Grove, the quicker way.

I stare at the tunnel of Killer's Grove looming in front of me, staticky with falling snow. The trees and their gnarled boughs reach for me, clawing at me. I've been here dozens of times since That Night, but never at night. Never like this.

"It isn't haunted," I tell myself as I get back on my bike and turn right. I don't believe in ghosts. All those stories about Killer's Grove being haunted are just a bunch of bullshit. Roads aren't haunted. Only people are.

Killer's Grove is black, no streetlights around. I flick my bicycle headlight on. It lights a pale path, scattering shadows as I pedal. I finally reach the tree where we crashed, and I brake. In my bike's light, I can see the scar cut into the tree's flesh.

A thought flickers into my mind, then slips back out. I try to grasp it, to hold on to it, but the more I do, the more shadowy it becomes.

Suddenly, my ears fill with a strange rushing sound. Goose bumps chase up the back of my neck. I hear a noise, a twig crackling, and whirl.

There's a flash of blonde hair, and then my head is filled with a pressure unlike any I've felt before.

I'm standing on a wet road, rain pounding the ground at my feet. My hair drips wet tracks down my checks. Shadows move in front of me. Trees bow and sway in the howling wind. Water roars.

A bright crack of lightning illuminates the shadows, making them take shape. The water gets louder, filling every gap in my mind, a horrible, agonizing roar. And then someone is screaming.

"Run!"

My eyes snap open, and I'm back in Killer's Grove, the frozen ground solid under my feet. Fear and frustration balloon in my belly, launching up my throat. What the fuck is happening to me?

My pain curdles into anger, and I bend over and scream, letting loose a wail that goes on and on, bouncing off the trees in the lonely forest. I hit my thighs with both fists over and over. I want to rake at my eyes and tear at my hair. And then a sound fills my head. A beep. Once, then a long pause. Again, then a long pause.

That nagging thought is back, too slippery to get hold of. I almost have it, but it shifts, again sinking beneath the black waters of my mind. *Beep.* Pause. *Beep.*

And then it clicks into place. A piece of the jumbled puzzle that's been floating inside my head.

"Oh my God," I whisper.

I get back on my bike and start pedaling.

Chapter 42

Laura

December

And so here I am. A traitor. An embezzler.

A murderer.

And I think back to that day, going into the grocery store for that milk.

I've had a lot of *if onlys* in my life, but that *if only* is by far the most profound. Because if I hadn't gone into that grocery store for milk, maybe I wouldn't have met Theo. Maybe I wouldn't be in this mess now.

It all goes back to that fucking milk.

I've called in sick to work the whole first week of December, using my injured arm as an excuse. I know Jack probably wants to talk to me about the money I stole, and Pete's worried I'm angry about him drinking too much, but I can't face those problems right now.

Instead, I spend my days writing in this diary, filling the pages with my messy, slanting scribble. I've always kept a diary, ever since I was a girl and my dad left. It helped me process my feelings, just as it does now. As an adult, I've been inconsistent about it, but now I'm making up for it. I write every day. Sometimes a few times a day. Going back to that first day, the day Jack sent me to get milk and I met Theo, working through everything that's happened since.

Thank goodness it's my left arm that's injured, not my right arm.

And then, for the first time in months, I start painting. My emotions leak onto the canvas in broad, manic strokes, splattering the canvas in vicious reds and blacks. It's my own face that emerges from the brush, my loathing for these things I can't undo emerging like a ghost.

When I've finished, I carefully create a false back for the painting and fill it with the cash I've withdrawn, nearly emptying what's left of my account. I feel anxious and fearful, every movement, every decision deranged, like I'm not fully here, like I've been taken over by a robot.

Mel pops by every day. She's been so supportive, but what I really want is to be left alone. I have panic attacks. My stomach is in knots. I can't stop throwing up. I don't understand how she isn't falling apart, too. How she's so calm. It makes me angry and resentful.

When she's around, I break down, letting all my pent-up emotions out. Mel reassures me that everything will be fine. She tells me we should take pictures of the bruises on my body. She forces me to strip off my top, to stand while she captures what I've become, light streaming down on me from the skylights above.

She prints the pictures out and tells me to hide them. "They're a case for self-defense if you ever need it," she says.

"If I ever need it?"

"You *won't*, but it's good to have a backup. There's a reason why flight attendants tell you to put your mask on first, Laura. You have to look out for yourself first. That's what we're doing. Don't forget, Theo *kidnapped* us. It was self-defense."

"I should turn myself in." My teeth are chattering. How long is it possible to be in shock?

Something flashes in Mel's eyes. It takes me a minute to define it. Mel is a good person, compassionate, charitable, loyal to a fault, but the look I see in her eyes now is fear. It makes me feel even worse. Because Mel doesn't like being scared, doesn't like being backed into a corner.

All her hard work to be healthy, eat organic food, meditate, do yoga, it's all to help her feel like she has some control in a world that can be very, very uncontrollable. But Theo's out of the picture now. He can't hurt us anymore.

And then I have a horrible thought.

"Theo's paycheck!" I bend over and start to howl, hot tears scalding my cheeks. "If he doesn't pick it up from the office, people will start looking for him."

"Shut the fuck up, Laura!" Mel snaps, glancing over her shoulder. "Do you want everyone to hear you?"

I'm momentarily silenced by the wild fury in her voice. The Melanie I know is calm, thoughtful. This Melanie is hostile, nasty.

I fight to calm myself. She's scared. Panicking. Like me. I need to pull myself together.

"You have to go into work," she says, calmer now. "Pick it up."

"I can't!" I moan.

"You can and you will," she says.

And for the first time, it sounds like a warning, not a suggestion.

I wait as long as I can. Another week and a half passes. It's almost Christmas, and I still haven't done any shopping. The girls will be out of school in a few days. Tomorrow, or maybe the next day, I'll rent a safe-deposit box and put this diary inside. I see the sense in what Mel says: it's good to have a backup.

The next morning, shortly after Mel leaves, Mrs. McCormack stops by holding a vibrant red orchid.

"Everything okay?" she asks, taking in my damp face.

"My arm . . ." I give a weak laugh, but I'm sure she can see through the lie. "Do you want to come in?"

"No, thanks. I'm off to yoga. Just thought I'd drop this orchid by." She hands me the orchid, which is magnificent, its petals so red, so lush and moist, they appear like living flesh.

"Ruby mokara," she says. "Its red petals represent determination, courage, perseverance."

"It's stunning, thank you."

She looks at me steadily for a moment. "If you ever need anything, I'm here, okay?"

"I know."

"A word of advice, my dear. Don't be one of those people who goes through life with their eyes shut. Time can change relationships, just as the sea reshapes the sand."

I swallow back tears. Like the doctors and nurses, she thinks Pete hurt me. And I can't say anything to defend him.

"I won't," I say.

She gives me a gentle hug, as if I'm as delicate as the orchid I'm holding. The sound of the front door shutting echoes in her wake.

My first day back at the office is awkward as hell. Jack knows I stole money from him. So does Rose. I feel her eyes on me, glaring at me, but I still manage to sneak Theo's check from her desk when she's at lunch.

To my surprise, Jack isn't in. Not that day or the next. When he does appear, he doesn't talk to me. That goes on for a week. Finally, I can't bear it anymore, and I burst into his office. My brother is sitting behind his desk. Tall. Lean. Tanned, even in winter. His face darkens when he sees me.

"I'm sorry, Jack." I shut the door behind me. "I know you trusted me and I've betrayed that trust. I could explain all the reasons why, but all you need to know is that I'm going to fix this."

I've been planning this speech all week. Obviously I can't tell him about Theo, but I can make this right.

"I don't have it all yet, but when I do, I'll pay you back. Every cent, Jack, I swear."

A muscle twitches in Jack's jaw. He tugs one earlobe, staring at me for a long moment. I see something in his eyes then, something darker than hate, something black and sinister, and a shiver of fear pulses through me.

Jack won't let this go. It would look bad for him to his employees, who I worry Rose has told; to his competitors, who might hear it through the grapevine; to the mayor, Nick Greene, who would look at Jack differently, like he's weak, ineffective. Jack won't allow that.

It won't be obvious. I won't see it coming. Jack isn't that type of man. He is shrewd, calculating. He'll wait, figure out how he can benefit; then he'll take me down. For him, the end always justifies the means. In business and in life.

After a moment, when Jack still hasn't said anything, I quietly let myself out.

That night when I get home from work, Ella bounces toward me, a grin on her face. Behind her, Alice is smiling shyly.

"Mel bought you a dress, Mommy, look!" Ella exclaims.

She drags me to the dress, which is draped over the couch in the living room. Pete is there, the Christmas lights up, a fire roaring behind him. He does a silly hand wave, showing off the dress like he's Vanna White. It's lovely, a shimmery gold with a deep V neckline and a long, mermaid-style hem.

"She said it's for the Christmas party," Alice says.

My stomach twists. Christmas Eve. It's only a few days away now. Pete's done everything this year, decorating the house, taking the girls ice skating, doing the Christmas shopping. I've been completely useless.

I stare at the orchid Mrs. McCormack brought, now sitting over the fireplace. Life is about opportunities. Our lives take shape from brushstrokes of chance and calculation. But now the canvas of my life has been punched through with holes.

Suddenly, I burst into tears. The girls and Pete stare in shock as I run upstairs.

After a little bit, Pete follows. He sits quietly next to me on our bed, not touching me, not talking, just sits there until my sobs subside.

"You need to tell me what's going on," he finally says. "Are you leaving me?"

"What?" I sit, wiping my eyes. "No! Pete, I swear. It has nothing to do with you."

"Then what does it have to do with?" he exclaims, frustrated. "I thought things were getting better, but you're acting like you can't stand being around us. You treat us like you wish we'd disappear. I mean, what is it, Laura?"

He's right. I've been punishing my family, and it isn't fair. I take a deep breath, and I tell him everything. Everything that happened that night and everything that led up to it. The whole unvarnished truth.

When I'm done, he looks at me solemnly and says, "We have to go to the police."

I look into my husband's eyes, and I flash back to that day, a hot August morning, when my brother texted, asking me to get milk.

The simple truth is, Theo could've found me anytime. If not that day, it would've been another. I can't blame it on him or the milk. It's my fault. All of it. And I have to make it better.

"You're right," I tell Pete. "I have to turn myself in."

Chapter 43

Jess

"I ran the DNA from the fingernail we found on Theo Moriarty's body against a cheek swab Maya Shepherd gave last year, and it isn't a match," Khandi tells Lieutenant Galloway and me.

She wedges one boot against the door and leans out into the courtyard as she talks, rubbing her bare arms. Snow sticks in her twists, and she shivers.

"Who's the DNA from?" Galloway asks.

"We don't actually have a match yet." The diamond in Khandi's nose winks in the pale yellow lights. "It'll take a little longer . . ."

I curse under my breath.

"*But* I also got a hit from that partial fingerprint on the suitcase zipper."

"In AFIS?"

"No, that was a bust. But Laura used to volunteer teaching children painting a number of years ago at the local elementary school. She had a full background check, including fingerprints, done then."

"So the partial is from Laura Harper?" I ask.

"Yeah, but here's the interesting thing. The fingerprint and the DNA from the fingernail are *not* from the same person. Laura Harper put Theo Moriarty in that suitcase, but she wasn't alone."

I turn to Galloway, heart accelerating. "There was a second killer."

Galloway's eyes burn with something I recognize: that buzz you get when a case starts to click. The aura.

"Maybe that's who killed the Harpers," she says. "They wanted to silence Laura."

"The family was just collateral damage."

"Killers tend to kill again when they need to cover their tracks."

Somewhere deep inside my spine, creeping along the palms of my hand, something is humming. A warning. A notice. Like a tuning fork stuck into an electrical socket. There's that pressure in my ears, that cold trickling down my spine.

I look up, and there's Isla, standing on the other side of the courtyard, blurred by the falling snow. And then that sound, the beeping of a fire alarm battery that's dying.

This time, I don't brush it away. I focus on it. Isla is trying to show me something.

"The beeping," I murmur.

"What?" Galloway and Khandi look at me.

"Alice said when she woke up in the car after the accident, there was a beeping sound. I thought maybe she'd imagined it or that it was the car itself making that sound. But what if it wasn't?"

I look up at the darkening sky, my body practically vibrating. My skin is hot despite the chilly winter wind. I'm filled with that restless sensation, like my skin is fizzing, like adding lemon to baking soda. I tighten my grip on my cane and start pacing, a thought tugging at me, something else Alice said, shifting and jumping around. I pause, close my eyes, trying to focus.

And then, suddenly, it's there.

"I know who was there that night." I thump Galloway's shoulder and head inside. "I gotta go. Alice Harper's in danger."

Chapter 44

Alice

My house is shrouded in shadow. Not Mel and Jack's monstrosity of a house. *My* house. My family home.

It's quiet. Dark. An icy wind has risen, swirling snow swallowing my neighborhood. But as I get closer, I see a thin light on in the living room.

I throw my bike on the snowy front lawn and climb the porch. The door is unlocked. It's ice-cold inside, my breath fogging. A lamp in the living room is on. I wonder if Jack's been paying the electric bill.

"Hello?" I call softly.

Her voice comes at me from the living room. "In here, Alice."

Mel is sitting at the dining room table, still wearing her coat and bobble hat. She's sipping a glass of water. Another glass of water sits across from her, leaving a damp ring on the pale wood. Next to it is a small, amber-colored bottle. Mel's Ativan.

"I thought you'd be here," I say. "Jack said you come back sometimes."

Mel looks pale and worn. Sometimes—maybe more than sometimes—I forget how much she's suffered. How devastated she's been by their loss, too.

"It's where I feel closest to them," she says.

She motions for me to sit, so I do. She slides the glass of water to me and picks up the little bottle. The pills rattle inside. Mel's hands are shaking, I realize.

"I know you've been taking them," she says.

"I'm sorry—"

She cuts me off. "What I'm more interested in is *why* you're taking them. Why you aren't coping and what we need to do about it."

A gust of wind raps against the window. Mel shifts in her seat.

"It's your fault, isn't it, Alice."

I bend my head, tears tightening my throat. A bone-jarring tremor is spreading up my arms, into my shoulders, rattling my teeth. Pain fills me, that old wound cracking open.

"Yes," I whisper.

She tips the bottle into her palm. Two tiny white pills tumble out. She pushes them toward me. "Take these. They'll help."

I do as she commands. The pills are acidic, sticking to my throat like bugs in a flytrap. I gulp down the whole glass of water. I've never taken two at once. I wonder what will happen.

"I shouldn't have told him," I say.

Mel cocks her head and raises her eyebrows. *Go on.*

"I saw Mom go into Theo Moriarty's house. I was so . . . angry." A tear slips out, and it's like the floodgates open and I can't hold them back anymore. Hot tears fall, splashing onto my cold hands. "I told Dad, and they fought about it. But they seemed to get better. I thought everything would be fine, but at the Christmas party, something was off. They weren't arguing, exactly, but . . ."

I dash at my tears.

"If I hadn't told him, maybe he wouldn't have done it. Maybe they'd be alive. It's all my fault."

Mel closes her eyes and takes a deep, centering breath. When she opens them, I see a sheen of hatred there. Mel blames me, too. Maybe as much as I blame myself.

"Wouldn't it be nice if all the pain could just go away?" She stares at me, her face blank. "I think that all the time. How do I get rid of this pain? And I wonder if you ever think that way, too. Because it *is* your fault, Alice."

I slump in my chair, feeling boneless. Hearing my own blame externalized like that, maybe it's a relief, like lancing an infected wound. I stare at the painting behind Mel. It's one my mom did of our family standing in front of the lake, the sun setting in the backdrop, Mom, Dad, and me smiling down at Ella, who's grinning up at us mischievously.

Mel tips more of the pills into her palm, a whole fistful, and pushes them toward me. I look down at the pills. Mel is giving me a choice. A way out.

Do I want to take it?

Already, I feel the two Ativan taking effect, combining with the one I took earlier. A blissful, warm sleepiness winds through my body. It's like riding a gentle wave, floating free as it carries me under a blue summer sky. How good it would feel to just dive beneath the surface, to let it engulf me.

I sweep the pills into my hand and lurch to my feet, palming them into my mouth as I press the glass of water to my lips.

"I need to lie down," I croak.

Mel's eyes are hooded, impossible to decode. "That's a good girl."

I stagger toward the battered brown couch in the living room. The floor rocks under me like I'm riding a ship in a stormy sea. I sway, trying to stay upright, but crash into a wall. I rebound off it, nearly falling to my knees. The glass flies out of my hand and shatters against the hardwood floor.

Mel scoops up the fragments of glass, sets the pieces on the table.

"Here." Her voice comes at me from very far away. She grips my elbow and guides me to the couch.

I curl onto my side, fold my hands under my chin, and close my eyes, riding the narcotic wave. Darkness creeps in at the edges of my mind, swallowing the living room light until all that's left in my mind is a dark, blank emptiness. Sleep threatens to take me under.

Someone sits at my feet. I think it's Mel, but when I slit my eyes open, it's Isla.

"Why are you here?" I ask her, my words already slurring together. But Mel is the one to answer.

"This is my safe space," she says. "I come here all the time. Ever since that night."

Mel kneels next to me, her icy hand brushing the hair from my forehead. I shudder. My eyelids are so heavy. I let them close, stop resisting the sandbags weighing them down. Silence falls, like the snow settling outside.

"You understand, don't you, Alice? Why I had to do it?"

I fight to open my eyes and peer at her, groggy and dazed. That nagging thought that had been bugging me as I cycled over slams into me again. The beeping That Night. And then again earlier, as Mel was standing outside my room. The scent of cigarette smoke. The crackle of shoes over broken glass. The photo of my mom and Mel at the Christmas party, heads bent together.

The thought had leaped out of the dark, crystallizing. And now: confirmation.

"You were there." My voice is a raw whisper, scraping over my throat like it's been raked at with a cheese grater.

Her eyes glisten in the thin lamplight. "Do you remember?"

"The beeping . . ."

"My pacemaker malfunctioned. But it made for a pretty good alibi. You really never saw me?" she asks. "You came back. I saw you."

"I didn't see anybody else. Only Dad. I thought . . ." Tears fill my eyes. I thought he would come after me next.

"I wondered, when I saw you in the hospital, if you had seen me, but you never said. You were talking nonsense about a dead little girl, completely unhinged."

"You . . . killed them?" Tears are flowing now, silent, sticky sobs that feel like they're being ripped from my chest.

"It was an accident." Mel inhales deeply. "I only wanted to stop the car. To talk some sense into them. Your mother was going to go to the police. She wanted to tell them the truth about what we did to Theo. She told your dad everything, and he convinced her to turn herself in. We argued about it. That's why she wanted to go home that night instead of staying like you usually did. I had no idea you and Ella were in the car; you were supposed to be at my house! I went after them, but Pete lost control on the ice. I didn't mean to hurt any of you. I just wanted to talk some sense into her."

"But why do you want to hurt me now?" I whisper. "I won't . . . tell anybody."

"I'm so sorry, Alice." She bends her head, and she really does look sorry. Just not sorry enough. "I can't risk you going to the police, like your mom wanted to. After everything I've done. I can't let you ruin it."

She grips my hands, too tight, her eyes burning intently. "But it'll be okay, I promise. I'll stay here with you the whole time. You'll just slip away peacefully."

She traces a finger over the scars on my wrist. *F R*

Hot tears leak from the corners of my eyes. Nobody will even question it. She'll say I've been stealing her Ativan, mixing them with my new antidepressants. All my friends will say I've been a mess since my family disappeared, drinking, partying, smoking pot, running out of class. *Unhinged,* as she's just said. Dr. Pam will say I've skipped my counseling sessions. Plus there's my episode in Killer's Grove.

I've been my own worst enemy.

"Tell me . . . what happened," I slur.

Mel sinks onto the floor, sitting cross-legged next to me.

"Tell me . . . everything."

She waits, her eyes bright, her cheeks flushed. She has time, I'm sure she figures. Time for the pills to dissolve in my bloodstream like tiny bits of sand.

Finally, she takes a deep breath and begins.

Chapter 45

Mel

December

Mel stares at Laura, completely stunned at what she's just said. That her best friend would betray her this way.

"I can't keep doing this," Laura says again. She's looking down, picking at a loose thread on her sling.

Blood rushes fast and loud in Mel's ears, the twinkling Christmas lights a pulse in her peripheral vision.

"Shhh!" Mel grabs her friend's arm and drags her over to the dessert table, where she begins straightening the cakes and cookies. "You can't do that."

Laura lifts her chin, almost defiantly. "Pete says—"

"Wait," Mel cuts her off, heart accelerating. She puts a hand on her chest, takes a long, calming breath. It's a habit she's had since she got the pacemaker fitted. "You told Pete?"

"I had to, Mel! You don't understand what this has been doing to me." Tears glitter in Laura's eyes. "I'm not like you; I can't deal with it. I can't sleep. I can't eat. My stomach hurts and I cry at the drop of a hat. I dream about it, and then I wake up and it's true and I think about it some more. He's my husband. Pete *knew* something was wrong!"

"You shouldn't have told him." Anger foams inside of Mel, a bitter taste gushing into her mouth. Her mind churns over how to fix this problem. "All you need to do is act normal, Laura. It isn't that fucking hard."

"It *is* that fucking hard!" Tears fill Laura's eyes, and Mel has the irrational urge to slap her. Laura turns away from the others, who are now dancing in front of the Christmas tree on the other side of the room.

"This isn't just a run-of-the-mill homicide anymore," Mel hisses. "We *concealed* it. Do you get that? We *covered up* a murder."

Mel has been nothing but good to Laura. Strong and steady and loyal. All the things she values in a person. She's been a good friend. *Better* than a good friend. Mel put the body in the suitcase she found in Laura's trunk and hid the evidence with it. She came up with the plan to hide Theo's body in the new property Jack had recently purchased.

Mel's done *everything* for Laura. She got rid of a fucking body for her! It's not like she's the one who shot Theo. And she can't believe that now Laura wants to repay her by getting her sent to prison.

Mel is aware of all she has to lose. Her business, which she's built from nothing. Finn would grow up never knowing his mother. Jack would walk away. Would he find somebody else? She'd have nothing.

Mel feels fury fizz in her veins. She's felt this fury ever since she found out Jack was cheating on her with his receptionist like some bad, cliché pornographic movie. Maybe it's been since before that, since she almost died when she was pregnant, the whole obscene, arbitrary unfairness of it building into a fury that now feels as dense and dark as stone.

"I'll say it was me. I shot him. I hid his body. I did everything. I won't say anything about you," Laura says, "but I have to turn myself in. Tomorrow. I can't keep going like this."

Mel stares at Laura, incredulous. "Have you lost your fucking mind? They'll know someone else was involved. How will you explain hiding his body the way we did? You couldn't do that on your own with a dislocated shoulder. *They will find out!*"

"I'll never admit it. If I don't say anything, they'll never know."

"What will this do to Alice and Ella?" Mel changes tack. "They'll know their mother's a murderer."

Laura's eyes shimmer. "I know. And I hate that. But at least they'll know I did the right thing. That's a more important lesson for them to learn."

Mel remembers being a girl, long before her father left, and seeing a hitchhiker by the side of the road. She told her father they should help him, take him where he needed to go.

Why would I unnecessarily put myself—and you—in danger like that? he'd asked. *Rule number one, Melanie, self-preservation always comes first.*

As the years went by, Melanie would think about rule number one a lot. If she was out drinking with friends, she wouldn't get into their car. If she was driving, she wouldn't text. Although she dabbled in dealing drugs, she certainly never took them. If something, or someone, threatened her, she'd strike first.

Mel glances across the room at Finn as Alice finally snaps the much-coveted picture with Santa. He's only four. He needs his mother, even if his father doesn't anymore.

She *has* to convince Laura to change her mind. She can't let somebody else's shitty mistakes take her down. Not after everything she's been through.

"Don't do this, Laura," Mel pleads, but Laura's gaze has already drifted away. She's no longer listening. She's made up her mind.

"Pete and I are going to leave in a little bit. The girls can stay. We won't tell them yet. I just want one last night at home."

Mel walks unsteadily to the liquor table and pours rum in a glass, then tops it with eggnog. Will is there, Shelby's husband. He's a detective, and she's careful to keep her face calm and composed, to act as if nothing is wrong.

She drinks and drinks and drinks until the room is spinning, the walls closing in. She thinks she's going to vomit. She stumbles out the back door in her bare feet. Snow has started to fall. It isn't sticking yet, but the cold is shocking.

The door flies open behind her, yellow light tumbling onto her shoulders. "Hey, Mel! There you are!" Jack roars in his drunk voice. The loud, obnoxious one she's grown to hate. Mel sees the cute little elf he's been flirting with all night hovering behind him.

Mel shoves past him. "I hear Finn crying," she lies.

Maybe he's going to the garage to fuck the cute little elf. She doesn't care. She runs inside, up the stairs, to her bedroom. She thrusts her hand under her mattress and pulls out the gun she's hidden there. Theo's gun.

Laura was such a mess after everything that happened, she didn't notice that Mel had gone back and found Theo's gun before they left. That she'd kept it. It was practically prescient of her, knowing that an untraceable gun would come in handy.

She knew that a guy like Theo would never have a registered gun on him. He just wasn't that type of a person. Laura had always given Theo more credit than he deserved. He was a lowlife degenerate even back in college, easy to manipulate. Easy to use.

Laura had never guessed that it was Mel's drugs Theo had peddled to Cody. That Mel was the one in charge of the entire operation. Like she'd told Laura, she didn't do it because she needed money. She did it because she liked it. She liked being in charge of something so successful, and she liked running the operation right under the noses of those who thought they were in charge. People often underestimated Mel, but she didn't mind. Being underestimated is a gift. It allows you to take risks others wouldn't expect of you.

But Theo was greedy. And stupid. He'd tried to grow too fast, had trusted the wrong guy to help him. Cody was an addict. You can never trust an addict to sell drugs.

One thing Laura never learned: trusting the wrong people can have deadly consequences.

Chapter 46

Jess

I go directly to Shane in the bullpen.

Maybe he isn't the partner I want, but he's the one I've got. I need him.

"I'll get a team on standby," Galloway says from behind me. "Call me when you're ready."

I fill Shane in on what Khandi told us as we head to the cruiser.

"Hurry. We're running out of time," I say urgently.

Shane flicks the lights on, pointing the car toward the O'Briens' house.

I peer through the whirling snow as I tell him about the beep Alice heard the night her family went missing. "It's been bothering me. And then I remembered something Alice told me the day I found her in Killer's Grove, when we were at Bea's Teas. Melanie O'Brien met us there, and Alice said Mel had a pacemaker fitted after a difficult pregnancy a few years ago."

The windshield wipers batter the glass, barely able to push the snow out of the way.

"What does Melanie O'Brien's pacemaker have to do with this case?" Shane whips around a corner. The rear tires spin, working to get a grip. His fingers are tight on the steering wheel, so tight they've gone white.

"Alice said that Mel had a checkup to make sure her pacemaker was working properly. Most pacemakers issue an alert if there's something wrong, like an electrical lead has come loose, if the battery is dying, or if the user is too close to a magnetic field, like a store's security system. It starts beeping. I once took a call out on a farm and a cop I knew, his pacemaker was set off by the electric fence. *That's* what Alice heard that night. Mel's pacemaker was beeping."

Isla set it off, I think, but I don't say it out loud.

"Shit." Shane turns the car into Killer's Grove.

"The list of people who gave DNA samples? Melanie wasn't on that list. We don't have her DNA on file, so she wouldn't match any of the evidence we have."

"She was in the hospital for observation for a heart problem." Shane glances at me. He's gone sheet white. "We thought she was sick. We had no reason to suspect a woman with a heart problem would be the killer."

"It was a good alibi. I didn't question it either at first. But Mel wasn't having heart pain. She went to the hospital because her pacemaker was acting up. Mel O'Brien and Laura Harper killed Theo Moriarty; then Mel killed Laura to keep her quiet."

"And now you think Alice is in danger."

"I'm sure of it."

I look out my window at the snow swirling around us. And then I see it. The scarred tree that the Harpers hit. And standing in front of it is Isla.

"Stop!"

Shane wrenches the steering wheel and pulls onto the shoulder. I throw the door open and slam my cane into the road, heaving myself over the snowy ground to the tree.

But Isla is no longer there.

I look to my left and right, peering into the black shadows. Snow has turned the world to static. The only sound is the howl of the rising wind, the low rumble of the car's engine, the beating of the windshield wipers.

Shane comes up behind me. His eyes are wary, but he doesn't speak.

I don't *feel* anything. Alice isn't here. Neither is Isla.

The road is empty. It's just a road, after all. Haunted by nothing but me.

"We're running out of time!" I spin in a circle, my heart revving. "Which way do we go, to the O'Briens' or to the Harpers'?"

"We split up," Shane says decisively.

I hesitate. "Are you sure?"

"I trust you."

"Why?" I don't deserve his trust.

"Because we're partners. Partners trust each other."

There's a flicker in my peripheral vision, something moving deep in Killer's Grove. I nod. "Okay. I'll cut through here and go to the Harpers'."

"I'll go to the O'Briens'."

We agree to call each other as soon as we arrive at our destinations and know more; then Shane gets in the cruiser and floors it, engine roaring.

I limp through the frozen forest. The wind and cold make it slow going. My leg is aching, a steady, hot thrum that gets more and more painful with every step. My jeans quickly become soaked. I huddle in my winter parka, freezing wind and snow battering my bare cheeks as I lean on my cane, driving it hard into the ground.

My breath is huffing out of me in great gasps, the cold slicing at my lungs like glass. I finally reach the house where we found Theo Moriarty. I hurry across the field to the paved road, moving deeper into the neighborhood, in the direction of the Harpers' house.

My phone rings. It's Shane.

"Jess, neither Melanie nor Alice is here!" he shouts. "Clarissa O'Brien said Alice's room is empty. Melanie isn't there, either."

I round the final corner, and there's Alice's bike slumped on the snowy front lawn. Parked on the curb is Melanie's sleek black Jaguar.

"They're here," I say. "At the Harpers' house."

"Galloway has a team ready. I'll tell her to send them to the Harpers' now. Do not engage. Do you hear me? Melanie is likely armed and dangerous."

"They won't get here in time," I say.

My heart is pounding urgently, worry and fear pinging every nerve ending. "Alice is inside with her!"

"Jess, listen to me. Just wait—"

But I've already hung up.

Chapter 47

Mel

Mel takes Jack's company truck.

Thank goodness the site manager dropped it at their house while he's away visiting family for the holidays.

A plan is forming. She's inebriated, but it doesn't stop it from unspooling like cotton candy in her mind. Mel has always been good at thinking under pressure, at planning, at organizing. She's cool in a crisis, and this certainly counts as a crisis.

She finds a couple of orange construction barriers and a ROAD CLOSED sign in the back of the truck. She uses them to block off the main road, hoping to force Pete and Laura into Killer's Grove, where she'll be waiting to confront them. Maybe if she can get to Pete, then Laura will come to her senses. She can't understand why he's convinced his own wife to go to the police. Doesn't he realize she'll go to prison? With actual criminals? He's always been annoyingly moralistic, but this is where she draws the line.

Mel just wants to talk sense into them. And if they won't listen, well, that's what the gun is for. They have no idea how far she'll go to protect the life she's built.

Mel pulls the truck off the road in Killer's Grove. The tires skid a little on a patch of ice, but she wrestles it into place and throws the truck into park.

Mel unlocks the hardtop canopy and climbs into the back, rooting around until she finds a high-power strobe warning light.

And then she settles in to wait.

It doesn't take long. She sees a pair of headlights coming toward her from the snow-blurred road and jumps out of the truck. She's perhaps still too drunk to be doing this, but needs must and all that.

The snow whirls around Mel, disorienting her. Her drunk fingers fumble with the strobe light, struggling to find the on switch. The minivan is getting closer. It's coming too fast, or maybe she's moving too slow.

It's nearly upon her when she finally manages to flick the switch. The strobe light is brighter than she expected. Blazing yellow light bursts into the black night, strobing too fast, a rapid succession of dazzling flashes.

Mel is temporarily blinded. She blinks furiously, working desperately to adjust to the light. She can't see, but she hears it, the sound of brakes squealing over icy pavement, then metal crunching and glass shattering. The car has clipped a tree and catapulted into the air.

"Noooo!" Mel screams, dropping to her knees and covering her head as the car flips into the air.

Metal scrapes against pavement, a horrible, bone-splintering squeal, and then the car finally comes to a rest on one side.

"No, no, no, no, no." She says the word over and over, hoping that this is a dream, a nightmare, that none of it is real.

Mel drops the light, her fingers numb with adrenaline. It settles in the snow, giving off a pale, anemic yellow light. Enough for her to see the crumpled vehicle.

She walks slowly toward the car. Glass glitters in the snow, reflecting yellow in the murky light. The passenger's-side front and rear wheels are still moving, rotating like the car thinks it's still going somewhere.

Mel brushes snow from her eyes and notices something, a small bundle, on the road's narrow shoulder, maybe fifteen feet from the car. She steps tentatively toward it, stomach churning. She drops to her knees next to the bundle, bile burning in her throat.

It's Ella. She must've been thrown from the car. Her head and face are a mess of blood and gravel. Her neck is tilted at an unnatural angle. Mel presses two fingers to her throat. Dead.

Mel buckles over, sobbing. Acid eats away at her insides. She thinks she will vomit, but nothing comes out. Her heart is jackrabbiting in her chest, too fast. Erratic. Faster and faster it goes, racing like a greyhound. Spots dance in front of her eyes. She feels like she's going to pass out, that she'll have a heart attack.

Mel snaps back, wipes her eyes as a thought presses in, cold and slimy, a hard slap that shakes her back to reality.

Where are Pete and Laura? And Alice?

Mel thought the girls were staying at her house, but if Ella was in the car, maybe Alice is somewhere nearby, too.

Mel stands on shaky legs, scanning the swirling snow for Alice. She's just standing on tiptoe to peer into the back seat of the upended car when her pacemaker goes off.

Beep. Beep. Beep. There are sixteen of them before it goes quiet again.

"Fuck," she hisses under her breath.

People mistakenly think that a beeping pacemaker means a failing heart, but that isn't true. Pacemakers beep for all sorts of reasons. A failing battery, a broken lead, a strong magnet. Once she got too close to the magnetic field of a store's antitheft system and it went off. She makes a mental note to call her electrocardiology office tomorrow.

Mel needs to get her heartbeat under control. She takes a steadying breath, like she's learned in yoga. Mel loves yoga; it is the one stabilizing factor in a life that often feels on the brink of falling apart. Then, because sometimes it takes more than just yoga, she pulls a cigarette out of a crumpled pack in her back pocket and lights it.

Beside her, the car's windshield wipers are still going, *swish, swish, swish*. Mel wipes her eyes. She should turn them off, but she doesn't. She just stands there, the wind whipping strands of her hair against her cheeks as she sucks at her cigarette, smoke curling into the snow-blurred air. After a few minutes, her heart calms, a cool detachedness draping itself over her. She inhales a deep, centering breath.

That's when she spots a splash of red hair splayed across the snow behind the car. She freezes, knowing instantly it's Laura, knows also that she's dead, just like Ella.

A sound. Rustling. Then glass crunching.

It's coming from the opposite side of the car.

Mel drops her cigarette in the snow and slips the gun from the waistband of her pants as she peers around the front of the car. It's Pete. He's climbed out of the broken windshield. Blood streaks down his face from a deep gash in his head.

He's bent over Ella's body, a wild, grief-stricken keening coming from his mouth. The sound is so horrifying Mel feels goose bumps prickle up and down her arms. His coat is wrapped around his hand, Pete using it to try to stem the blood coming from Ella's head.

Mel is frozen in the shadows of the car, but she must make a noise, because Pete's head swivels, his eyes landing like bullets on her.

"You." He looks at Mel, tears glistening in the yellow headlights. "You did this. Why?"

"*Me?* No, this is all *your* fault, Pete." Rage fills her, eats away at her insides. "None of this would have happened if you hadn't told Laura to turn herself in!"

She takes a step closer, hand tense on the gun. Her father's voice echoes in her mind. *Rule number one, Melanie, self-preservation always comes first.*

Rule number one taught her common sense, caution, safety. It taught her to survive. She would always be grateful to her father for that.

Because now she knows exactly what she must do.

"Where's Alice?" she asks, training the gun on Pete.

Her voice is controlled now. Her hands are steady, her breathing calm. She sees understanding on Pete's face. He knows what she has to do. He accepts it. He would do the same in her place.

A noise comes from the tree line, twigs crackling under shoes. It's Alice, her gaze bouncing between her dead sister and her father with wide, horrified eyes.

Pete glances at Mel, his face a mask of hatred and fury and rage, and then he turns to Alice and screams a warning.

"Run! We're next!" He tries to get to his feet, sways, lifting one hand, like he's trying to push her away. "Alice, run!"

"I'm sorry, Pete," she whispers.

She takes three swift steps from behind the car so she's directly behind Pete.

From this distance, there's no chance she'll miss.

Chapter 48

Alice

Mel's voice breaks as her story cuts off, sadness rising off her like dry ice.

"I chased after you but couldn't find you," she tells me. "And then I went back. I had to . . . clean up, and . . . Pete and . . ."

She swipes angrily at her tears and stares off into space. When she speaks again, it's like she's alone now, talking to herself. "I tried to hide Ella's backpack with Theo, but I lost my nerve. I couldn't bring myself to open the suitcase, so I stuffed it into the trunk. I didn't think anybody would ever find it."

She turns to me, pleading with me to understand. "I never meant for any of this to happen. I only wanted to talk some sense into them. But I had to protect myself. And Finn! He's only little, he needs his mom."

From where I was standing at the tree line, I never saw Mel hidden behind the crumpled car. Only my dad bent over a body. The fury on his face wasn't for me; it was for Mel. He knew she was responsible for his wife's and daughter's deaths. What a massive betrayal he must've felt. And then, seeing me standing there, he must've been terrified, afraid for my life.

He didn't shout, "Run, *you're* next" but "Run, *we're* next." A warning that Mel was going to kill us, not that *he* was going to.

My heart is breaking, shattering like glass smashed against the pavement. I was wrong about everything. About everyone. Jinx, who is kind and honest, and Maya, who betrayed my mom and me, and my dad, who wanted to warn me, not kill me, and Mel—worst of all, Mel—my aunt who pretended to love me but killed my family.

All this time, I thought she was grieving, because she *was* grieving. But her grief, the scent of torn leaves and lightning strikes, it wasn't just grief. It was *evil*. It floats around me now, sticky, like black mold spores filling the air, blotting out the light.

I want to say something, want to ask where they are now, where she hid their bodies. But the air has turned brittle. If I speak, it will shatter everything, millions of razor-edge shards that will slice us both until we are torn, bloody strips of nothing.

And anyway, the drugs have paralyzed my tongue. It lies fat, thick as a slug inside my mouth. I let my body relax and my breathing go steady and even.

"Go to sleep." Mel drags a blanket from the back of the couch over me. Her lips brush my forehead, her breath icy cold, mingling with a sudden draft that whooshes through the house.

My eyelashes flutter open. But instead of Mel, I see Isla.

My guilt, my conscience, this girl who died before my family disappeared, getting all tangled and twisted in my mind. As an emotion, guilt has so much power. It's the strongest sense I feel in people, the color, of bruised aubergine; the scent, of cracked winter bark and mildew; the weighted feel in the air, hot and heavy, like stepping out of a shower.

It's so conflicting, so contradictory. Because I *am* glad to be alive. But when someone dies, when you blame yourself, even though now you get to live, that guilt, that *regret*, is a heavy, heavy burden.

So how do you set it down?

I want so much to fix what happened. To mend the past. But I guess the truth is, you can't fix things. You can only carry them.

But maybe, one day, maybe I'll be able to set them down. I see that now.

That cold breeze stirs again, pulling at Isla. The edges of her wobble and sway, and she begins to disappear like ripples in water.

"Don't go," I mutter. I don't want to be alone.

Her voice is a whisper in my ear. "Hold on."

But I can barely hear her. I am a bird, soaring on a white cloud. But the cloud bursts, drops of water splattering me. And then I'm falling. Down, down, down to the sea. I hit the surface and I'm no longer a bird. I'm just me. Just Alice. All alone, diving beneath the rough waves. Something is pulling on my ankle, tugging at me.

I try to scream, to kick against it, to get back to the surface.

"It's all right, sweetheart, I've got you. Just let go."

I'm sinking down farther and farther beneath the cool black water, into the darkest, darkest place.

I don't even bother fighting it. I let the sea take me under.

Chapter 49

Jess

Time.

We can do time, kill time, save it, spend it. It can heal all wounds or teach us just to live with them. We lose time and have all the time in the world, but the truth is, time is the thing that eventually kills us all. Because time waits for no one. And nobody is powerful enough to stop it.

I feel it now, the steady drip, drip, drip of the sand in the hourglass. We're running out of time. My chance to save Alice is slipping away.

I don't have time to wait for backup.

I limp up the driveway. Visibility has gone from bad to worse. Giant, fat blobs of snow are falling fast, hustling to the ground. The footprints leading toward the front door are barely visible now. I climb the front porch and peer in the window. There's something there, a shadow on the other side of the blinds.

Alice?

I set my cane on the porch and slip my hand up my sleeve, bunching the material and smashing it into the panel of glass by the door. The glass shatters. It isn't a quiet entry, but speed is more important than stealth right now.

I reach through and open the door, drawing my gun as I shuffle inside. I'm unbalanced without my cane and press a hip into the wall as I scan the room.

The house is deathly quiet. Dark, with a dim light coming from the living room. I limp toward the light, and there she is. Alice.

She's lying on the couch, a blanket pulled to her chin. She's bone white, utterly still.

Panic licks at my belly, my breath sticking in my throat. My world narrows, and time slides away from me as I hurry to her.

"No! Alice, wake up, sweetie. Wake up!"

I drop awkwardly to my knees. Alice's hands are curled under her chin. I wrench them away, fumbling to get to her neck, to check her pulse. Something tumbles out as her palm opens. A necklace. A heart-shaped locket with a musical note attached to the bottom.

I drop it into my pocket and thrust my fingers into Alice's neck. And then a miracle. Her pulse, butterfly-wing soft under my fingertips.

Something prickles over my back, and there's a faint rustling sound. I spin, just in time to see wild eyes. A knife swinging down toward me. Melanie.

I bring my arms up to protect myself. The knife buries into my forearm. Hot pain lances through me. I scream. Mel kicks my gun away, then levels another kick to my temple. Fireworks explode in my head. Everything goes blurry, and I crash into the floor.

I twist and instinctively lash out with my good leg, catching Mel in one ankle and bringing her to the ground. Blood is gushing out of my arm, the slash near my elbow. I'm losing blood fast and it's making me dizzy. I grit my jaw and blink, trying to get my eyes to focus.

Mel scuttles away from me and gets to her feet, knife still in hand. Another stab. This time she misses. Fear like boiling water bubbles inside me. I can't get to my feet without my cane. I weave on my knees, bring one hand out to steady myself. I'm at a complete disadvantage, unarmed, no gun, no vest, one disabled leg, and losing blood too fast.

She jabs with the knife again. But she's off-balance, moving too quickly. I take advantage and lash out again with my good leg. I get her in the knee, and she drops to the floor. I throw my weight against her, taking her to the ground. The knife clatters out of her hand, landing a few feet away.

We scrabble, slipping in blood. I'm stronger than her but weak from the loss of blood. She gets an arm free, and her elbow cracks into my skull. My vision sparkles, and I crash backward.

This time, I can't get up. The world around me sways like I'm on a boat. Mel gets to her feet, scoops up the knife again.

"That's it." She hovers, knife poised over me. "Just close your eyes. You'll be with your daughter soon."

That catches my attention. She knows who I am.

I look down at my arm, the blood pouring out of me. Is that what I want? To join Isla?

The answer hits me like a punch to the teeth. No. I don't want to give up. I still have so much to live for. Mac. My job. All the victims I can help. I owe it to them to stay alive.

But maybe, now, I don't have a choice. Blood is squirting out of me too fast, matching the beat of my heart.

Mel lifts the knife above her head, readying for the last, fatal stab.

A shot explodes in the night. Glass shatters. Mel's eyes widen. A splotch of blood blossoms on her white coat. She drops to her knees, releasing the knife. It clatters onto the hardwood floor. Mel grabs for her shoulder, howling.

Voices fill the air as cops pour into the house. I let my eyes close. And then Shane is at my side, pressing his jacket to my bloody arm.

"Get an ambulance in here now!" he roars.

I blink at him. "How'd . . . ?"

"Dispatch called Galloway. The neighbor across the road had called in a break-in. The team was already on the way when we spoke on the phone."

Behind him, one of the cops is cuffing Mel, reading her rights.

I struggle to sit. "Alice."

"Jess . . ." Shane tries to stop me, but I shake him off. I keep the pressure on my arm, but my blood has already drenched Shane's jacket.

"Alice. Wake up, sweetie."

And then, another miracle. Alice's eyelids open. She reaches up and stuffs her fingers into the far reaches of her mouth. They emerge slimy and covered in white.

"You clever girl," I whisper, relief bashing at my lungs. "You never swallowed them."

"Tried . . . not . . . to . . . ," she slurs, then retches, spitting the rest of the spit-slicked white pills onto the floor.

I follow her gaze to a small pile of white huddled on the floor under a painting of Alice and her family. She'd spit some of them out earlier, too.

Alice lies back on the couch, her eyes fluttering.

"They're here," she whispers. "My family . . . is here."

"Alice, look at me." How much of the drugs has she ingested? "You need to stay awake, okay?"

She pries her eyes open and stares at me groggily. I try to hold her gaze, but the room tilts. I can't stay upright anymore. I slump to the floor. I hear Shane shouting my name. I blink up at him, unable to answer. The edges of my vision have started to soften, the darkness tugging at me.

I close my eyes, letting it win. But then, right before I pass out, I hear the whoop of an ambulance.

We're going to be okay.

Chapter 50

Jess

Two days pass before I see Alice again.

She's still in the hospital, meant to be discharged today. I was released after just a day, a couple of stitches, a bag of blood, and a bandage later.

When I arrive at the hospital during visiting hours, Alice is playing Uno with a cheerful-looking goth girl. Maya is conspicuously absent.

When we brought Maya in for questioning, she'd immediately told us her manager and Theo were selling stolen goods from the sports store. It had been a slick operation until they decided to include guns.

The robbery was reported, and the manager had asked Maya to keep one of the guns until the heat died down. He'd threatened to make sure she was the one who took the fall if she didn't.

Maya came home one day just as Laura was stuffing the suitcase with the stolen items into her trunk. Terrified Laura would take everything to the police, she'd started texting her threatening messages.

It remains to be seen if the DA will press charges.

Alice tidies away the Uno cards as her friend leaves. The TV in the corner of her room is broadcasting the news. It flashes to a close-up of Shane at the press conference earlier this morning. I'm standing next to him, my arm in a white bandage, Galloway a few feet back. Shane is wearing a suit and tie, looking calm and confident as he answers questions.

I shed my parka and sit next to Alice.

"Maybe you'll have a cool scar." She holds her forearm up to mine. "We'll match. Sort of."

"Mine looks like an I," I say.

"Fir."

"Fried?"

She giggles. "Fire?"

"Friends."

We share a smile.

"How are you doing, Alice?"

"Dr. Pam changed my antidepressants. She thinks they were making me hallucinate."

There's a movement in the corner of the room. Pete. He's watching his daughter, his expression filled with love and sadness and longing. Alice follows my gaze and looks at me quizzically. She doesn't see him. I don't think she ever did. It was just her own brain trying to cope with the trauma of what had happened.

For the first time, Pete meets my eyes. And I finally understand why he never spoke to me. He didn't need anything from me. Pete knew he was dead. He knew the truth. He just wanted Alice to know it, too, so she could find closure. So she would know what really happened that night.

Pete gives me a small smile and lifts a hand. He walks toward the door. His body shimmers, becoming more translucent with every step. And then he is glowing light, glittering and twinkling as he slips from the door into the next world, moving into the space where dreams grow and memories dwell.

My heart physically hurts as I think of everything that awaits Alice. Her first boyfriend, the light in her eyes when she falls in love for the first time. Her graduation and then college, taking those first steps into the big, wide world as a new adult. Her wedding and then her first child, clasping her warm newborn to her beating heart. But all of it will be without her family to cheer her on.

Time. We never have enough of it with the people we love. Never. All we can do is appreciate the moments we do have. Live in those moments. Be present. Be grateful for every one of them.

"I wanted to tell you, I'm moving to Florida. With my grandma," she says.

"Christmas on the beach." I smile even though it makes me sad. "Nice." I take a deep breath. "Alice, your family . . ."

This is the hard part. After this, Alice will never be able to cling to the idea that maybe things could go back to the way they were. "I thought about what you said about them being there at your house. I wondered if you meant it literally, not figuratively. We got sniffer dogs in and they . . . they've picked up a scent in the shed out back, under the floorboards. We believe your family members are buried there. We'll be digging up the floor tomorrow."

Unsurprisingly, Melanie lawyered up the second we arrested her. More surprising, Jack is sticking by her. She's claimed she was trying to save Alice after finding her unconscious. That she was calling the police when I came in and had attacked me after finding me with my hands on Alice's neck.

But we're piecing everything together, running her DNA against the evidence we have, like the cigarette butt found at the scene. So far, the evidence shows they died that night. Melanie moved them to the trunk of her car, where she kept them for a few days. We had that brutal winter storm and the ground was frozen solid, so she couldn't bury them. Once we'd finished searching the Harpers' house, she took them there, pulled up the floorboards in the shed, and buried them.

Her very own telltale heart.

Alice's eyes are shiny with tears. "That's why she kept going back." I nod.

"Dad loved it in his darkroom. I'm glad he was there."

I touch her hand. "I'm so sorry."

"She wanted me to kill myself. That's why she gave me the drugs." Her voice is ripe, swollen with remembering this terrible thing her aunt did to her.

"What made you spit them out?"

"My mom's painting of our family in the living room. I saw their faces, and I knew I couldn't just give in." Her eyes meet mine, glossy and red. "I had to survive. I had to be the one person in my family who didn't die. I owed them that."

"I'm glad you made that choice, Alice."

When I get home, I go straight to my bottle of Jack Daniel's. I pour two fingers in Isla's Snoopy cup.

"One little drink," I mutter, but for once, my mind isn't on the alcohol.

It's on the necklace in my pocket.

And the diary I found because of it.

I had finally gotten home after being released from the hospital yesterday morning when I remembered the necklace in Alice's palm. It was heart-shaped and held a family picture of the Harpers wearing matching Christmas pajamas. The musical note at the bottom was a slightly different shade of silver. When I held it up to inspect it in the kitchen light, I realized it had been welded on, a messy homemade job. And printed in tiny letters were three little numbers: 135.

That's when I knew. It wasn't a musical note. It was a key.

I spent yesterday and today visiting banks in town with safe-deposit boxes. This morning, on the way to visit Alice, I got lucky. I found one registered to Laura Harper. Inside was a leather-bound diary filled with tiny, looped writing.

I head out to my living room. Last night, Will stopped by with a Christmas tree—courtesy of my dad—and he and Shelby helped me decorate it. I sit in my reclining chair, the lights twinkling, and pull the diary onto my lap. I've waited until now to read it.

I scan the pages, flipping through to the night Laura and Mel killed Theo Moriarty.

Ice scatters down my neck as I read, as one more piece of the puzzle clicks into place.

◆ ◆ ◆

. . . *a flash of light illuminates the river thrashing violently to our right. Theo presses the gun to Melanie's head.*

"Get the money out!" he shouts over the howling wind.

I reach into the empty space at the bottom of the tree. My fingers close around a handful of mud and twigs.

Everything moves in slow motion then. I throw the mud at Theo.

"Run!" I shout at Mel.

Theo flinches, his hands coming up to protect his eyes from the mud. I yank the gun out of my waistband and squeeze the trigger, hitting Theo in the chest. He looks down at the blood blossoming, then at me, stunned.

Blood bubbles out of his mouth. He staggers backward, tries to run. He only makes it to the road before collapsing onto his back. I stand over him, the gun still in my hand. Mel is saying something, but I can't hear what. There's a loud buzzing in my head. A ringing.

I think I'm in shock. I should call Pete. No, he's too drunk. I should call the police. But that doesn't seem like a good option, either.

And then Theo's eyes flutter. He tries to sit up. It startles something in me, jolts me into motion.

I shoot him in the head.

Melanie is screaming. "You fucking killed him!"

I stare at Theo. The top half of his head is missing, blackness mingling with the rain.

That ringing grows louder. Spots speckle my vision. I drop the gun and lurch backward, falling to my knees and vomiting violently. Rain streams down my face. I'm shaking.

And then we hear something. An engine. Headlights glimmer, a vehicle coming around the bend.

I freeze, realizing exactly what's going to happen and yet unable to stop it.

The truck slams into Theo. His body goes flying. The driver overcorrects, wheels squealing. It flips into the air, lands against the boulders with a sickening crunch, then slides down the muddy embankment toward the rising river.

Mel and I scramble over slippery rocks to the truck. A woman and a little girl are inside. The woman hangs half out of the driver's-side window. Her leg is mangled, shredded by the glass. I yank her arms, trying to pull her out.

"Mel, help!" I howl.

Mel climbs out of the back seat, her face sheet white as she looks at the little girl.

"She's dead," she says. "There's nothing we can do."

"No!" I'm sobbing now.

Mel shakes me. Hard. She tells me all we can do is help this woman. I move on autopilot, reach for the woman's arms as Mel lifts her leg. She shrieks in agony but eventually passes out, going limp and boneless as we carry her up to the road.

Mel pats her down, finds a wallet in her jacket pocket. She flips it open and hands it to me. Inside is a detective's badge and ID card.

Printed on the ID card is Detective Jessica Lambert.

The words slide down my skull. I feel sick, breathless with shock.

Not a deer. A body. *A dead body.* Isla's death wasn't my fault. Not the way I thought it was. One drink or none, on that darkened, storm-slicked corner, I never would have seen it.

Would I have?

So many things make sense now. The old man who'd claimed Boudica had flagged him down. The sound of women's voices. How I'd been pulled out of the car, carried up to the road, away from the rising river. Not Isla, as I'd thought. Laura and Mel.

And yet some things still don't fit.

My mind fizzes the way it does. *It never stops, does it,* Mac used to say ruefully.

Something is tugging at me. A question, maybe, or a knowledge. I stare at the empty coffee table, that slippery feeling pulling at me. And then, there it is.

If I hit Theo on the road, why did he have milfoil on his clothes?

There are no answers. Will I ever have all of them? Do I *need* all of them?

I've been carrying the weight of this for so long now, I never imagined what it might feel like to set it down. And yet here it is. *Can* I set it down?

I pick up my phone to call Mac, to tell him what I've learned. But the words I've whispered to myself for so long rise from my belly, up my throat like vomit.

You're worthless. A killer. They deserved better than you.

We think we'll find forgiveness, closure, somewhere out there. Maybe in another country or another job or another case. But it isn't out there. In the end, nothing can absolve us but ourselves. Because the past is with us, baked into our cells, stirred into our DNA, rising into the person who steps into each day.

I think of Shane looking for a girl he'll likely never find. Is it better to have hope, to feel it like a grain of sand rubbing against your gums, or closure? I know Isla is dead, but still I chase her ghost. That, I know, isn't closure.

I'm floored suddenly by that terrible mix of guilt and grief that sent me spiraling into alcoholism after she died. I know I'm supposed to move on, let go, explore the idea of a life without Isla, but maybe a part of me still isn't ready. Maybe I'm scared that if I move on, I won't see her anymore, and that will be too much like forgetting, like moving into a new life, one where Isla is a character in a book I read a long time ago.

And if I don't see her, then her face will fade, and then the sound of her voice, and then maybe one day I'll look at a picture of her or hear her voice in an old video and I'll be taken off guard. Surprised. By the freckle she had near her left dimple or the way she could move her right eyebrow, as if it were entirely separate from her, by the pitch of her voice and the cadence of her speech and the shout of her laughter and the way her skin felt when she leaned against me and whispered, *I love you, Mommy.*

And that is unacceptable; forgetting means she's really gone.

But reading this diary, it reframes things for me, like looking at one of those optical illusions, a bunny this way, a duck that way. What's philosophically interesting about those is what happens when the aspect changes, when we shift from seeing the bunny to the duck. The change isn't the image on the page or the photoreceptor cells within your retina. The change is in you.

So then, can I move on, find a new lens to look through?

Closure is a myth. Consigning someone you love to the past, never to be in the present again, it isn't voluntary. I don't want to do it. But maybe I can move to a different frame of mind, empowered by my memories rather than decimated by them. Because I find now that, though I'll never stop being sorry, I do want to stop punishing myself. Maybe that's enough.

I set the diary on the coffee table and cross to the window, stare outside at the falling snow. Across the street, the neighborhood children are building a snowman. One shrieks as another launches a fat snowball. Another child, an adolescent boy, stands a little ways away, watching. But there's something about him. Something nebulous, hazy. He isn't alive, I realize. A ghost.

There's a sound, and then Isla is standing in the living room with me. She's smiling, her front teeth still missing, her Hello Kitty headband slightly askew.

The past is never dead. It's not even past. But I wouldn't have it any other way.

It's only because of Isla that I know love never dies; it only changes form. That I learned being a mom is a privilege, that life is a gift and to take nothing for granted.

Because of Isla, I'm a better person. I can't regret that. Not ever. And whenever I feel like I've been singled out, like I'm being tortured, I remember that: I'm the luckiest woman alive because I got to have her.

"I'd do it all again," I tell her. I'm weeping now, sobs wrenching out of me, my heart suddenly both full and light, a whirl of cotton candy. "I'd go through all of it again, if it meant I got to have you. Every drop of pain, every memory that hurts, every time I see your face, it reminds me of the treasure I got to hold for eight years. I love you, Isla."

"I love you, too, Mommy."

She sets something on the coffee table, then reaches a hand out to mine, closing the distance between us. I expect to feel the iciness of her skin touch mine, and I do, but it isn't solid, it's like mist, cool and soft, the feeling seeping into me, as though she's stepped inside of me.

And then she's gone and all that's left is a familiar, heart-shaped worry stone sitting on top of the diary. I pluck it up, wiping my tear-streaked face.

And I realize what I want to tell Alice, the words I'd say to help her in this terrible future she faces. If you love someone enough to feel the pain of their passing, it is the love that lasts. That love outlives memories and faces and sounds. It outlives pain and heartbreak and anguish. That love is what will carry you through.

I balance the worry stone in the palm of one hand, my phone with Mac's number on the screen in the other. Outside, the sounds of children shrieking with laughter chime in my ears. I glance up. The ghost boy is looking in my direction with dark, sunken eyes, hollows beneath his cheekbones.

My dad was right. Solving more cases won't make me feel any better. But I can't turn my back on them, all the victims who have no voice to speak for them.

I set the worry stone on the diary, my phone next to it. I slide my arms into my parka, and I step outside, looking for the boy.

Is he looking for me? I don't know.

But I'm going to find out.

Chapter 51

Now

Claire Parker sips a mai tai on the patio of a beachside bar. She's wearing a navy sarong, sandals, large sunglasses, her short, jet-black hair ruffled by a gentle sea breeze. The drink is refreshing, the shade from the palm tree she sits under cool after her day spent in the hot sun, painting pictures for tourists on vacation.

She's gazing across the bar at a TV behind the counter. There's an international news show on. The yellow ticker tape at the bottom reads: *Missing Harper Family: Found at Last?*

Claire's heart begins beating hard and steady. She gathers her things and slips inside, closer to the TV. The scene shows the Harpers' house, winter snow piled high on the roof. Police tape surrounds it, flapping in the breeze.

The story is just breaking. A helicopter thuds overhead. The scene shifts to an aerial shot. Christmas lights are strung around the neighborhood, sparkling snowmen and flashing reindeer decorating the lawns. Police uniforms and vehicles with flashing lights line the road, barricades blocking the street.

Claire recognizes Detective Jessica Lambert leaning on her cane in the front yard of the house the police are focused on. She stares at her phone, her expression tense. She has a coffee in one hand, a slouchy black beanie on her head, her long, dark hair trailing down her back.

There's a flicker at the edge of the camera. It's Alice Harper, cycling up the road. She throws her bike onto the snowy grass and sprints across the yard, her gaze fixed on the detective's face. Detective Lambert gives a short nod, and Alice's face crumples. Her body follows, and she collapses to the ground.

Detective Lambert's coffee arcs through the air as she drops it, rushing to Alice. The camera captures her wrapping her arms around the girl, whispering something in her ear.

The news reporters are speculating on what she told Alice, but Claire already knows.

We found them.

But has she told Alice everything?

Because Claire knows there are only two bodies hidden in the Harpers' shed.

Laura's isn't there. It never was.

Claire's cell phone rings from her purse. She drags it out. An unidentified number.

"You should've told me the truth last year," Mrs. McCormack says on the other line. "Laura."

"It's Claire now," she hisses, glancing to either side of her. But nobody is listening. There's only one other person at the bar right now, and the bartender is busy flirting with her.

"You let me think your husband did it."

"Would you have helped me if I didn't?"

Mrs. McCormack doesn't answer. Maybe there isn't an answer. Claire let her think the rumors about Pete were true because she knew then Mrs. McCormack wouldn't go to the cops. After all, her daughter's husband had been a cop when he'd killed her.

Now she knows everything. Almost.

"Are you watching the news?" Mrs. McCormack asks.

"Yeah," Claire says. "Have you been watching Alice like I asked?"

She's been worried for a long time about Alice living with Melanie.

"Yes. Fortunately, the code you gave me for the O'Briens' front gate still works. And so does the key." She chuckles. "Although I think Alice nearly caught me following her a few times. The girl is too perceptive for her own good."

"How is she?"

"She's . . . struggling."

"I wish . . ." Claire stops. Wishes are granted only in fairy tales, after all.

Neither speaks for a moment, watching the news from their respective locations. But Claire's mind has wheeled back to that night, to the person she used to be.

After the accident, Laura woke slowly, her shocked brain not quite able to process what had happened. She'd pulled herself out of the upturned car, her head swimming. Snow turned her vision to static. Her arm was covered in blood, a ragged wound near her wrist. Her mouth was filled with blood. She spat, crimson splattering the snow. She was so dizzy, everything whirling. She fell to her knees in the snow as blackness swept over her.

When she woke again, she heard Mel's voice.

"None of this would have happened if you hadn't told Laura to turn herself in!"

A pause. Pete shouting. And then a gunshot split the night.

Laura staggered to her feet, blinking to clear her vision. She lurched around the side of the car just in time to see Mel disappear into the forest.

On the ground, Pete was bleeding from a gunshot wound to the head. Underneath him was Ella. They were both dead.

Laura had looked around wildly for Alice. There was no sign of her.

A slow, hot panic filled her, like boiling water in a teapot. Mel would come back soon. Her best friend who'd killed her family to stop Laura from going to the police.

Mel would kill her, too.

And so she ran.

But she had a plan in mind. She ran into Killer's Grove, dripping blood from the wound in her arm into the snow, a trail leading to a chasm that cut deep into the forest. And then she wrapped her arm tightly in her coat and hid in a hollowed-out tree, where she waited until Mel crashed through the snow, following the drops of blood to the chasm. Minutes later, she turned around, returning to the car.

Laura's plan had worked.

After that, she slipped through the trees, veering toward the clearing, their little suburban neighborhood, all the way to Mrs. McCormack's house.

Mrs. McCormack had cleaned up her wounds, tucked her into bed like the daughter she lost so many years ago. The next day, she told Laura Alice was in the hospital. She was safe. Mrs. McCormack went to visit, but she wasn't allowed in Alice's room. Laura's mother told her that Alice would live with her in Florida.

And so Laura had fled. She had money, enough to live off for a while. With it, she bought herself a new identity. Claire Parker. A woman who paints for tourists and spends her evenings quietly drinking at a beach bar.

All that time daydreaming about being a different person, and now here she is and she'd give anything to go back to what she had. She closes her eyes, longing desperately for a past she can never get back. Pete, how exciting it felt at the start, the tedious normalcy of their years with young children, their pride as they grew older. The Christmases and camping trips and cups of coffee in bed. The moments of passion and tenderness, of anger and resentment. But mostly, the days that tumbled into months and then into years. How a solid and ordinary life can actually be exactly what you need.

She remembers once, when the girls were small, she and Pete had taken them for a walk in Killer's Grove. They'd come upon a small field covered in a vibrant, radiant carpet of bluebells and had been completely astonished by their transcendent beauty. They'd sat amid those bluebells, their velvet blue petals brushing their thighs, and their fingers had twined together as they watched their children play, and it was its own kind of magic, the kind you only get with someone who knows all of you.

She wishes so much that things had been different. That she could have grown old with Pete, or at least sat next to him when he died, holding his hand and whispering how much she loved him.

Do you remember the bluebells, my love? she'd say as he dropped from consciousness, from life. *Meet me there.*

But all the things she longs for lie in darkness now.

When she'd learned all those months ago that Alice hadn't gone to live with her grandmother and was instead living with Mel, she freaked out. She'd almost turned herself in. That was the first time she'd called her. She'd wanted to warn her that she wasn't safe, hoping the static from an old radio would distort her voice.

"You're going to leave Detective Lambert the evidence?" Claire asks Mrs. McCormack.

"Yes," she confirms. "The gun Mel used to kill Pete is still in her car, hidden in the tire well, so I'll leave an anonymous note, along with her clothes from that night."

"It was smart of you to get them after I left."

"I'm lucky I had your keys. I've grabbed a few things for you from your house. Should you ever need them."

Claire sips the last of her mai tai, watching Detective Lambert comforting her daughter on the screen.

"You can tell Alice the truth now." Mrs. McCormack's voice on the other end of the phone crackles, static down the line.

"You said the detective found my diary."

"Yes," she admits. "I saw her get it myself. But I still don't understand why you wrote it if it's all bullshit. You could've just told the truth and had Melanie arrested."

Claire drops her eyes to her mai tai. The ice is melting at the bottom of the glass, turning the liquid a soft pinkish orange. She debates ordering another one as she thinks about how to answer Mrs. McCormack.

Yes, she could've told the truth. That Mel was there that night. That she helped cover up Theo Moriarty's murder. That to hide it, Mel had killed her husband and daughter.

But then she would've had to tell the truth about everything leading up to it.

That Alice shot Theo Moriarty.

Alice had woken to the sound of Laura talking to Theo. She hadn't seen Mel and had thought Laura and Theo were having an affair. Alice snuck downstairs, ready to stop them, when she heard Theo tell Laura to get in the car. Alice had climbed into the back of the minivan.

She'd blamed herself for telling Pete about Theo, for the ensuing fights, and had decided this time to take matters into her own hands.

While hidden there in the back of the minivan, Alice found the gun Laura had stolen from Maya, the gun Laura had never put under the front seat. Another fabrication for her diary.

When Laura, Mel, and Theo exited the minivan, Alice had followed. She knew she had to stop Theo. And she had.

For good.

But she had no idea what chain of events she would set in motion. That Detective Jess Lambert was driving home with her daughter right then. That she would hit Theo and crash into the river. That Isla wouldn't survive.

Alice freaked out when they found Isla dead. And then when she'd seen Theo's crumpled body thrown to the side of the road, she'd insisted they had to get rid of it—had tried to pull him into the rushing river before Mel had stopped her.

After that, Laura had written the diary, intending it to be a confessional for the police to find. An alternate ending to what had really happened. To protect Alice.

She watches her daughter embrace Detective Lambert on the TV and wonders if this is her penance. Or maybe it's just plain old karma. She's responsible for everything that led up to Detective Lambert's daughter's death, and now Detective Lambert gets to comfort Alice while she watches from afar.

Karma's a bitch. And sometimes you just can't outrun the past.

Even when she left the diary in the safe-deposit box and gave Alice the key, she knew the truth of that.

Her choice back then was clear: tell the truth and lose Alice forever or take the blame for her. It was only when she woke in Killer's Grove, after Mel had killed her family, that she realized she had a third choice. Take the blame and run. Let them all think she was dead.

She had promised Alice she would protect her no matter what, and in return she made Alice promise she would never admit the truth. So far she'd kept that promise. Hopefully she continued to. There was no statute of limitations on murder.

Claire glances again at the TV, where a photo of Mel is on the screen. The monster who turned her into a ghost. What will the police say when they find only two bodies in that shed? Will Mel tell them Laura fell into that chasm? Will they look for her?

"Your orchid is blooming, you know," Mrs. McCormack says. "The red one. It means good fortune. Maybe it's time to come home. Or, at least, time to tell Alice where you are. She should know she hasn't lost everybody."

Claire sucks down the last watery dregs of her mai tai and stands, tucking her phone under her chin. She throws one last glance at the TV, then walks out into the hot, shining sun.

"Maybe," she says as she heads back to the boardwalk. Back to painting portraits of tourists on their tropical vacation. "One day."

ACKNOWLEDGMENTS

Thank you so much to my readers. I'm grateful every day I get to do my dream job, and it's all because of you. I am forever grateful.

Writing a series is an interesting journey that can be tricky to navigate. A big thank-you to my editor Jessica Tribble and developmental editor Charlotte Herscher for helping me find my way, and for pushing me to write my absolute best. Thank you to the team at Thomas & Mercer for your hard work and for getting my books into the hands of readers. And thank you so much to Sharon Pelletier, my amazing agent, for always believing in me, even when I don't.

I wouldn't be here today if it wasn't for the support and enthusiasm of a number of book friends, reviewers, and bloggers who've taken the time to read and talk about my books. There are too many to name, but a few on Instagram I'm grateful to are Gare (@gareindeedreads), Sonica (@the__reading__beauty), Linzie (@suspenseisthrillingme), Robyn (@robyn_reads1), Briana (@brianas_best_reads), Cindy (@groundedinreads), Kim (@itsallaboutthethrill), Lauren (@findapassion1114), and Jenni (@tarheelreader). Also, thank you to Tonya Cornish, who works tirelessly to promote my books, and to everybody on my author Facebook page (there are too many of you to name!), who read, engage, and cheer me on every day. You are the best!

A special thank-you to DeeAnn Magboul, Judith Collins, Jen Jumba, my gym peeps at Westcroft, Ningthi Mangsatabam, Daniela Petrova, Colin Steel, Jamie O'Brien, and my in-laws Rachel, Jo, Sue, and Mick, who are always so excited to read every book I write. And to all of my IRL friends who are endlessly patient when I disappear into a new book, thank you.

Authors are pretty amazing, and I'm grateful to call a number of them friends. Thank you to Lisa Gardner, Jeneva Rose, Samantha Downing, Alex Finlay, Greg Wands, E. G. Scott, Debra Webb, Wendy Walker, Ashley Winstead, Marcy McCreary, Kaira Rouda, Kimberly Belle, Heather Gudenkauf, Danielle Girard, Hank Phillippi Ryan, Hannah Mary McKinnon, Megan Collins, Vanessa Lillie, Jaime Lynn Hendricks, and Robert Swartwood for being supportive, fabulous cheerleaders whom I adore and aspire to write as well as.

And last but not least, thank you to my family, Richard, Adam, and Aidan. I've been lucky in life to be blessed with people who lift me up and have faith in me. I love you.

Did you enjoy *What Lies in Darkness?*

Then check out the first in the Jess Lambert series, *These Still Black Waters*, about Jess investigating when the body of a woman is found floating among the reeds in the lake behind a local house, forcing her to confront a horrible truth.

Or try the prequel novella, *The Stranger at Black Lake*, about a young Jess Lambert when she first moves to Black Lake and gets drawn into a deadly cat-and-mouse game after a young woman's mysterious disappearance.

And make sure to sign up for my book club newsletter to hear more about my books, as well as win thrillers every month: www.Christina-McDonald.com/book-club.

ABOUT THE AUTHOR

Christina McDonald is the *USA Today* bestselling author of *These Still Black Waters*, *Do No Harm*, *Behind Every Lie*, and *The Night Olivia Fell*, which has been optioned for television by a major Hollywood studio. Originally from Seattle, Washington, she now lives in London, England, with her husband, her two sons, and their dog, Tango. For more information, visit www.christina-mcdonald.com.